THE
ARCHER
AT
DAWN

THE TIGER AT MIDNIGHT TRILOGY

The Tiger at Midnight

The Archer at Dawn

THE
ARCHER
AT
DAWN

SWATI TEERDHALA

KATHERINE TEGEN BOOKS
An Imprint of HarperCollins Publishers

Library of Congress Control Number: 2019957881
ISBN 978-0-06-286924-1

Typography by Carla Weise
20 21 22 23 24 PC/LSCH 10 9 8 7 6 5 4 3 2 1
❖
First Edition

TO MY FAMILY, FOR LETTING ME DREAM.

Beware,
oh Archer,
your enemies
are as near as the dawn.

—FROM THE TALES OF
NARAN AND NARIA

CHAPTER 1

Esha brushed aside the leaf as it tickled her cheek, notching an arrow in her bow.

The rosewood tree she perched in shook gently in the breeze but held steady. In front of her lay the open road, bracketed by a row of trees. Esha pulled the string of her bow taut with slow precision, her eyes narrowing in focus as she aimed down the long road.

Kunal had said he'd spotted the caravan about a mile away. It was too soon—they had crossed the Jansan border only a day ago—but she was taking every precaution. The last thing they needed was to let the caravan with Reha slide past their noses.

A rustle came from the tree across from her, and Esha glanced up to catch a pair of amber eyes staring back at her.

She made a face at Kunal, who was gesturing wildly. This wasn't the first time Kunal had forgotten that she wasn't a Blood Fort soldier, with their special signals. He paused and pointed down the road, motioning an "X" with his hands.

"You can talk, Kunal. The caravan is far enough away that no one will hear us," Esha said. "And your newfound dancing skill would probably draw more attention than our brief conversation."

Kunal gave an exaggerated sigh. "I've been trying to motion that it's not the caravan."

Esha slackened her bow and relaxed into a squat.

"It's not her." The breeze tousled his hair.

"How can you tell? Could you sense her?" she asked. Hidden in the jungle for the past week, Kunal had been able to experiment with the new shape-shifting powers in his blood. So far, he had discovered sharpened senses—keener eyesight, better hearing, a sense of the animals nearby—but his shifts were unpredictable.

"No, it's an open cart. A fruit seller," he said. Kunal rubbed the spot between his eyebrows, pain that plagued him whenever he used his sharpened eyesight. "Why he's taking this road instead of the Great Road, I don't know."

"Fruit? Mangoes?" Her eyes lit up.

Esha scrambled down the tree and landed with a soft slap, the hardness of the ground below a reminder that they were back in Jansa, where the land thirsted. Kunal landed next to her, his presence warm at her back. This new closeness between them was still something she was getting accustomed to. Normally, her missions were alone.

But she didn't mind having him around.

"Mangoes. I bet he has mangoes," she said.

Kunal only groaned. "I think I'll know you for years and still not understand this obsession of yours."

"We've been waiting for hours for some sign of the transport that might have Reha. My hands are cramped, my legs are aching, and I haven't had real food, aside from these horrible rations you brought, since we left Mathur. You wouldn't even let me steal anything in the last town," she said, throwing in a pout that she knew would soften Kunal's expression.

It did, but it was accompanied by a raised eyebrow. He was catching on. Smart man.

"We don't want to draw the attention of soldiers, and you scampering out of someone's bedroom with an armful of fruit would have certainly been something to remember. I'll plant you a cursed mango tree so you can stop buying them at every stand," he said.

"Think about it. Some hot food. A nice bed instead of these scaly trees." Her words were soft, needling. "What about letting me sneak into an empty house at the next town? We won't be hurting anyone."

"No. We'll get by on rooftops." He paused. "Though I can't deny I would love a hot bath. Or even a hot spring for us would be wonderful." A faint blush crept up Kunal's skin.

"You've been thinking about us, soldier?" she said. Esha stepped a bit closer.

His breath hitched, and she held back a laugh.

"No need to look so horrified. You've already kissed me. I think a bit of flirting is allowed."

"It's not that— It's not about being allowed— I'm—"

Esha held up a finger to Kunal's lips.

"I'm teasing," she said. "But I do want those mangoes."

And with that she ran off, throwing a challenging look behind her.

◦

Kunal had decided long ago that Esha might be the death of him, but he had never feared death. He shook his head at her even though she was long gone down the road.

It had been almost a week since the skirmish at the ruins of the temple, and they'd heard only murmurs of the caravan the soldiers had mentioned. The one that could hold Reha, the lost princess. Enough to suggest its truth, but not enough for them to have found anything yet. And though he was sure Esha had been on longer missions with less success, he could tell she was getting antsy.

There had been a hawk that had arrived with a note that she had quickly hidden away. He had meant to ask, once or twice, but each time they had a moment to themselves, other, more important things had come to mind.

At the thought of those moments, he grinned.

Kunal secured his pack before crouching and launching off down the road himself with inhuman speed. Within seconds, he had caught up with Esha, laughing as he grabbed her by the waist.

He held her steady as she careened forward, startled.

Kunal hadn't shown her this newfound ability yet—he'd discovered it only the day before when hunting for food.

She slapped his arm as he righted her. "You could be seen by someone," she whispered.

He shrugged, a sudden nonchalance taking over. "I'd fly us both away."

"And if that person had eyes and saw you shifting into an eagle? Would you be okay with me killing him? Because you know that would be the only option."

"What is with you and murder as the first resort?" he said.

"Well, apparently I have to be the sensible one right now, and I'm not particularly enjoying it."

He crooked a finger under her chin, tilting it up so that he could brush his lips against hers. "I don't like to be teased," he said.

"You're going to have to get used to it."

A smart reply was on his lips when the earth wheezed farther down the path. Kunal and Esha broke apart as the fruit seller came around the bend. The man was startled by the presence of two strangers on the previously empty road, his askew turban nearly falling off. But within minutes, Esha had charmed him while purchasing a mango and Kunal had started to fix the creaky wheel on his caravan.

Kunal bent lower, straining to lift the wheel out of its socket.

"And why are you two on this path instead of the Great Road?"

"I could ask you the same thing, *emenda*." Esha smiled. "Though I'm sure I can guess. Tariffs on the Great Road have increased. My brother and I heard as much in the last town."

Kunal choked back a cough. He'd had enough of surprise relations recently.

They'd agreed earlier that their story would have to change in different situations. The old fruit seller would be more likely to help them as traveling, bumbling kids. Kunal didn't know how Esha immediately read people with such clarity that she could shift her story at a moment's notice. He envied her skill.

"Yes, yes, those cursed tariffs. My brother's wife's cousin didn't have the money and is now paying double taxes for the season—it's the vultures if they can't comply."

"Vultures?"

"The king's newest method of execution." There was an undercurrent of fear in the man's words that Kunal recognized. He'd heard it before while traveling up Jansa.

"As for us, we've lost our travel caravan at the last rest stop and have been trying to catch up. Have you seen it?" Esha took a deliberate bite of her mango, her tone light.

The man shook his head but then paused. "There was a private, armored one I passed a day ago. Wealthy merchants, by the looks of it." He glanced between them, and a crinkle appeared in his brow. He'd probably realized that the two of them looked nothing alike.

Kunal stood up, letting the wheel fall with a thud.

"Fixed," he said. The fruit seller blinked a few times before beaming.

"Thank you, my son. I have been struggling with this cart for a day, and my back is aching." The older man placed a hand over Kunal's head in blessing, as Kunal pressed four fingers to his heart and bowed. "I hope you find your caravan."

Kunal nodded as Esha rushed to help the man back into his cart. They waved off the fruit seller, making sure he was safely down the road before turning to face each other.

"An armored caravan. It's got to be the king's royal caravan," Esha said.

"Agreed. It's possible we're not the only ones who know of this. It'll be best to be on alert and devise a plan. We could trail the caravan, find them in the next town, and create a diversion—"

"Already have a plan," Esha said. She slung her bow across her chest and fixed her uttariya. From it, she drew a small pin, one of a Fort soldier, and presented it to Kunal. "I nicked it off Amir before I knocked him out."

Kunal shook his head, though he couldn't help but smile. "Lead the way."

———◃◦▹———

It took Esha only a minute to realize the caravan wasn't a caravan at all.

She edged slightly to the right to get a better look. She recognized a military chariot when she saw one, having helped Harun design a few. This one was designed to transport important goods quickly, unlike the plodding tread of a caravan.

Esha cursed under her breath. Her plan was useless now, if that was the case.

But maybe the wheels . . .

She bit her lip, shifting her head to squint at the two rows of soldiers that surrounded the chariot. It had come to a stop in a well-covered part of the nearby jungle, close enough to the path to escape, but surrounded by trees so no one could take them by surprise.

A few steps forward, and the first line of soldiers would be in her line of fire. Two shots, two soldiers down. Kunal shook his head at her, as if he could read her thoughts.

He really was no fun.

Esha decided to concede this one to him and changed the aim of her bow. Two soldiers down would make her happy, but it would alert the others to their presence. However, she might be able to create a distraction.

She raised a hand in signal to Kunal, pointing at the wheels and then her eyes. He furrowed his brow, concentrating as he used his eyesight to narrow in on the wheels, a power of his that Esha was getting rather used to. Kunal's brow relaxed, and he nodded at her, drawing a wheel in the air and pointing at the bottom two spokes. She returned the nod, readjusting her bow and focusing in.

It was . . . pleasant. Having a partner, someone to watch her back. A small part of her still wondered, worried, how much she could really trust a soldier who had turned. A bigger part of her realized how unfair that was.

She focused, taking aim and drawing her bowstring taut. Esha let the arrow loose, her gaze unwavering as it sailed through the air and hit the bottom spoke. A sharp crack punctuated the air as the wheel broke off and the entire chariot pitched forward, landing heavily into the dirt.

The commotion came from the driver and the foot soldiers, who reacted as most people might—with confusion and annoyance. The Senaps reacted as she expected. Within seconds their bows were drawn, their swords at the ready.

The chariot driver got down from his perch and waved at one of the Senaps, who came over to help inspect the wheel. Esha could make out only the faint notes of conversation, but from the way Kunal was cocking his ear he could understand what they were saying.

Two of the Senaps, both wearing jeweled armbands, signaled at the others to move.

"He's assigning them off in twos to patrol the perimeter. Basic protocol—I don't think they suspect anything," Kunal whispered.

"But they will, once they find the arrow," she said.

He nodded. "Once they find the arrow, they'll lock down the surroundings and encircle the caravan. Naria herself would find it difficult to get through that shield maneuver. Our best bet is to distract the two guards before that happens."

Esha turned to Kunal, pulling out the pin she had nicked off Amir. She undid the clasp and pinned it to the waist sash of Kunal.

"It'll have to be you," she said.

"Makes sense. I'm not sure these soldiers will be so kind happening upon a girl in the jungle." He flashed her a wicked grin.

"Oh? Because you were so kind?" She tilted her chin at him as he leaned in.

"*Kind* might not be the right word. . . ."

He leaned in for a kiss, and she let him get closer until the last second, when she pulled away, tapping a finger to his lips.

"Mission first. Think of it as a reward," she said before she tossed a wink at him and climbed down the tree.

CHAPTER 2

Kunal blinked into the midday sun. He wiped his hands on his dhoti and adjusted his armband, making sure it faced outward at the right angle to show off the jewels that indicated he was a Senap. It fit the bronze armor he now wore, which Esha had made sure to pack.

A cold sweat dripped down his back, and his hands were clammy. He hated lying. He had no idea how Esha did it so easily. Kunal pushed into the clearing where the caravan and the Senaps waited, coming face-to-face with the arrow points of two spears.

He immediately threw his hands up, taking quick account of the scene before him. *Sun Maiden's spear*, he hadn't even noticed them from his spot in the trees. They must have been hidden in the shadows.

Kunal did a quick count in his head. Two Senaps in front with spears and the two before with the swords. Which meant that they were following standard procedure for high security. But if Kunal remembered correctly, there would be four pairs of two soldiers with this procedure. . . .

One of the soldiers jabbed his spear forward again, and Kunal didn't have much time to linger on this realization, quickly deciding Esha could handle it.

As he looked at the soldiers before him, their expressions suspicious, their spears unmoving despite glances to his armor and armband, Kunal decided he was rather more worried for himself.

———⟨○⟩———

Esha crept along the edge of the road, hidden by the half-cast shadows of the approaching sunset.

Two soldiers were checking the jungle to the west of the caravan. She'd have to split them up. The shorter soldier kept looking over his shoulder, as if to make sure the other hadn't gotten lost. He had to be the more senior of the two.

She crouched low, grinding her sandals into the dirt to remove any trace of her footprints, and thumped the tree trunk behind her before darting out of the way.

The taller soldier stilled and then tapped the shoulder of the other, tilting his head in her direction. They crept over, their bows drawn, hands on their knife hilts.

She saw in those movements why the Senaps were known for being the best—the most elite soldiers and trackers within Jansa. They were methodical and deliberate, moving together seamlessly as one unit.

Esha notched two arrows on her bow and sent a quick

prayer up to the Moon Lord before letting go. The first arrow found its aim, in the small gap between the soldier's shield and his cuirass, which he kept exposing. The taller soldier immediately ducked out of the way and pulled his comrade down. The arrow dedicated to him barely missed.

Any element of surprise was gone now. And Esha realized her grave mistake. When the taller soldier had turned to dodge her arrow, the rusted double silver brand of his armband glinted against the setting sun. He was a Senap captain. The other soldier must have been the newer one, turning around to watch the actions of his superior officer.

The captain unslung his bow and was aiming into the tree, directly at her.

Esha scrambled higher, up the sturdier branches, and jumped onto the tree to the right. She tumbled down the tree, using her momentum to ram into the captain and knock the bow out of his hands.

The shorter soldier was sitting to the right, a bloody hand to his throat as he scrambled to use jungle moss to stanch his wound. Smart soldiers were always so annoying.

Esha tumbled over the mossy, wet jungle floor and scrambled back up. The captain was getting up as well, and he didn't look perturbed by her appearance, or that she was a she. He had the same gleam in his eyes as all good fighters. He drew out his knife and charged at her.

Panic seized her, and she rolled out of the way, grabbing the bow off the ground and shooting arrow after arrow at him. Only one found its aim, in his arm, but it barely slowed him down.

Esha decided to hold her ground as he came again at her. She dropped to the floor at the last second, slashing at his leg with the knife she had hidden on her. The captain grunted, stumbling, and Esha heaved forward, using the momentum to land a crack against his skull with the hilt of her knife. She struck one blow, but before she get another one in, he grabbed her wrist.

He seized her neck with his other hand, using his height and weight to lift her off the ground. The air escaped her lungs as she struggled to reach for the whip tucked under her waist sash, hidden so as to not give away her identity.

But it wouldn't matter who she was if she wasn't alive.

Esha fought against his hands, driving her foot into the soldier's groin. He dropped her, grunting in pain, and she fell in a heap, gasping as she dragged herself away.

She took in a welcome breath and got to her feet shakily, preparing to square off with the captain again. A noise sounded from behind her, but Esha kept her eyes on the captain. That is, until he let out a piercing whistle.

Esha spun around and decided it was a good thing she had kept the whip in her sash.

———◄○►———

Kunal let out a nervous chuckle.

"Where did I come from?" he said, repeating the question. His hands were still up, the two spears still pointed at his jugular. "A few of us soldiers are returning to the Fort from a mission and have camped farther into the jungle. I got a bit lost, I'm afraid."

The soldier on the left scoffed, his spear wobbling. "Lost? Fort soldiers should be trained better than that."

The soldier on the right shot a recriminating look at his partner and dropped his spear, offering an arm. Kunal grasped it, forearm to forearm. "Mohit, drop your weapon. I'd heard that there was another squad on its way back from the coast."

Mohit didn't look happy, but he did lower his spear a few notches, giving his fellow guard a half nod. Kunal lowered his hands but made sure to still keep them in Mohit's sightlines as he moved forward.

"So, what is this?" Kunal asked, keeping his tone light as he assessed the caravan. "A weapons shipment? I heard there was a new set of Harran steel being sent to the palace before the start of the Sun Mela."

The chariot was tilted, leaning against a tree. Kunal furrowed his brow, trying to see if he could make out any sounds from inside the covered chariot.

"No, nothing of that sort. Would've loved to get a look at a set of new Harran steel—those desert blacksmiths are unparalled," the soldier said. "Though we are on our way to Gwali."

Mohit gave his partner a sharp look, but Kunal pretended not to notice, stumbling a bit and using the side of the caravan to catch his fall.

And that's when Kunal spotted it. The caravan wheel

had an extra compartment that indicated the cargo being carried wasn't cargo at all. And in the back, he saw the metal pin that every royal transport had, one that would separate the chariot from the caravan.

Mohit was now advancing on him, suspicion across his face as he ignored the sputtered words of his partner. Kunal straightened himself and pushed away from the caravan after reaching a hand behind to yank at the metal pin in the corner of the broken spoke. The pin tumbled to the ground, outside of Kunal's grasp.

"Tell me, if your squad was returning to the Fort, why are you on this road? Wouldn't it be better to go south?" Mohit asked.

"It would. But my comrades wanted to avoid the Tej rain forest, so we took this longer route."

"That will delay you."

"We planned on making up the time," Kunal said, walking to the left as if he was aimlessly pacing. But he was positioning himself closer to the edge of the jungle. Away from the caravan, which was teetering now, the latch and small metal pin having loosened.

Another minute and the pressure alone from the caravan would cause them to weaken.

Mohit finally gave him a nod of approval. Kunal gave him a nod back, feeling the slow warmth of shame filling him. If he hadn't agreed to find Reha, if he didn't know what he knew . . . Mohit might have been a friend.

Suddenly, a shout pierced the air. It took him a few seconds to realize it was Esha's voice.

And she was shouting his name.

Esha burst into the clearing, her hair flying, blood streaked across her clothes, a deep welt around her neck. He didn't even have time to feel shock at the bruising around her throat.

Behind her were four soldiers, the pairs that Kunal had hoped weren't there.

Kunal reacted before he could think. He rushed at the nearest soldier and tackled him to the ground, only to look up and see Esha sprinting toward the caravan.

It was poised to topple over.

Mohit was running toward the caravan as well, his eyes on the wheels. And another soldier was heading after them both. Kunal landed a well-placed blow to the soldier's face, hearing a crack as he fell to the ground. Before he could get up, Kunal was tackled and hit the ground, hard.

Hard enough that his extra senses erupted around him and Kunal had to hold back a scream. He heard the labored breaths of every person, saw the pores on the face of his attacker.

And it was the only reason he heard the pin being slotted back into the chariot.

Sun Maiden's spear. Kunal took another blow to his cheek, but he didn't stay down. Gathering up his strength, he lifted and smashed his head into his attacker—a Senap captain who looked vaguely familiar. Kunal pushed away the terror at having hurt a ranking member of his—*the* army—and focused.

Two down.

Kunal ran back to the caravan. Mohit jumped into the chariot driver's seat as Esha battled the remaining three soldiers. One of them turned, and Kunal followed his frantic glance to see Mohit lashing the horses to get away.

"Mohit," the soldier yelled. "Mohit, help us!"

But Mohit didn't spare a second glance.

The chariot sped away, and Kunal's heart plummeted. The remaining soldier, the one who had first offered him his forearm, let out a frustrated yell before turning to look at Kunal. Mohit had followed the rules, put the mission first.

"Traitor," the soldier spat. He charged at Kunal.

◆

Moon Lord's fists.

Esha took a ragged breath, cursing softly in Dharkan and Jansan.

Ahead, a soldier advanced on Kunal, and they circled each other. Esha tried not to let panic set in—Kunal would be able to run after the caravan. This was their last chance. They were supposed to rescue Reha, not let her slip through their fingers while battling a bunch of cursed annoying soldiers.

Esha brushed sweat away from her eye and felt a sticky wetness against her brow. She looked down at her hand, noticing the red that dripped from her fingers but not registering it.

The short, squat soldier pulled a knife, and Esha snarled.

She unleashed her whip, deciding then that none of these soldiers would be able to leave alive, and circled the attacker's arms with the metal tip. He let out a cry as he went down.

She cracked her whip again, almost as an invitation. The second soldier pounced forward from the left. Esha spun out of the way before the soldier could land, then lashed upward with her whip, wrapping around his torso and launching him forward.

He flew into the nearby tree, groaning.

Something rammed into Esha. She pitched forward but couldn't roll into the fall. Instead, she landed in a sprawl. Kunal took down the soldier he had been facing diagonal to her, cracking him over the head.

She turned back around, scrambling in the dirt away from the first soldier, who looked angry.

Well, that made two of them.

Esha reached down her leg and grabbed the secondary knife she wore on her calf. She threw it, knowing it wouldn't kill her attacker.

But it would slow him down.

He gasped as it found its mark in his thigh. Esha got to her feet and lashed her whip again as her attacker grunted and yanked the knife from his thigh.

He tried to throw it at her, but she knocked it out of his hand and then lashed him. Once. Twice. He fell back on the second one and she bounded forward, using the momentum from her running start to take him down.

Before he could get up again, Esha wrapped her whip around his neck and pulled tight. She waited. *One, two, three, four*, and the man collapsed.

Esha rose to her feet. Kunal was facing the last soldier, in a deadly dance of knives, before he took a deep breath and simply barreled the attacker into a tree.

The soldier slumped down the bark and Kunal stepped back, catching sight of her. Kunal backhanded him with the hilt of his sword.

"Are there any others?" she said.

Kunal shook his head, dragging the three attackers together. "No, and I can't hear any other troops in the area. I think we're clear."

Esha stopped behind him, a faint pain climbing up her side. She ignored it and grabbed her knife to slit the soldiers' throats. A strangled sound came from Kunal.

"They're liabilities if they're alive. They've seen us."

Esha looked up and felt the weight of judgment in his gaze. She had become more aware of her own code now, how it differed from and converged with Kunal's.

But she was protecting them. She would always protect the people closest to her first.

"They're near death anyway." When that didn't seem to shake the frown off his lips she tried another tack, already thinking about the soldiers who had gotten away. "If a few soldiers in Gwali mention us, it could be ignored. But a squadron? We won't be able to set foot in the city."

"We shouldn't be killing anyone. I've seen enough death recently."

"Kunal, you're a soldier. Don't go soft on me now."

Kunal looked as if he was going to turn away.

"It'll be painless."

And before Kunal even fully turned away, Esha had slit the soldiers' throats. There was still one more in Gwali, which she'd have to clean up later.

"We let him get away," Esha said.

"They ambushed us. It was ten men against two and we still managed to hold our own."

Esha sighed, rubbing her eyes. "You're right. I don't have to like it, though. Do you think we should try to catch up?"

"They'll be on high alert. It'll be suicide," he said. "They won't be taking any breaks until they get to Gwali. Protocol will demand the shield formation I mentioned—it'll be impossible to get through."

"It sounds like we're going to need help. They'll be sure to double protection after encountering us," she said. Esha looked down at her torn and bloodied clothing. "I don't think we can do this alone anymore. Not after being outnumbered like that, even if it was mostly just infantry."

"You know, infantry still train a lot. They're decent fighters," he said.

"Not enough." Esha snorted. "You're too kind, Kunal.

How did you become a top soldier at the Fort again?"

Kunal gave her a sly grin. "I'm good with my hands."

Esha let out a laugh, but she knew it must be hard for him to be on this side, fighting against men he had seen as comrades for years.

"I sent a hawk earlier," she said slowly.

Recognition alighted in his eyes—he had noticed. Good for him.

"The rest of the team—Bhandu, Arpiya, and the twins, Aahal and Farhan—are accompanying the royal procession to Jansa. We can debrief together, figure out a new plan."

"You could've mentioned you had written for backup. But I agree. We can't do this alone anymore."

"The note wasn't about backup, actually. I had promised to keep Harun apprised of our relative location." Esha raised an eyebrow at Kunal. "He's furious with me, especially when another squad found our contact murdered and us missing."

"He'll survive," Kunal muttered.

Esha held back a laugh.

"Let's clean up and then head west toward their camp," she said. Esha glanced back at the fallen soldiers. "Grab their weapons as well."

Esha moved away, making a face as she realized she was a filthy mess. She loosened her tight waist sash and a sharp pain shot up her torso, adrenaline finally leaving her body. Her hands flew to her side as another stab of pain followed, a dull ache spreading through her torso. And when she lifted a hand, it was streaked in red.

Blood began to soak the side of her shirt, her waist sash no longer acting as a tourniquet.

Her vision began to blur, and Esha pitched forward.

CHAPTER 3

Esha woke up to the scowling face of Harun. She rubbed her eyes, willing the image away. It remained, and it might have been her imagination, but even his beard quaked in anger.

"How—how did I get here?" Esha asked, her voice hoarse.

"Your soldier found our camp," a woman's voice said from the back of their small tent. Arpiya. She'd recognize her friend and fellow Blade's voice anywhere. "Apparently, Kunal was able to track us from the directions we sent in the note."

Kunal winced as Bhandu came up behind him and clapped him on the shoulder. He must've shifted into his eagle form, large enough to carry her, and flown her here after she fainted. A risky decision, especially because the rest of the team didn't know of his parentage—and she wanted to keep it that way.

"Care to explain what happened, Viper?" Harun said through gritted teeth.

A sigh came from behind. "Give her a few moments, Prince. How would you feel if you were startled awake by a snapping turtle?" Kunal said.

Bhandu's deep laugh rattled through her hazy fog, and Esha's eyes eased open. She took in the full sight—angry Harun, a pleased-looking Kunal, Bhandu, Arpiya, Farhan, and Aahal.

Everyone was here. Esha groaned.

"Is it necessary for you all to be in this tiny tent? What have you been doing—staring at me?"

A chorus of weak noes went up in her team, and Harun continued to stare daggers at her.

"I've been waiting for you to wake up so I can get a report. A full one. Not the spotty communications you've sent so far. And I expect an explanation for this injury and why you let a soldier escape a week ago. Remind me again why I even sent you out on this mission."

Harun was at the top of his fury now. His hand flew to pinch the bridge of his nose, and he took a deep breath. Esha tilted her head at Kunal to speak before she realized they hadn't agreed on their story.

"We were set upon by Fort soldiers before we reached the meeting place, and that's where we found out the contact was dead," Kunal said. "I was captured while standing watch."

Kunal filled them in on the rest. How they had discovered the new Jansan rebel group run by Dharmdev and how Laksh turned on them—leaving out anything to do with Kunal's newfound parentage or his relationship with Laksh.

"—and then Esha came into the battle and killed two of the soldiers."

Harun looked at the blood-soaked bandage around her waist. "While *you* let a soldier escape. Not the best way to convince us you're not also a spy, like this Laksh. Somehow Dharmdev got a soldier to turn while within the Fort. That's pretty great work."

"Kunal wants to help our cause. Would he have saved me otherwise?" Esha said, aiming for a patient tone. Harun looked at Kunal sharply, as if he knew another answer.

"And how does that account for the past week, then? Gods above, if you tell me you've been doing anything but trying to capture this Laksh, I'll—"

"Harun, if you'd give us a chance, we could tell you the most important part," Esha said, a heaviness returning to her chest. "It'll explain everything. Why we've been gone, why I'm like this." She waved weakly at her torso.

Harun huffed and gave her a terse nod.

"The soldiers were moving back to Gwali for the truce, but also to protect something. Someone." Harun's eyes narrowed as she spoke, and she could see his mind calculating all the possibilities.

"We heard something similar—rumors of a marriage. A noble-born girl from the east, maybe?"

Esha shook her head, staring at her old friend, hoping he saw what she wasn't saying.

"That's not it," she said.

"Then what?" Harun said.

Esha hesitated, uncertainty flooding her. What if they were wrong? This news would hurt Harun, but it'd also give him hope. A direction to go in.

"Spit it out, Esha," he said.

Esha inhaled and stared her old friend in the eye. "We found her. We found Reha." And before Harun could say anything, before a glimmer of joy could shift across his face, Esha continued. "And Vardaan has her."

———◄○►———

Kunal knew in theory the lost princess Reha was the prince's younger sister, but it wasn't until he saw the raw despair on the prince's face that he understood what this could mean to him.

What if he had a sister? Maybe someone to care for would have changed his path, given him something to fight for. For a fleeting moment, Kunal understood what had shaped the young prince.

Esha scooted to the bottom of her bed before enveloping Harun in an awkward hug, her movements hampered by her bandage.

"No," he said. "No. If Vardaan has her in his grasp . . . There's no time to spare. What if he hides her away, hurts her in his pursuit of power? She's only sixteen. She won't even realize she's being used."

He looked at Esha as if she were water in the desert. It annoyed Kunal, even though he knew Harun deserved that comfort right now. The others moved forward, offering their own comfort.

"We're not sure, Harun, but it makes sense. Why else would Vardaan have come to a truce? He isn't worried about us anymore, not when he has Reha and her blood. He'll try to do the renewal ritual for the *janma* bond with her blood and keep ahold of his power over the country." Esha took a deep breath, which made her wince. "We've been gone for a week because we were trying to end all of this, chase down the caravan we suspected had her. I wanted to come back to you with your sister in hand. That's why we're late."

"We'd followed the caravan and were closing in on it when we found ourselves outnumbered," Kunal said, coming around the corner of the cot.

"More soldiers?" Harun asked.

Kunal nodded. "We—I underestimated the security. I assumed there would only be ten but there were more than protocol dictated. Too many for us to take down, but they were protecting something important. That many guards wouldn't be placed even on the most expensive Harran steel shipment."

"Kunal also confirmed that the caravan was designed for a passenger." Esha's voice grew insistent. "It had to be her. Reha had to have been in the caravan. And if she was there, then she's on the way to Gwali. We can't let her be held there. Harun, she's sixteen, and this is when her shape-shifting powers will come in. She won't have anyone to guide her but that monster, and he'll only use her. She needs us."

"If you're right, then my sister is on her way to Gwali right at the same time the Dharkan royal retinue has been invited for the Mela. The first time in a decade. Add in the peace summit at the end of the Mela and this is a camphor-soaked rag waiting to be lit," Harun said.

He stood up and moved to the window. He paused there, the room in utter silence for minutes, before he turned around.

"We'll have to scout out her location once we get to Gwali, confirm it's her, and then coordinate a rescue. All while making sure it can't be tied back to us—not with the peace summit at stake." He looked at Esha, the team, and even Kunal. "If we let Reha fall into his hands, Vardaan will control the magic and the land. Worse, he might decide to kill her and our land will fall to the drought next if the *janma* bond fails and the Bhagya river fades."

Esha struggled back onto the bed and into a sitting position, her face fierce.

"This is our next mission, team," she said. "We'll get her back, and we'll bring balance to the land. We won't let the bond fail. We won't let Vardaan use her."

"Esha, you have a hole in your stomach—"

"We're doing this, Harun." Esha's face was stone, resolute in her decision. "I'm all in. I'll bring Reha back, no matter what."

"We are too," Aahal chimed in, followed by nods from the others. Harun merely nodded, his shoulders sagging down, a burden released.

The prince turned to Kunal. It was the first time Harun had looked Kunal straight in the eyes. His hands were down by his sides, palms open, and he waited. He asked no question, but Kunal knew that he was expecting an answer, and, to his surprise, Kunal had already decided.

Reha was the key to saving his land, but in the wrong hands, she was also the key to its destruction. He might not be a soldier of the Red Fortress anymore, but he was still sworn to protect his land and his people. And after all the wrongs he—and his uncle—had done, this was one thing Kunal could do right.

Kunal gave a short nod.

———◦———

Esha hadn't expected that. A moment of hesitation as Kunal weighed both sides, analyzing everything behind those amber eyes—*that* she had expected.

"First, we need to find out where that caravan is going," Harun said.

"There will be a shipments room in the military garrison of Gwali," Farhan said, moving forward. "I've been reading up on the recent renovations the king did to the royal and martial sectors of Gwali ever since the start of the War of the Brothers. Some light reading for the journey."

"*Light reading,*" his twin, Aahal, mocked, using air quotes. Farhan was the more serious and studious of the two, while

Aahal was glib enough that he could charm anyone.

"Perfect, book brains has already figured it out. We break into that room," Bhandu said.

Kunal shook his head but held back from saying more. Harun cocked his head at the other man.

"Why are you shaking your head, soldier?"

Kunal hesitated for a moment. "It could easily be falsified. Many of the infantry are trained to have multiple versions of such records to protect the army's goods."

"Then we bribe them for the real records," Bhandu said.

"Won't work. They won't have access to the real records."

"Then we threaten them," Bhandu finished.

"Martial punishments are gruesome already. Not sure any threat you delivered would outweigh their desire to save their skin."

There was a beat of silence in the room.

"Okay, then what? If all records in the palace could be falsified and we can't outmatch the army in cruelty or money, what do we do?" Arpiya asked, breaking the silence. Everyone looked at each other before finally turning to stare at Kunal.

"The Fort," Kunal said. "The Fort keeps detailed records of every caravan and shipment."

"You want to go back to the Fort?" Esha said before she could stop herself.

"No," he said quickly. "You asked what could be done. I'm just saying the most accurate documents will be there."

"If the soldier says the only place to get that information

is the Fort, then that's where we'll have to go." Harun walked toward Kunal, considering him. "Normally, I'd say it's a mission for the Viper but . . ."

"They'll be on high alert after the general was killed, especially as they believe it was at the hands of the Viper. Probably have new protocols that you don't even know of, ones designed to look for rebels and the Viper, in particular," Kunal finished. Harun nodded.

Esha looked between the two of them, narrowing her eyes.

"What if . . ." Kunal cleared his throat, a bright look on his face that Esha didn't trust. "What if I went back? Got the information. Saw what the new protocols are."

"Why would we let you go back to the Fort?" Esha said, her lips pursing.

Harun leaned forward. "I second that question."

"Third," Farhan said quietly, Aahal nodding next to him.

Kunal looked Esha full in the face, his amber eyes trained on her.

"You did turn me, didn't you? I'd like to be useful."

Esha tried not to make a face. He was using her own words against her, and, she had to admit, she didn't particularly like being on the receiving end. "I can be your eyes and ears on the inside. I'm not suited to being idle."

"How can we trust you?" Arpiya asked, arms crossed.

"I'm your best option for finding out where the caravan went," Kunal said, though now his brow was beginning to furrow.

"I trust him," Esha said. She trusted Kunal, but having him return to the Fort, be among his fellow soldiers . . . the idea didn't exactly excite her.

"Why would you do that? For us?" Harun asked.

Kunal's eyes flickered to Esha. "I want to . . . bring back balance. Reha is the best chance for me to make my country whole again. So if this is what it takes to get her back safely, then I will do it."

Harun frowned, and Farhan and Bhandu wore matching looks of worry. It was Arpiya who spoke next.

"It's dangerous, and it's a risk. But he's the only one who can get into the Fort—and he's volunteering. Let's not discredit that. Esha is out of the question after her last venture to the Fort, and the rest of you would be made in moments."

Bhandu scoffed in the corner.

Arpiya continued. "We don't have a lot of choice here. Esha can put together the best rescue plan this side of the Ghanta Mountains, but it won't matter if we can't find Reha once we're in the city."

"There's always a retinue of soldiers that go to the Mela. We can plan to meet in a week's time in the Pink Palace in Gwali, at the start of the Mela. By then I'll have confirmation of where Reha has been sent," Kunal said, color rising to his cheeks.

Esha tried not to shake her head. Soldiers. The minute he saw the outline of a new mission he was chomping at the bit. She hoped that's all it was.

"How will you get yourself sent in the retinue, soldier?"

There was a lightness in Kunal's movements now, a bounce almost. "Senap," Kunal said. "I'm not just a soldier. I'd just been promoted to Senap before leaving on my miss—leaving the Fort. And my new post was to be Gwali. The retinue will be a backup."

Something flashed across his face, a tension, that Esha had gotten used to noticing in her soldier. She took note of it. Part of her thought the Fort wouldn't be so kind to a soldier who failed a mission, even if it was an impossible one. But he knew the Fort better than she did.

Harun considered Kunal with those shrewd eyes. "But you're no longer part of the Fort. Or at least, that's what you keep telling us."

"No one else knows that," Kunal said. "For all they know, I've merely been busy. If I fail to check in three times, they'll mark me missing or dead. But if I get to a garrison soon—"

"You'll be back on the books," Harun finished. "Gwali, you say?"

A slow grin coiled around Harun's face, one that Esha didn't care for. She knew the way Harun thought, if only because it was so similar to herself.

Kunal nodded once, firmly.

Harun tapped the edge of Esha's bed, tracing his fingers over the blanket. "I'm surprised you didn't think of this, Esha. I'm assuming the soldier told you this when you turned him—it must have been one of the reasons you attempted something so risky, right?"

Harun's voice was casual, but she detected the under-current of his words.

"Yes, exactly why." There was more she wanted to say, how he shouldn't be putting himself in this position, not when Laksh was still out there looking for him. Not when he was one of the only remaining Samyads alive. But she couldn't say any of it, not without revealing Kunal's secret.

"This is no simple task we're asking of you. I can't say I trust you, soldier. Reha is my little sister. She's also the best chance both of our nations have at healing the land. Will you be able to do whatever it takes, even against your for-mer comrades?" Harun asked.

The two men looked at each other, something unspoken passing between them. Something Esha couldn't under-stand, and that annoyed her.

"Yes," Kunal said. "I'll do whatever it takes to ensure Reha is safe. And to save my country."

Only two weeks ago, Kunal had almost left when Esha had given him the choice to go back to his life. No one in the tent knew that. Was she enough reason for him to stay? To betray everything he had known?

Or was he truly a part of the team?

She knew which one she wanted to believe. Esha tried to catch Kunal's eye but instead caught Harun's penetrating gaze, which asked her the same question.

—◄◦►—

The hawk landed on Kunal's outstretched forearm, and he inhaled sharply as his body thrummed. Kunal reread his scribbled note to Alok once more before rolling it up and attaching it to the hawk's claws.

He was going back to the Red Fortress while Esha and the team would continue on as part of the royal retinue, taking on roles within the nobility. Once they were all inside the gates of the palace, they'd meet again and proceed from there.

He'd leave in an hour, making a stop at the nearest garrison to check in. If he rode fast he should make it back to the Fort within a day and a half.

Kunal had made up a story for Alok, stretching the truth a bit, but letting him know the bare bones of what had happened—Rakesh had been captured, Laksh and Amir had run away, and he was the sole soldier left. He also sent a similar note to General Panak, with a few of the details omitted.

He hoped it would set the stage for his return and minimize the questions he'd receive, though it would still be dangerous. He'd have to keep his story close to him. From one angle, he was the de facto winner. From another, it was quite suspicious that he was the only one who had returned alive.

Unfortunately, that was the sort of realization that would only make him more popular at the Fort. Kunal tried not to shake his head at the idea that being thought of as a murderer would add prestige to his name. He'd always looked away when the other soldiers talked like that, resolved that *he* wouldn't act that way, think that way. But after meeting Esha he could see that that wasn't enough.

It was as if a part of him he had buried had been able to breathe fresh air. This desire to set things right, to make a difference—it wasn't new, not really. It felt unearthed. As if the years of loneliness and obedience had buried it under armor and bronze.

Kunal watched the hawk take flight, soaring through the reddened sky of the early evening, imagining how the air would feel against his skin—his wings.

A new beginning. A chance to do something, for once.

It was all he could really ask for.

CHAPTER 4

Kunal sneaked into the small tent, looking around before darting inside.

Esha was lying on her side, facing away from him, but he heard her soft snores and trod lightly inside the tent. In a flash, she sat up, her body twisting in what must have been a familiar way, the knife in her hand threatening. But instead of a knife flying past his head, he saw Esha double over, groaning in pain. Her knife fell to the ground.

Kunal rushed to her side and she swatted at him. "Don't sneak in like that; I might've carved a hole into your chest."

"I noticed," he said. "Though it doesn't look like you'll be carving holes into anyone anytime soon."

Esha gave him a look. "Injury or no injury, you know I could cause my fair share of pain."

"Indeed," he said mildly. "But maybe now you should

focus on resting and healing. Then you can threaten me standing up."

"You sound like Harun," she said. She pulled herself to an upright, sitting position with a grimace.

Kunal could tell she didn't mean that as a compliment, so he said nothing. Instead, he helped her, using his hands to steady her. Her skin was soft and warm under his touch, and despite her state, he could feel the heat in his belly rising. It had been a while since they were alone together.

He knew he should drop his hands, let her sit back and keep resting, but his hands stayed on her waist, trailing up her arms and shoulders.

When he looked up, Esha was staring back, an eyebrow slightly raised. Color was slowly rising into her cheeks.

"Just checking to see how you're healing," he said.

Esha was lucky the knife wound had been clean and that Kunal had been able to get her to a healer quickly. By the time he had flown them close to camp, her wound had been sewn shut.

"Then you'll see I'm healing quite well. So well, that you should really let me get some fresh air. Walk around camp, that sort of thing," she said.

"Arpiya already warned me that you'd say something like that. Apparently, last time you got wounded you sneaked out and managed to run half a training session with the squads until she caught you."

"And my injury then was much worse." Esha tried to

move up, but Kunal's arms around her proved an obstacle. "So you should really let me go."

He chuckled. "Arpiya also mentioned that when she found you, you had undone a quarter of the stitches, earning you a tongue-lashing from the healer."

Esha sank back against the cot frame. "Also true."

"Look, the more you rest now, the more useful you can be once we're all in Gwali."

"Are you leaving?"

"Tonight," he said. "I told them it was so I could arrive by evening tomorrow but . . ."

"You mean to arrive in the morning," she said, her voice quieting. "I'm not too fond of the idea of you leaving. Again." A hint of something shy crept into her voice, and Kunal felt his conviction soften.

"I'll find you," he said.

Esha chuckled low. "Just like old times? But I'll be in the Dharkan royal retinue."

"I know," he said. "But would it really be so strange for a young, beautiful Dharkan girl to catch the eye of a Senap guard?"

Esha leaned into him, before wincing in pain at the movement. "We can't be obvious. Perhaps I'll catch your eye, but nothing more."

She paused.

"At least not in public," she said softly, the hint in her voice enough to set a low simmer to Kunal's blood.

<hr>

Esha noticed the way Kunal's eyes flashed; his body tensed, and she held back a little smile.

"We'll have to set rules," she said, lowering her voice.

"Harun already gave me a list—"

"Not for your communication with the team. For us," Esha said. "We can't tell the others."

Kunal's lips momentarily pursed, but he nodded. "I've just gained their trust. Plus, I have no interest in facing down an angry Bhandu."

"How will we communicate? You and I?" He traced little circles over the skin of her knuckles. Esha shivered.

"I'll leave you notes," she said.

A quick glance around told her that no one was outside the tent. She leaned forward to cup his face, fighting back a groan of pain. She drew a thumb over his lips, her eyes flickering to them.

He took the hint and kissed her, slowly, gently, taking care not to put pressure on her left side. Her frustration and annoyance faded to the background. She could live in these moments, bathe in them, wear them like armor.

She might need to for this upcoming fight.

Esha tensed up again, and Kunal pulled back, looking at her. "Are you okay? Did I push into your wound? I knew I shouldn't have—"

She shushed him with another kiss, a quick one. "I'm fine. I just started thinking about the task we have ahead of us. Do you remember being at court?"

"Not much."

"Understanding the politics, making alliances, will be important. Tensions will be high with the Sun Mela now open to Dharkans. Not to mention the peace treaty looming over everything."

"You're really making me look forward to this mission," he said.

"What's not to like? Subterfuge and schemes. You've dealt with vicious vipers and snapping turtles. It'll be fun," she said. "Your first mission as a rebel."

He shook his head.

"I'm not a rebel, Esha. I'm not sure I can do this," he said softly, revealing the fear that had begun prickling at his chest.

"You're not. You're a soldier. And that's why you're perfect for this role. Just be yourself."

Kunal chuckled, but she could still see a flicker of worry in his eyes. Esha felt it too, a needling thorn under her ribs.

CHAPTER 5

Kunal strode toward the Fort, wincing as he rolled his shoulders. He hadn't mastered landing when he flew and always managed to hit something—this time it had been a series of towering rosewood trees. He picked a few leaves out of his hair before he came into view of the Fort.

Kunal spotted two soldiers at the watchtower and raised a hand in greeting. Before he could even lower his hand, a conch shell was blown and two more soldiers ran up the gatehouse steps to the top of the watchtower, peering down at him.

They shielded their eyes as they looked at him and for a moment Kunal worried—would he be accepted back?

But then they waved him in, away from the official entrance.

He had barely knocked on the soldiers' entrance to the Red Fortress when it flew open and he was barreled into.

It took Kunal a few seconds to realize that he wasn't being attacked but, rather, embraced.

Kunal patted Alok awkwardly on the back, unused to such affection from his friend. But gods above, was he happy to see him. Alok pulled away, coughing a bit as he straightened and pretended like he hadn't just squeezed Kunal within an inch of his life.

"Kunal," he said. "It is good to see you in fine health, comrade. Praise to the king that we received your hawk in time."

Kunal raised an eyebrow at the formal tone and was about to remark on it, when footsteps turned the corner and Commander, now General, Panak appeared. It was quite the welcome party.

"Soldier, glad to have you back," the new general said, echoing Alok's words. "Especially after what happened to the other men on your mission."

Kunal dropped to his knees, crossing an arm over his torso, four fingers to his chest. "General, it's with my sincerest of apologies that I come back empty-handed. I've failed the mission, and I accept any judgment on your behalf for my punishment."

Kunal had prepared for this. He hoped it would be something light—extra menial labor in the Fort or to the journey to Gwali, at worst a demotion. It was only now that his heart seized and he thought of all the other punishments that might be befitting his failure. Kunal had assumed his standing as a loyal soldier, as a recently made Senap, would help him. The Fort couldn't afford to lose another soldier after losing three, but nothing was for sure.

"Kunal." He looked up, startled by the use of his first name. "There was no failure. We sent you on an impossible task. Three of your fellow soldiers didn't return, yet you were wily enough to escape. You'll eat with me tonight at the main table and give me your full debrief."

General Panak clasped Kunal around the arms and dragged him up to his feet. "And we'll discuss your commission day tomorrow as well."

He clapped Kunal on the shoulder once before turning away. "Alok, make sure this soldier gets a hot bath and food." It wasn't until the general's footsteps faded away, disappearing into silence on the stone floors, that Kunal faced Alok.

"Has it been like this since I left?" Kunal didn't try to hide the bewilderment in his voice. His uncle would've imposed some sort of punishment, even if it was light, simply to make an example of failure.

"Don't be fooled," Alok whispered. They walked down the hallway toward the training courtyard, where soldiers milled about. There was a lively lilt to the air, and Kunal realized what it was—conversation. They had never been allowed to have conversations during training.

Alok stopped in a small alcove that overlooked the training courtyard but was still half shrouded in shadows.

"If anything, the Fort's become more dangerous," Alok said.

"Really?"

"At least before, you knew what to be scared—to be aware of. This new veneer of being friendly, not just comrades, it makes me uncomfortable," Alok said.

Kunal chuckled. "Well, there are a lot of reasons that could be true—"

"No, don't be fooled. It seems the general has plans for you, or you've caught his eye. But things haven't really changed around here. Punishments are just as arbitrary, but they're no longer solely based on the rules."

A rustle of feet on the stone moved up toward them. "Be careful tonight. I don't trust General Panak."

"Like you trusted my uncle?" Kunal said, a little more sharply than he intended.

Some of the tension in Alok's shoulders dropped. "Don't be a pillock, Kunal. Your uncle had his issues, but he ran this Fort like a well-oiled wheel. People understood their place, understood the rules."

Kunal looked closer at his friend, saw the truth in his eyes.

"And you're worried about what happens when highly trained and well-armed soldiers no longer understand the rules?"

"With clear rules, even unspoken ones, there's order. I don't know, Kunal. Something has changed."

Kunal looked around, thinking back to the new feeling in the air. Change was a good thing, in his mind, especially after all he had learned about his uncle and the Fort's role in Sundara and the Night of Tears. Maybe Alok was right. Or maybe he was being paranoid after being alone in the Fort for months.

It wouldn't hurt to be careful tonight, however skeptical he was of Alok's fear.

"I'll be on guard during dinner, then, and I'll report back to you," Kunal said, unable to resist throwing in a wry smile.

Alok scoffed. "You'd probably get by pretty well in life answering to me."

"You know, you sound like someone I met during my mission."

"And from the look on your face, this is a person who didn't make it into your notes back to me?" His voice was rather accusatory.

Kunal chuckled. "Oh, definitely not. She wouldn't have liked that."

"She?" Alok grinned, slow. "So you finally put that face to good use."

"Not that again."

Alok shrugged as if to indicate he couldn't be blamed.

Kunal looked at his friend, his wide-eyed gaze, the perpetual smile that graced his face even when he frowned.

It was a familiar face. Home.

"Alok, I wanted to say—"

But Laksh had been familiar too. Kunal took another look, a longer one at his friend, assessing him like he would a battle plan. His friend looked a little worse for the wear.

Alok would be different—Kunal wouldn't take him for granted, wouldn't miss those signs. As it was, Kunal would need help at the Fort. Needed someone to confide in about Esha and the Blades and everything that had happened over the past two moons.

"Yes?" Alok prompted.

A memory of Laksh's face, of him holding a knife to Kunal's throat, stopped him cold.

"Nothing important. Glad to see you."

Alok gave him a sidelong glance. "You too, Kunal. You too."

———◄○►———

Esha gently lowered her feet to the floor as shades of violet streamed through the thin canvas of the tents. She tested her movements, putting weight onto one leg and then the other. Her legs worked fine. A sharp pain stabbed into her as she accidentally twisted. It was just her entire torso that burned.

It had been a few days since Kunal had left, trying to make it to the Fort before the end of the moon cycle. If he missed his commission day, he wouldn't be inducted into the Senap guard. Esha didn't want to admit it, but she already missed his presence. She had spent the time since he left confined to her bed, alternating between replaying their goodbye and planning out the steps of her mission in Gwali.

The Sun Mela would be scheduled and set for them, with parties and competitions and events. Esha would have to make friends quickly with the palace staff and find the best ways in and out, as well as be at court. Esha took another step, her body stiff from disuse. She had only gotten to the front of her tent when the flap blew open and Arpiya almost ran into her.

"And what do you think you're doing out of bed?" Arpiya demanded.

"That isn't really a bed. It's hard as stone, and I'm sick to death of being cooped up in here."

"I don't care. Get back in there. I'm under strict orders to keep you rested. Do you want the wound to heal improperly and then to start bleeding through your sari during one of the Mela dance performances?"

"No," Esha mumbled.

Arpiya gave her a look, her hands on her waist. "Then get back in bed. If Harun hears—"

"If Harun hears about what?" a deep voice asked. Harun's head ducked into the tent.

"She got out of bed," Arpiya accused.

Esha shrugged. "Would you expect anything else of me?"

Harun smiled. "No."

Arpiya let out a deep, weary sigh.

"It's okay, Arpiya. I came to get her anyway," Harun said. He came in and took Esha's arm, holding her up. His arm snaked around her waist, and despite her grumbles of protest, she sagged against him. The scent of almond oil, of Harun, enveloped her, and she felt herself relax. She'd forgotten what it was like to be back at home—or the closest approximation of it.

Arpiya came up on the other side of her.

"I can walk just fine," Esha said in protest. Arpiya glared at her.

"I'm sure you can. But knowing you, you'll reach for something or try to lift something, and then we'll be back to stitching you up."

Esha groaned but couldn't help the surge of warmth in her chest at being so well looked after. Cared for.

"Fine, but you can only help me out to the campfire. I'll struggle from there. I don't want the squads to worry."

Esha thought she heard Arpiya mutter "Too late." The three of them somehow got out of the tent together and to the campfire. Arpiya moved away, already focused on something new, but Harun held on to Esha.

Esha looked up at him. "So why did you come to get me, defying your own order?"

His face broke into a grin. "I have something to show you."

Arpiya bounced on her toes. "Oh! I have something too. I'll be right back." She ran away before either of them could respond.

"What is this thing?" Esha asked, letting Harun guide her through the camp.

"You'll see."

Harun kept his arm around her, and she glanced up at him. "You can let go now."

"How do I know you won't collapse?"

"It'll take more than a knife wound to knock me out of the game," she said. His hand tightened around her waist, pulling her close to him for a second, before he let go.

"All right, my little Viper. I'll let you stumble across the rest of camp to assuage your ego."

Esha scoffed, waving a hand. "I'll need more than that for my ego."

Harun laughed but stood aside, walking slowly next to her. He led her into his tent, evident from the regal lion crest and numerous red-and-gold clad guards outside, and toward the back, where a large mahogany table stood proud. A long scroll of paper, stained from age at the edges, was unfurled across the table, little figurines of silver on top.

"Remember that map we always envied in Father's war room?" Harun bounded across the room.

Of course she did. That's where she'd spent many a morning after archery practice with Harun, tracing her finger along the map and imagining all the wondrous places her father had gone, might have gone if he were still alive.

"Well, I stole it," he said. A childish smile lit up his face as he waggled his eyebrows at her. She laughed, mostly at the expression on his face, one she hadn't seen in years.

"And your father didn't notice?"

"By the time he does, I'll be long gone." He grinned. "Plus, we have more use for it right now. It was just hanging there, dusty and unused. Thought I would give it a new home for a bit."

"Obviously," Esha said, grinning back. Harun had been a serious young boy—the events of his childhood had made him that way—but when he acted out, it had been legendary.

Clearly, he hadn't grown out of that yet. She was glad for it.

He sat down at the table, chattering with excitement about something on the map. Esha smiled and nodded, knowing she should pay attention. But really, she was just happy to be back and with her friend.

The mission to kill General Hotha had taken up nearly three moons of her life, and it had been shadowed with loneliness and fear, wondering if she'd make it back alive to even see her team again or if she'd die alone in Jansa. Meeting Kunal had changed all of that, and yet, Harun and the team were her family. It was a different sort of comfort.

Esha drew closer to him, looking at the map he had laid out on the table. She peered over his shoulder to get a better look when Harun turned suddenly to say something. Their eyes met, their faces only a hairbreadth apart. His eyes flickered down to her lips, and a memory of their last kiss flashed across her mind. It had been before her mission, on a rare cool night in Mathur on a balcony of the Palace, the river shimmering below them.

Arpiya emerged from the side room with an annoyed expression at that exact moment, coughing.

"The boys never clean the dust off their gear," she grumbled. She glanced at them and then sighed wearily. "Can your reunion wait? I have something important to tell you."

Harun's cheeks reddened a bit at that, and he pulled back. Esha did too, wondering why she hadn't before.

"Anyway. I sent out notes to the spymaster in Mathur and my contacts in Gwali the minute you came back. Their intel on Dharmdev is quite illuminating."

Harun nodded at her to continue.

"Apparently, he's been a figure in some of the smaller towns for quite a while. Made a name for himself by stealing from garrisons and taking down soldiers who were corrupt."

"A regular folk hero," Esha said.

"Kind of," Arpiya said. "He's won the support of some of the common people with the stealing and aggression, but there are whispers of them being radicals ever since he moved to Gwali and started gathering followers. I don't think he'll be content with stealing, not if the reports are true. He's determined to take down Vardaan, put a new government in place. I believe it. This is a man who's built himself into a folk legend without ever showing his face."

"Sound familiar?" Harun asked, raising an eyebrow at Esha.

"So he has a group? How many? What's the organization?" It couldn't be too big or they would've heard more chatter from the Crescent Blades stationed in Gwali and the surrounding towns. Or perhaps he was just that good.

"Started out small, according to my contacts. But he's been recruiting the smaller resistance groups, those that lost leaders during Vardaan's last raid."

"Taking a page from the Yavars' book," Esha said. The Yavar horsepeople lived in clans, separated from each other. But after the War in the North thirty years ago, one man had united them under his one banner.

"Because of that, Dharmdev's numbers are strong. His followers call themselves the Scales of Justice."

"Dharmdev's Scales," Harun said. "Catchy."

"Organization is unclear, but I can confirm that he has at least a second-in-command. Don't know how many are in his inner circle yet."

"Laksh might have been," Esha said.

"The soldier?" Harun asked. "If he escaped, he's a liability. He knows your face, Esha. And the soldier from the caravan saw Kunal."

That wasn't even the worst of it, though she wasn't about to tell Harun that.

"I have a plan to take care of it," Esha said. She'd track down the soldier from the caravan in Gwali. As for Laksh, her poison-tipped knife would have slowed him down, even though it had only grazed him. That poison worked quickly, and they'd be able to get to Dharmdev before he did.

"What are you thinking?" Harun asked her.

"The Scales tried to frame me—to draw me out or to distract Vardaan; it doesn't matter. They put my life in danger, and they did it well. It took me almost two moons to unravel their scheme." Esha hesitated for a moment, an idea hovering in her mind. She took the leap. "I think we should try to talk to them. They want Vardaan off the throne; so do we. We should at least reach out to them. See if we can be allies."

And keep an eye on them. But she wouldn't voice that thought, not when Harun didn't know all that had transpired in the jungle with Laksh, or that Kunal was a Samyad, the *heen rayan*.

"Only you would suggest allying with the group that framed you," Harun said, snorting. He moved a silver figurine across the board, placing it in Gwali from where it had been, languishing in the outer towns of central Jansa.

"Speaking of alliances," he said. "We'll need a few."

"Noble houses will be the best, right?" Esha said, excitement filling her. She loved the thrill of the chase, but she also loved planning. Assessing and plotting and dreaming.

"Not the nobles. I hate working with nobles," Arpiya said, groaning.

"Says the girl from one of the most blue-blooded houses in Dharka," Harun said.

Arpiya glared at him. "I thought we agreed to never mention that."

"If we want to be successful," Harun said, "we'll need political support, money—"

"And troops," Esha finished. "All things nobles can give us easy access to. We just need one house, maybe two, in Jansa to support us. Perhaps Ayul or Rusala."

"Maybe Pramukh," Esha and Harun both said at the same time.

They grinned at each other. She had forgotten how easy it was with Harun sometimes.

"What?" Arpiya asked, exasperated. "I don't speak Harun. Why do we need support? I thought we were rescuing Reha."

"Yes. We rescue Reha, fix the *janma* bond, but then?" Esha said.

Harun stood up, taking the large silver figurine in the shape of an eagle and knocking over the small kinglike figurine that was in Gwali. He placed the figurine approximately where the Pink Palace of Gwali would stand.

"Then we take the throne back from Vardaan," he said.

CHAPTER 6

Esha bit her lip as the horse jostled, knowing full well that if she let her pain show through, Harun would put her back in the travel palanquin.

She blew out a frustrated sigh and pulled a bit tighter on her waist sash, which cinched the hard bandages around her waist. Esha glanced at the sky for the third time, checking for signs of a hawk. She'd started sending out a few notes to her contacts in Gwali, laying the groundwork for her return there. She had unfinished business in the city. She hadn't lied to Kunal when she had said the general had been the first step of her plan.

She was going back to Gwali, the place of her parents' murder, and this time, she'd leave the city with better memories.

"Esha, a word?" Harun said, trotting up next to her and shooting a quick glance at her side. "I saw you left the palanquin. Hard to make friends in there?"

"Well, you haven't made it easy. Half of them are eyeing me warily, wondering where I've been and why I haven't been at court as much the past few years. The other half managed to remember I was introduced to court years ago as the king's ward and now see me as a potential path to you. Which is annoying."

"You *are* a path to me," he said. "It's smart of them to see it."

"You're condoning such behavior?"

Harun snorted. "Don't pretend you don't love it—the scheming. You'd have every one of them eating out of your palm in weeks if you were truly at court."

She raised an eyebrow. "Like you?"

"I'd like to say I'm the only one immune to your charms." He grinned at her, one of those ones that always made her stomach flip a little. "But we both know the truth."

"Maybe you're right, but part of me wishes I could own the role I've had in protecting our country. Maybe then they'd stop pestering me with questions about your favorite color of silk," she said.

"Indigo," he said, smirking. "And I know what you've done, Esha. This cease-fire, this potential for peace, none of it would be possible without your years of sacrifice."

"That's nice, but I wouldn't mind having those ladies in there know that I was the one who made sure their borders and trade routes didn't get disrupted," she grumbled.

"Well, you won't always have to be in the shadows. You don't always have to play that role."

"What?" Her head shot up. "That's my whole life."

"That *has been* your whole life. But what about in the future?"

"What about it?" Esha frowned. The Viper would always be needed to ensure peace.

"Have you considered a role at court? My council?" Harun said.

"I already turned you down. It'll be easier for me to move around unnoticed during the Mela if I don't need to be attached to your side as your adviser."

"Like that would be so horrible," he said.

She stuck her tongue out at him. "Anyway, I'm unofficially one of your advisers. And I don't think I'd ever want to be on your council, trapped in a room, arguing over grain rations. I'd rather be in the field, ensuring we have those grain shipments for our people," she said.

"Maybe not the council, then. But something—"

"Harun, I was trying to complain about how no one appreciates me," Esha said. "Not take on another job."

His voice softened. "I appreciate you."

Her throat went dry as she tried to figure out how to reply.

Harun straightened in his seat, clearing his throat. "It's why I feel that I should apologize to you, again." Esha quirked an eyebrow at his tone.

"For what happened at the last donor function? I'm past it, Harun. I've done worse to you before," she said with a wry smile.

"No, not that." He winced. "Though that was wrong of me. I was upset, angry, and I should've acted with a clearer head. But the soldier . . ."

"Kunal."

"Kunal," Harun agreed, drawing out the syllables of the name. "I should've trusted you more on him. Moon Lord knows how he managed to get you back in time when you were so severely wounded, but he did. He brought you back. I'll always be grateful."

"Thank you," she said. "Does this mean you'll start being nicer to Kunal?"

Harun made a face. "I said I trusted him, I didn't say I particularly liked him. But he's doing us a huge favor by being our eyes and ears on the inside. Because of him we're one step closer to finding Reha."

"One step closer to bringing back balance."

They exchanged a glance, and she knew he was thinking of the same thing as her—the first time they had decided to join the rebels and had made the same vow, under a banyan tree in Mathur.

"Who would've thought we'd end up as the leaders that day?" she asked. The night of their first mission and decision to change the world. "We were so young."

"We weren't young," he said. "Our innocence left us both earlier than most. The gods decreed this was our path."

There was something reassuring about the way Harun believed so firmly in his path—their path. After having grown up seeing his uncle betray his father, murder his aunt and cousins, and then bring a vibrant country to its knees, Harun had dedicated his life to Dharka.

His people before everything. Always.

It was why they had clicked. Her thirst for revenge had melded with his need to bring back balance, and together, they had dreamed of a new world.

And tomorrow, they'd arrive in Gwali. They'd be one step closer to ending all of this.

Finding Reha. Deposing Vardaan. Bringing back balance to the land.

"Do you think she'll be happy to see me?" It took a few seconds for Esha to realize Harun was talking about his sister. "Or will she curse me for not looking harder for her? For abandoning her."

"Harun."

"Last time I saw her she was learning to play the veena." He chuckled. "She had also just started climbing everything, and it was my job to peel her off trees and bring her safely down every day for dinner. I wonder if she's the same or . . ."

His voice caught.

A wellspring of sadness rose in Esha, one that mingled with her own grief-tinged memories of the city they were traveling to.

"It's been ten years, Esha," he whispered, his hand going to the locket he always wore. It had a small oil painting of his family inside, and she'd never seen him without it.

"It'll be as if nothing has changed," Esha said. The future would be better once they had righted the wrongs of the past. It had to be.

He nodded slowly, setting his shoulders as they crested a tall hill. The moment had passed, and the prince had returned, steeling himself for the task ahead.

"Look," he said. He grabbed her reins and tugged her horse into a canter, breaking off from the rest of the retinue. "We're almost there."

She pulled her horse to a stop next to his, looking out over the vista. Gwali was spread out below the cliff they were on, leagues in the distance but visible. It shone in the buttery yellow of the midday sun, which cast a glow around the pink sandstone of the palace in the center, the ocean past it.

Gwali. The city of the murderous king, usurper of Jansa. Also the city of ancient lore, the birthplace of Naria and the ancient games of the Sun Mela.

"Are you ready?" Harun turned his dark gaze on her. They were heading into an unknown, but she wouldn't be alone this time. And soon, Kunal would be there too.

"As I'll ever be."

———◄◦►———

Kunal had to admit being back at the Fort wasn't as easy as he had thought. He half expected General Panak to jump out at him, demanding to know his whereabouts, and he hated having to lie to Alok.

How did Esha do this so often? He felt like his insides were on fire, and yet his skin was clammy whenever he saw Alok. He'd taken to turning the opposite way the past few hours whenever he heard Alok walking toward him.

And now? He definitely needed to be left unseen.

He peeked his head around the corner, checking both directions before he walked over to the records room. It'd be his first stop, among many, at the Fort.

Kunal took care to ease the door shut—he knew it squeaked. A summer banished to the records room for unauthorized oil painting had led him to become very familiar with the archival system and how the Fort maintained its communications.

Not much had changed since that summer. The room was still musty, like old leather and seawater combined. He found the cabinet he was looking for and flipped through a stack of old notes neatly tied together.

The ones he'd be looking for would be on top. He nudged an older stack over, straining his neck to see over the organized piles.

There.

Kunal moved forward, sidling along the narrow gaps between the shelving. These notes were used to pass from transport to transport as record and confirmation, especially as squads were restationed and moved around. One authorized note would be sent out and the copy would be stored here. A process his uncle had started.

He found the one he was looking for, from only a few

weeks ago, and flipped through until he found a note that was for a squad that had been restationed from the coast to the center of Jansa. And then another from the Hara Desert to Gwali. Then another from Faor to Gwali.

One wasn't enough, two was a coincidence, but three was deliberate. Kunal checked the destination for each of them, squinting at the parchment notes.

Gwali. Martial sector. The citadel.

Kunal sucked in a breath. It was expected that Reha would be taken to the martial sector of Gwali, but he supposed he had been holding out hope that she would be in the palace. That perhaps Vardaan had different plans for her than captivity and numerous guards.

Kunal took out a small piece of chalk and paper, jotting down what he found. He rolled up the small notes and tucked them into his waist sash before carefully putting the original records back. He'd send a hawk to Esha when he got a chance, though he felt himself hesitating. He shook his head. No, they needed a heads-up before they entered the city.

The citadel.

Walls of stone the height of three men, squads of elite Senaps inside and outside, night and day. One of the most heavily guarded, well-fortified buildings in the entire capital city.

Kunal could only hope Esha would be as good at breaking into citadels as she was forts.

CHAPTER 7

Kunal relaxed into conversation with the new general, telling him as much of the truth as he could over their dinner of cumin- and coriander-spiced vegetables and warm, crusty flatbread.

Alok had been paranoid. The general was perfectly nice, inquiring about the mission and the towns he had been to, which garrisons. He didn't have too many questions about the Viper.

The hall was as Kunal had remembered, the same din of noise as the soldiers chatted and ate, clinking goblets and knocking the wooden table legs. He had left Alok somewhere in the middle with his squad of charioteers. They'd been celebrating the mastery of a new maneuver, one he remembered his uncle had tried to teach them for almost a year.

Kunal wanted to ask questions, see how the Fort had

changed, but he had to focus. He had made a promise to the Blades, and though it made his stomach burn to lie to the men he had trusted for so many years, the past two moons had taught him that trust wasn't as solid of a currency as he had believed.

The specter of Laksh still hung over his conversations with Alok, who hadn't noticed anything, thankfully. Kunal didn't want to suspect him. But until he had proof Laksh had acted alone, he couldn't confide in Alok.

The last of the food was cleared from the leaders' table, and General Panak turned to clap Kunal on the back.

"You've always been a breath of fresh air, Kunal. I can see why your uncle enjoyed having you at the Fort. Though he regretted bringing you here first, not giving you a choice to explore more of what was beyond these walls."

Kunal didn't try to hide his shock.

General Panak looked solemn. "We became closer before his passing, when I took on the mantle of commander. I knew you were important to him. He wanted the best for you."

Kunal swallowed roughly. Somewhere, somehow, his uncle had turned from the right path, becoming the feared general instead of just stern Uncle Setu. Kunal wished he had known him before, seen the man behind the armor.

"That's why it pains me to tell you this," General Panak said.

Kunal's body tensed.

"I know we set you on an impossible task, but you failed

to bring the Viper back. If I let you off without a punishment, it'll be chaos here. My soldiers need rules and order. You will be demoted, stripped of your Senap armband and position."

Kunal kept still, trying not to betray any emotion, let alone his worry. If he couldn't become a Senap, he couldn't get to Gwali in time for the Mela.

"Unless—" General Panak paused, scanning the room, searching for something before he turned his gaze back to Kunal.

"Unless what?" Kunal asked. "I know I failed, General, but I'm willing to do whatever it takes to make it up to the Fort. I've worked to become a Senap for almost a decade now."

General Panak nodded, looking out to the soldiers who sat in front of their dais, scattered around the room and oblivious to them. Only a few looked up, whispering and pointing at Kunal.

"You see what I mean?" General Panak said. "To quash these rumors, we'll need a spectacle. If you want to keep your position, Kunal, you'll need to undergo a Battle of Honor."

Kunal gripped the hilt of the knife at his side, the sharp edges digging into his palm. A Battle of Honor was the way they settled disagreements at the Red Fortress, a time-honored, ancient tradition.

Trial by combat.

———◦———

The gates of Gwali were as majestic as ever. A thick sandstone wall encircled the city, with tall watchtowers dotted along the way. Two eagles with their wings unfurled were carved into the outer wall of the city, their sharp eyes on any intruders—or guests.

The ancient guardians of Naria's city.

And just behind the legendary eagles were corpses hanging from the two watchtowers, a reminder of one's fate if Vardaan is displeased. Esha and Harun's retinue hurried past, and as soon as they entered the gates, they were thrown into the maze that was the center of the city. Throngs of people fitted into every corner of the old city, milling about like crashing waves.

Ancient marble buildings mixed in with new sandstone towers. The city's denizens approached it with a combination of reverence and casual indifference, throwing out their refuse in the same streets where they put idols of the gods. Esha had uncertain feelings about the place as well— her first childhood memories of the city were of the palace, as well as the palace's dungeons. She was familiar with Gwali—the wealthy town houses, the merchant and trade quarter, the artisans' way, the thieves' den, and the beautiful temples and city halls dotted throughout.

It was the palace, and the people inside, that worried her.

Their procession made its way through the most narrow labyrinth of streets before coming out onto the martial quarter and the Queen's Road. Even Vardaan's attempts to change the name to the King's Road hadn't changed the hearts and minds of people who still referred to it by its original name. The ancient road expanded, curving right and up a ramp that led to the Pink Palace of Gwali.

The Pink Palace was bordered by the ocean to one side, a forest to another, and the city to the next. A perfect situation for a palace, the stronghold of the warrior queens of Jansa. Esha's retinue traversed the ramp up to the palace, arriving outside the massive doors as they were opened by a dozen Senaps in ceremonial regalia.

Harun drew to the front of the procession, having switched to riding in his chariot. His driver pulled forward so that they drove in parallel with the entrance of the palace, the tall, solid gold doors carved with ancient myths and tales.

They waited, and Esha began to grow impatient. She admired and hated this part of court politics. Vardaan was showing his dominance in making them wait, but in another few minutes it would be outright disrespect.

Harun and his uncle Vardaan hadn't seen each other since Harun was a child. What would that interaction be like—would they embrace and play the roles of family? Or would they choose a more true path?

Esha was about to start counting when the doors creaked open and Vardaan, the Pretender King, walked out.

She felt her blood rise in answer to her grief. That old, familiar hatred. Her heart quickened in time to the thudding in her head, everything else receding but that hot, dark feeling. This was the man whose greed had torn apart Jansa. Had killed her family.

Esha pulled at her horse's reins, urging him forward to catch up to the front of the crowd. She didn't trust anyone in this court, certainly not this Pretender King. She readied her knife under her uttariya, just in case this welcoming party grew out of hand.

Vardaan was at the front of the crowd, flanked by a cadre of officials in crisp white uttariyas. He was resplendent in a gold-threaded silk uttariya and dhoti, both the color of fresh blood. Long and short necklaces of gold adorned his neck, ruby-encrusted armbands encircled his upper arms, and he wore a thick gold circlet around his brow.

Understated for his first appearance.

Harun had matched him, though he wore no circlet or crown. As the representative of his father, King Mahir, Harun had chosen to dress down. He was the crown prince, but he was his father's emissary first.

"Welcome, nephew," Vardaan said, walking forward. He threw his arms open as Harun descended from the chariot. Harun dropped to his knees, touching his fingertips to his uncle's feet in reverence. A deft avoidance.

Harun had shown him respect, as was due to his uncle, and taken control of the situation in one move. Vardaan reached down and brought Harun up to his feet, as an elder would do, and Harun bent forward, his palms together in greeting.

"Salutations, Uncle."

"Ah, none of that, my nephew."

Vardaan slapped his hands aside and, before Harun

could react, pulled him into a hug. Her friend's face showed an expression of shock before it quickly disappeared. Esha's fingers tightened over her knife.

Vardaan pulled back but didn't let go of Harun, beholding him instead, throwing glances out to the crowd of nobles behind them. They gave little gasps of happiness at the warmth from Vardaan. As if they believed his little show.

They both shared the same angular jaws and sharp features, a thick head of hair—Vardaan's streaked with white—and short beards. Even their eyes held that same deep, penetrating gaze. As if they were constantly sizing you up. She knew they were related, but to see it in person was unnerving. How could two people from the same family turn out so different?

"You've grown so much, my boy," Vardaan said loudly. "I remember when you were just a toddler, running after me with your toy sword, begging me to show you sword fighting."

He gave a small laugh, and a chorus of titters went up behind him in the crowd of Gwali nobles.

"I remember as well, Uncle. So long ago. What, has it been fifteen years now? A lifetime," Harun said.

Vardaan didn't take the bait, instead clapping an arm on his back. "It has been too long, it's true. I'm sad your father couldn't make it." A storm clouded his face. "Is he doing well?"

"Better," Harun said. "Just a passing illness, but we didn't think it would be right for him to travel until better." There was lightness in his tone, but it was clear Dharka was still off-limits. What confused Esha was the look on Vardaan's face.

"I hope my brother gets better. Looking at you is like looking at a copy of him." The Pretender King's face softened. "I have missed so much in your life—your first archery lessons, your first reading of the royal history, your shifting ceremony."

His voice sounded sincere—and Harun took a second too long to respond. "There will always be more firsts, uncle," he said. "Maybe now we have a chance to see them."

No more than a couple sentences and a decade of pain in them. Esha had been the one to sit with Harun, listen to his heartache over his sister, the pain of having his uncle leave and betray them so deeply. Harun had only been eleven when the coup had happened, but he had been old enough to have formed a bond with his uncle.

Esha wanted to believe this was another manipulation, another court move on the larger chessboard. But she'd seen enough pain in people's eyes, felt it enough herself, that she recognized it in Vardaan's. Esha knew about Vardaan, had studied his every move, watched his every battle tactic and political ploy. But she had missed a crucial element to the picture she had painted of him—reality.

Reality was usually never the same as stories—as the Viper she should know that better than anyone. And the reality here was that Vardaan was utterly, completely normal in real life. He was charismatic, attractive even.

Esha no longer knew where to put Vardaan, the nightmare from her dreams, the monster they hated.

And that terrified her.

————◆————

A breeze gusted into the lower courtyard of the Fortress where Kunal, and the other soldiers of the Fort, were arrayed.

His upcoming battle had drawn many soldiers away from their precious free time. There were rumors Kunal had gone up against the Viper and survived, or that he had killed the other soldiers to get the prize for himself.

Kunal finished stretching and rose to his feet, bouncing on his toes to warm his muscles. To his left was a table of weapons. What would be the best to use? They'd get one weapon for the fight, but it would all depend on what his opponent chose. Alok was to his left, his second-in-combat.

"Why is it that I'm always trying to prevent you from getting yourself killed? And that you never listen?" Alok said.

"Maybe you're getting old," Kunal replied. Alok's five years on him meant nothing to him, but he loved to rib him about it. "Losing that sense of danger and fun."

"You sound like Laksh," Alok said. He scratched the end of his short beard. "I still can't believe he ran away. Especially without telling us."

Kunal shrugged. "Perhaps he was scared of the consequences of failing."

"You came back, and you failed. Even a demotion is

better than certain death from desertion," he said.

"Some people are scared of failure."

"But that wasn't really Laksh. He had things he wanted to do here."

"Well, maybe we don't always know people as well as we think," Kunal snapped.

"Okay, maybe we don't. I'm beginning to realize that too," Alok said, raising his hands in defeat.

Kunal sighed, turning to apologize, but the conch shell blew. His opponent walked in, a towering statue of muscle and ferocity.

Kunal took a deep breath and centered himself, focusing on the fight ahead and his goal.

Stay alive. Get his commission as Senap to Gwali, meet with the team, and rescue Reha. Save the country.

But the thing he was looking forward to the most was seeing Esha. Four days at the Fort and he was missing her fiercely. He painted her in his mind, the careless toss of her curls, and the small dimple at the corner of her lips when she smirked.

The conch shell blew again and his opponent, Urvan, grabbed a long-handled mace and swung at him. Kunal immediately ducked out of the way. Alok grabbed a spear and threw it toward Kunal, who caught it handily.

Perfect. Long range enough that he could hit his opponent without getting in range of his mace. He hated maces. They were weapons of brutality, with no finesse.

Kunal lunged low, stabbing his spear into Urvan's

thigh. The soldier cried out but didn't go down. Kunal spun around, aiming to land a blow on Urvan's side, but the man moved quicker than he anticipated.

He caught the end of Kunal's spear and threw him to the ground. Kunal tumbled to the sand of the Fort courtyard, his spear clattering out of his hands.

Urvan approached, breaking into a run now. Kunal scrambled to reclaim his spear and get to his feet. He dodged the heavy end of Urvan's mace, sprinting out of the way at the last second. Kunal spun his spear in his arms, gaining momentum as he approached, knocking Urvan in the jaw with the blunt end and stabbing him in the arm with the other, before ducking out of his mace's range once more.

Kunal did that a few more times, until he could see Urvan getting frustrated—and confused. The Battle of Honor was till the death, and Kunal seemed to be playing with him. But ferocity and brutality had never been Kunal's style.

Urvan's frustration caught up to him, his face growing red. Kunal waited as the soldier charged at him, a fierce yell tearing out of his throat.

Kunal didn't move a muscle. Not until the last second, when he thrust up his spear, using the force to knock the mace out of Urvan's hand. Kunal dropped his spear and grabbed the mace, spinning and knocking the soldier to the ground.

He went down hard. Kunal dropped the heavy mace onto the sand, happy to be rid of it.

Kunal picked up his spear again and approached the

soldier. To his credit, Urvan held his chin high even as he struggled to sit up, a deep crack in his armor displaying the gash in his side. Even when facing his death, he didn't beg or ask for mercy.

"Why were you chosen for this, Urvan?" Kunal raised his spear.

"I skipped out on my patrol to visit my mother," the soldier said, his voice low.

Kunal stepped forward, swinging his spear and aiming.

He threw it down a pace away from Urvan's head.

"I've won the battle, but I'll hold no claim to this man's life. That's for the Sun Maiden to decide," Kunal said loudly for all to hear. He turned to face General Panak, who stood on the floor above the courtyard.

A hush of whispers ran through the crowd, the soldiers unsure how to react.

"Accepted," the general said.

Kunal sagged with relief, and Alok ran to him, catching him before he stumbled.

He'd still be able to meet the team in Gwali for the Mela.

He'd still be able to help save Reha.

But beyond everything, he was glad he was still a Senap.

CHAPTER 8

The Pink Palace itself was a majestic dream, one that rivaled the halls of the palace in Mathur. The opulent pink stonework, pearl-encrusted ceilings, and intricate gold tapestries of Jansa's ancient history were stunning as always, causing the main hallway to shimmer with light. Murmurs of appreciation could be heard from a group of young Dharkan nobles, those who had been too young to have seen the palace before the war. Esha should've acted as if she were one of them. Instead, she was stuck in an onslaught of memories.

They were ushered into a guest wing Esha hadn't been in before. One blessedly free of memories. When she had last been at the palace, during her dad's final trip as Dharkan ambassador, they had stayed in the royal residence, closer to the center of the palace.

Esha walked into her room behind the royal housekeeper, nodding in thanks to the woman. It was opulent, befitting a member of the royal retinue, with a large, plush bed, expansive windows, and an armoire. Vardaan was treating them as true guests.

She checked the exits and entrances—there were two—and moved toward the closet to see if there were any hiding places, when a small noise came from behind her.

Esha started and turned around, realizing there was a maidservant still in the room. She was a pretty girl, with a round face and a wide smile that instantly put Esha at ease.

"My lady, I'm to be your maid."

Well, that was a surprise. She hadn't had a lady's maid assigned since she had been the king's ward. And she had dismissed her last one over three years ago—no one needed to know her comings and goings at court, not if she couldn't be sure of their loyalty.

"I have no need for a maid."

The girl didn't move.

"I'm sure there are other nobles who would like your services."

"The prince assigned you a maid. I won't get in your hair if that's what you're worried about, my lady. But I will say, getting dressed in some of the latest court fashions will require some extra help."

Esha frowned but couldn't very well tell the girl that she had spent years doing her own hair and styling herself as the Viper and her many faces.

"Most noble ladies are quite excited," the girl said.

"Most noble ladies haven't been traveling for years,"

Esha said, deciding on a modicum of honesty. "I'm no longer used to a lady's maid."

"Traveling?" The girl clasped her hands together in delight. "Then we'll have a lot to talk about while I get you ready. You'll need help; the whole palace is buzzing about you," the girl said, before seeming to realize she had revealed too much. Her face reddened.

"About me? Why?"

The maid started playing with her hands. "I shouldn't have said anything, my lady."

Esha chuckled and waved a hand at the girl to sit down. The maid eyed the chair but remained standing.

"What's your name?"

"Aditi, my lady." She hesitated. "I didn't mean to speak out of turn."

Her voice was deferential but there was something in the set of her shoulders that Esha recognized, a hint of steel.

"I have no problem with you speaking plainly," Esha said more softly. "If anything, I require it, Aditi. The prince requested a maid for me, and I shall accept one."

Aditi nodded, relieved, before bowing low.

"None of that," Esha said, waving her hand. "Tell me, when will my luggage be brought in?"

"It's already been brought in, my lady, and I've laid out two outfit options for tonight's dinner. It'll only be in the residence quarters and the king won't be attending, so I've picked an ivory pure silk sari with a big maroon border. It has peacocks on it, no house emblems, so you should be able to stay neutral the minute you walk in the door," Aditi said, clearly unable to hide a hint of excitement.

Esha had forgotten there would be smaller dinner parties this entire week before the Welcome Ball and looked at Aditi with new appreciation. Perhaps it wouldn't be so bad to have help.

Aditi smiled. "It's been a while since you've been at court, hasn't it? I heard as much."

"From 'the palace'?"

"From the textile trader, my lady. The Dharkan prince and his court are the talk of the town."

"Is he?" Esha said, wondering what that'd do for Harun's ego. "It has been a while, Aditi. I'll accept a maid but—"

The girl looked up.

"Only if you are my friend first. This is a new court in a new country, and I could use some help aside from dressing," Esha said, giving a sigh of reluctance. She liked the girl and the way she held her head up high, but it would be better for her to assume Esha wasn't too keen on politics.

"It's not my place, my lady. . . ."

"Please," Esha implored. "I'll not tell anyone what you say."

"All right, my lady," she said. "If we're friends, then I have to say that you should really eat some food before the dinner tonight. It will be hosted by House Manchi, and I saw their chef sneeze into the jaggery syrup earlier today."

Esha made a face and laughed. "Thank you."

"I'll fetch you some chai and snacks." Aditi moved to the

door, whispering in the ear of a servant nearby, who nodded and bowed.

"Will they always be here?" Esha asked, moving about the room and resuming her calculations.

"The servants outside? No. But if you'd like—"

"No, no, I'd prefer them not to be. And the prince's room? Where is that?"

Esha continued her surveillance, trying to figure out the easiest way for her to leave her room at night. Window or the door? If Harun was nearby, it would be easier for them to meet with the team.

"Just down the hallway in the next wing," Aditi said, still hovering over the seat Esha had offered. "He isn't too far, if you're worried, my lady."

Good, then. She'd also be able to keep a close eye on him. She didn't trust Vardaan and— Esha's head snapped up, realizing what her words sounded like.

"Oh no, I didn't—"

Aditi's face was still, but there was faint amusement in the tilt of her eyebrows and mouth.

"It's all right, my lady. I understand your concern for your prince." Her voice was light, but Esha sensed an undercurrent of interest. Aditi was one of the prince's many admirers.

Esha didn't have time to ask anything more, as the tea and food arrived—two pots of ginger chai alongside plates of pistachio cookies and thick slabs of dried mango jelly. Aditi bustled about, directing the servants to place the pots of tea and food on the various tables and then started to unpack Esha's saris. There were scars on the maid's hands, ones that looked years old.

Aditi cleared her throat. "My lady, if I am to be your friend, I feel it's my duty to let you know that the palace is buzzing about you because of the prince. It seems Lady Mati of your own court has told many others that the prince favors you and rumors have spread."

"Favors me?" Esha blinked in confusion.

"For marriage."

Esha felt her cheeks warm and pressed a hand to her face. Months ago this sort of comment would have put a smile on her face. Now it was . . . confusing. She had given up on Harun, decided he was a path closed off to her.

"We're just—" Esha paused.

"Friends?" Aditi finished, neatly folding over the pleats of Esha's second-favorite sapphire-colored sari. "I'll tell anyone who brings it up."

Before she could even thank her, Aditi bowed and left. Esha looked around at the cavernous room that was now hers, sitting down on the bed as she chewed on a pistachio cookie.

Rumors she could handle.

The question was, what else did Vardaan have in store?

———◦———

Kunal brushed aside the linen cloth that separated Laksh's room from the rest of the soldiers' barracks. He didn't know why he came here. Laksh wouldn't have left anything, not with everything so out in the open and visible to all the other soldiers in his squad.

Maybe Kunal wanted answers. Laksh's betrayal had left him warring between anger and a fierce sadness. And in between, loss. His best friend had deceived him, torn an unstitchable rip into their relationship.

Laksh technically had another moon before he would be declared "dead" to the Fort, so his section of the room was left untouched. A stack of building blocks in faded colors, a memento from his childhood. The gold comb he had been so excited about winning in a game of cards before realizing it was actually just painted gold. It was all there.

Kunal sat on the cot, reaching underneath and patting the wooden frame to look for any secret compartments or hidden scrolls. He went on like that for a few minutes, carefully inspecting every nook of Laksh's very untidy corner.

A noise, a dozen paces away, startled him. Kunal stood up quickly as the door creaked open.

"I thought I might find you here," Alok said. "You've been avoiding me since you returned, acting as if everything's okay."

"Everything's fine. I'm fine."

Alok gave him an unamused look. "Good thing you haven't changed too much, Kunal. You're still a horrible liar. You know, something about Laksh's story hasn't sat right with me since the beginning, and now you're here, in his room."

He came over to where Kunal stood, grabbing a small figurine of a Harran dagger that was on Laksh's nightstand.

"Why are you here, Kunal? You've barely said anything about Laksh, *our friend*, leaving. At first I thought you were disappointed in him for leaving the Fort. But there's more to it than you're telling me, isn't there?"

The torrent of emotions Kunal had kept at bay since Laksh's attack in the jungle came to a head.

"Laksh could be dead now for all I care," he said, rage nipping at his tongue.

But the minute the words left his mouth, he knew it wasn't true. Alok's eyes widened but he said nothing.

Kunal quieted and made a decision. "I saw him before he left. More accurately, before he betrayed my trust, tried to blackmail me, attacked me, and fled into the jungle. He's been secretly working for Dharmdev, a new rebel leader based out of the backwater towns in central Jansa. He tried to convince me to join but I said no. . . . And still I covered for him when I got back here."

"I . . . I don't even have a joke for that," Alok said.

Kunal snorted.

"You could've told me sooner." Alok's mouth was a grim, straight line.

"I didn't know if I could. He didn't just desert, Alok. He's been a double agent for moons. I didn't know if anyone else was involved. I still don't."

Alok walked over and punched him in the arm. "Yes, you do. Do you really think I could lie for weeks, let alone moons? Remember that one time I tried to challenge Laksh to cards?"

A smile came to Kunal's face. "That was difficult to watch."

"You can trust me, Kunal," he said quietly. "You're my true friend. You've been by my side from the beginning. If you knew the things I've done . . ."

"That we've all done," Kunal said.

Alok straightened and pulled a face. "I'm loyal to the Fort, soldier." There was the faintest hint of wavering in his voice.

Alok thought he was upset with Laksh for leaving the Fort. That Kunal expected that loyalty from him too. It was the small stone that cracked his armor.

Kunal didn't want to lie anymore, not to Alok. He wanted to be honest about Laksh, about Esha. He wanted someone he could trust.

"But if you think I'm going to buy that's the only thing that happened on this adventure of yours, then you're taking me for a drink-addled horse trader. You mentioned a girl, and now you're telling me Laksh was a double agent? There's more to the story, Kunal." Alok set his chin, staring Kunal down. "And I'll find out, even if I have to knock you around."

Kunal sighed, rubbing the side of his jaw.

He no longer worried about trusting Alok but rather about keeping him from this messy web he had found himself in.

"Let's go for a walk."

———◄○►———

Kunal walked into the armory, shooting a quick glance behind to make sure no one had followed him in. Confirming the fact, he moved inside.

Kunal kept an ear out for any changes in the sounds outside, having put a few well-placed, sharp rocks around the pathway and entrance to the armory. The armory was tucked into the farthest corner of the Fort and surrounded by thick walls of stone. It was the only time of day no soldiers would be in the area, most of them using their free time to go to the ocean or play dice in the courtyards above.

But he stayed alert. There was only one soldier he did expect.

"Need some help?" Alok said in greeting, turning the corner and deftly hopping around the rocks. "Want me to be lookout?"

"No, we should be good. Close the door quietly and lower your voice."

He was surprised at how well Alok had taken the news. Clearly, discovering his best friend was a deserter and had feelings for the Viper, the Fort's sworn enemy, wasn't as bad as Kunal had thought.

Alok had been shocked when Kunal first told him about what had happened during his mission. He was devastated about Laksh. Then annoyed he had missed out. And giddy when Kunal had mentioned Esha. And now he kept hinting at being a part of whatever Kunal was going to do next in Gwali.

Kunal moved toward the back part of the room, where

the knives and special weapons were kept. Alok followed behind him, looking over his shoulder.

"You know, shortly after you left, a contingent from the palace arrived. They were hidden in a room for days."

"Probably just to outline the details of the Mela, Alok."

"All right, but wasn't that good information?" Alok asked eagerly. "You know, I still can't believe that you almost left. I've been thinking about it since you told me—if I could do it too."

Kunal moved away from the shelf of sheathed knives to shush Alok. "Yes, being scared for my life is really a lot of fun."

"I've got to meet this Esha, need to find out her trick," he said. "The old Kunal would break out into welts if he were talking about desertion. Certainly wouldn't have made a joke."

"It wasn't a trick, Alok," Kunal said, sighing and running his fingers over a long, thin knife. "And it wasn't just her. You didn't see the people, the land out there beyond these walls. People are suffering, and we're doing nothing about it."

Alok's voice grew quieter. "I did, actually. I saw it on the last campaign. Why do you think I picked fights after we came back? I saw the drought. I saw people starving, and the army looked the other way. We raised taxes, took away the local courts, and hoarded our own gold. It turned my stomach."

"Then why didn't you leave? Try to do something?"

Alok laughed. "Leave and go where? My family would be in danger if I left, Kunal. Deserters' families are targeted. And try to do something? What could I do? I was no one, not even a captain."

Kunal heard what Alok didn't say—that he wasn't the previous general's nephew.

"And, Kunal . . . you don't know what I've had to do in this army."

Something bleak crossed his face, as transient as a shooting star.

Kunal shook his head. "Who cares?" he said, thinking back to his conversation with Esha by the ocean. "It's not about the past, but the future. Do you respect and love this land? Its people? Do you want to build a better future?"

Alok's brow furrowed, his hands clenched. "Yes."

"Then fight for it," Kunal said.

"You're right."

Kunal looked at his friend, who came around to pick up a long ax. He hefted it and placed it into the pack Kunal had sitting on the table.

"But you still haven't really said why you're back or what you're planning to do. It's happening in Gwali and has to do with the Mela. I'm not stupid, Kunal. So I'm telling you now, I'm in, whatever it is."

Kunal sighed. Alok's jaw was set, and he knew him well enough to not try to argue.

"You might regret this."

"Oh, I surely will. But isn't that what friendship is?"

Alok said, grinning wildly. He took a look at the weapons Kunal had accumulated—three knives, a handful of throwing stars, a quiver of arrows—and clapped him on the back. "Looks like we're going to war."

———◆———

The moon hung low in the sky, like a babe in a sling, as Esha crept out of her room and into the silence of the night.

She slipped past the night guards and down the side staircase. Soon enough, she was winding her way through the gardens, the best way in and out of the palace without notice. No official patrol within the mazelike paths, and the gardens connected to two of the other wings.

Esha climbed up the rope she had tied the day before on the outer gates during her morning walk with Lady Suchitra of House Rusala. Within minutes she was up and over. She crept along the wall, keeping to the shadows until she got to the shade of a large banyan tree. She tugged out the extra knife she had hid there, strapping it to her back, as well as a few short daggers, which she added to her forearm guards.

She had one goal tonight—find that soldier from the jungle. Mohit. She wouldn't let another soldier go, not after Laksh.

Esha knew what Kunal would say if he knew—she still remembered the look he gave her when she had slit the remaining soldiers' throats. But her lemon boy was too noble-hearted and didn't understand the realities of the world they lived in. If one soldier lived who might recognize him, that was one soldier too many for their mission to succeed.

Esha sneaked down the narrow lanes of the merchant quarter, readying her whip.

———◄◦►———

The second-story room she climbed into was small and unoccupied, a perfect vantage point to listen to the conversations downstairs.

Her contact had told her that this inn had been frequented by the soldiers of Mohit's squad and that Mohit was a fan of the establishment's specialty, cardamom rice pudding.

She tried not to think much about him, whether he liked the sweet because of his childhood or if he had a spouse who made it for him. It didn't matter if Mohit did. He had to be eliminated to protect her team.

Esha pressed an ear to the door and let her mind settle, sifting through conversations for key words—*Mohit, caravan, traitor.*

Finally, something perked her ears.

"I don't see your friend here today," the owner said, his voice reedy.

"Which one? Sunil? Jaiprakash?" a deep voice replied. There was a clink of glasses.

"No, *emenda*. The other one, the one who never seemed quite happy."

"Oh, yes. Mohit." There was fondness in the soldier's voice. Esha leaned closer, hand sliding to her whip. "He'd only come here for your specialty dish, that's true. He wasn't one for drinking or gambling." The soldier laughed hollowly. "He won't be coming back. None of that squad will be coming back."

A beat of silence. "I'm sorry to hear that, *emenda*. Is there anything I can do to entice them back? I can have my chef make double the rice pudding, with dates and nuts. Oh, and exotic fruits from the west."

"No, no. The king has taken them." There was a clear bitterness in the soldier's voice. Taken them? Esha racked her brain for where they could've gone and why Vardaan would've ordered them there.

"Ah, I see." The owner didn't sound surprised. "May their souls escape this world. Was there a reason?"

"It's the king's will, isn't it? We all live and die at the king's will." The soldier coughed. "As it should be. His Highness is our savior. Fetch me some wine, will you? These things are done—no point talking of them."

Esha sat back on her heels. The squad that brought Reha in hadn't been ordered anywhere else. If what the soldier was indicating was correct, Vardaan had killed Mohit to ensure his silence.

The surprise that hit her was unexpected. Vardaan was known to take good care of his soldiers, even if he didn't care for the rest of his people. She could think of only one reason strong enough to kill a loyal soldier—a secret that needed to be protected at all costs. Reha.

Shuffling footsteps came from below. The sound of

wine pouring and a clink of glasses followed, but the conversation was muffled. Esha ventured out of the room, wrapping her turban tight around her head. She winced as the cursed breast band she wore poked into her ribs and doubled back as she reached the bottom of the stairs, hiding behind another man as if she had been there the whole time.

She lingered near the bar, eyeing the crowd as she tracked down the soldier from before. He was near one of the tables now, talking to a few other soldiers who were drinking and playing dice.

"It's so unfair that the soldiers aren't getting as many entries as before due to those Dharkans. Our best should be out there in the stadium, trouncing those weaklings."

"Well, did you hear about the Falcon Squad? Our king is bringing them back to deliver the prize at the Victor's Ball."

"The Falcon Squad?" The admiration was unmistakable. "Weren't they the ones who helped the general take control on the Night of Tears?"

Everything slowed down around Esha. Esha turned toward them, her hands clenched into fists.

A third voice answered, "Yes, that's them." This voice was less enthused, flat even. "They'll be the king's guests of honor for the Mela. I think they just arrived—they'll be shooting the first bow at the archery tournament. I think our captain mentioned a medal ceremony as well, before the final competition. Picking this squad is an interesting choice, given that the Dharkans will be in town for the peace summit. Doesn't quite signal peace to have your commando force that led the coup as your guests of honor."

"Ignore him," said another. "I can't wait. Do you think we'll be able to meet them—"

Esha had heard enough, but her legs were unable to move. She wanted to grab one of the soldiers, demand to know more about the squad that killed her parents on the Night of Tears.

She'd never been able to forget that night—the soldier with his curved sword and the general behind him. The soldier's owl eyes underneath his helmet. The way the general gave the order with a smile.

The soldier had hesitated, and for a moment she had thought he wouldn't follow the order, but then he had moved forward like a wraith, knocking her father down and grabbing her mother's hair. The general stood behind, watching it all.

He was gone now, though not by her hand.

But the wraith?

He was alive, celebrated, and in this city. He'd be in the Mela.

A hand waved in front of her face. "Little fellow?" a soldier said, waving his hand once again. "You're blocking the way to the wine."

"Sorry," she said, moving away from the bar and into the corner. She placed a cold hand to her chest, trying to calm her frantic heartbeats.

The gods had finally spoken, after years of unanswered pleas. After arriving to find the general already dead at the Blood Fort.

Esha had a chance to get justice, to fulfill her vow to her parents' ghosts.

And Moon Lord help anyone who stood in her way.

———◄◊►———

The commission ceremony took less time than Kunal thought, and by the end, he had a newly made Senap armband, one that denoted his station and rank.

One benefit of being the only survivor of the infamous Viper mission was that he now had a modicum of influence. Enough to get Alok assigned to be his charioteer for the drive over to Gwali. Only half the Fort was allowed to leave to participate in the Mela games, as they still needed soldiers defending the Fort.

Kunal tossed the last pack into the back of the chariot. His friend's wavy head of hair could be seen peeking out of the space between the chariot and the wooden wheels.

Kunal grinned and then yelled loudly, "You all right down there?"

Alok hit his head on the inside of the chariot bottom and pulled back to glare at Kunal.

"I liked boring Kunal better," he muttered.

Kunal felt his grin growing wider at that. "What was that?"

"Nothing," he said, shaking his head. "We're good to go. Wheels are on tight and no pin loose. You're going to tell me why you were worried about something so specific, aren't you?"

"At some point."

He'd given Alok a brief sketch of his plans in Gwali—take on his role as a Senap, be the eyes and ears for a rescue mission. He had promised to tell him more, but if there was one thing the past two moons had taught him it was that he could never be too careful.

Alok clambered into the front of the chariot and grasped the horse's reins, grumbling to himself about "friends who think they're so high and mighty after meeting a girl."

Kunal stepped into the chariot behind him. He was finally going to the Sun Mela, and as a Senap no less. He could remember how much he longed for such a day when he was younger.

But Kunal dreamed of new things now.

CHAPTER 9

The streets of Gwali were anything but quiet. Esha wound her way through the labyrinth that was the thieves' den, looking for one sign in particular.

A white horse with a crown of flames was emblazoned on a rusty building sign, swaying slightly in the evening breeze. Esha breathed a sigh of relief. She crept up to the side of the building and knocked on the entrance, making sure her mask was in place. A rectangular slab of wood slid open, only a pair of bloodshot eyes visible.

"Knowledge is?"

"Costly," Esha said.

The door opened to reveal a short middle-aged woman.

Esha followed her into a scented hallway dimly lit. The woman said nothing as they moved past closed rooms, some with curious noises coming out of them. That smell—Esha struggled to place it, except that it was floral.

The woman held her hand out to stop Esha before ducking inside a room. A minute passed, then two, and Esha started to fidget. The woman appeared again, just her head from behind the door.

"They're ready for you," she said.

Esha raised an eyebrow at all the secrecy. Dharmdev had good reason to keep his identity hidden, but this was ridiculous.

The room itself was a stark contrast to the rest of the building. Plush throws covered every inch, and the walls were decorated with gold-threaded tapestries.

A tall woman rose from the floor, her sari opulent in a way that even court nobles wouldn't wear—it was too ostentatious. A long scar carved the outline of her right jaw outside the edge of her panther mask, and as she came closer, Esha saw her arms were corded with muscle. A fighter.

"I bow to the sun in you, sister," the woman said, echoing an old Jansan greeting. She indicated that they move to the floor, gliding over and taking one of the pillows for herself. A handful of people, who Esha figured were members of the Scales, hung around the fringes of the room, hands on their weapons. They each wore a mask that covered the top half of their face, black and gold, in the shape of different animals.

The woman noticed Esha's gaze and turned to her people, giving them a signal to leave. Once they were gone, Esha took a pillow opposite the woman and adjusted her own cobra mask, green and gold. It was the terms of their agreement, to keep their faces hidden. Harun was already not keen on the idea of them meeting. He had set that term to protect her, or so he said. She hadn't told him that it was possible the Scales already knew who she was.

"Greetings . . ." Esha peered at the woman, who chuckled.

"I'm Zhyani, second-in-command of Dharmdev's Scales. Dharmdev sends regrets about missing tonight. I'll have to be enough."

"I'm sure you will be. I'm Palak." She hadn't actually expected Dharmdev to show up. In fact, she had hoped for someone else, a face she could befriend and negotiate with. The tales of Dharmdev didn't indicate that he was a particularly open man.

"I was intrigued to hear from our mutual contact that an emissary from the Crescent Blades wanted to meet. He didn't say much else."

"We just found out about Dharmdev's—your—group," Esha said, deciding to lay her cards on the table. "While news of Dharmdev has been filtering in through our networks, it wasn't until recently that we came to know more of you." Esha paused, waiting to see if Zhyani would give any indication that she knew about Laksh or Kunal. The woman made no movement. "After his recent speech in Jubilee Square, of course."

"It was a rousing speech," Zhyani agreed. "But get to the point, Blade." She leaned forward, the long white scar on her jaw flickering against her brown skin in the dim light of the room.

"Our two groups want the same thing, to take down

Vardaan." Esha paused for emphasis. "We should work together. The Crescent Blades and Dharmdev's Scales. We'll be the scourge of the Pretender King."

Zhyani tilted her head, tapping one finger against her lips.

"I think not." She leaned back among her pillows, put a pipe into her mouth, and blew out a perfect ring. "A tempting offer, but we'll pass."

"Don't you want to—"

"Check with Dharmdev? You don't think I have the power to make my own decisions?"

Esha sidestepped the question. "Why not work together? We *both* want Vardaan off the throne."

"And then what? We step back and allow you to put a Dharkan puppet of yours on the throne?"

"A puppet? Why would we do that?" Esha asked, her surprise genuine. Of all the objections, this one hadn't crossed her mind.

"You forget that Vardaan is a Dharkan. We have had enough of Dharkans on the throne."

Esha tried not to let her shock show in her eyes. So many years of hatred had blurred the fact that Vardaan was Dharkan. He had become a traitor the minute he had laid a sword to Queen Shilpa. That others felt differently was something she hadn't considered.

"He's no Dharkan. He's a traitor."

"Pretty words," Zhyani said. "But perhaps he just isn't doing what your king wants. What if he complies? Becomes an ally? The peace treaty signed? Will all be good with Vardaan then, Blade?"

"No," Esha said. "The *janma* bond—"

She stopped, unsure of what to say. Esha had come here only to get their support to take the palace back. She couldn't mention Reha, not if Dharmdev believed her to be a myth, though now Esha couldn't be sure they'd accept her even if they knew. There was a certain zeal in Zhyani's eyes that she'd seen before—in those rebels who tended to burn bright and die fast.

"The *janma* bond has been a noose around our necks," the woman said. "Our people would be better off without it controlling our access to the land. Free to make their own future without interference from the royals or gods. Bonds are meant to be broken, are they not? Or that's what our dear king would say."

Broken? Esha wasn't sure whether this woman was being literal. The bond could be broken only by the gods. And the scholars said that could mean disaster for her own people, an unending drought that would destroy both their lands, decimate the population. But the woman didn't seem concerned, which was either malice or knowledge.

What did she know that Esha didn't?

"We don't want a repeat of Vardaan," Zhyani continued. "And we have no proof that you will be any different. Your government is so keen on peace, how can I trust you Blades? I've heard rumors that you've become aligned. Though with peace on the horizon, I can't blame you. Much." She stared at Esha then, her onyx eyes hard. "We need someone on the throne who understands our struggles. And that isn't another Dharkan like you."

"Then you're aligned with another Jansan house," Esha countered, trying to understand. "A new group like yours couldn't have raised the funds alone. Who wants the throne for themselves? House Ayul? I heard the second son has spent most of his inheritance, though. House Rusala? Oh no, Pramukh. The young heir-to-be is quite desperate, isn't he?"

Zhyani raised a single eyebrow above her mask, the movement almost as cutting as a sharp word.

"I'm surprised, Viper."

Esha blinked, keeping still. It was a mark for Zhyani, that she had guessed and guessed correctly.

"At what?"

Zhyani traced a finger over the top of her steel cup, flicking a droplet of condensation off.

"How small your mind is," she said with a mocking smile. "Provincial, really. I expected more from the great Viper, breaker of blockades and killer of generals."

Esha narrowed her eyes, her hand going to her knife at her waist. Zhyani wagged a finger at her.

"Naughty. Sly. Prideful. This is more in line with the legendary rebel. You are the Viper," she breathed. "I figured you'd send someone as the Viper, but I didn't know if it'd really be them. You."

Esha swallowed a curse. Novice mistake to get baited.

"I do admire you. You came here in good faith, I believe

that. Especially since you knew we set you up for the murder of the general. And yet you were still willing to ask us for help. But one of our men is missing because of you, and your prince is here trying to make peace with a demon."

Zhyani pulled out her own knife and flicked the sharp point of it.

"We refuse your offer." She pointed behind Esha. "The door is that way."

———◆———

The training courtyard of the Pink Palace was nothing like the one back at the Fort. This one was outfitted as was befitting the capital of a militaristic nation like Jansa. Kunal had arrived only a half hour before. He'd barely had a chance to register his own excitement at finally being in the mythical city of Gwali, walking the halls of the fabled Pink Palace, before he had been whisked away by servants. He had been able to swipe the note from Esha he knew to be waiting for him in the courtyard.

I've been dreaming of you, soldier. . . .

Kunal repeated the words in his mind as he walked through the double courtyards, weaving his way past soldiers shooting at targets, heaving and hurling weighted balls, and going through drills with their spears and swords. No one spared him a second glance. It was the perfect sort of welcome for Kunal.

Kunal had already sent a hawk off to Esha about the citadel and his discovery that the caravan had been sent there. They'd need to confirm that Reha was indeed there, but it was a good start. All Esha had sent back was that he'd get new info soon, with when and where to meet the group.

Kunal was glad his role was mostly done. He'd been in Esha's shoes for a bit, sneaking around, and he wasn't too fond of it. But more important, he would see Esha again. Even if it was with the rest of the team. He'd steal whatever moments he could.

"And this is your new training area. Different from the one at the Fort, I'm sure, but we like it well enough," the captain said, throwing a proud grin toward Kunal. "We run exercises in the morning and at night. Full meals in the dining hall."

Kunal nodded along, trailing behind the captain.

"We might be in Gwali, but we're not that different. Still a soldier's life, eh?" the captain said.

Kunal couldn't help but smile a little at the captain's enthusiasm. He wasn't what Kunal had expected for a newly made Senap captain. A bit more like Bhandu than Rakesh.

"Though I heard you've just been on a mission and returned to the Fort."

"I was," Kunal answered slowly. "Unsuccessful, unfortunately."

"Can't have been that bad, otherwise you wouldn't have been sent here with a letter from the general."

Kunal said nothing, clasping his hands behind his back.

"We're happy to have you here. Senaps will be on a different schedule, but all soldiers train together in the morning.

We'll run our drills at night, near the citadel. Until the Mela starts, at least."

"What's happening then?"

"You've never been to a Sun Mela?"

Kunal shook his head. "I've always been on campaigns or training."

Captain Gajra frowned. "Senaps get assigned new duties when it's Mela time. We normally increase the infantry presence around the city and assign the Senaps to guard the palace. This time around, with the foreign delegations—"

"Foreign delegations?"

The captain's eyebrows shot up. "Sun Maiden's spear, I forgot it was supposed to be a surprise. Don't tell anyone, all right?"

"Of course," Kunal said, tucking away the information to send to Esha. "Where are they staying, though?"

"The palace, of course."

"But don't the Mela champions usually reside there?" Kunal asked.

"Well, there will be changes. It'll be a lot easier to house everyone now that the royal and martial sectors have been united. But that's talk for later."

The captain introduced him to the other Senap squads, running so quickly through the names that all Kunal could do was nod and smile. Kunal committed a few faces to memory, and though it left a bad taste in his mouth, he paid particular attention to those who had roles that would be important for his mission.

Captain Gajra finished his round by introducing Kunal to his new squad. Most of them were the same age as him or slightly older. One soldier walked over to Kunal and they clasped forearms in greeting. He had a welcoming face, brown skin crinkled at the corners of his eyes from laughter.

"We're glad to have you, Kunal. I'm Chand. You've come at the best time, right before the Mela," he said.

"I've never been. I was just telling the captain."

"Speaking of the captain," Chand said, turning to face the man. "We'll show him the rest of the yard."

Captain Gajra sighed. "Have him back in a quarter hour. We need to get him outfitted for his regalia before the Welcome Ball."

"As you wish, Captain," Chand said, giving a quick salute. He beckoned to Kunal, the other men not far behind. A tour followed, one that made Kunal itch to take a sword in his own hand. It'd been awhile since he'd been able to train, especially with top-of-the-line weapons. They were all joking with one another, the way he, Alok, and Laksh had once done.

These men were . . . normal. Friendly, even.

If he hadn't been a snake in their nest, he might have let himself relax, but one slip and he'd jeopardize the whole mission.

Chand tossed a sword at Kunal and his reflexes reacted, catching it easily.

At least not everything had changed.

CHAPTER 10

Esha grabbed one of the gold goblets being passed around and lifted it to her lips, scanning the room as the man across from her prattled on.

The meeting with Zhyani the night before had set her on edge despite revealing a happy piece of news. Laksh hadn't returned. One of their men was missing—Laksh was the most likely, which meant one fewer thing to worry about. But without the Scales, they'd need to garner more support within the nobility to put Reha on the throne. She'd been hoping to avoid that.

At least Kunal had discovered where the caravan had arrived. The citadel. Only the most heavily guarded and fortified building in the military sector.

A plan was forming in her mind, though, one in which Kunal would play a large role. She smiled to herself, thinking of different ways a Senap on their team would be useful—especially one with superhuman abilities.

Harun was in a corner talking to a noble or councilor. Since his meeting with Vardaan, there had been a noticeable weight on his shoulders. One that was painfully obvious to her.

She knew how she'd normally get him out of his moods if they were alone, and Moon Lord, if he didn't look handsome tonight. The thick circlet around his brow, studded with diamonds and garnets, glimmered. The downturn of his mouth made him look more serious, highlighting the angles of his cheekbones, and compared to many of the other noblemen, it was clear he was young and in his prime, his body lean and honed from daily training.

There was a whole flock of ladies hovering, darting glances at him and whispering—Jansan and Dharkan alike. It looked like the two countries had already found one way to bridge the divide. Otherwise, the Jansan and Dharkan nobility were separated within the cavernous ballroom, each keeping to their side with only a few narrow-eyed glances tossed the other way.

So much for peace.

She supposed there was a decade's worth of war, rhetoric, and suspicion between the two nations and friendship. This was one step. There were a few brave souls who had breached the divide and were now making small talk and laughing.

Esha was one of them. She nodded at her companion, a young nobleman from Jansa who didn't need much help in their conversation, waving his anguli, his sigil ring, around as he carried on. Exactly why she had picked him.

Out of the corner of her eye, she saw a Senap guard, half hidden against one of the pillars, and Esha wondered if Kunal had arrived yet. His last note said he would be on patrol within the banquet tonight, now officially a Senap. One of the palace guards.

It had been a little more than a week since they had parted at the camp, and Esha was eager to see Kunal again. Esha felt around for the small note she had tucked into her pocket. She would deliver this one in person, instead of asking Aditi to drop it off in the loose stone outside the banyan tree in the palace gardens. Aditi thought she was leaving love notes for the prince, which was fine by her. It'd been the only way Esha had been able to communicate with Kunal since arriving at the palace, especially with his new schedule as a Senap.

There was something about the idea of seeing Kunal in his full Senap regalia that made her uneasy. She still saw Kunal, the man she had begun to know, the soft mouth and pale, kind eyes, but the armor unnerved her more than she liked to admit.

Esha had never been able to forget that a Senap had killed her parents, but now, since she had discovered the Falcon Squad was somewhere in this palace, the thought was like a fierce vise around her heart. Her eyes trailed over the group of soldiers, keeping an eye out for any falcon emblems. The guests of honor were surprisingly absent from tonight's festivities.

She shook her head a little, trying to disperse the nightmares that threatened to become vicious daydreams.

Her companion stopped his monologue and looked at her. "Are you all right?"

"Yes, I'm fine," she said, throwing a quick smile on her face.

"I heard a delegation from the Yavar is coming," he said excitedly. "Apparently, this Sun Mela is to be one of the most open in years." Esha had been about to leave, and, instead, she paused.

"Really? Who will be in this delegation?"

"A few of the leaders of the top clans, a few of the nobles," he said, proud he knew something others didn't.

"Will Seshirekh be attending himself?"

Seshirekh had been the one to unite the Yavar after the War in the North. These individual rulers often didn't last very long, but his rule had been an exception so far. He'd reigned long enough that he was in the process of choosing his successor now. As per the Yavar traditions, anyone in his clan could put forth an heir, despite Seshirekh having a daughter.

And it would be a perfect time for that daughter to be brought to Gwali, to the gathering of all the nobility of the Southern Lands, as a test. Curiosity itched at her and she wanted to pepper the nobleman across from her with questions.

"It's unlikely that he's coming." He thought for a moment. "I believe he's sent his potential successor, though."

He began to prattle on, explaining the way the Yavar succession happened. If he had bothered to ask her any questions, he'd have known she was well aware of the details of the Yavar succession process, probably more familiar than him. She resisted the urge to roll her eyes and interrupted.

"Who exactly is going to be here? Do you know?" she asked. At the look on his face, Esha pulled back. "You know, no one else knew this. Can you believe it? I just assumed you might know more. . . ."

"Ah, yes. You're right to ask me, though I'm sorry I don't know everyone. I do remember that Lady Yamini will be in attendance."

Lady Yamini, the daughter of Seshirekh, the heir presumptive. She wondered what it would be like seeing the Yavar, Jansan, and Dharkan alike mingling, the ghost of the War in the North thirty years ago hanging over them. The Yavar had accepted the Aiforas as the natural border after the war and agreed to stop pushing forward. But now they'd be able to come and watch the Jansans and Dharkans snipe at each other. How much had changed in thirty years.

Esha nodded before making an excuse to escape and walk over toward Arpiya. She pulled Arpiya aside, and her friend kept her smile on until they turned away. Then she let it drop.

"I don't know how you do it, Esha. Being charming, the flirting," Arpiya said.

"You seemed to be doing a fine job. That man keeps looking over."

"I wasted my efforts on the wrong man, who knew absolutely nothing of importance. Certainly nothing about the newly arrived 'shipment' from the coast."

"Same," Esha said. She stepped to the side and around, making it look as if they were taking in the beauty of the tapestries on the walls. "Though I have learned that the Yavar are arriving for the Mela. Something our dear Jansan friends forgot to tell us. It might be good to find out more."

Arpiya nodded. "On it." She winced. "These shoes were not a good choice."

"I told you to pick the other ones."

"Yes, yes, mother hen." Arpiya was clearly resisting the urge to stick out her tongue at Esha.

"Isn't that your job?" Esha asked.

"I'm on break for tonight. Tonight, I'm Arpiya, lady of mystery." Arpiya fluttered her lashes at her.

Esha couldn't help but snort. "You're in a fine mood tonight. Okay, lady of mystery. Have at it. Get me some information."

"As you wish," Arpiya said, before sweeping away.

Esha grinned, looking around to find her next target as she sipped her rosewater lassi.

To her left, a lower Jansan nobleman. Too young to be useful, but potentially a good asset. Ahead, two Jansan noblewomen making loud comments about everyone's attire. Gossips were useful, but these ladies had frayed sandals that were a season out of style. They hadn't been to court recently, which meant their houses were out of favor.

To Esha's right, someone more promising.

She was about to insert herself into the conversation with the Jansan nobleman, from House Rusala, as his anguli, his sigil ring, indicated, when Harun caught her eye. He had been watching her, and a small smile was on his face. She smiled back, happy to see his mood lifting.

As if her thoughts had conjured him, Vardaan entered the room. A fanfare of trumpets and drums sounded through the vast space, and silk-clad dancers led the way, welcoming him into the hall. They tossed jasmine and rose petals at his feet, creating a pathway onto the dais.

Ah, this was the pomp and circumstance Esha had been expecting when they had been greeted at the palace gates earlier.

Harun let it all happen around him, not moving from his spot, sipping at his drink. Strength was shown in the small moments.

Vardaan didn't go toward his throne, though. A boy holding a mahogany box followed him as he strode over to Harun and grasped him by his shoulders.

"Welcome and blessings of the Sun Maiden to you," he said.

"Blessings to you as well, Uncle," Harun said, repeating the welcoming salutation of the Sun Mela. Esha edged up the side of the crowd that was growing around them.

"I come with gifts—"

"No, Uncle, you shouldn't have."

"But of course. I haven't seen my only nephew in over a decade."

Neither of them mentioned the reason for that. The bloodshed and violence and broken lives. Esha's hands curled into loose fists at the mask of pleasantry on Vardaan's face.

"And we are celebrating potential peace between our nations," Vardaan continued.

Vardaan snapped his fingers again and the boy opened the box to reveal gold jewelry, armbands, and short and long necklaces. They were resplendent, befitting of kings.

And studded with blue sapphires, the most inauspicious of stones according to the lore of their Southern Lands. Not just inauspicious, but deadly and painful to those of royal blood. Harun still had a nasty burn scar from accidentally holding an uncut blue sapphire. The practice of mining blue sapphires had been ended decades ago—a joint decision by the Samyads and Himyads of the time. A matter not known to many.

Esha walked closer so that she was parallel to the royal pair, hiding behind a woman's large hairpiece in the shape of a peacock.

"Oh, Uncle. Thank you for this gift, but we cannot accept," Harun said.

"Of course you can. We're family, and our countries are about to be allies once again. Unless, of course, you're not deferring out of respect but rather fear?" Vardaan offered a thin, slimy smile. "Come now, nephew, we no longer have those silly beliefs about the gods here. We don't believe in those old folktales of the ill luck of blue sapphire, do we?"

Harun bowed his head, looking as if he was, in fact, scared. "I have no desire to turn away your generosity, Uncle. We'll gladly accept. But let's not assume too much of the gods yet, yes? They know and see all, weighing our actions."

Harun looked up, every ounce of deference fleeing as he locked eyes with Vardaan. "We will all be accountable, whether in this life or the next."

Vardaan hesitated, but before he could decide whether to take offense, Harun unleashed a blinding smile.

"Please, Uncle, do not let me slow down the festivities. My mother always said the rules of the Sun Mela must be announced before sundown, as per tradition. Did I learn this correctly?" Harun asked out to the crowd, drawing them in with one waving hand.

Many of the Jansan nobles nodded slowly, warmed by the mention of the late Queen Gauri.

"Then let us begin," he said, bowing out of the way.

Esha shook her hands out under her uttariya, steadying them as she turned away. Didn't this Pretender King have better things to do than threaten her prince? And to offer blue diamonds, the stones of the Lord of Darkness.

He wasn't worthy of Naria's image, of her legacy. But she wasn't the only one who felt this way. Even some of the Jansan nobles seemed to be shocked.

"—what will he do, the young prince? It is an insult. I wouldn't—"

"—the prince is no older than King Mahir was when he inherited the crown—"

"—I can't look. Doesn't our king know he is inviting bad luck—"

Esha threaded her way through the crowd, taking care to pick up any information she could. Just as she got to the front, the doors opened and the conch shells were blown, announcing the newest arrival.

The Yavar clanspeople.

Their retinue swept into the large hall, about a dozen strong, excluding their warriors. Esha's view was partially blocked by a tall nobleman who kept fidgeting, moving back and forth in front of her vision.

Esha threw a few elbows and cleared a line of sight for herself again, but the Yavar had taken up a spot to the side, hidden under the balustrade of the ballroom. The warriors at the front wore fierce expressions; the rest of the retinues' expressions were rather blank. A few of the younger members of the retinue looked around in awe.

"Welcome, Yavariya. You've arrived just in time. I was just about to gather our guests around to announce the rules for the Sun Mela," Vardaan said, voice booming throughout the cavernous space.

A figure emerged from the group of fur-draped Yavar. A brown-skinned lady, no taller than Esha, with a pleasing round face and a strong nose. She was beautiful, as evidenced by the reactions of many of the noblemen. Her chin—it gave her away as the heir. She held it too high, either from years of arrogance at her birth or years of having to feign it. Her long, straight black hair was braided back, falling to her waist.

This was Lady Yamini of the Yavar, heir to Seshirekh's throne.

Lady Yamini bowed to Vardaan, in the way that was customary to the Yavar, but not as low as one might expect. "Thank you for your invitation again, King. Jansa was a sight to behold on our journey here, though much changed from my last visit," she said.

Esha heard the undertone to it—about the drought in Jansa. The Yavar didn't have the same connection to the land as they did. Their forebears had eschewed the gift from the gods, choosing instead to roam the lands and find their sustenance as they pleased. The Yavar prized their freedom, and their ancestors had been no different.

She was still unsure why the Yavar were here. Judging by the looks around the room, many others were, as well. Their clans hadn't attended a Sun Mela in years.

"This Sun Mela marks a new chapter, with all the people of the Southern Lands united once again. It has been my greatest regret that I have not been able to bring us all together," Vardaan said.

Not for lack of trying. Vardaan's idea of bringing the countries together was under his own banner and his own rule.

"I'm glad to have the Dharkan and Yavar nobility with us this year," Vardaan said. He grabbed a goblet from the gold plate near him and raised it high. "To a new beginning."

Esha murmured along with the crowd, raising her goblet, all the while thinking of one thing. The gift, this show of peace, the happiness that Tana had hinted at a moon ago—it confirmed in her mind that he had Reha and that he felt confident.

Well, she'd do her best to strip him of that confidence. Piece by piece.

Vardaan walked to the throne at the front of the room, solid gold and towering. A gold eagle statue was curled around its back, his wings protecting whoever sat there. A prickling feeling grew in her chest as memories swarmed her. That wasn't his throne to sit in.

"And now for the rules of the Sun Mela, our time-honored tradition," Vardaan said, taking a seat. "Our tournament of athletics to find the mightiest in the land. This year the competition will be open to all men—Jansan, Dharkan, and Yavar."

He didn't say women, which wasn't a surprise. Nor did he use the proper salutation for the Sun Mela, instead focusing on the athletics. The Sun Mela was also the start of festival days throughout Jansa, and in the city of Gwali, families gathered and celebrated the return of the Sun Maiden to the land. It was a sacred time, a time of the gods. Vardaan had never been one for the gods, though.

"As always, we will hold initial qualifiers open to all men tomorrow to pick our one hundred champions. From there we will have three major competitions to crown our mightiest, and the winner of the prize. A boon from me. A king's boon," Vardaan said, throwing a wink at the crowd. Esha resisted a scowl at his charming smile. He should have warts or hideous scars to show his true colors, not this appearance of friendliness.

"First, our archery tournament. Then mace fighting, and, last, the chariot race, until there is only one champion. And, of course, we'll be hosting musical competitions throughout, and a number of our venerated houses will host the champions' parties within the royal sector. But this year, there will be some exciting new additions to the competitions."

The crowd buzzed at his words, and Vardaan quieted them with a raised hand. Was she the only one who felt a shiver of dread at his words?

"You'll find out soon enough. Trust me, it'll be . . . thrilling."

Definitely not good.

The crowd of nobles was excited, though there were a few confused faces in the House Ayul and in some of the Dharkan houses, like House Panchala and House Drivedi.

"Due to the larger crowd at this Sun Mela, we will have to restrict access to the citadel to just the champions to ensure their safety and comfort. The training courtyard in the palace will be open to any men, however." Vardaan clapped his hands. "And we're done." He turned his head up to the sundial that hung from a corner of the room. "More time for all of you to drink and enjoy yourselves."

Some of the younger Jansan noblemen from House Man-chi gave a hearty *Hear! Hear!* as they swayed. Esha looked away and tried to digest everything, listening as many of the Dharkan nobles tittered in excitement at seeing their first Sun Mela games.

This wasn't her first Sun Mela—her first had been fifteen years ago, when she had wandered around the grounds of the palace with her hand tucked into her father's palm. When her mother and she would pick new jasmine garlands to wear and new outfits with the colors of their favorite players from the markets, which would churn out new saris as favorites emerged.

Esha took a deep breath in and out, unclenching her fingers from the goblet.

There was so much to do. Information to find, nobles to charm.

Esha eyed a target and slithered over, goblet in hand and laugh at the ready.

CHAPTER 11

Esha looked around the room for Kunal, but the throngs of people refused to budge.

"Do you think House Pushpal will have the victor again?"

"There's no way the Blacksmith's Guild will show their face after that abysmal mace fighting from last year."

"I've heard rumors that Dharmdev will be at the games."

That stopped Esha. When she looked around to identify the voice, she couldn't. She cursed inwardly, moving through the crowd again. Esha whipped around and bumped into one of the servants, a young woman. She began to apologize when the girl looked up.

"Aditi," she said, recognizing her own maidservant.

"Sorry, my lady. I should've been more careful."

Esha snorted. "I ran into you."

She'd lost the voice in the crowd, and Esha frowned. As

she looked around one last time, she saw the Yavar again, now mingling with the other nobles.

"Tell me, Aditi. How long ago did the palace know that the Yavar were arriving?" Esha asked, finally putting words to the question that had bothered her all evening.

"We only found out recently." Aditi straightened her back as another servant passed by. "Our king makes many last-minute decisions, and we, of course, are here to oblige his wishes."

She gave Esha a pointed look.

"I thought as much."

"Have you seen the prince tonight, my lady?"

"Yes, I saw him earlier," Esha said, still caught up in her thoughts.

"I'd advise you to go and speak to him before he's overrun with the other ladies. Perhaps leave another note," she added, grinning wide.

"How do you know the notes are to the prince?"

"I didn't till now."

Esha barely had time to laugh before the girl gave her an impish smile and bustled away. She watched her go, noticing how the Yavar were drawing a little crowd and the tentative way the Jansans and Dharkan nobility were talking to one another, using the Yavar as the buffer.

But she was looking for one person now.

She saw him standing with his fellow Senaps, completely oblivious to the gaggle of ladies near him. No wonder the ladies had singled him out. Tonight he looked like a commanding soldier straight from the ancient tales, with his uttariya thrown over one shoulder, concealing yet also highlighting the strong, sculpted body underneath.

Esha studied his face, the strong jawline and faint beard that skimmed it, admiring the way his full mouth contrasted. Hard and soft.

It'd been a little over a week since they'd seen each other—their longest time apart in the past moon.

Esha looked away, not wanting to draw attention, as she caught the tail end of one nobleman's comments, bursting out into laughter at the joke about the fisherwoman and her disobedient husband. She glanced at Kunal only to see that he was staring back at her, his gaze intent. Her skin flushed as their eyes met, lingered, and broke apart.

All the thoughts in her brain fled, replaced by a sudden need to talk to him.

◆◇◆

Kunal pulled at the new Senap armband he wore. He had clasped it too tight and hadn't had a chance to fix it before his squad had been called to their patrol.

The hall was resplendent in silver and indigo that evening, sheer reams of silk draped from the ceiling, diamonds and aquamarine hanging as well. The silver of the moonlight outside mingled with the jewelry decked around the necks, arms, and waists of the guests, looking as if the heavens themselves had been brought down.

Esha was in the corner of the room, her mass of curls twined together like a crown on her head, her sari a deep indigo that moved to a light indigo as it flowed to the ground. A gradient fit for the night sky and one he would love to paint, especially if Esha was in it. She glanced up, and he caught her kohl-rimmed gaze across the room, his heart skipping a beat.

Beautiful. As always.

He longed to march right over and whisk her away, someplace where there would be only the two of them, away from the eyes of everyone.

She had a mischievous smile on her face as she glanced over the shoulder of the noble across from her. Something in her eyes flickered, the quickest of movements, a glance to the side. What was she trying to tell him?

He turned to the left and looked back at her in confusion. But Esha wasn't facing him anymore, instead laughing throatily at something the noble had said.

A voice startled him as he realized a few of his fellow soldiers had gathered around him.

"Of course the Mela games will be won by a Jansan," Chand said.

"With the Yavar here? They're expert horsepeople; one of them will be guaranteed to win the chariot race," said Alok, who had basically become the sixth member of Kunal's new Senap squad, considering the amount of time he spent with them.

"But the archery? Mace fighting? No one can match us," said another, a smaller man who had recently joined the Senaps.

"I think the Dharkans might surprise you," Kunal

said. "Their training is similar."

Alok nodded. "That's true. My weapons master at home was a Dharkan, before the war." Kunal glanced at his friend. He had never bothered to ask about his life before the war, not wanting to pry.

Esha flitted on the edge of his vision, never completely leaving it. She turned at one point, glancing toward him with a frown, probably due to the group he was standing in.

He understood her misgivings about the Senap guard, especially after what she had told him she had suffered at their hands. He had his own misgivings, and yet, many of the Senap were not at all what he thought. They were different from the soldiers at the Fort—Chand's calm drawl of a voice, Porus's frantic way of eating. Even Alok had mellowed in the city, though he was still being a pest about joining in on "all the fun you're having."

These men had chosen to commit themselves to a higher level of training, like Kunal had, and he saw how careful and analytic they were, kindred spirits to his own way of thinking.

If only they weren't bound to a man who couldn't be trusted.

Esha's stare lingered a little longer this time, hard and penetrating. Alok noticed and appeared a bit uneasy.

"Why is she looking at me like that?"

Kunal sighed inwardly. Where was the charming girl he knew? An idea struck him, a way to get back at Alok for all his nagging. "Maybe she fancies you. Some girls are just bad at showing it."

His friend nodded slowly, as if Kunal was right. Porus and Chand nodded along as well, glancing a bit uneasily between themselves. Kunal hid a little grin, knowing that it was all bravado.

Alok puffed up his chest a bit. "She is quite pretty, despite the scowl. Maybe I should go over there. See how long it takes me to make that scowl disappear."

"I think that'd be a bad idea," Kunal said immediately.

"Really?" Alok said, the air deflating out of him. He looked relieved, though, and Kunal realized that despite all the talk, he'd never seen Alok approach a girl.

"Yes. Also, she's a Dharkan by the cut of her waist sash," Porus said.

"Nothing wrong with that," Alok said.

"I mean she's a Dharkan noble, and you're . . . you."

Porus ducked Alok's fist, laughing.

Esha came into view again, her motions a bit more insistent. "Follow me," her lips said. Kunal excused himself from the soldiers and followed behind her, coming to a stop on one side of the massive fountain in the middle of the hall. He expected her to stop as she came toward him, but instead, Esha walked past him.

He sharpened his senses, tracing her through the crowd as she threw a look back at him. He hesitated and then followed. Hoping he hadn't misinterpreted that soft, warm glance.

She was walking through the crowd, toward the center, and his brow furrowed, confused that they were going farther into the room. Esha moved faster until she was about a half circle of the room ahead of him.

And then she stopped. Her fingers flicked out and down, a signal.

Esha did the motion again until Kunal realized she was telling him to stop.

Here?

She tilted her head in response, unnoticeable to anyone else. She had positioned herself at one end of the oblong room so that they were at opposite ends, the fountain between them.

A soft whisper filled his ears and then—

"Kunal." Esha's voice surrounded him. Kunal started and looked around, but no one else seemed to have heard her. The lady to his right was picking at a rose-syrup-drenched pastry; another to his left was searching for someone in the crowd.

"Kunal, don't move. You're standing right above a diamond." Kunal slid the toe of his sandal an inch, seeing a black diamond the size of his palm on the floor. "It's the match to where I'm standing. The whispering points," she said. "I wanted a moment alone with you."

Across the way, she lifted a glass to her lips, looking unconcerned as her gaze swept the room. But she kept her mouth covered.

Kunal followed suit.

"Do you know why it's called the Whispering Room, this hall?"

"No," Kunal said. His shoulders tensed until the sound dissipated. The softest of smiles curved up Esha's lips.

"There was once a pair of lovers, forbidden to one another. One was a servant, the other a noble, and here was the only place they could be together."

"Here? We are hardly together."

"It's a story, Kunal. And they were together, the only way they could be. If you are quiet enough, you'll still hear their conversations in this room," she said.

"A pretty tale. What happened to them?"

"Only the gods know. But I doubt they're willing to tell."

His smile curved against the rim of his glass. "I'd like to think they ran off, somewhere where they could be together and be free."

Silence for a moment, but Esha hadn't left. "I'd like to think that too. A life for them. Somewhere."

Kunal didn't know when he had begun to hold his breath, but he let it go at her words.

"Or maybe they stayed, maybe they fought for their right to be together," Esha said.

"I suppose it's the one thing worth fighting for—above all," he said.

"Above your duty and honor?" The teasing note in Esha's voice carried over as well.

Kunal didn't immediately respond. "I would hope they wouldn't be in conflict."

"Life isn't that simple, is it?" Esha's voice faded a little. "Someone's coming toward me. Check your pocket, soldier."

Her last words blew away like breaths of smoke, and Kunal wished them back in an instant. He lowered his eyes, tilting his glass as if it were empty before stepping away from the diamond. A quick glance around confirmed that no one had been listening or had noticed.

But even if they had, their conversation had revealed nothing.

Except to the two of them.

As always, Esha managed to cut to the core of who he was in just a few words. He patted his pocket, and, sure enough, a small folded-up note was tucked away.

Kunal ducked into the shadows behind a pillar, unraveling the note and scanning it quickly.

It feels as if it's been years since I've seen you, soldier. . . .

And at the bottom:

Meet us tonight. The door of the swallow at three conchs blow.

He smiled to himself and walked back toward the other soldiers.

CHAPTER 12

The last time Kunal had been in a palace, he had been running for his life. Now he wasn't running, but he still felt like he was hiding.

He sneaked a look down the corridor to make sure no one was following, and crossed. Kunal had kept on his Senap uniform—sturdy, pure silk uttariya and dhoti, jeweled armband, gold cuirass, and spear. If anyone found him crawling around the guest quarters of the palace, he'd be able to make up some excuse about hearing a noise and patrolling.

Kunal couldn't deny that he was excited to see the team, even though he wasn't really a Blade. Yet they had welcomed him. Kunal turned another corner, having finally reached the room. It was as described, a tall mahogany door with a swallow carved into the right half of it. He knocked, once, twice in a half beat, three times in a quarter beat.

The door opened, and a head of curls greeted him.

Kunal's heart sped up as Esha grabbed his hand and pulled him inside. The rest of the team was there already, scattered around the room. The twins lounged on two chairs, their long bodies thrown across them in rather uncomfortable-looking positions. For some reason Arpiya was poking Bhandu, who was pacing the room. Harun faced the window, looking out into the darkness.

At the creaking shut of the door, Harun turned. Esha immediately dropped Kunal's hand, and he tried to hide his frown at the lost contact.

"Glad you finally made it, soldier. We don't have much time. The patrols have been doubled for tonight, and I can only be gone from the Welcome Ball for so long before drawing notice." He stared at Kunal. "You found where the caravan went?"

"Yes," Kunal said. "I sent a hawk—"

"I received it this morning," Esha said. "Haven't been able to get the whole team together."

"And?" Harun prompted.

Esha sighed, rubbing her cheek with her open palm, her arms crossed. She hesitated, though Kunal didn't know why.

"The citadel. The caravan was delivered to the martial sector and the citadel," Kunal said for her.

———◄○►———

The team burst into noise, everyone talking at the same time. This was why Esha had hesitated. She had been trying to find the right way to deliver the information. She sighed, pressing a finger to her temple.

Farhan's grip tightened on the table. "Moon Lord's fists."

"We're done for," Bhandu said, throwing up his hands.

"I second that," Aahal said.

Esha held up a hand and they quieted with only a few more comments. She'd spent the entire day trying to figure out a plan so that the news wouldn't hit the others like a brick, and she had still come up short. Esha had decided to wing it, which wasn't a leadership tactic she normally employed. But now Kunal's blurting of the truth was forcing her to think even faster.

Arpiya looked down the room at Esha and Harun. "The citadel isn't a place you just waltz into and case. What are we going to do?"

"Can Kunal get us in?" Farhan asked.

"I don't have the authorization to get into the citadel without clearance from the Senap captain, or the general," Kunal said.

There was a pause, a moment of silence that hung heavy.

"But we might be able to get access," Esha said once everyone was silent.

Harun had that look on his face, like he was pulling through a million threads to piece together an idea, and when they locked gazes, she knew they had thought of the same thing.

"We just need a Mela champion," Harun said.

Arpiya bounced on her toes. "Yes," she said, clapping her hands. "All Mela champions will be housed in the inner tower of the citadel."

"So if we just got someone through to the Mela, we could get access and scout out if she's being held there!" Bhandu said, happy to be making a contribution.

"Exactly," Esha said, suddenly excited. She'd always wanted to be in an archery competition. "I'll do it. I can dress as a man. I've done it plenty of times before."

"The soldier is our best option," Harun said.

Kunal stiffened a bit. Esha wrinkled her nose at Harun. So much for being in step with one another.

"Kunal will have to be at his post," Esha said.

"Kunal can enter the archery competition. If anything, it'll solidify his status in the Senaps if he does well. Shouldn't be too hard for him if he's as good as you say, right?" Harun said, his voice curiously light. Esha narrowed her eyes at him.

"Kunal shouldn't have to be the main fighter of every step of this mission."

"Kunal should have known what he signed up for."

"Kunal is right here," Kunal said, exasperated. He stepped forward, away from Esha, forcing Harun to have to sidestep him.

"I'll enter." He paused. "I've always wanted to be a Mela champion anyway."

"Have I mentioned that I'm great with a bow and arrow?" Esha said.

"Would you tell us if you weren't good at something?" Arpiya said.

Kunal cleared his throat. "It's too dangerous. What if

you're discovered? And what if your wound opens up?"

"I agree with the soldier," Harun said.

Six heads whipped around to look at the prince in unison, including Esha's.

"It feels weird when they're agreeing," Bhandu said to no one in particular.

"You should stop calling me soldier here, Prince," Kunal said, his teeth slightly gritted.

"Much better." Bhandu smiled.

"Harun is right, Esha," Arpiya said. "You are the only one who can play your role in the court. We have others on this team who can enter the Mela and are better suited to be champions. Especially since Vardaan isn't allowing women to even compete."

Esha sagged. Anyone else and she might've fought more. "Fine."

Harun nodded. "And it won't be just the archery tournament. If we want to be thorough and make sure we have time to get her out, we need access to the citadel throughout the Sun Mela's festivities. Fourteen days. You won't be able to hide for that long, Esha. The soldier has an advantage."

"Can you do that?" Harun asked, turning back to Kunal. "If my sister is in the citadel, the distraction of the Sun Mela will be our best opportunity to case the citadel, break in, and rescue her. But we can't do any of that if we don't have a Mela champion."

Kunal shifted in place. "Understood."

"We do need a Mela champion," Esha said. "But keep

a low profile. Mela champions can become celebrities. We don't want to risk exposing you—or us." There was more at stake for Kunal than the others could imagine. "And if our mission is discovered, it could put a target on the Dharkans in this city and the king will have a reason to end our peace talks."

"Farhan, you'll be backup in case something happens," Harun said. "Make sure to get through the qualifiers. If Kunal doesn't make it into the archery tournament, we'll put you in. Bhandu, we'll need you to steal some more soldier uniforms. Arpiya, Aahal, you know what you have to do. Esha?"

"I'll be backup," she sighed.

"Don't worry, Viper. We'll tell you all about it," Bhandu said good-naturedly.

But Esha had already moved on, realizing that the archery tournament would be the perfect time to set her own plan in motion. The Falcon Squad, including her parents' murderer, would be there to shoot the first arrows.

Perhaps being backup wouldn't be so bad.

———◦———

Esha looked around the hallway corner to confirm no one had seen her escaping the afternoon tea that Lady Irvani of Manchi was hosting.

She arranged the pleats of her sari, like a noble lady would, before walking purposefully toward the Great Library doors. One knock and they swung open for her.

Silence, and then a small man shuffled forward, his head bowed.

"My lady, we just opened the library after morning lessons. Please come in."

Esha bowed, her palms together as she bent. "Thank you."

He ushered her in, and she stepped inside the cavernous hall. The doors shut behind her, closed by the tall servant she had spotted hiding behind it, and she took in the splendor of the Great Library.

Rows upon rows of scrolls were tucked into wood and stone diamond-shaped shelves. The entire floor was laid out in multicolored stones, the walls etched with reliefs of the tales of Naran and Naria, the history of the royals. One thing Vardaan hadn't destroyed.

Esha hurried into the room behind the scholar, trying to match his quick pace. The main entrance narrowed into a smaller room, and the scholar led her to one of the long tables in the center. Stacks of opened and unopened scrolls teetered on the table, their musty scent overpowering everything else in the room.

She glanced at the upper level, where she had spent so many days as a child. Where she had spent her last days in the palace with Reha.

The scholar turned around quickly after realizing Esha was following him. "My lady, feel free to look around. You can see how we've categorized the books by subject over there in the library scrolls, or you can ask Ishaan over there. Family scrolls are in the corner, as is modern history and cataloging. If you need anything—"

"Actually, scholar, I'm looking for texts on the *janma* bond and arcana."

"Scrolls on the bond and magic are over there," he said, pointing over at a small corner with a few hexagonal holes. Last time she had read the Great Library's arcana texts, they had taken up half a floor of shelving. Vardaan's work, she'd bet.

"I'm looking for ancient texts. I've been here before, you see. Before the war."

The scholar's eyes shifted. He peered more closely at her.

"Anything you might have, I'd love to read," she added.

He looked as if he was going to ask a question but didn't. "I'll look into it, my lady. There might be some renowned texts still around. This library is so big, you know."

"Indeed. I'll send my maid, Aditi, to check in tomorrow morning."

He bowed to her with his palms closed and disappeared into the stacks. Esha breathed a little sigh of relief. After Zhyani had mentioned the Scales' desire to break the bond, Esha had sent a hawk back to the scholars in Mathur to get more information. But she had also encoded it, and it would take days before she could expect a reply.

She had been feeling a faint sense of unease since Zhyani and the Scales had turned down their offer. Perhaps she just wasn't used to being told no, as Harun had said. But she had sent a note to Kunal to meet her at the library, so she figured, one stone, two snakes. She'd take the time to do some research of her own.

Esha walked over to the section with the family and personnel records. Since the War in the North, Vardaan had taken to giving commendations to his favorite squads and holding events in their honor. The royal chroniclers were sure to have taken notes about the king's generosity. If she could find one of those scrolls, get the names of the men on the Falcon Squad, she'd be one step closer to her goal.

Esha tugged an armful of scrolls out of their shelving holes and juggled them over to the table, where she spread them out. She glanced out the windows at the sun and a large dial hanging on a nearby wall. Kunal was to meet her right before sundown, so she didn't have much time.

She scanned the scrolls, looking through sporting events, commendation ceremonies, parties, more parties, going backward through the years. She had come to the month of the coup, when Vardaan had begun to set up his royal chronicler, purveyor of all propaganda, and hoped the information would still be as strong.

It wasn't. The names and dates trailed off, whole months gone, but at the end of one of the scrolls was a section about the Falcon Squad—and their disbanding. The squad had come together in dire circumstances, commingling General Hotha's tried-and-true men with promising young soldier recruits from around the country.

Esha felt the heat in her blood rise as she read on. She

found no mention of the original members. Now she'd have to get the information the Viper way.

She swallowed a sigh. It was never easy, was it? She was about to comb through the records another time, just to be sure, when a quiet gasp at the front of the silent library drew her attention.

Kunal stood inside the doors of the Great Library, staring up at the massive structure with wide eyes. Esha smiled, remembering being that full of awe once. Perhaps tonight she'd be able to recapture some of that magic the Mela and this city used to have for her.

She closed the scroll and put it back in its place, walking forward to meet her lemon boy.

CHAPTER 13

Kunal's dhoti was a tad too small for him, but he couldn't really complain. Esha had arranged it all—a secret passage, clothes that would let him slip by unnoticed.

He tugged at his uttariya, feeling bare without his cuirass. He was used to going bare-chested, but it felt odd wandering the streets without armor.

"Relax, soldier," Esha whispered. She reached for his hand, her touch warm against his palm. "No threats here. Just the citizens of Gwali celebrating."

He tried, but his training held fast. And despite being together, Kunal couldn't help count down the time till it would end and he'd have to sneak glimpses of her at parties. Even now, it was improbable that they were here, together.

The general's nephew and the Viper.

A soldier and a rebel.

But here and now, they were just a boy and a girl,

sneaking out of the palace to join in the revelries of the Chinarath, the first day of celebrations during the Sun Mela. There would be a special bazaar, mouthwatering food, and general merrymaking. He had never been.

"Well, you apparently are horrible at taking orders," Esha said. "So I guess I'll have to force your hand." She pulled him into a throng of people, drawing him behind her. He moved to grab her hand but hesitated.

This felt different from their stolen kisses in the jungle or in the healer's tent. They were in public. What if someone saw them? True, he wasn't dressed as a Senap, but what if Aahal or Bhandu were in the crowd?

Someone bustled into them, and Esha fell back against Kunal with an *oomph*. Her skin was warm, warmer than a summer sun, and her soft curls tickled the bottom of his nose. She tilted her head up at him, mischief in her eyes.

"Crowds," Esha said, wrinkling her nose. "Stay close."

The Chinarath was exactly as he had imagined. Bright and joyful, with a cacophony of multicolored clothing and patterned art, the latter done by the ladies of every household in the morning to ward off evil spirits. He walked past one of the houses, the bright pink and cerulean rice on the doorsteps used to intricately create a design of a lotus in a lake. He wondered if anyone might teach him this style of art, so different from the oil paints he loved.

Music thrummed through the air, the steady rhythm of hand drums punctuating the notes of a multitude of veenas.

Despite the encroaching drought, the citizens were celebrating. Perhaps they didn't want to think of the date juice in their hands instead of the traditional sugarcane, the crop now decimated up north. Or perhaps this was their show of hope. Colored glass shaped as mangoes and dried herbs hung over the doors of homes and the streets covered in twinkling diyas and garlands of marigold and jasmine. The old traditions were still alive.

Kunal's stomach gave an aching groan as he was bombarded with the smells of spicy fried chickpea fritters and syrupy fried milk-dough.

"This is your first time seeing this, isn't it?" Esha sent him a bemused look.

"The Fort didn't really have celebrations like this," he said, eyeing a bright pink sweet shaped like a rose.

Esha stepped forward and exchanged a few coins with the sweet seller, handing Kunal the rose. He reached for it, but she lifted it away at the last second.

"I demand payment," she said, staring him down.

"Oh? So generous, you are."

"I'm extremely generous, soldier," she said, the tone of her voice changing. "In many ways."

Kunal flushed. She always managed to make him feel like a young boy again. He leaned forward, drawing close to her ear.

"I prefer lemon boy," he said, grabbing the sweet from her hand. "If you're determined to not call me by my name."

She laughed, her entire face lighting up like one of the flickering lamps surrounding them.

"Some things never change."

"Some things do," he said, pointing between them. He bit into the sweet, and it tasted as pink as it looked, like a creamy rose dipped in spirals of sugar.

"You're quite the warrior poet," she said. Apparently, he had said that last part out loud. "I love that about you."

His brain sputtered at her words. *Love?* No, she had just said she loved *that* about him. Him being a poet. That was all.

"You're a bundle of contradictions, Kunal."

"So are you," he said through a mouthful of the sweet. "It's why we're suited."

"Oh? We're suited?"

"Yes," he said as if he had just decided, though he had determined it the minute he had turned around in the jungle weeks ago. "We understand each other."

"My lady's maid understands me."

"We challenge each other."

"That is true."

"We've made each other grow. Look at us together now."

"Haven't particularly enjoyed the growth part," she quipped. "Life was easier when I hated all soldiers."

"And we found each other again," he finished. "Lemon boy and demon girl."

"Demon girl?" she said, looking affronted.

"That's what the maids called you, didn't you know?" he said as innocently as he could. It was the truth, actually, though it had been said with affection. Esha tried to look angry but was unable to keep from sliding into a smile.

"Fine. Lemon boy and demon girl."

"I'll allow our circumstances aren't the best," he said slowly.

Esha gave him a look, picking up a set of bangles and inspecting them. She put them down with a shake of the head and selected long, forest-green emerald earrings instead, tapping the gems.

"Our circumstances aren't the best? That seems like a massive understatement. I had to lie to my lady's maid to get clothes for you so we could sneak out of the palace, hide from our teammates—not to mention our countrymen—and enjoy a few hours together."

"I said I'll allow our circumstances aren't the best."

And they weren't. It had been only a few weeks ago that Kunal had wondered why the gods had put Esha in his path, when theirs were destined to cross but never travel together. But things had changed.

The team had accepted him, a Fort soldier, and there were peace talks between their nations. He couldn't help but hope that the rift between their nations would truly heal and they'd not have to hide anymore. What had been a fantastical dream seemed . . . possible.

"But we're here now."

Esha tilted her body toward him, looking up at him through her lashes, and he felt as if he were about to come undone.

"We are."

———◦———

Esha felt her body move instinctively to match Kunal's.

"How has it been, by the way? Being back at the palace?" she asked.

"Different."

Kunal paused and took her hand. The contact sent a spark of fire through her body.

"In a good or bad way?"

"Just different." He sighed, looking up at her, his amber eyes resembling burnished gold in the pale moonlight. He traced a pattern over her knuckles, weaving his fingers through her own. "Haunted."

Esha gave him a wry smile. "Everywhere I go, I feel as if I've been there before, only to remember I have."

"I don't even remember much, just flashes. But I keep wondering, keep wanting to know more—the palace was my family's residence for years. It would've been my home."

"It is your home."

He shrugged, looking away for a moment. "Perhaps. I still have so much to learn about my past. About my . . . new talents."

"One step at a time, Kunal."

His fingers hadn't stopped trailing her skin, but his eyes grew darker.

"No more talk of the past or the unknown. I don't want to waste our time. Not when I finally get you to myself for a few hours," he said, a hint of annoyance in his voice.

"You know I'm one of Harun's advisers now, right? I'm an important woman. Sought-after. My time is highly valuable."

He grinned, pulling her closer as people moved around them. They were just two more besotted lovers in the crowd, and people rolled their eyes but moved away. His hand was splayed across her back, like embers against her skin.

"Did I mention I'm a prince?" he said, his voice low.

"Oh, really?"

"Long-lost. Apparently, that beautiful palace is my home." He pointed at the outline of the Pink Palace in the distance.

"Is that supposed to impress me?"

"Does it?" he asked, cracking a smile.

"I think you're going to have to try a little harder."

It felt as if something was pulling her toward him, an invisible thread that kept being tugged between them, insistent, demanding. Kunal said nothing, simply staring at her, sending shivers down her spine.

"What, no clever retort, soldier?" she teased.

"You're just so pretty," he said softly.

Esha had heard more elegant and intricate compliments, but the sincerity with which he said it—the way his voice lightened and his eyes became butter—did her in. She drew closer to him. It never ceased to astound her, this connection between them.

"Watch out!"

A young girl and two of her friends barreled into them, pushing Esha over into Kunal's arms. They stopped and turned around to apologize, but then proceeded to giggle at them.

"What's the hurry, little one?" Kunal asked.

"The dancing! It's starting!" she said, hastily adding, "*emenda.*"

"Then I suppose we better follow her," Kunal said, a gleam in his eye.

———◆———

They were thrust into a large circle of dancers, chaotic and full of life. Even by Esha's standards, Kunal picked up the rhythm of the dance quickly. The circle moved together as if they took the same breaths, bending and bowing and jumping in time, the men across from the women.

Kunal's face was so bright he was channeling the sun, his eyes wide like he never wanted to stop drinking in the scene around him.

Her heart pounded as the music started to crescendo and partners drew closer to each other. Kunal pulled her in, after a quick look at the other dancers. She reveled in the feeling, the closeness of his body, and the warmth of his touch. The way his hips brushed her own.

The music dipped and, soon, came to a close. They let go of each other and she instantly felt cold without his warmth. The drums started up again, and Esha checked the sky and the nearest sundial. Their time was almost over.

Esha dragged Kunal out of the crowd despite his protests.

"Where are we going? There's more dancing."

"But if we're dancing we can't do this," she said in turn. Esha pulled him into an alleyway and stood on her toes to kiss him.

"An alleyway?" he said.

"Old habits die hard."

She pulled him so close she could feel his breath on her cheek, his stubble against her lips, her neck. The heat between them intensified and twisted, turning from a low simmer to a raging flame.

She winced suddenly, a slight pain lancing up her torso where her wound was. He pulled back immediately, brushing the hair away from her face.

"Too much?"

"Never."

He raised an eyebrow. "If you're in pain, tell me."

"It was nothing," she said, before pulling him back in. "We don't get these moments very often, Kunal." She grinned against his mouth. "So please shut up and kiss me."

He did as she asked.

———◦———

The next day, Esha woke up to the sound of Aditi's struggled breathing.

She quickly dressed and opened the door to her sitting room, where Aditi was dragging in a huge basket of lily and jasmine garlands—and mangoes.

"For you, my lady," she said. "From an admirer?"

Esha smirked but said nothing, and Aditi handed her a letter. Aditi whistled an old Jansan love song, and Esha shook her head.

She unfurled the note, sinking into the armchair that looked out a tall window and into the courtyard below.

> *When I think of you, Esha, I imagine the monsoon.*
> *Warm and life-giving. Fierce and powerful.*
> *A contradiction, just like a warrior poet.*

Esha smiled to herself, rereading the note again.

A monsoon.

She flipped her knife and cut into a mango, carving off a huge chunk. Perhaps they were well suited.

CHAPTER 14

Kunal followed the other Senaps into the locker room of the stadium, marveling at the pink sandstone courtyard and the spiraling, white marble citadel that loomed over it.

The Mela had officially begun, and with it the city was changed. The festivities had started yesterday, during Chinarath, and the city hadn't stopped celebrating since. It had taken Kunal almost half an hour extra just to make it to the locker room of the stadium from the palace, winding his way on the Queen's Road through the procession of people dancing and whooping, waving the flag colors of their favorite house or guild.

The qualifiers had been in the palace courtyard, but that day's archery event would be in the ancient stadium, built by the Jansan queens during the Age of Dreams.

A thrum of excitement shot through Kunal at the

prospect of participating in such an old tradition. His uncle had never allowed him to, which he always believed was because his uncle thought him unqualified or a disappointment.

Now he wondered if it was to keep him hidden. He'd never know. But Kunal did know he'd have to be careful, good enough to win but forgettable enough that he didn't draw attention. His life was at stake—if his parentage was discovered it would make him a target. Vardaan would want him dead, and Vardaan's enemies would want him as a pawn.

Kunal dropped his pack on the sandy ground and grabbed a cloth with which to clean his bow. He set to work checking the tightness of the string and ensuring each of his arrows was properly fletched.

He strategized ahead, laying out all the various ways this part of the mission could go wrong. There was calm in those moments. He could feel his breath coming a bit easier. Satisfied that everything was in order, he slung his bow across his shoulder and walked out to the small courtyard to the left of the locker room, where there was a water pump. Kunal pumped water into a thick stream, taking a drink and splashing his face to cool down.

"Thirsty?" someone said. Kunal shot up, his hand on the knife in his waist sash.

He'd recognize that voice anywhere.

"What are you doing here?" Kunal moved backward, making sure his back was to the wall.

Laksh followed, raising an eyebrow at him. He came out of the shadows, an uttariya thrown over his head and across his shoulders, hooding his face.

"Not much of a welcome for one of your oldest friends."

"*Friend* is an interesting term, Laksh," Kunal said.

"I saw Alok earlier. I'd suggest a reunion, but somehow I don't think you'd be agreeable to one," his old friend said, taking a step forward.

Laksh was the same, and not. His voice was rougher, but he had that same look in his eyes, as if the world were a joke and if Kunal came just a little bit closer, Laksh would let him in on it.

Or stab him in the back.

Kunal could make out a faint line of purple across Laksh's temple, reaching down his face, neck, and collarbone. Laksh noticed.

"That was a gift from your lady friend. That poison was quite difficult to find an antidote for." He grinned, but it wasn't a pleasant one. "I'll have to thank her for that in person."

Kunal's body stiffened at the thought of Laksh anywhere near Esha. The first pricking of shifting closed in on him, and Kunal hummed to himself in his head to calm down.

"What do you want?"

"Were you always this bad of a conversationalist, Kunal?"

He growled at Laksh in response. The former soldier sighed and moved closer to Kunal, his hands up.

"I'm not here to hurt you. I came to help." Laksh looked Kunal up and down. "You might need it. You don't know what's in store for you during the Mela."

"Archery."

"Always so literal. Did you notice that Vardaan mentioned 'additions' to the tournament? Did you wonder what they were?"

He had, in fact. But he wouldn't let Laksh rattle him again.

"I just want to help you win, Kunal."

"*Just?* I'm learning there is never 'just' anything with you."

Laksh laughed. "I've missed you. You were always the moral compass for me, did you know that? Even though you were dutiful, you never went to excess. You didn't enjoy the horrible things you had to do, unlike some others."

"I still did them," Kunal said. "It doesn't make it right."

"Nothing was ever right at the Fort. The only thing good about my time there was you and Alok."

There was a sincerity to Laksh's voice. A moon ago Kunal would have said with full confidence that he would know when Laksh was lying. That Laksh would never lie to *him*. But Kunal no longer trusted himself when it came to his old friend.

"I wish I could believe you, Laksh. But I've seen you lie easier than breathe."

"I haven't revealed your true identity yet," Laksh said, as if it should absolve him. "I haven't told my leader—"

"Dharmdev."

"—or anyone else. Do you know why?"

Kunal wanted to hear Laksh say that he hadn't told them to protect him. But there had to be more. He looked closer at Laksh, inspecting his clothing, the gauntness of his face, the way he leaned to one side.

"They won't let you back," Kunal said, throwing out a wild guess.

Laksh flinched. "We were brothers once. I haven't revealed you, believe me or not, because I still care for you, Kunal."

"Brothers do not lie to each other."

"Is that so?"

"Don't mock me, Laksh."

Laksh sighed. "You make it too easy."

He grinned, but Kunal glared back.

Laksh's face twisted. "Have you considered how I might feel? You've deserted, and yet you joined the Blades. You're willing to forgive Dharkans like the Viper, whose mission it was to kill your uncle, but you haven't forgiven me. Your brother in arms. Your own kind."

"We're all descended from the same gods."

"And how little that matters in the real world."

"I don't want this world, then. I want to build a better one," Kunal said.

"Then let's build a better one."

Kunal was about to retort back but hesitated.

Laksh swooped in. "Let me help you. Let me show you

we can work together. You shouldn't trust the Crescent Blades."

"I trust them more than you right now," Kunal said, but the vehemence he had before was fading the more Laksh spoke.

"You wound me," Laksh said, clutching a hand to his heart. His eyes hardened. "That Esha, she is a beautiful girl. Quite a catch. I'm assuming you'd do anything to keep her safe."

"She doesn't need anyone's help for that."

Laksh waved a hand. "Yes, of course. But unforeseen things happen all the time, right?" He paused, letting his words sink in. "You've entered the tournament. Win this round. You can make an excuse to your Blades, slip of the hand or whatever."

"And why would I do that?"

"I'm sure you can think of a few reasons, Kunal Samyad. Have you had a chance to talk to the king recently?"

Kunal drew his knife now. His heart raced at the idea of his secret out there. But he steeled himself. "Fine, reveal my identity. No one will believe you."

"You think I haven't done my research?" Laksh pulled out a small, jagged blue stone the size of a robin's egg. A raw uncut sapphire. "Do you know what this is?"

"It seems like you've been carrying around bad luck for a while. Is that why Esha almost killed you?" Kunal said, finding some fight in himself.

Laksh laughed fully. "I rather like this new Kunal. I'm

going to have such a good time working with you." He walked closer, getting into Kunal's face. "I don't want to do this. You've left me no choice."

Laksh pressed the sapphire to Kunal's throat. Fire surged into Kunal's veins, and the shift rammed into him, threatening to take over. Kunal wrenched himself away from Laksh, falling onto the ground.

He looked up at Laksh, gasping, a hand to his throat.

Laksh inspected the blue sapphire in his hand. "Inauspicious for most, dangerous for you. Not known to most people, though I'm sure the royals know, and that's why it was outlawed to mine. They're rarer than a blacksmith's good mood."

Shock lanced through Kunal. He wasn't ready to give himself up, not yet, even for the good of the country. He got to his knees and then his feet, still holding a hand to his throat. When he removed his hand, he felt the edges of a burn, the skin sore to the touch.

"If you're going to kill me, just do it now."

"I have absolutely no intention of harming you again, Kunal," Laksh said. "I'm merely showing you that my threat isn't an idle one. And if you don't care about yourself, perhaps think of others. Esha. Alok. What about them?"

Kunal was on Laksh in a second, his knife digging into his throat. "If you touch one strand of hair on either of their heads, I'll—"

Laksh's throat bobbed against the steel of Kunal's knife.

"It wouldn't be me. I wouldn't even need to. Anyone

close to you will become a way to control you. Don't you see? You can protect them, though. Just win this round and I'll keep your secrets safe."

"Why?"

Kunal didn't drop his knife, and he considered following through. But he couldn't guarantee Laksh hadn't built in a fail-safe with the Scales in the event that he didn't return.

Laksh remained silent.

"I won't be threatened by you for life. I'd rather die," Kunal said, stepping back and handing Laksh the knife.

Laksh brushed aside his hand. "Always so dramatic. Follow my requests for the Mela and after that, you're free. I'm not asking you to become an assassin. Just my eyes and ears."

Kunal noticed he didn't say "our."

"Your eyes and ears? I thought you wanted me to win the archery round. Tell me why, or no deal."

Laksh glared at him, his eyes squinting. "You've become better at asking the right questions. I need you to win this Mela."

"So you can control me more," Kunal said.

"Not everything is about you." Frustration, anger even, coated Laksh's words now. "I want the king's boon. And you're going to help me. I'm sure you'll make the right choice."

Kunal looked at him warily. What choice did he have, though? Even if he didn't believe a word out of Laksh's mouth, he knew he could believe the threat behind his words. If he said yes now, Laksh would be appeased. He'd figure a path out of this later.

"It's not as if I have much choice," Kunal said, his voice flat.

Laksh shrugged, unconcerned.

"But at the end of this, you'll get out of my sight. Forever." Kunal's voice shook as he said the words, but the anger and betrayal he felt surpassed the sorrow, fueling his spite.

"You drive a hard bargain," Laksh said, some of the easiness having left his voice, a hint of something else creeping in. "But I can make that happen."

The two stared at each other until Laksh turned and walked away.

"Win the Mela, Kunal," Laksh tossed over his shoulder.

He didn't need to finish the sentence. Kunal could already hear it.

Or else.

———◄◊►———

Esha slid through the side gate, latching it behind her. She checked her quiver and bow, pulling her uttariya down to cover her eyes. She wore the plain clothes of a trader, hoping not to catch attention, which might be easier than she had thought.

The area below the stadium was stuffed with potential fighters of every age and class. Most of them were focused on warming up or checking their bows. It was clear who were archers and who were simply hoping for a chance to say they'd participated in the Sun Mela.

The soldiers were off to the side, their status obvious despite not wearing their armor. That was one aspect of the Sun Mela she had always enjoyed. All fighters were welcome and treated the same, despite their background. The winner could be one of the elite Senap or a farmer who had been training all year.

Esha had no intention of competing. She was there for one reason—to find her parents' murderer.

The cursed soldier would be in the stadium, as would his squad, to shoot the first arrows. All she had to do was wait, hidden, until the soldiers left and the Falcon Squad came back in after their ceremony. They'd be in their regalia, helmets and all.

Esha had never forgotten the image of the soldier in his helmet.

Someone jostled into her, and Esha straightened, letting her memories drop away. She needed to focus. Esha found a corner in the side of the large hall, directly across from a row of targets. She sat against one of the short stone columns, which offered a view of most of the room. The others joked with each other or ignored and glared—though that was mostly the blacksmiths and the sailors, who had a rivalry.

Esha spotted a small nook where she could hide until the Falcon Squad came back. Cheers erupted from outside the room, and Esha perked her ears. They'd be inside soon. She moved quickly, ducking bows and limbs, when a hand grabbed her and yanked her back.

"What are you doing here, boy?" the man said, his face

red as he shook his head. "I knew we were missing one."

"I'm not—"

"You're lucky. They just shut the doors and aren't letting in any more qualifiers."

"Late qualifiers?" Esha repeated, her heart stilling.

"For the archery competition," he said, looking at her as if she had lost it. He pointed down the hall to where the room opened into a large courtyard and beyond it, the arena. "It's starting now."

CHAPTER 15

A weight had settled on Kunal's shoulders since Laksh had left, once he had realized what he had agreed to.

He'd have to do whatever Laksh asked. But once he found a way out of this, he'd tell Esha. If he told Esha before he had a plan of his own, she would charge right in and probably start a war between Dharmdev and the Blades that neither one of them needed. Not when the real enemy was up there in the royal box.

Kunal looked out at the crowd, shielding his eyes in the heat of the midday sun. The arena was filled to the brim with people from every walk of life. The Jansan and Dharkan nobility sat together in the top box of the arena, beside the king's own box.

The excuse would come to him, but now he needed to focus on winning this round, when he had been planning to just get by. Winning this competition would mean ranking as one of the top five in archery. It would mean drawing attention to himself.

Chand slapped him on his back as he took the spot next to him.

"Ready?"

Kunal twisted his mouth. "I hope so."

Ten fighters at a time, shooting at a target fifty paces away. The goal was to get five in the center of the target for this round to qualify for the next.

Kunal scanned the rest of the participants. He saw a tall, rangy man built like an archer and a smaller one to his right who had kept his turban on even in this heat. Two portly men who held their bows as if they hadn't touched them in years, and an eager young lad who was nearly chomping at the bit to start. No one looked particularly skilled in this round, but talent could be deceiving in its package.

The first conch blew, and the fighters took aim.

Kunal managed the first one quite easily. And the second. The third veered off a bit and missed the center by a few rings. He did the same with the fourth, and the fifth was a bad shot. He took a moment to fix his bow position and peer around the stadium.

Chand had already made three and was grinning. Two of the men to his right struggled, and three to his left were out. The small man with the turban hung back—with five arrows neatly in the center.

Huh. Kunal had underestimated him.

He refocused and let two more thud into the outer ring

before remembering the rules. In the event of a tie for the third round, scores would be tallied from the first two. If he wanted to guarantee being in the top five, he'd have to make the next three perfectly.

Sun Maiden's spear, he was stuck now. He couldn't take any chances.

Kunal took a deep breath and focused into the target, his eyesight growing sharp. He saw nothing but the center of the target, and everything else faded away as he took aim and shot the next three in rapid succession.

Kunal stepped back unsteadily as he let go of his bowstring, a wave of weariness hitting him. One more round.

The crowd was already cheering, picking their favorites, and Kunal heard a few shouts behind him.

Kunal and the other fighters stepped back, returning to the starting line as the targets were rearranged by a row of servants, a few of which ushered the remaining fighters into a smaller ring within the circle, presumably to make the next round harder.

A few minutes later they were lined up again, targets at the ready. Each of the men stood closer now, their numbers thinned. Stacked in a line they looked like a row of targets themselves.

The small man was back as well, and next to Kunal, shifting on his feet, his turban low enough that he had to keep pushing it back up. The conch shell blew, thunderous cheers echoing through the arena, startling Kunal, as did the chants and cheers from behind him. He froze for a second, overwhelmed. But a glance up at the boxes reminded him that Esha was there, somewhere, and that he wasn't alone.

He felt eyes on him and looked to his right just as the small man looked away.

Kunal took a deep breath and centered himself. Five center shots and he was into the next competition, mace fighting. Seven and he'd be in solid position for winning the archery round entirely, as Laksh wanted.

He toed the line that marked his spot, raised his bow, aimed.

And let his sharpened senses take over.

———◦———

The sun flared overhead, giving Esha an excuse to pull her hood down over her eyes. She lifted her bow again after hitting the center with her first shot.

Moon Lord's spear. She had been so close to the Falcon Squad. So cursed close she could taste it, and now?

Esha glanced over at the other fighters and Kunal. She needed to get herself out of there, especially before he recognized her. She hadn't told anyone about her search for her parents' murderer, not yet. And this turn of events was not what she had envisioned.

There was a corridor nearby that would at least get her to the stables, where she could run to her rooms and switch out her clothes. *If* she could get through the guards, which she'd be able to do only as an official competitor now.

Esha tried to relax, knowing that the frustration and tension in her body wouldn't help her. She closed her eyes, breathed in and out. The memory of her first archery lesson came to her. She'd learned to shoot in the shady groves that surrounded the palace in Mathur and wished she was back there for a moment, with Harun by her side. Esha looked up at the box and found him sitting to the right of someone who hadn't been there before. She squinted before her eyes widened in recognition.

King Mahir was here.

More incentive to get back up there. Harun was good at lying to everyone except his father. The last thing they needed was for the king to realize his brother was holding his lost daughter hostage.

Esha drew her bow and let an arrow loose. It hit just on the edge of center. A cheer went up in the section of the arena that was closest to her.

She had just shot her fifth arrow, taking her time, when a commotion to her left drew her attention. The left-middle section of the arena was going wild, stomping their feet and clapping together. In seconds, she understood why.

Kunal had shot five arrows in a row after his first two. Dead center, two of them splitting each other.

She gritted her teeth. What was he doing?

It had to be a mistake. Maybe he had used his sharpened senses and hadn't meant to. She'd seen the shifting take over Harun, often in situations where he hadn't intended it to. Esha had received more claw marks on her hips than she cared to admit. And Kunal wasn't trained.

They'd have to figure out what this meant for their rescue mission.

A cheer went up through the crowd, clearly loving the drama of Kunal's archery. He looked around suddenly as if he had forgotten where he was, a hint of worry flashing through his eyes.

He must not have realized. It didn't matter, though. Now no one would forget him.

The competitors who hadn't made it through were ushered out of the gates, the guards still in front of the only entry to the corridor that would get her back to her room and out of these clothes.

Esha sighed. One more round and she'd be able to make a run for it.

She started to walk to the next line marked in the rings, to get as far away from Kunal as she could before he recognized her and began to ask questions, when the floor began to shake.

Esha was so startled she jumped up slightly, her uttariya knocking back just as Kunal looked up.

He knew it was her.

Even from where she was standing she could see his grip on his weapon tighten, his brow crease. He strode forward to her just as she began to turn away, his jaw set in confusion—and anger?

But before he could catch up to her, the unmistakable roar of a feline bombarded the arena, filling it.

Esha slowly turned, and there, where the previous targets had been, stood two huge lions.

The crowd had gone deathly still. But as the animals began to move, the voice of the crowd grew again, now in fear and agitation. The competitors stepped back, throwing harried glances at each other as they bunched into two groups, each facing one of the fierce cats.

Was this Vardaan's way of welcoming them? When had this been introduced? A hundred more thoughts ran through Esha's head, but one came into focus.

Survival.

Something brushed against her, and Esha jumped. Kunal was at her side the next instant, grabbing her shoulder and pulling her to him.

"Esha, what in the Sun Maiden's name are you doing?"

"What are *you* doing?" she countered. "You weren't supposed to have shot five arrows in a row like you were pretending to be the cursed Archer at Dawn."

"I hadn't meant to, but I lost control."

"You? You lost control?" Esha's voice was skeptical, until realization hit her. "Oh, you lost control of *that*."

"Yes," he said. "And now everyone will be suspicious if I leave and don't make it into the competition."

"I suppose you're right," she said, her bow at the ready. She shot an arrow at one of the lions, but it batted it away, not even turning its head. She cursed, thoroughly.

"I am," he bit back, his own bow up as well. "And stop angering them."

"What are you talking about?"

"The lions, they've been riled up. They're angry."

"Well, let me just roll over and let them maul me and everyone else."

Esha raised her shoulder to shoot, nudging into the space behind another competitor who was sending arrows at the lions. He was aiming for the wrong area, though, and she was about to tell him when the lion finally roared and charged.

Kunal grabbed her as the animal leaped past them, landing with claws out, right where they would've been.

She went back-to-back with Kunal, crouching for her next shot as he stood tall.

"I'm aiming for the belly, you aim for the neck." He nodded against her, and she felt his muscles shift as he changed his aim.

"Can you calm them? If I grab their attention?"

"I don't know how," he shouted, the din of the arena crowd growing deafening. Esha tried to tune it out instead of turning her head to see what was happening to the others. If they didn't succeed, they'd have two lions on their hands.

"Don't you talk to your cursed horses or something?"

"They just tell me things sometimes. Like that they're hungry or thirsty," he said. Without looking behind him he took out a knife from his belt, handing it to her just as the lion turned again, drawing closer to Esha's side.

She grabbed the knife and threw it, wishing she had her whip on her.

By the Moon Lord's luck, it hit its mark in the animal's side, and the lion reared up, roaring in pain.

"If there was any time for your powers to be useful, this would be it!" she yelled.

"I'm trying!"

The lion circled them, but Esha and Kunal didn't break their position, each taking turns to shoot, slowing it down. Two of the other competitors were on the ground, blood flowing around them.

"Kunal!" A stocky Senap appeared, drawing the attention of the lion.

"Chand, get out of the way," Kunal said.

But the lion had already been distracted. It leaped at Chand, sending him sprawling to the ground with a sickening crunch. Kunal looked as if he was about to run forward toward the soldier, but Esha grabbed his shoulder.

"We need to stop the lions," she said.

Kunal took a step back and nodded.

"When I tell you, go for the belly," he said.

"And what are you going to— Kunal!"

Esha lunged after him, but he was too fast.

Kunal sprinted for the lion, a blur as he leaped and tackled the hindquarters of the beast, its claws scraping against the metal of his cuirass. "Now!"

Esha ran as fast as her lungs would allow her, sliding down and under to send three arrows deep into the beast's belly.

She landed on the sand heavily, grunting as every bone

in her body rattled against the ground. Her vision swam, but she was able to look up to see Kunal still holding on to the now-wounded animal. It looked like he was speaking to the animal, subduing it.

To anyone else it looked like Kunal was going to be the new favorite.

The lion tamer. The Archer.

Esha groaned, getting to her feet as four sharp conchs blew.

She drew a bloody hand against her brow as she looked over to see the other lion, badly wounded in the corner. The other group of fighters was scattered, a number on the ground with injuries. A few were slowly getting to their feet, while two didn't look as if they'd ever get up again. Their blood stained the sand.

Esha staggered up, making sure her turban was low as she glanced up at the royal boxes.

This was only the first competition of the Mela.

What did Vardaan have planned next?

CHAPTER 16

Kunal strode out of the stadium wearing a new black armband that signaled he was a Mela champion. He also had a new name from the crowd, who had dubbed him "the Archer." As if he needed another problem.

The arena was emptying out below, after the competitors had been named and heralded. Fifty in total, and Kunal had caught only some of their names—Tushar Inyar, Punohar Pramukh, Narotham Suresh. Chand made it through, as had Esha. But she'd disappeared before the heralds could discover the young man's name and add him to the next competition's list, the mace fighting.

Kunal walked toward where the nobility and merchant boxes would empty out, hoping Esha had made it back before anyone realized.

"Senap Kunal," a voice called out. Kunal turned to the prince.

Harun caught up to him quickly, with Arpiya, Esha, and the rest of the team trailing behind. Esha was in a fresh sari now. She wouldn't meet his eyes, but he was glad she had made her way back. She had told him she had been working a lead in the city when she had gotten into a spot of trouble and ran into the waiting hall. But she skirted around any specifics.

Not that he was one to comment on hiding something. Her disguise had been enough of a distraction that he had been able to put off her questions about his stunt.

"Congratulations on an incredible feat of archery," the prince said loudly, as other nobles passed. Once they had turned the corner, the prince's face transformed into fury.

"What in the Moon Lord's name were you doing? What happened to our plan to not draw attention to you?" the prince whispered through gritted teeth. Even the rest of the team looked grim.

"It was probably just an accident, right?" Aahal said.

"An accident? He was leading from the first round. If I knew you wanted to show off, I wouldn't have put you in," the prince said.

Kunal looked to Esha, who was still silent, a vacant expression on her face.

"It wasn't just your call. It was Esha's too."

At her name, Esha woke up. "Harun, it seemed like a mistake," she said.

"Am I the only one who thinks a mistake like that is impossible?"

Bhandu raised his hands up a little, looking at Kunal.

"It seems unlikely, cat eyes."

"Don't get me wrong," Esha said. "I'm not happy he disobeyed a direct order, and it does change our plans. But maybe not for the worse. He'll have more access now. Kunal, do you realize that your name is already on everyone's lips? They're calling you 'the Archer'—after the mythical Archer who slew a dozen lions."

"Didn't he die from a snakebite?" Bhandu whispered to Arpiya.

Arpiya shushed him.

Kunal blinked rapidly, the realization finally hitting him. It was the last thing he wanted.

"See, he didn't think of the prestige. He didn't try to sabotage," Arpiya said. "I think."

"I didn't," Kunal replied. "I don't know what came over me."

"I do," a deep voice said, approaching from the shadows. The man had thick black hair, with a white streak through the left side, and a sharp gaze like Harran steel. He wore an opulent, jewel-encrusted crown. "I know what came over him."

"Father?" the prince's voice questioned.

The others immediately dropped into bows with their palms together, but King Mahir held up a hand and they rose.

"Your sense is usually keener in these matters, Harun. Have you really not seen it? Or felt it yet? I'm surprised. Something must be on your mind."

His son looked at him in confusion.

"He's one of us, son. More precisely, he's one of them. A Samyad."

A ripple of shock went through the team. The prince looked horrified. He must have realized this meant they were cousins.

"I thought there was something off about him, but I assumed it was because he was a soldier," Harun said.

"How did you know?" Kunal asked, his voice quiet.

"It's the song of your blood. We can hear the songs of other blood that is akin to ours. Yours is fast, fierce, free. The song of the Samyads and the eagles of Naria." King Mahir pointed at his hand. "Put your weapon away."

Kunal hadn't even realized he was gripping it. Esha stood still, looking between the two of them but saying nothing.

"Cat eyes? Is what?" Bhandu said.

"I'm sure Kunal had a reason for not telling us," Aahal asserted.

Kunal gave Aahal a small, grateful smile.

The prince was silent, and his eyes weren't on Kunal. They were on Esha. "I'm sure he does," he said. "Apparently, honesty is an easy currency with this team."

King Mahir put a hand on his son's shoulder, and the touch drew the prince back into himself. "His song is new, his power uncontrolled. The poor boy must be suffering. I take it you only recently discovered your parentage?"

There was no point in dissembling. "Yes, sir. Only a few weeks ago."

The king stared at him for a few moments, and Kunal straightened, feeling as if he were at inspection at the Fort. They had exchanged only a few words, but Kunal liked the king. And anyone who could make the prince stop talking.

"Another one of our kind. We're dwindling now," the king said, wistfulness and a deeper note of sadness entering his voice. They all knew why, but it was easy to forget the Night of Tears had torn the fabric of an ancient family, one that had been entrusted with powers direct from the gods.

"Of course, if my son would give me heirs, I might not be so sad," the king said, raising an eyebrow at the prince, who turned a bright shade of tomato red. Kunal didn't miss the quick glance the king had thrown at Esha, whose impassive mask cracked.

Bhandu snickered a bit before Harun shot him an angry look.

"Father—"

"That's a matter for another time. Harun, we must take Kunal under our wing." The king walked over to Kunal, clasping him on the shoulder. "Who were your mother and father, child?"

Kunal felt as if he were eight years old again, arriving at the Fort and having to tell his story. He felt small, lost. Who were his mother and father? He thought he had known, but there was still so much he didn't know.

"Nirbhay Hotha and Payal Dhagan—Payal Samyad," he said quietly.

"Dhagan. Interesting last name choice for her." The

king's eyes were kind. "Payal. She was a bright ray of sunshine and my wife's source of joy. She loved her sister, and she would have loved you, nephew."

Nephew.

Kunal swallowed heavily, suddenly overwhelmed. The king's words were like water in a desert. They hit him in the depths of his soul, where he believed he would always be alone.

"I can't let your power grow like a weed, Kunal. It'll be a danger to everyone if you're not in control."

A danger? Kunal wanted to ask more, but the king pulled away. "Report to me tomorrow, early morning. I'll put in a request for a personal guard while staying here, but it's up to you to get yourself assigned. We'll start lessons then."

Kunal nodded and the king swept away.

Aahal and Bhandu looked to be bursting with questions. Arpiya was talking to Harun in a low voice. Farhan was standing close to Esha, who looked a bit struck, frozen even.

Kunal cleared his throat.

"Where should I start?"

———◄○►———

Esha closed the door behind them, but Harun didn't even wait.

"You knew," he said, his voice low and accusing.

She thought about denying it, pretending that she had been as shocked as he was. But they had agreed to no secrets between them. She winced. No *more* secrets.

"I knew."

"You knew, and you never mentioned. Never hinted. This wasn't some cursed game. This is my sister's life—"

"I weighed the benefits of you knowing versus the chance of you storming—which you are doing, by the way—and secrecy won out. There was nothing we could do with the knowledge, Harun."

Harun looked as if he were going to tear his hair out. "Nothing we could do. Nothing we could do?"

"Nothing we could do with him that wouldn't make the Blades lose our souls," Esha said, her voice quiet. "What would we have done with him? Used him as a bargaining chip with Vardaan? It wouldn't have worked, and we would have become as bad as him in the process. Worse even, for at least the Pretender King has had loyalty to his men."

"You speak of loyalty, Esha, but I'm wondering if you know the meaning of the word," Harun said.

Esha swallowed. "I deserve that."

She reached for Harun's hand before he could storm away, forcing him to look at her. He stared back, his long-lashed gaze unblinking.

"Harun, my loyalty is to Dharka, to you, and to him. Do you remember my stories of lemon boy? My friend from before?"

"Yes," he said, some of the hardness in his mouth softening. "The boy who played Naran to your Naria."

"That's him."

"That's him?"

"Yes."

His face tightened in disbelief. "Then you've been compromised since you met him."

"That's unfair."

He refused to meet her gaze again.

"That's unfair, Harun," she repeated, angry now. "Just because I promised to keep someone else's secret? I wasn't compromised, I was trying to hold on to a bit of my past that was still alive."

"I'm not faulting you for that—"

"Then what?"

Harun grabbed her arm, tugging her closer. "You and I made a pact, years ago, and it wasn't just to the Blades or to Dharka. It was to each other. You will always be a part of the Blades. But do you even want to be?"

How could he even ask that of her? The Blades were her family. He was her friend—he was more than her friend. The ties that bound them were strong, laced with steel.

"Of course I do," she said. She had never forgotten the pact they had made, under the banyan tree that stood proud in the center of Mathur.

Harun lifted her chin up with a finger, till their eyes were level. "Esha, you are the original Blade, steel forged from the fires of loss. But if you want something—else . . ."

Esha searched the depths of Harun's gaze.

"I want to be here. I fought for years to see this through. But, Harun, it was Kunal's *life*. You would've kept him in Mathur, and he deserved the chance to live. We've already been forced into roles, all of us."

Harun should have known that more than anyone. But the openness in Harun's face faded at the mention of Kunal's name.

"You don't know that," Harun said softly. "You don't know what I would have done. You assumed—but you've been gone often, Esha. Not everything has stayed the same. I haven't. You certainly haven't."

"Harun, I—"

"I deserved your trust. But apparently, that has been given away to someone you've known for barely three moons," he said, bitterness slipping into his voice. Esha saw him tucking it away, fighting to maintain his composure. Something he did as the prince, around people he didn't care to let in.

She reached for him, but he pulled away.

"See to your soldier. Make sure he gets his training with my father so that he's not a liability."

"Harun, let's talk about this—"

"No," he said. "We needed to talk before. There's nothing else to say now."

He left the room without a single glance back.

CHAPTER 17

The Dharkan king's quarters were magnificent, showered in pink marble, gold filigree, and encrusted rubies and emeralds. Kunal noted that there were no blue sapphires.

Kunal had convinced his captain to put him on the king's guard, expressing a desire to prove himself as a new soldier. He knocked on the door of the inner chamber, and a servant welcomed him in. The king sat at a small desk farther into the room.

"Reporting for duty, sir." Kunal pointed at the antechamber. "My partner is stationed outside, while I'll be stationed inside for the morning patrol. Just to be extra careful."

The king rose from his chair, tidying a few things into the drawers, and walked over, dismissing his servant from the room. A slight tremor ran through the king's hand.

"I'm impressed. Hotha wouldn't have trained you any other way."

A mix of grief and betrayal hit Kunal, as it always did.

"You knew my uncle?"

The king nodded. "He was one of Vardaan's closest friends. I also believe he was the worm in Vardaan's ear before the coup. But that's another matter I won't burden you with."

"I'd like to know," Kunal said softly. "Not necessarily this, but I want to know more. I spent so many years unseeing and unhearing. I want to make up for it."

King Mahir considered him for a moment before nodding. "Understood. But I can't promise you'll like what you hear. Come inside."

Kunal put down his spear against the wall and followed the king's lead in taking a seat.

"What do you know so far?" King Mahir asked.

"Not much," Kunal admitted. "I began to shift only a few weeks ago."

Kunal quickly summarized the discovery of his parentage and how his powers had grown over the past few weeks, leaving out any details as to why he was in Gwali or what the team was doing.

"You didn't have your first shift until recently, yes? What caused it?" King Mahir asked.

"I lost control," Kunal said. "My uncle had taught me that I must have control over myself at all times."

"So this control that your uncle taught you. How did you employ it?"

Kunal considered the question. "It was like holding

a tight vise around the neck of a snake. Hold it far away enough from you and you know it's there, but there's no worry of being bit. That's how I experienced my emotions, as if they were the enemy."

"But they're not, are they?" the king asked softly.

"No." Kunal's fingers played with the fabric of his dhoti. "It wasn't until I accepted them and felt them that I began to feel free, feel my power."

King Mahir nodded, rising from his seat on the small chaise under the window. He tugged at a rope, and a curtain of silk tumbled down over the glass. He motioned for Kunal to stand up.

"The gods gave humanity the power to think and to feel, and when we cut off one of those two, we cut off a part of ourselves. What makes us human. In our case, it's our connection to the land and its every inhabitant."

King Mahir took a deep breath and let it out, repeating the process. When he looked up at Kunal, his eyes were the dark gold of a lion's, and claws flashed dangerously where fingernails had been.

"You need control, but not over the parts of you that are human. Finding the connection within your soul, your personal song, will allow you to pull on that connection when needed. As I've just shown. This is called phasing, being able to hold on to human and animal forms at once and at will. It's difficult to master but essential."

Kunal shifted his weight, uncertainty creeping over him. Could he do this?

"We won't be starting with phasing, though. First, you'll have to find your own song, your connection to the gods. Then you'll be able to master your powers."

"So far, whenever I've turned fully, it's normally been out of my control. Why is that?" Kunal asked.

With slow precision, King Mahir began to transform his hands back. "Because you aren't trained to find the balance in the connection. There's a balance in everything—light and dark, sun and moon, fire and water. That same balance is in the land too, and we are the keepers of that. Our ability to shape-shift is a gift from the gods, but it is our burden too."

"Burden?"

"You know about the ritual." Kunal nodded. Everyone in the Southern Lands had some knowledge of the ritual, the blood sacrifice required to keep the land whole. "There is much to the ritual and the arcana of the ancients. It is our job to understand and protect that lore aside from maintaining the balance."

"I thought it was just the scholars who studied it."

King Mahir shook his head. "It's passed down to every generation of Himyad and Samyad. It's a sacred duty we have to our people. If we are to be the rulers of the land, shouldn't we be the servants as well?"

Kunal felt himself nodding. The more he had considered his newfound heritage, and his old duty as a soldier, the more he had been wondering how they fit together. The nature of a monarchy was inherently unequal, the way

Vardaan employed the term. But in the tales of old—or even of a decade ago—monarchy ruled hand in hand with the people. Local courts, tribunals, guild laws were all owned and perpetuated by the people.

The people were entrusted with their own governments, and the royalty was entrusted with their protection. And in his chest, Kunal felt a fierce need to protect, aside from the oath and role his uncle had forced on him.

"I'm glad you agree. When we abandon our duty, catastrophe follows. It happened during the Blighted War and even ten years ago. Vardaan weakened the old bond, though mankind had been putting stress on it for decades, and the connection we used to have with the gods is now tenuous. I've been able to keep the bond together, barely, with my blood and the knowledge I've acquired about the original ritual. I've been searching for—" King Mahir looked away, his face blank when he turned back, like he had made a mistake.

"Your Highness?"

"Sorry, I got caught up in a memory. The privilege of the old," King Mahir said with a chuckle, though he was barely over forty. Kunal saw it for what it was—a pivot—and allowed it.

"You've been able to shift under emotional duress, and you've noticed some of your senses and powers finding you, but you can't control it. You must learn to connect to your powers, find your song. But once you start down this path, you won't be able to turn away." Kunal understood. He wouldn't be able to turn away from his birthright anymore after this. He would be a Samyad.

"I'm ready," Kunal said.

"Then let's begin."

———◀◇▶———

Another party, another noble's boring life story. Esha smiled and gave a titter of encouraging laughter, her eyes alight with feigned interest.

Esha fidgeted in her marigold embroidered sari, the thick gold belt around her waist digging in. Today's party was hosted by the House Ayul, the room dripping with ribbons and saffron marigolds, one of the many parties held between each Sun Mela event. Aside from the nobles' parties, a number of unofficial events had popped up around the city for the competitors who wanted to practice or for those who narrowly missed the cut. A grand time for those willing to gamble away their money—or for those who were there to facilitate it.

A hand tugged at her, and Esha spun around. Arpiya was decked in a peacock-blue sari, her short hair pinned up into waves that framed her round face.

"Lady Esha, I've been looking for you," she said before offering her apologies to the nobleman.

"Thank you," Esha whispered as they quickly walked away. "How could you tell I was dying to get away?"

"You were grasping your goblet a bit too tight. You know these ceremonial goblets are made of pure gold, right? They bend with pressure. That one will have the imprint of your fingertips for a while."

Esha looked down at it and then at her. "Oh."

Arpiya chuckled and beckoned at her to follow as she wove through the groups of people standing. One circle was full of young noble girls who looked infinitely bored, glancing at everyone with disdain over the rim of their chilled glasses of lassi. A Yavar warrior held court in another circle, telling the story of a battle with large hand motions.

Harun was in the corner, deep in conversation with Lord Mayank of House Pramukh's adviser. He hadn't looked at Esha the entire evening, barely nodding his head at her when she had entered the room.

It pained her to think that there was a wedge between them. She had assumed he'd be annoyed, maybe angry. But hurt? She hadn't seen it coming.

He was right. She *had* assumed the worst of him. She was worse than the dirt on the bottom of a Fort soldier's shoe.

Arpiya peered at her again, and this time, Esha didn't have the heart to pretend that she was okay. Her conversation with Harun had been playing over and over in her mind.

"I told you to tell him," Arpiya said. Esha could see from the way her lips were pursed that she was clearly trying not to say more.

"I told him what I thought was relevant," Esha said.

Arpiya clucked her tongue at her. "You're digging your heels in, and that won't help anyone. Just apologize—"

"I did—"

"Spend some quality time with him—"

Esha turned red. "I can't do that here," she said quickly, and then thought of Kunal. "Anymore." Or at least she thought. Kunal and she had never declared themselves.

Arpiya raised a single eyebrow. "I didn't mean in that way. But interesting that your mind went there first." Esha made a strangled sound. "Anyway, I just meant time. You keep sneaking off when you're not on the mission. You think he hasn't noticed? We all have."

Esha closed her eyes. That had nothing to do with Kunal—she'd only seen him maybe once or twice and only for a few moments.

She had been trying to track the Falcon Squad after the archery event failure. How could she tell the team that? They were supposed to be focused on Reha, but Esha couldn't get her parents' killer out of her head. Her mission was to sneak them into the citadel, rescue Reha, and make alliances that would help them gather troops to put her on the throne. Not revenge.

She blew out a sigh, looking at Arpiya. "It's not what you think."

"Not my business what you do at night." Arpiya leaned in. "Well, actually, I have so many questions. Is Kunal—"

"It's not Kunal!"

"Fine, Harun—"

"Not Harun either!" Esha sputtered. Arpiya's eyebrow rose even higher as she waited for a real answer.

Esha groaned. "It's another man. The one who killed my parents. He's in town for the Mela. I overheard that his squad, the Falcon Squad, was going to be the guests of honor when I went to meet the Scales."

Arpiya's eyebrow dropped, replaced by a look of such sympathy and love that Esha felt like breaking down and telling her everything. "I'm not here to tell you to do anything. However, if you asked, I would remind you that we all have our ghosts and nightmares, Esha. Every single one of us on the team. And we've each handled it our own way, which also means you can handle this another way. If you so choose," she said gently.

"I can't," Esha said. "I made a promise to their souls in that dungeon in Gwali. Their deaths couldn't have been for naught."

"Didn't they die to save you and the princess?"

Esha looked down at her goblet, the fingerprints now firmly dented in. "They shouldn't have died at all."

Arpiya reached over to grasp Esha's hand, somehow knowing that she was struggling to hold back her emotions in that moment. They smiled at each other, and Esha was about to say something, consider that Arpiya might be right, when Harun crossed her vision.

Arpiya nodded at her.

"Go talk to him," she said. "He'll forgive you. He cares too much about you not to."

Harun? He cared about her as much as he cared about anyone on the team. They had always edged around the issue of their feelings for each other. Every time she had tried to speak of more . . .

Esha shut down that line of thinking. There would be nothing between them if she couldn't fix this. Esha hurried over before someone else took the open spot next to Harun.

Esha noted the position of the Yavar heir—Yamini—and Vardaan as she walked over. Vardaan had been mainly absent from the parties, causing the ones he was at to become spectacles—probably what he wanted.

Harun didn't look like a prince tonight but a king in the making. King Mahir was there as well, the solidity and maturity of wisdom in his face. But Harun shone through, like a freshly polished pearl—their future.

He looked over to his right briefly, his jaw tightening as he spotted her.

"You've been a hard man to get ahold of," she said in greeting, hoping to lighten the thick air between them. He was standing straight, his hands clasped around a goblet as he surveyed the room.

"Well, I am the prince," he said, still facing outward. "I've been busy preparing for the first day of our negotiations."

"And I'm one of your advisers."

Something flickered in his face—disappointment?

"Is this official business, then?"

She was about to answer, but he didn't let her start. "If it is, have you had a chance to spend time with Lady Yamini? Or with the Jansan nobles? There's one from House Pramukh, Lord Mayank, who might be amenable to our cause. He's apparently the talk of the town—"

"Harun," she said softly. "I'm sorry."

His posture sagged, and he finally looked at her. "I know you are. But it's not that simple."

"I know, you want to see action. And I'm working on it. I went to the library, and I think we might have information on the ritual soon—"

"Esha, that's not what I meant."

"Then what? We've had arguments before, we've played stupid games, and we've been able to get through it all, and that's never been simple," she said, unable to hide the frustration in her voice.

"This isn't just an argument. You should know that," he said, simmering.

"Then what is it?"

Esha wanted him to say it. If only so she could cursed well fix it.

"That you don't know the answer to that question . . ." Harun sighed and ran a hand through his hair.

"Tell me what I have to do."

"Esha, how can you not know how I feel—?"

His voice broke off as a shadow approached.

"Have I interrupted something?" King Vardaan walked

up to them, waving between the two of them. Lady Yamini was behind him in an exquisitely painted sari, a few other Yavar at her side.

Harun straightened, and Esha turned to face the newcomers.

"No, of course not," Harun said, his voice a tad flat.

"I heard from your adviser that there have yet to be formal introductions between you and the Yavar. I haven't made your acquaintance yet either, my lady," Vardaan said, a smile on his lips as he looked Esha over.

Something tightened in Harun's body, and she resisted the urge to calm him. She could handle herself.

Esha bowed forward with her hands clasped in greeting to the king. "It's a pleasure to meet you, Your Highness. And our most esteemed friend," she said, turning to Yamini. Yamini bowed back in return.

"This is Esha Amara, the king's ward and my longtime friend," Harun said, a low note of warning in the way he said *friend*. It gave her a little hope that he was still using that word.

The king inclined his head at her in acknowledgment, his fingers lightly tapping the goblet in his hand. "A pleasure."

At that moment a nobleman walked over and bowed to them. Vardaan narrowed his eyes at the newcomer. He was a strapping young man with a strong chin and black hair that curled around his ears, one lone curl lying against his forehead. Esha's gaze was drawn to the crest on his sword—House Pramukh.

This was Lord Mayank.

"I'm sorry to intrude, but I have yet to meet the esteemed Dharkan prince," he said, placing four fingers against his chest. "I'm Mayank Pramukh." He moved with surprising grace for a Jansan.

"Neither of you intruded at all. My prince and I were just arguing over whether the jaggery dates or mango custard was better. I think it was the custard, but my prince disagrees," she said, tossing a look at Harun.

"I'd have to agree with the prince, my lady," Lord Mayank said. "Though I'm not fond of disagreeing with someone as beautiful as you."

Esha smiled.

"My lady," Esha called to Yamini. "What are your thoughts?"

She pondered the question. "I'd have to agree with you, Lady Esha."

"Two to two. Your Highness?" Esha said, turning to look back at Vardaan, keeping up this little game of courtiers. He hadn't stopped looking at her, something thoughtful in his eyes.

Her heart stopped. Did he recognize her as the girl in the dungeons, the one who was thought to have helped the princess escape?

Esha kept the fake smile on her face. Someone brushed her hand, and she didn't look, already knowing by the shape of the calluses on his fingertips that it was Harun. It tugged her back into her body and out of her memories.

"I'd have to agree with you, my lady. Mango custard has been one of my favorites since I was a young man. It seems we have something in common."

Esha demurred, trying to look pleased at the notion, before turning to Harun. "Looks like the mango custard has won, my prince."

"Looks like it has. I suppose you'll want my jeweled dagger. I'll send it to you by servant tonight."

Esha tried not to look surprised. She always forgot how good Harun was at these games—with a few words he had revealed her strength, accepting that she was right and indicating that she knew how to use a dagger and understood its worth. "I'm looking forward to it, my prince."

"And why would someone as lovely as you need a dagger?" Lord Mayank asked. "I'm sure you'd be able to cut through your enemies' hearts with one sharp glance."

Vardaan lifted his goblet as if toasting to the words. "What poetry, Mayank."

If Esha wasn't so annoyed at the idea that a woman wouldn't need to be armed, she might have been charmed. Lady Yamini stiffened at Vardaan's toast.

"The Yavar believe every woman should be armed."

Lord Mayank dipped his head. "I was merely trying to give the lovely Lady Esha a compliment."

An adviser showed up at Vardaan's elbow, and he excused himself for a moment.

"Lady Yamini, I would love to hear more about the

Yavar training camps for girls. Would you care to take a walk? Lord Mayank, you're welcome as well, unless you'd rather stay here with the men. Don't want you to get cut by my gaze," she said softly.

Lord Mayank choked a bit on his sip of wine, and Harun reached out to hit him on the back, hiding his grin poorly.

"I would love to," Yamini said, depositing her goblet on one of the trays.

Esha was burning to know what Harun had been about to say before they were interrupted. But more than ever, Dharka needed a united front.

So Esha held out a hand to Lady Yamini as she approached, a smile high on her cheeks.

———◆———

A curved blade hovered in the darkness above Esha's head, like an executioner's tool.

Bronze cuffed hands held her back, her screams rending the air, but she couldn't break free. She couldn't run to her parents, and she drowned in her agony as she watched the soldier blink his owl eyes and move with focused precision forward. She kicked and bit and snarled, and when the inevitable came she tried to avert her eyes, but the hands kept her still, pushed her head forward.

Esha saw and heard it all. The slow, graceful way her mother fell into a heap, as if she had only gone to sleep. Her father's cries and how they faded into silence.

How everything went breathlessly quiet.

And the soldiers turned toward her, dark ichor eyes burning beneath their bronze helmets. And General Hotha, smiling.

A scream tore from her throat, piercing the silence.

She would make them pay. She would find every one of them and watch—

Movement jarred her awake, and Esha shot up, grabbing the knife under her pillow.

Aditi gasped. "My lady."

Esha recoiled. She scooted back into her covers, shoving the knife under her pillow again as if Aditi could unsee it.

The girl stared at Esha.

"You were having a nightmare, my lady."

Esha pressed a cold hand to her face, calming the rage in her blood.

"Another minute and you might've woken up the whole wing."

"I'm sorry, Aditi," Esha said. "Thank you."

Aditi nodded, averting her eyes as Esha rose out of bed.

"My . . . sister. She gets the dreams too. Terrors, more accurately." Aditi hesitated. "Are you all right, my lady?"

Had she revealed anything? Esha's mind shifted through five different lies she could tell, but she was tired. And heartsick after another reminder of her unfulfilled vow to her parents.

"No," she said quietly. "I'm not."

Aditi sat on the bed next to her and laid a light hand on Esha's shoulder.

"Let me get you some tea."

———◄○►———

Kunal marched down the palace pathway to the outer wall. He'd been annoyed since he awoke—perhaps from disrupted sleep due to carousing champions or from not having a moment to himself.

If it wasn't the new patrol schedule, or meeting requests from houses that wanted to sponsor him for the Mela, then he was in training for the Mela—locked in a room with the king. He already felt as if he was connecting to a past he thought he would never know. And that was due to King Mahir's generosity.

The more time he spent with the older man, the worse he felt about leaving King Mahir in the dark about their plan to rescue Reha. He'd tried mentioning his concerns to Esha in one of their notes, asking what their plan was, but she hadn't responded—in fact, she had completely ignored his question.

It was beginning to feel like there was a growing list of things Esha was holding close to her chest since the jungle. Since she had reunited with her team—and with Harun. Alok said Kunal was just being an arse because he was used to being in charge and in the know.

Which only annoyed Kunal. The king had a right to know his daughter might be alive. It was as simple as that.

195

Kunal took up his post outside the western outer wall. He set his spear on the ground, trying to calm his mind as he waited for the morning patrol to come. Footsteps pattered across the stone, and Kunal straightened, relieved to hear the soldiers approaching.

But it wasn't the footsteps of soldiers. Laksh moved into the light, and Kunal let out a deep groan.

"What? Thought I forgot about you?"

How was it that Laksh was able to keep finding him? Was he being followed? Or did he have access to the Senap's patrol schedule?

Laksh's face had gained back some of its fullness, but that hunger was still in his eyes.

"Tsk. No need for that." Laksh smiled, thin as ice. "This is a quick meeting. You might actually enjoy it."

"Unlikely," Kunal said.

"Are your manners always like this? No wonder the Viper has been spending more time with the prince."

He narrowed his eyes at Laksh, trying to figure out what he was playing at, but the man's face remained mostly impassive. Just that infernal smirk.

"I wonder what people would say if they knew she was the legendary Viper. The death bringer to the Jansan army," Laksh said. "And your new captain? He'd be so disappointed to know the newest addition to his team is not who he thinks. Is working against him."

The sun flared into Kunal's eyes as he circled around

Laksh, making sure to get his back to a wall.

"Stop playing around, Laksh. These half-truths and innuendos don't suit you."

An emotion flashed over Laksh's pointed features—annoyance or anger, Kunal couldn't tell. "And they suit you?"

"Not at all. I hate this. All of this."

"Your Viper doesn't."

"And that's her choice. She has a knack for it, but she is true to her core. Loyal to her people. What are you?"

Laksh cracked his knuckles, the smirk sliding off his face. "Are we really going to talk about who is more loyal to their people? Look at yourself, Kunal. Would-be deserter, working with those Dharkans."

Kunal gave him a grim smile. "Maybe if you hadn't tried to capture me and use me as a bargaining chip, I'd be singing a different tune. And I have broken a few oaths," he said, swallowing the lump in his throat that still formed at those thoughts. "But my first oath was to this country, this land."

"And you believe the Dharkans will do better? Do they know who you are, Kunal? How do you know they won't leave you behind, the poor bastard Samyad?"

Something snapped in Kunal. He walked toward Laksh, and to his credit, his old friend didn't flinch in the face of Kunal's anger.

"I would never work with Dharmdev's group."

"Really? Have you even talked to them? Or Dharmdev? Your own countrymen? Or are you making assumptions and judgments? Typical for the Kunal I knew."

"I might have felt your words if you hadn't chosen to insult and discredit good people. I don't know what your problem is with the Blades, but I'm not getting into something that's clearly personal," he said, trying out a thought that had just occurred to him.

"Handing the reins over to those foreigners?" Laksh said, his reaction fierce enough to confirm Kunal's suspicion. There *was* something personal.

"Those foreigners? How is that any better than what Vardaan is saying? 'Might is right, the queens were weak, only I knew best.'"

Laksh paused. The silence cooled the heat between them.

"You may have a point, Kunal, I'm big enough to admit that," Laksh said softly. "I may have my own issues with the Blades. But the others—Dharmdev, the Scales—they've suffered under Vardaan's rule. They're scared."

Laksh's concern was so sincere that it caused Kunal to do a double take.

Made his heart ache.

This was the friend he had known and loved. The jokester, the one who saw both sides and argued for both. He had been the balance between him and Alok.

"I need you to do something else for me."

"And what's that?"

"I need to get into the palace."

Laksh had clearly drunk the traders' moon-touched herbal drink.

"Impossible."

"Nothing's impossible."

Kunal gave him an impatient look. "Why, then? It'll be crawling with soldiers who might recognize you. You're supposed to be dead."

"Concerned for me?"

Kunal sputtered in indignation.

"I'll be fine," he said. "Worry about yourself. I just need a door that I can slip through."

"What could you possibly gain by me getting you into the palace? I thought you wanted me to win the king's boon. Not get yourself killed."

"I'd tell you, Kunal. I'd let you in on everything—a full debrief—if you joined us."

Kunal flinched. Not this again.

"I thought as much," Laksh said. "You know I can't tell you why. And honestly, it'd jeopardize you."

Kunal peered closely at his former friend. What could Laksh need to do in the palace? His first instinct was to warn the team, to set up Aahal and Farhan as lookouts while Laksh moved around the palace. But he couldn't do that without revealing his initial deception.

"I'll get you into the palace." Kunal straightened as he heard footsteps in the distance. "But I need you to get out of here. Now."

Laksh gave an exaggerated bow and left.

Kunal rubbed his temple. He'd find a way out of this mess. If he had the steel in his heart that his uncle had, he'd be able to just get rid of Laksh with a quick swipe of his knife.

He needed to find something to turn the tide and put him back on solid land.

But what?

———◆———

Esha found herself wandering the palace in the early morning, the dark skies above her reflecting her mood. The stars hadn't bothered to come out, and it was so early that even the birds were silent. The image of the soldier in her nightmare had been playing again and again in her head like an unending song.

She stepped out of the palace corridors into a small courtyard that bordered the edge of the palace gardens. Moonlight spilled over an empty marble bench, casting odd shapes across the grass. Once, on a morning like this when she had woken from a bad dream, her father had taken her into these gardens and they sat under the blooming ashoka tree, counting the petals on each flower until she fell back asleep.

Esha closed her eyes, fighting a wave of grief that threatened to overwhelm her. If only she hadn't gone to the library that night. There had been rumors of danger, but she had been so adamant. Such a stubborn child.

And now she was back in this city.

Her father used to take her to the bazaar in Gwali every moon to see the dance troupes whirling in mesmerizing circles. Her mother would take her to the temple, picking marigolds from these gardens beforehand to bring as an offering.

She'd once felt at home in this city.

She'd once almost died in this city.

That was when she had made her vow, after she had been thrown out of the dungeons of the citadel. To honor her parents' memory by getting justice.

And what had she done so far in the city to honor them? Nothing.

"Are you all right, Lady Esha?" a voice asked.

Esha jumped and turned to face the newcomer, swallowing the lump in her throat as she quickly adjusted her sari and patted her hair flat. Lady Yamini walked into the moonlight and it cast a misshapen halo around her head.

"I'm fine," Esha said before hastily adding, "Your Highness."

Yamini waved her hand. "Don't bother with the title. I can't abide all this protocol and preening anyway."

Esha chuckled. "You and me both."

"My mother felt the same way when she married into my father's clan. She is not one for pomp. Was," Yamini said, her brow furrowing for a moment.

"I'm sorry," Esha said. "It's never easy to lose a loved one."

"It's the way of life, isn't it?" Yamini's voice was steadier than Esha's would have been.

"I wish it weren't."

"You know, some Yavar believe there exists a path to

eternal life. A way to avoid the Chariot at Dusk. It's become a new fad to search for the treasure of Vasu the Wanderer."

Esha chuckled. "I'm not sure I'd want eternal life. I just want a full one, well lived."

"We can agree on that, Lady Esha," Yamini said, a grin splitting her face. "Having to deal with all these courtiers for eternity?" She shuddered.

"Are you not a fan of court, my lady?"

"I wasn't brought up in it, this lifestyle of half-truths and full lies. I grew up in the north, with my mother's clan in the tallest peaks of the Aiforas," she said, a hint of pride in her voice. "I was brought up as a warrior and tactician for our clans." She didn't say anything else, but Esha could tell by her tone that she didn't think court life matched up.

"Impressive. I was trained to fight as well. I'd love to see you in the sparring court." Esha paused. "But the king doesn't condone such behavior here. Another time and place."

Yamini made a noise. "These rules are stupid. We would never handicap half the population back home."

"I'm of a similar mind," Esha said, pausing and looking around. "Though please don't repeat that."

Yamini looked affronted. "Of course not. I can hardly fault you for being sane."

Esha burst out laughing, which she hadn't expected to do that morning. Yamini's lips twitched as well, a crack in her otherwise stoic armor. Esha found herself relaxing a bit in the young woman's company.

"I can't wait to see you on the battlefield one day, Lady Yamini. For that matter, I'd love to see you among a group of noble ladies at court. I'm sure you'd fare much better than you think."

"You know, it's not the ladies I have trouble with," Yamini said, indicating to Esha that they should continue walking. "It's the men. They never seem to know what to do with me."

"Really? I would've never thought," Esha said, laughing. Yamini gave her a look before realizing Esha was joking.

"That right there. That ease and charm, it's not something I have naturally," she said, no trace of embarrassment on her face at revealing a weakness. Esha liked the honesty with which Yamini faced life. It reminded her of Kunal, in a way.

"I'm sure charm is not necessary on a battlefield."

"It doesn't hurt when leading soldiers." Yamini gave her a wry grin.

"You lead an army?" Esha asked before she could rein in her surprise.

"The northern division. A league between three of our clans," she said dismissively.

Esha kept a neutral smile on her face, storing the information away to tell Harun later.

"May I inquire what was causing you distress before?" Yamini asked, a stiff formality over her words, as if she wasn't sure how to get the sentiment across.

"Nothing of importance."

"My mother often said, 'That which seems unimport-ant is typically of the most importance,'" Yamini said. It was clear she had loved her mother, her tone softening in memory.

"Your mother was a wise woman." Esha tried to remember more about Yamini's mother, the daughter of another clan's chieftain, but she couldn't recall much.

"Yes. She was." Yamini interlocked her arms behind her back. "Except at the end," she added, almost as if to herself. Her face looked lost in thought, captured by an old memory.

"Hm?"

"The young prince is clearly taken with you."

Esha startled at the sudden shift in the conversation, then considered Yamini more closely than she had at the start of their walk. Yamini's expression had tightened.

"That's what they're saying." Esha laughed it off, trying to assuage the doubt Yamini had inadvertently given away and let the woman know that she could trust her. "But we grew up together. And I think we both just enjoy sporting events, whereas I can't say the same for some of the other nobles."

Yamini's eyes lit up. "You do? I thought I was the only one who was genuinely interested in the tournament so far. My father has always been a patron of sports, but he can be insufferable about them. Always acting as if he understands the rules better, just because he happens to have been born a man."

"Now that is a frustration I can empathize with. When

I first started training in fighting at the palace, I was placed with a group of mostly boys."

Yamini groaned in sympathy. "I was as well."

Esha felt a sudden kinship with the girl. "Then you know exactly what I mean when I say, sometimes, the best defense is offense."

"I hope that means what I think it means."

"I got very good at wrangling frogs and snakes and relocating them. Often to new beds."

Yamini burst out laughing, her face filled with delight.

"Tell me everything," she said. "Some of my friends could still do with a frog in their beds."

"Oh, well, that's my specialty," Esha said, grinning.

◄◇►

Esha slid into the steamy water of the bath, letting the heat surround her like a cocoon.

She should try to relax. Kunal was in the citadel, she had befriended Lady Yamini, and they were a step closer to finding Reha's exact location and rescuing her. But Kunal had also become a crowd favorite, endangering himself. And Harun barely looked at her anymore, that one moment of friendship at the last party disappearing the next day.

She wished Kunal were with her. He had a way of speaking and seeing the world that both annoyed and calmed her, and it was that calm she sought now.

But she wouldn't be able to see him anymore, now that he was into the next round. He'd be surrounded by other soldiers and fighters, and she'd only see him at the champions' parties, if then. He had been leaving her worrisome notes, though, asking questions about King Mahir and their plans after they rescued Reha—when she needed him to focus on the immediate task. They'd planned to have Kunal and some of the team case the citadel tonight, when the champions would be at the party.

The party tonight was hosted by House Rusala, and Esha had prepared blue and black clothing to wear in their honor. She took out the blue sapphire ring she had pilfered from Harun's gift, wondering if it would match. It was a bit reckless, but after Vardaan had taken notice of her during their last conversation, Esha wanted some extra protection. She'd be careful to hide it from Harun, but if anything happened and Vardaan was there . . . she would be prepared.

Aditi had brought in a table full of steaming tea and bath oils, and Esha was enjoying the rose and jasmine soak in the tub. There was a small crash of metal against stone and Esha looked over to see that the flower vase had tumbled over and Aditi was clutching her hand.

"Are you all right?" Esha asked, clambering out of the tub.

"I'm fine, my lady. Just a burn," she said quickly. "The water was hotter than I thought."

Esha reached for her, but she deftly moved out of her way, picking up the vase and signaling to one of the other servants.

"Leave it, Aditi," she said. "Don't worry about it."

"No, no," the girl said, bending to the floor.

"They're just flowers. I'll help—I don't want you to slip."

"You're too kind, my lady."

"Kind, my arse," Esha grumbled, pulling on clothes to join her on the floor. Aditi had bent over to pick up the fallen rose petals and Esha kneeled beside her. Her lip was trembling and it seemed her maid was in more pain than she was letting on. Esha placed a gentle hand on her shoulder.

"Don't worry about this," she said. Aditi looked up. "Go on, go to the infirmary. I'd walk you there myself if I thought you'd allow it."

"My lady, I have to finish—"

"You've done more than enough. Anyway, I've been dressing myself for longer than you've probably been alive."

"That's hardly correct. I'm only a few years younger than you," Aditi said, snorting.

Esha took a closer look at the girl and realized she was right.

"I'll blow the lamps out and put away my clothing neatly. I promise," Esha said.

"All right, my lady," Aditi said, a glimmer of a smile on her face. "If you insist."

"I do." Esha pushed Aditi toward the door.

And she did, though it wasn't just for Aditi.

An idea had come to her. And she'd need the room to herself.

CHAPTER 18

Kunal had spent the last two hours training in the pal ace courtyard with Chand, who had agreed to form a partnership with him until the end of the Mela. They had gone over the proper forms for mace fighting, and Kunal was a sandy, dirty mess, but this was what he was good at, what he enjoyed. What'd he'd missed.

And now, it was for the right reasons. It was up to him to make sure his team had access to the citadel tonight— he almost relished the pressure. It was the fame that he could've done without. Now he had to cover his face when he went into the streets and fight off calls in the palace hall- ways. One weaver in the artisans' sector had even woven his face into a blanket.

Kunal shook his head as he walked to the washroom, determined to get at least one layer of grime off him before the end of the day—though at least the dirt was a good disguise. As he turned the corner, something familiar flashed in the distance. He stopped and turned around, quieting his footsteps.

There. A movement against the open windows across the gardens. Kunal crept down the hallways of the palace, speeding up as he went.

He found Esha in the darkness of the west wing, his sharpened eyesight the only thing keeping him from bumping into every wall and corner. She hovered close to the window in one of the alcoves that overlooked the courtyard, her hair blowing in the soft breeze, tendrils escaping her loose braid. She was in her training gear, but it was dyed black.

In two strides he was at her side and took hold of her hand, tugging her to him. She spun into him, landing hard against his chest.

"Going somewhere?"

He took advantage of her moment of confusion to look at the setup around her. A long rope lashed against the side of the palace.

"Tell me you're not sneaking out."

"I'm not sneaking out," she said immediately.

"Esha . . ."

"Kunal."

"Why are you sneaking out? When there are normal entrances?"

"Don't like them. Or the guards."

He made a hurt face and she waved her hand.

"You're all right," she said with a grin. "Don't worry about it, Kunal. I'm following a lead."

"That's what you said at the archery tournament."

"I made a mistake; my disguise then wasn't good enough."

"That may be, but what were you doing? And does Harun know?"

Her face instantly shuttered.

"No, and you're not going to tell him."

A gust of wind flew through the open window, and Esha pressed up closer to him. The annoyed words he was about to speak died on his tongue. They were a hairbreadth away from each other, had been in this position a number of times recently, and yet tonight the moon was shining and there was a tendril of hair lashing her face.

Like the first night they had met.

This time, he didn't hesitate and tucked the curl behind her ear, cupping her face in his hand.

"I'm not? Is that a threat?"

She sighed, her eyes turning a darker mahogany as he brushed his fingertips against her cheek. "Please, don't."

Esha stepped back, tugging Kunal so that he had no choice but to follow her. Not that it was a chore. The darkness was a welcome cover, giving them privacy in a way they hadn't experienced in days.

She pulled him into a deep kiss, replacing all the thoughts he was having with the feel of her in his arms. He entwined his arms around her small frame, feeling her soft skin under his touch—and checking for hidden weapons. He pushed her up against the open window of the alcove, not caring who might be below. But while he wanted to stay there, with her, like this, he hadn't forgotten that she was sneaking out to do something.

"You know I have another knife," she said, her voice husky.

They broke apart for a second, staring at each other. Kunal made the mistake of looking down at the one he had drawn from her waist sash. In seconds, she grasped the sides of the windows, and pushed herself into the alcove like a swing.

"I'll be right back, I promise. There's something important I have to do."

The look on Esha's face was Viper, through and through.

Esha tugged at the rope behind her and launched herself through the open window to land on the outer wall of the palace.

Kunal leaned over to see where she had gone, but she had already disappeared into the darkness.

―――◄◦►―――

Esha winced as she took a seat in the large, oval room, her bangles cutting into the gash she had gotten in last night's hasty exit. Her information gathering had gone well, except for the initial interruption by Kunal. She had gotten a location—the Falcon Squad was staying in the garrison. Brute force over stealth worked, but she was paying for it now with a number of new scrapes and bruises.

She brushed her hair out of her eye and tucked a loose curl back into the ornate braided crown that Aditi had done that morning for the peace summit. The meeting room was spectacularly decorated, with the crests of all five Jansan houses and the eagle of the Samyads towering above them on the ceiling. Esha imagined many war councils had been held there with the Samyad queens. What she would have given to see that.

She was supposed to be conversing with her prince, perhaps checking on terms before the negotiations started. But as it was, Harun was avoiding her and she was one of the only women in the room, drawing curious and hostile glances. Not the best choice for keeping a low profile, but Harun had insisted that she deserved a seat at the table.

The doors flew open and Vardaan entered, winged by a cadre of advisers in stark white dhotis and four Senap guards at his back. Harun was swept toward the long table in the center of the room by one of his advisers. Esha moved to take a seat farther down the table, but Harun held a hand up to her, stopping her in her tracks. He turned to his adviser.

"Make a spot for Lady Esha next to me."

"But, Your Highness, that spot is for Adviser Kulkar," the man said, looking nervous.

"Give him another spot."

"Your Highness, I'd advise against that. We can't have a—"

A what? Esha felt her lips tighten into a thin line. *A woman?*

"I don't care," Harun said, an edge to his voice.

"Harun, it's fine. It'll be better for me to be down there. I can observe more," she said quietly, stressing the latter part. He stared at her, searching for something.

"All right, if you think it's best," he said, turning back to face the table.

The adviser looked relieved. Esha sent him a look that made it clear that he owed her one. She took the seat she had pulled out before, sliding into it as a trumpet was blown and the official talks began.

"Greetings, Uncle," Harun said, bowing slightly to Vardaan and his advisers. "Thank you for setting up this peace summit for our countries. Dharka seeks peace and friendship from its neighbor and sister country. We're glad to be here to discuss the best future for both of our people."

"Welcome," an adviser to the right of Vardaan said, tilting his head. "We're honored to have the delegation from Dharka here to negotiate a peace treaty." His voice hitched, and he looked over at Vardaan, a rough swallow going down his throat. Vardaan nodded at him. "However, an important matter has come to our notice. One that must be immediately resolved."

Esha glanced around, trying to see if anyone else on their delegation knew what the man was referring to.

"This morning, one of our Senaps was found dead."

"My condolences," Harun said, putting four fingers to his chest.

The adviser bowed his head in response. "Thank you.

Senap Ronak Undhiya was a great warrior, and a rising star in the king's personal unit."

Esha's tapping finger stilled, and she quickly pulled her uttariya over the cuts and bruises on her arms while panic flooded her body. She had merely thrown a few blows to get him to speak. She definitely hadn't killed him.

He had been alive and breathing, though spitting curses, when she had left.

"I'm very sorry," Harun repeated, a hint of impatience in his voice. "But may I ask why you're bringing this up?"

"We're worried there are those taking advantage of the Mela to harm our soldiers. And when we thought about what has changed from previous Melas, your delegation . . ."

"Are you insinuating something, adviser?" King Mahir asked, his deep voice rumbling.

The man looked nervous again, glancing over at Vardaan.

"No insinuations, brother. We thought you should know that there might be some forces in the city who are not happy with us meeting. The disturbances only started after your arrival. Another soldier had been poisoned at an inn."

Esha gripped the table tighter.

"Uncle, I'm still unclear how this affects us," Harun said. "Forgive my bluntness. But if your soldiers are being targeted, it could be anyone. You can be assured it's no one from my court. They're as committed to peace as we are."

"That's the thing, we can't be sure," Vardaan said.

"Dharkan rebels have previously targeted my army."

He trailed his finger along the table, drawing the shape of a whip.

"And what about the Jansan rebels?" Harun asked.

"Jansan rebels? We have none. My people are loyal, and those who aren't, aren't true Jansans," Vardaan said, his tone almost bored. Esha thought back to the corpses swinging from the city walls and drew her uttariya tighter around her body.

If Vardaan was going to pretend Dharmdev was inconsequential, there was nothing they could do. But Esha knew how dangerous the Scales could be. Was this their work? Framing the Blades, once again?

"We think it prudent to postpone signing the peace agreement until after we get to the bottom of this," the adviser said.

"Really?" King Mahir asked, his gaze sharpening on the man. "And this isn't an excuse to cancel our talks, which we traveled here in good faith to have? We've been nothing but gracious since the truce, despite your previous general being the constant aggressor."

King Mahir realized the mistake when Vardaan's tapping fingers stopped abruptly.

"My general? The man killed by your rebel group, the very one you claim you can't control?"

"I have no affiliation with them. We only heard recently—"

Vardaan scoffed. "He was my general. A sworn soldier.

My friend. If you think I've—"

His adviser put a hand on his forearm, and Vardaan retreated, but they'd already seen the anger underneath Vardaan's mask.

Mahir leaned forward, matching Vardaan's anger with his own.

"Your sworn soldier. Do you know what he did to our civilians in Sundara? He wasn't a general, he was a common murderer."

Harun tensed next to his father.

"What was that?" Vardaan's voice was a low simmer.

"You heard me, Vardu. A murderer."

Vardaan flinched as if he had been hit. "I hate that nickname, you know it."

"You hate everything about us, don't you? You left our parents, our people, our land."

"It wasn't really *ours*. Was it, brother? No, everything was for *you*," he spat out. Heat flared between the brothers, something unspoken sparking against old wounds. Esha had expected a difficult conversation, but it was different seeing the decades of pain and anger between the two royals.

A second later, Vardaan's face was back to being placid and pompous. "Well, all that's changed now. Hasn't it, brother?" He swept a hand out. "I've my own kingdom now."

Esha could almost feel the fire coming off King Mahir, but somehow he managed to fight it, and when he spoke his voice was as cool as ice.

"Indeed."

It was a good reminder that Vardaan hadn't been born a vicious, lying monster. He had been formed. She had always thought that it was due to greed, a singular motivation from a singular monster of a man. But Esha couldn't hold on to that idea now. Not when she had seen her nightmare in the flesh.

Vardaan was human—cruel, scheming, angry. But also charismatic, protective of his men, loyal.

Rather like the Viper.

Silence reigned in the thick air. The advisers on both sides wore identical expressions of fear and worry.

Vardaan frowned, dropping the indolent smile he had been wearing. "My men are important to me. And there's no assurance that your men will be safe either. Someone is trying to stop our talks."

"Isn't that more reason to continue?" one of Mahir's advisers tried.

"Yes," Vardaan said. "But I won't risk my men or your safety." And something about the way he said it made Esha almost believe him. "Not if I have a choice."

King Mahir nodded. "I understand," he said, his voice softer. There was a pause between them, a moment that they both recollected, but it passed.

"We can agree to hold off on the signing, but let's not delay our negotiations. If this is indeed a threat, we cannot be cowed," King Mahir said.

Vardaan looked pleased with the outcome.

Esha felt her panic shifting into anger and confusion. Someone had killed Ronak after she had left. Someone was trying to punish her country through her. She needed to stop, reassess the situation. But rage and grief still battled inside her heart, curling into the empty spaces in her chest.

Esha took a stilted breath, drawing herself out of her head and turning her attention back to the talks. They had moved on to the terms of the agreement—how they'd share the border and trade routes—but Esha couldn't focus.

She'd made a vow to her parents that night, and one couldn't forego something written in blood. Esha felt her heart torn in two, her duty to her past and future colliding.

Esha didn't know which she would choose.

Kunal allowed himself a small frown as he lounged against the palace wall. He'd already had to dodge a group of young noble ladies in the training courtyard and now he had to figure out how to lie to Arpiya.

Arpiya had been working every night to set up an exit plan from the citadel to the palace. Tonight she'd requested his help, and though he had already sent a note to Laksh that he'd let him into the palace, he had no good excuse to say no to Arpiya.

"Why are we going this way?" Arpiya asked, sweeping her short hair out of her eyes.

"Are you all right?"

"I'm fine. Answer the question."

He shrugged. "I found this to be a better path to get to the lookout. Plus, I have a few Senap duties I need to fulfill tonight," he added, providing an excuse for what he was about to do. He was already tense and uncomfortable at the idea of letting Laksh into the palace, like a scorpion was on his back and he was letting it sit on his shoulder.

"Hmph," was all Arpiya said in response.

"Is something the matter?" Kunal asked, not really wanting to get into it. But Arpiya had been kind to him when she had no reason, and he wanted to return the favor.

Arpiya blew out a frustrated sigh. "That feeling is back. The feeling that I need to leave or run. It's been plaguing me ever since I got inside these damn walls."

Kunal looked at her thoughtfully. "I know what you mean." He paused before continuing. "I haven't painted or even thought about art since I set foot in this palace. It's as if it sucked all the art out of me," he said.

Or maybe it was all the scheming and lying. He couldn't be sure.

"I'm positive if you asked Esha she would change up your tasks. Maybe take on a few for you."

Arpiya shuddered. "She would, but I hate the parties more than lookout. And we need alliances, more soldiers. I can't wait till we're done with this mission and can get out of here. We'll take Reha somewhere safe while Harun figures out how to maneuver her onto the throne."

Maneuver her onto the throne? Kunal glanced at Arpiya, but she was looking down the hall. The goal was to save Reha and find a way to get her to the ritual in time. There wouldn't be time to get her on the throne beforehand. But perhaps there was some plan Esha had up her sleeve; he'd have to ask her when he saw her.

"Why did you ask for lookout duty tonight? If you've been stuck here for so long."

"I wanted to confirm our plan. I'm confident of the Senap and servant timings, and I've given enough gold coins to the traders to ensure they jump when I tell them. But there are always things that go awry, so here I am. Checking and rechecking."

Kunal nodded. He understood that.

"And I wanted to spend time with you, soldier," Arpiya said.

"Me?"

She examined him. "My best friend dragged you in and dumps you onto our team. It's clear to me she cares for you."

Kunal coughed, shifting his position. "She cares for me? Did she say that or—"

Arpiya rolled her eyes. "The two of you. I'm not here to be your messenger. Anyway, she broke her team's trust to keep your secret. She lied to us for you."

The tone of Arpiya's voice made Kunal realize what Esha had broken to keep him safe. His heart thumped fiercely. He'd do the same for her. He was doing the same, agreeing to let Laksh into the palace and more.

"Moon Lord's mother, you two are the same. Learn to control your expressions around others at least?" Arpiya said.

"Huh?"

"That moony look on your face and the steel that followed. I'm glad to see it. I came here to make sure you don't do anything to hurt my friend. Otherwise, I'd skin you from ear to ear."

Kunal winced. "I have no intention of hurting her."

"That's clear to me now, at least. But intentions aren't what the world is built on," she said. "You can have the best of intentions and yet . . ."

He wasn't sure what she meant by that. Wasn't good intention the basis of a good act? A tapping sound against the door nearby prevented him from philosophizing further with Arpiya.

"What was that?"

"Not sure," Kunal lied. "Let me check. Stay hidden around the corner until I give the signal."

Arpiya looked like she was about to question him, but she nodded. Once she had turned the corner, Kunal opened the door, yanking Laksh into the room.

"I said to tap once."

Laksh pushed him away, brushing off his uttariya. "I wasn't sure you'd hear me."

"I'm pretty sure everyone in this corridor heard you."

"Everyone? If you've set me up—"

"Oh believe me, I thought about it, but I don't betray my word. Unlike some—"

"And who is this?" Arpiya said, walking up toward him. She had pulled out her hair from its bun and untied her sari from around her waist, making her look like a regular courtier.

"I might ask the same question of my friend." Laksh

bowed to her in greeting. "Who is this lovely lady?" he asked, a twinkle in his eye.

Kunal felt stuck, unsure what to do. He couldn't warn Arpiya about Laksh without giving away his precarious position with him.

"This is Arpiya, a friend of mine. And this is Laksh," Kunal said through gritted teeth. "He was the noise we heard. He dropped his knife."

Arpiya gave him a look as if he was being odd, and Laksh moved forward.

"I was just passing by and thought I'd say hi to Kunal. I'm glad I did." Laksh's gaze was locked on Arpiya.

"Oh, do you not see each other often?" Arpiya asked, her voice an octave higher than normal.

"No, I see Kunal often enough," Laksh said, his meaning clear. "It was my luck I happened upon him and you." Arpiya blushed. Actually blushed.

Were they . . . flirting? Kunal felt nauseated at the thought. Esha would have his head if he knew what was happening—he had to step in.

"And my *friend* was on his way. He mentioned he had some urgent business in the martial quarter." Which was not only in the very opposite direction from them, but hopefully reminded Arpiya that he was—or had been—a soldier.

But the curiosity on Arpiya's face didn't waver. "Business? Are you a soldier?"

Laksh hesitated. "Retired," he said, pulling his turban

a bit lower. Kunal grinned at Laksh's discomfort. He must have remembered all of the Fort's horrible punishments for desertion. And how close he was to being discovered.

"I have a few dealings, but they're all rather boring."

"Nonsense, I'm sure they're exhilarating."

"No, they're boring," Kunal interjected. "Laksh, weren't you on your way? I'll walk you out."

Kunal almost sighed in relief as Laksh nodded, though Laksh was having a hard time tearing his eyes away from Arpiya. Which made Kunal want to tear his own eyes out himself.

Laksh approached Arpiya, tucking something into her palm.

"If you'd ever like to talk more," he said. She nodded, the curiosity in her face turning warm enough that Kunal looked away.

What in the Sun Maiden's name was happening? Had the gods disappeared or were they secretly laughing at him right now?

Kunal grunted and hauled Laksh off. After two more corridors, Kunal let him go and wheeled around, only to see Laksh in far-off thought, his eyes dreamy.

It made Kunal even more irrationally annoyed.

"You said I had to get you into the palace. You do not get to interfere with other parts of my life," Kunal said.

"Who is she?"

"None of your concern."

"Now, Kunal—"

"No. If you want all the details, the full debrief, I'd give it to you. If you joined us," he said mockingly, surprised at the depth of venom he was feeling. Esha would have been proud.

"Touché, friend," Laksh said, some of his normal expression returning.

"What did you give her?"

"Nothing, a token."

Kunal looked at him with disbelieving eyes.

Laksh sighed. "What? Every other person in this city is allowed to give a token of their interest but I'm not? I'm still a man, Kunal."

"If you hurt her . . . ," Kunal said, trailing off.

"You truly think you're better than me—" Laksh's voice rose, clear frustration on his face. "Just because you see everything in black and white doesn't mean the world is that way. And what hypocrisy. You and the Viper—"

"Don't you dare mention her, not after threatening her to my face. Oh and by the way, the lovely girl you met? She's one of Esha's closest friends," Kunal said, enjoying the way the color drained from Laksh's face.

"No matter. And by the way, my *occupation* doesn't preclude me from being a gentleman," Laksh said.

Kunal tilted his head. "We'll see, Laksh."

His old friend said nothing to that, merely grunting and picking up his pace to match Kunal's.

A half hour later, Kunal made his way back to Arpiya. He had tried to follow Laksh but lost him pretty quickly in the maze of the palace. Thankfully, Kunal had shifted some of the Senaps' posts to be near any of the important rooms or exits that night.

He might not know exactly what Laksh was up to, but he'd at least be safe in knowing he wouldn't be getting mixed up in their rescue plans. Arpiya was still on lookout, and the only benefit of them meeting would be that he wouldn't be able to slip by without her noticing.

She was facing the other way when he trotted up behind her.

"Sorry for that."

Arpiya nodded but didn't turn around from the open windows. To his relief, she didn't ask any questions about Laksh. She was too intent on something that was happening outside, in the courtyard.

"What's happening?"

"Nothing, so far," she said. "But something looks off. The camphor lamps are doused in the west wing of the palace. The servants never douse them before the king returns to his quarters. But by the positioning of the guards down by the receiving hall, he's still going strong at tonight's party."

Kunal peered out.

"We could find the others, see if they've noticed anything. The guards will be changing soon, and I've got a cleaner who's now indebted to me and will alert us if any-one moves a mustache between the palace and the military quarters."

Kunal did a double take, looking at Arpiya with a new sense of awe—and a little terror. If he let her stay here she'd be sure to spot Laksh, and he couldn't afford it.

"I'll keep an eye on it. Report anything odd at the team meeting tomorrow. Why don't you take off?"

Arpiya cocked her head at him. "That's kind of you." Kunal flushed. If only Arpiya knew. "I would love to get some sleep. All right. See you tomorrow, Kunal."

Kunal saw her off before turning back to the window. He hated to lie to her, but he had to protect Esha. Kunal scoured the darkness once more, looking for Laksh, hoping to the Sun Maiden that he hadn't invited trouble.

But he had no choice.

And now that his hands were dirtied, he felt as if they'd never be clean.

CHAPTER 19

Esha hated waiting. She'd been stuck in this little corner of the street, for what felt like hours.

Her legs were beginning to cramp, and annoyance was beginning to crawl up her spine. Her contact had said the Falcon Squad would be returning from a meeting at this time and she'd been staking out this entrance of the garrison for the past hour, waiting for them to return.

Just as she began to consider leaving, she heard footsteps. Pairs of them, probably five or six in total. The squad.

Esha straightened, knowing she'd only a moment of time to capture their attention in this disguise. She'd get a proper look at them, determine which one had the honor of meeting her knife later. She should kill them all, but after the peace summit, she was going to play it closer to the vest.

Plan better, be more cunning. The Viper's territory.

Esha fixed the turban on her head, twirled the fake mustache she wore, and checked the gold pouch on her waist sash, the mark of a gambling den owner, before straightening her shoulders and strolling out of her hiding spot.

———◄○►———

Kunal was late. He picked up his pace, patting his bag to ensure all the supplies they needed to case the citadel were still in there.

The citadel and garrison were nestled near each other, a tunnel and walkway connecting them for security purposes. The champions would be gone and Kunal had made sure the soldiers would be otherwise occupied. This time, Kunal was taking every precaution.

Kunal fixed the positioning of his Senap armband and tugged his cuirass, feeling more comfortable than he had in a while. He was close to the citadel when he heard a two-by-two cadence more familiar to him than his own heartbeat.

A Senap squadron, coming his way. But why?

The champions were in the palace for yet another party, and the soldiers' exercises were being held in the palace courtyard. He sped up, turning the corner so that the garrison and the towering marble citadel came into view.

And in the distance, trailing a carousing group of soldiers in ceremonial regalia, was a small figure dressed like a gambling merchant, gold belt, mustache, unearned swagger and all.

But Kunal had seen Esha in enough disguises to immediately recognize her.

He broke into a run.

—◁◦▷—

Esha was about to call after the laughing soldiers when something stopped her. The feeling of being watched, or worse—that feeling she got before something went wrong in a mission.

But this time, she ignored it. She was tired of waiting. It had been ten long years.

Her shoe snagged on a rock, and Esha tripped, slowing down. One of the soldiers, who looked the least inebriated, turned at the noise, and Esha thought she saw his owl eyes glancing back, skimming over her.

But she couldn't be sure.

One of the other soldiers shouted and pointed at a nearby inn to a chorus of agreement.

She moved to follow them when arms enveloped her. Esha started kicking, but the person was strong, lifting her off her feet.

"Shh," Kunal said. "Squadron of soldiers following you."

Esha froze and then nodded against his chest. He put her down, and they moved to run. Kunal leaped ahead, turning the corner in seconds, but Esha wasn't fast enough.

One of the soldiers broke off from the rest and sped after her, catching her arm as she rushed to escape. He yanked at it as she jumped to the left, trying to get out of his reach.

Esha felt her shoulder pop out and bit her tongue hard to keep her scream inside her mouth, tasting blood.

She reacted by instinct.

Jab with her other arm, knee to the groin, and kick to the head. The soldier staggered back, a hand to his face.

Esha ran without a clear direction, realizing her exits were blocked. Kunal reached out and pulled her into a dark corridor near the walkway that connected the garrison and citadel.

She took a ragged breath, dropping her head against his chest as two soldiers ran into the walkway. The soldiers stopped steps from where Esha had been a few moments ago, spears out.

They were trapped in this small alcove. Kunal held her close against him, waiting for the soldiers to pass.

To their left was the only way back to the palace, a tunnel that led to the throne room. It was completely blocked with two pairs of Senaps guarding the entrance. To their right were the walkways, leading directly into the heart of the military. Dangerous, but not more dangerous than four Senaps.

"No," Kunal said, reading her mind. "I'm already letting in Bhandu, Aahal, and Arpiya. They'll be waiting for me. I can leave the alcove, drive the soldiers away."

"That's stupid. We can't be found together. And we'd be sitting ducks here. I do have some experience getting in and out of fortresses, soldier," she said. "I'll be fine."

Despite her flippant tone, her breath came in a ragged burst. Her arm ached, not just due to her injury but from her memories of her last time at the citadel. She hadn't wanted to enter this place, be inside. Again.

This wasn't how tonight was supposed to go.

Kunal pulled her closer, taking care not to brush against her shoulder as he placed a tentative kiss on her fingertips.

"What's wrong?"

"Nothing, we're wasting time."

"Esha . . ."

Something in her broke. "The citadel, it's where I was taken after my parents were killed."

Kunal's lips formed a firm line. "Then we're definitely not going."

The conch was blown, ten short bursts. The meeting time.

She didn't have a choice. Esha took a deep breath, inhaling the crisp air and exhaling the dark memories. Esha was scared, but the Viper wasn't.

"The squad will be waiting, and I'll not be trapped here for them to find me in the morning, like some caught fish. You'll help me into the citadel, take me into your room, and reset this damn shoulder. I'll leave then," she said.

Esha steeled herself, layering her armor back on as she untangled herself from his embrace.

She tilted her head at the passageway. "You go first, and I'll follow."

Kunal gave her a lingering kiss before pulling away and disappearing into the walkway to the citadel.

———◄◦►———

Esha appeared behind him, her small body pushed against his as they crept into the citadel. It was mercifully empty.

He had set up everything for their mission that night, making sure that they had a window between switches in patrol squads. Kunal had spent days putting this together and now, with Esha here, she could endanger their one chance to confirm Reha's location.

Kunal ducked his head around the corner. "Stay here. The others are coming soon, and we only have a half hour before the patrols are reinstated."

"Let me help, then," Esha said.

"No," he said. "You're a liability." He lowered his voice. "What in the Sun Maiden's name were you even doing there, Esha? You're supposed to be at the party with Harun, keeping an eye on the champions."

Esha was silent. "There was a change in plans. I'm here now."

"Yes, you are, and you're going to *stay* right here—"

"If you think I'm going to let you have all the fun while I'm stuck—"

"I like her already," a voice said, cutting through their whispers. Kunal groaned. Alok appeared around the corner, his mop of curls bouncing. His wide-eyed gaze drank it all in, his grin brighter than normal. "This is her, isn't it?"

"And who is this, Kunal?"

Alok let out a slight gasp and gave her a little bow. "I'm honored to meet you, Viper," he said, his voice low.

Esha bounced to her feet, her right hand going to her waist sash despite her injury, where Kunal knew she had both of her whips. He stepped in front of her, easing her hand away from her sash.

"This is Alok. Alok, who I've mentioned. Alok, who likes to stick his nose where it doesn't belong," he said.

Alok shrugged. "I figured you forgot to tell me about your secret mission tonight. I know you don't enjoy partying, but I figured you'd at least be at tonight's. Especially because your lady friend would be there. I thought you said I could meet her." He threw an accusing look at Kunal, clearly having realized that Kunal had pulled one over on him about her before. "But she's here now! Which is exciting. I suppose you both plan on casing the citadel together."

"Stop. Talking," Kunal whispered. He turned back to Esha, ready to explain himself, but she was only looking at Alok with a curious expression.

"He was planning on casing the citadel without me," she drawled. "Which would've been a mistake. I'm excellent company."

Alok gave her a knowing glance. "He likes to leave me out of things as well."

"You were never supposed to be here. It's not safe, and the only reason I brought you here is because you're

233

injured," Kunal said, pointing at Esha. "And I still have to let Bhandu in."

"Bhandu? Is he one of the Crescent Blades as well?" Alok asked.

Esha raised an eyebrow, looking between Kunal and Alok.

"Seems we've all been hiding a few things, haven't we?" she said, her voice silky. She stepped toward Alok, putting four fingers to her chest in the Jansan greeting. "Esha. It's good to meet you."

Alok put his hands together and bowed in the Dharkan greeting. "Alok. Charmed. You're far too pretty for him, you know."

Esha chuckled and rested a hand on Kunal's arm. His blood warmed where her fingers were—and at the look in her eyes. "He's got a few things going for him."

Kunal made a noise between a grunt and a sigh. "We need to move."

"Is he like this around you too?" Alok said, whispering. "All honorable and brooding?"

"Oh, I like that description."

"Are you two done chattering? Can you please stay quiet?" Kunal barked. He sighed and put a hand to his head. "Please?"

Alok turned serious. "What's wrong?"

"We ran into a squadron of soldiers, outside of patrols. It's possible that—" He hesitated, looking at Esha. "It's possible we've been spotted, but they shouldn't know we're in the citadel. They'll most likely be covering the entrance to the palace. Either way, we need to be on alert. I don't have a good feeling."

Esha nodded, rolling her good shoulder. "Let's move quickly, then."

CHAPTER 20

Kunal and Alok helped Esha to the bed despite her best attempts to walk over herself. Once he was sure she was situated, Kunal ran to the window and slid open the shutters.

A large shape hit the window and rolled into the room with a thud. Kunal groaned at the noise and moved to shutter the window when a lanky figure slid into the room. Farhan.

"Took you long enough," Bhandu whispered, shaking off his uttariya and throwing it onto one shoulder. He started at the sight of Esha. "Viperess, what are you doing here?"

"Long story," she said. "Better question is, what is Farhan doing here? I thought Aahal was coming for this mission."

Bhandu made a face. "Aahal's stuck at the palace with Arpiya. One of their contacts is asking questions, so they're handling it. Also, I tried to get rid of him."

"I was getting bored in the library. And he was rather easy to follow. And to distract," Farhan said. "You should work on that."

"You should work on keeping your features together on your face because one punch and—"

"Boys," Esha said, her voice stern. They both stood straighter. "You're better than this."

"That's a neat trick," Alok whispered to Kunal. Kunal grinned. He loved this side of her, the commanding, powerful leader. It made him want to stand up straighter too.

"Not a trick. She's their team leader. They'd follow her unto death," he whispered back.

"True, cat eyes. Very true," Bhandu said, moving to stand protectively in front of Esha. "Which means you have a handful of seconds to tell us why you have another soldier with you. Isn't one of you enough?"

Farhan stuck a hand out as Kunal rushed to speak. He wasn't frowning at Alok like Bhandu was. He was actually . . . smiling. Alok caught Farhan's steady gaze, his cheeks flaming.

"He's not just a soldier, he's my friend."

Bhandu raised an eyebrow.

Kunal sighed, continuing on. "He's one of my oldest friends. He's been helping me, though the gods know I haven't wanted him to. The patrols and squad movements? He's been keeping an eye. He helped me arrange tonight. There's no way I could've done that and be in the tournament at the same time."

Kunal put a hand on Bhandu's shoulder, and tilted his head at Esha. "I'm sorry for not letting you know sooner, but I was protecting you as much as him. He knows everything about me, but I've only told him the barest of details about our plan."

Bhandu's eyes narrowed, but he looked toward Esha. Farhan walked over to Alok.

"Alok, is it? I'm Farhan." The tall boy put four fingers to his chest. Alok returned the gesture, unable to take his eyes off Farhan.

Bhandu grumbled, but Esha patted his shoulder. "We trust Kunal, Bhandu. Let's trust his friend too. And we could always use an extra set of hands," she said.

"Also might I remind you, we now have only twenty-five minutes to confirm whether Reha is here or not," Kunal added.

"Fine. I trust whoever she trusts," Bhandu said. "And if Farhan likes him, then . . ."

Something sparked in Esha's eyes as she and Bhandu turned back to the other two men, whose heads were close in discussion.

"We need to split up," Kunal said. "Bhandu, you're with me. Farhan, look for any sign that Reha's here in the upper levels. Alok, stay with Esha, make sure she's all right after we—"

Without hesitation, Bhandu was in Kunal's face, hands around his throat.

"What did you do to her?" he snarled.

"Nothing. She got injured while . . . following a lead," Kunal finished, pushing him away. Which was harder than he was happy to admit.

"He didn't do anything, Bhandu. This was all me. I followed a bad lead, hurt my shoulder, and Kunal was around to bring me here," she said, the set of her mouth grim.

"So fix her cursed shoulder, cat eyes," Bhandu snapped at Kunal.

"I—" Kunal paused. "I've never done that before." He had caused so much pain, and he was embarrassed to say he didn't know how to fix any of it.

"I have," Alok said, striding forward. "I spent time in the healing tents when we were on campaign. This will hurt."

Esha nodded.

"Do you want something to bite on?" Alok asked gently.

Esha shook her head, but her eyes flickered to Kunal. He was going to walk over and offer his hand, but the presence of the others stopped him.

"I'm going to go on three. One, two—"

A sharp crack sounded in the room as Alok wrenched Esha's shoulder back into place.

"You said three!" Esha said, rubbing her shoulder. Bhandu leaped forward to grab Alok, but Farhan stepped in front, allowing Alok to sidestep and clasp his hands together.

"Surprise helps with the pain. Sometimes the anticipation is worse than the act itself."

Esha stood up and tested her shoulder.

"It doesn't hurt," she said in awe.

"Glad to hear it," Alok said. But Kunal knew by the small smile on his face that he was more pleased than he let on.

Kunal leaned over to Alok. "You never told me about the healing tents."

"You've been rather busy."

He stopped his friend, pulling him to the side as Bhandu played mother hen with Esha, making her move her arm in different ways.

"I don't want to be too busy for you," Kunal said. "We're going to talk about it, all of it. Over whatever drink you want."

Alok's eyes lit up, though he shrugged as if he couldn't care less. "Sure, if that's what you want."

"Yes. After this, we're doing it."

"Bhandu, let go of me," Esha demanded irritably. "Alok, I'm fine, right?"

"You're fine."

Esha turned to face Bhandu, triumph on her face.

"But I'd say you should go easy on it tonight. And rest it for the next few days."

"You heard the soldier. What if your stomach wound had opened up again?" Bhandu asked accusingly.

"Don't worry, mother, my stomach wound is fine. Hasn't bothered me in a week."

Alok made a curious noise, leaning forward. "I'd love to learn how they healed that. Did they use—"

"Touch her without Farhan around and I'll break your fingers," Bhandu said.

"I can break his fingers if I want, Bhandu," Esha said lightly. Alok didn't look nearly frightened enough; in fact, the idea seemed to excite him more.

"You're so much more fun than Kunal," Alok said.

Kunal made an exasperated noise. "Let's go," he said to Bhandu.

They left, Bhandu pulling a Senap helmet over his eyes, tossing one angry look back at Alok.

———◁◦▷———

"Can this friend of yours be trusted?" Bhandu asked as they climbed their way down the narrow side staircase.

"I'd trust him with my life," Kunal said.

If he didn't trust Alok, he didn't know who he could trust. Alok had every opportunity to betray him over the past week and he hadn't.

That was good enough for Kunal right now.

Bhandu grunted, and they continued in silence, winding down the levels at a steady pace. Kunal had to nudge Bhandu a few times to slow down, as most Senap pairs were trained to walk in tandem.

"If he does anything—"

"Who?"

Bhandu made a face. "Don't pretend you don't know who."

"I don't know who," Kunal said. He was enjoying the tomato red Bhandu was turning.

"You know I know you know who," Bhandu said, his eyes narrowing.

Kunal shrugged his shoulders.

"Don't test my patience, cat eyes."

"Wouldn't dream of it," he said, keeping his face still.

"Alok!" Bhandu exclaimed. Kunal shushed him, holding a finger to his lips.

"What about him?"

"Cat eyes, if you so much as—"

"You could try to trust me," Kunal said.

Bhandu stopped and held a hand out to Kunal. "Don't go making this about you. And anyway, the fact that Harun and Esha have given this task to you says enough. We trust you."

Kunal shifted, uncomfortable and unsure if he believed Bhandu's words.

"Some of us even like you. I volunteered to come to the citadel with you, did you know?"

Kunal's head shot up, and Bhandu stared him down before breaking his gaze away.

"Really?"

"Yes, cat eyes." Bhandu rolled his eyes. They approached another intersection, and he leaned forward and blew a low whistle. Kunal sent him a questioning glance. "Helps draw out anyone without us having to show our face."

Kunal pursed his lips. It actually was a good trick. Bhandu whistled again, this time aiming the sound toward the opposite end of the hall. They darted away as two soldiers rounded the corner.

"They won't be gone for long," Kunal said. "Protocol

demands making a full round, which will take five minutes or less."

They crept down the stairs and came to one of the lower levels, which was teeming with soldiers. Soldiers who had not been on the patrol schedules or accounted for in the captain's log.

There were four of them guarding the entryway to the lower levels of the citadel. Kunal racked his brain, trying to remember what it looked like, but he had only been shown the entrance on his initial tour as a Senap. The captain had led him away, saying the lower levels were mostly unused.

Extra soldiers hidden, no mention in the captain's log. This had to be it. Where they were keeping Reha.

"She's here," Bhandu whispered, echoing his thoughts.

They hurried down the last few stairs, looking over the entryway into a circular room of dark dungeons. In the corner stood more guards, and Kunal yanked Bhandu back.

"There," Kunal said. "Those guards who didn't leave their post to make the security rounds. That's where she is."

"We need confirmation," Bhandu said, eyes darting below.

"Then let's get it," Kunal said, setting his jaw and drawing out his knives.

———◂◦▸———

Esha looked at the sundial again. Five more minutes.

The citadel had a number of fail-safes and only a few entrances and exits. Kunal had worked hard to set up tonight so they'd be able to confirm Reha was there before the next

Mela event, giving them enough time to set up the next part of the plan—breaking her out. And if they were able to get her out in time, Kunal wouldn't have to be in the spotlight anymore, and Esha could keep him safe.

So many threads rested on this, and she had nearly destroyed it all. Esha pushed down the shame, trying to focus on the positive.

All they needed was one thing to confirm Reha was in the citadel and tonight would be worth it.

Farhan slipped back into the room sooner than Esha thought he would, with a small object tucked into the back of his waist sash. He removed his helmet and shook out his long hair, closing the distance from the door to the bed with two long strides.

"I found it," Farhan said. Alok's head snapped up, and he stopped talking about the various applications of wound dressings, which had been doing nothing to alleviate the restlessness she felt sitting around while Kunal was down below.

"What is it?" Alok asked, taking the spot next to Farhan.

"Jasmine oil," he said.

Esha looked up at that. "Jasmine oil?" She stood and clasped her hands together.

"Am I missing something?" Alok said. "I feel like I'm always missing something."

"Jasmine oil was found in the Senaps' supply room," Farhan explained.

Alok still looked confused. "Okay, and . . . so?"

"Alok," Esha said. "Is there any reason a Senap or champion might need jasmine oil?"

"No, but who—"

"Noble ladies," Farhan finished. "It's the latest hair trend in court. And what's more, there were reams of silk and thread in the supply room. As if someone's been getting custom clothing."

"This is what we needed," Esha breathed. Now, Kunal and Bhandu just needed to get back safely. Her injury had lost them precious time, and if anything happened to them because of her . . .

"Oh, I see. I can confirm that there's no jasmine oil in the champions' or Senap squads' bathrooms."

Esha gave Alok a questioning look.

"Being Kunal's friend has some perks."

"Then it has to be for someone special," Esha said. She paused before adding, "Kunal's well liked?"

Alok raised his eyebrow. "I know, he's not particularly charming, but Kunal's become rather close with some of those men."

Kunal was close with those soldiers? She knew it meant nothing, and yet, a tiny kernel of doubt lodged in her heart.

"Good work on his part," Farhan said. "It'll make it easier for him to get us back in if they trust him. We still need schematics, a read on the number of soldiers defending the citadel, inside and out, and an exit strategy. Arpiya's working on the latter, but the first two . . ."

"Complicated," Alok said. "The way I like it."

"You enjoy puzzles?" Farhan asked, his voice a tad too casual.

"I enjoy excitement," Alok said. "You seem like someone who'd be fantastic at puzzles, though. All smart and . . . intelligent."

Esha stifled a laugh.

"You know, I've recently become interested in healing," Farhan said, leaning forward.

"Really?" Alok smiled. "I'd love to talk to you more about it. You know, after all of this."

Farhan nodded, and Esha knew by the look in his eyes that he'd go straight to the library after this and read everything he could get his hands on about healing. It's how he always was when he had a crush.

"I'll set up a tea for you both," Esha said. "Anyway, the jasmine oil is a solid lead, but until Kunal and Bhandu come back, we won't know for sure. Perhaps it's a gift for the Senap captain's spouse, or his daughter—"

"The Senap captain's not married," Kunal said as he entered the room. Bhandu wasn't far behind, and he immediately took off his helmet, grumbling about soldiers and their armor. "Lower level is swarmed with soldiers who aren't on patrols or recorded anywhere else. A secret army.

"She has to be here. In the citadel."

CHAPTER 21

Night fell on the palace gardens like a glittering veil, covering everything in an inky darkness.

The evening's musical contest was being held outdoors, under a sheer, shimmering tent of silk. Wooden floors had been laid around the garden, providing a solid ground for the many scattered pillows and tufted seats. Light blankets of the finest cotton were thrown about, the vibrant colors of magenta and teal and saffron contrasting harmoniously, adding to the air of luxury that the manicured gardens provided.

Courtiers had already taken seats around the garden and the stage in the middle, their shiny hair ornaments and brightly colored clothing like little jewels within the tent. It was all rather arresting, and Esha let herself bask in the beauty of it. She knew that Kunal would light up at the sight of the tent and garden, that faraway look coming to his eyes

247

as he transformed it into art in his mind.

She felt the same way about music. The strands of notes lofting through the air wove through her mind, creating a story. She could imagine the dance, the slow, methodical steps that would rush into a crescendo of footwork and then relax into long, graceful movements of her arms. She hummed along with the new song that had picked up, the drumbeat creating a new energy that lifted the room's eyes.

Harun walked in, glorious in peacock green and a white silk uttariya of such fine quality it was almost transparent in the blinking light of the camphor lamps. He glanced around the garden as he walked into view, throwing one end of his uttariya over his shoulder. Their eyes met for a moment but didn't linger—they'd have time to talk later.

This competition wasn't a required part of the Mela, but rather a chance to bring non-champions into the celebration. Contestants had been chosen and invited from around the country, others from their guild or family connections. And as always, there was a small number of attendees who were there after winning the drawing, from all walks of life.

It was one of the old traditions that Vardaan hadn't removed. He had the presence of mind to realize it wasn't always big things that caused unrest, but the little things. This was one of the traditions that would've felt like a slap in the face if it had been removed.

Who needed their liberties as long as they had their celebrations?

A Dharkan champion finished his song, and a new tune

started up, one from a Yavar clansman who played a wooden flute.

Harun took a seat on the dais across from Vardaan, on the other side of the stage. His movements were languid, in control. But Esha noticed his ramrod posture.

"Good to see you, nephew," Vardaan said as the clansman finished his song. "Let's take a break from the contest, shall we?"

The man next to Vardaan stuttered his objection, pointing at the schedule. Vardaan ignored him. "Let's give our performers a rest. Why not a little performance from you, nephew? I've heard you are a proud cultivator of the arts at your court in Mathur. It's your specialty, it's said."

"They've been saying too much," Harun said. "I have only taken an interest in the talent of many of our wonderful artists, which even a simple man like myself can admire."

"Simple man? You do yourself a disservice," Vardaan said. "Are you not the man I've heard you are? Sing for us."

Esha knew Harun's music had been his salvation after his sister's disappearance and his mother's death. He rarely let anyone hear it, instead investing in the talents of others as a way to continue his mother's love of music.

"I am my mother's son, always," Harun said, his voice quiet. "This song was her favorite. Perhaps you'll recognize it, Uncle."

The first note of Harun's song was unsteady, his voice shaking for a second before taking flight. But then a hush came over the garden. Even Vardaan looked struck, speechless. It was a song about a lone memory of love that had sustained a man across nights of loneliness and pain. Harun's eyes fluttered closed as his voice rose, strength in his low baritone.

Harun took the old song and made it his own, imbuing it with his loss. Esha felt wetness at the corner of her eyes and saw many others wipe their own. Harun's voice rose into an improvisational section, soaring over the high notes and deepening into the low ones. When he finished and opened his eyes, the entire garden was silent.

Harun looked up, staring straight at his uncle, his jaw set.

Vardaan stared back as if he had seen a ghost, his face pale and his eyes wide. He recovered quickly, raising his hands and clapping. Soon the entire audience joined in, many rising to their feet. Harun bowed to the audience, his hands clasped in front of him.

Trumpets of fanfare rang out, and King Mahir strode into the garden and up to the dais where his son sat.

"My son is quite talented, is he not?" he said, grasping his son by the shoulders. He turned to face his brother. "Rather like his mother."

A soft sigh went through the crowd—Queen Gauri Samyad had been loved by her fellow Jansans, even after she had left them for Dharka. The love story between Gauri and Mahir was still a legend to this day.

But Vardaan looked almost pleased that Mahir had shown up.

"He is. Good to see you're feeling better, brother," Vardaan said. A razor-sharp smile glinted on his face. "We're just getting started. You're going to love the entertainment tonight."

———◄◦►———

Kunal hadn't known the prince had such artistry in him. He had just arrived at the garden and he hastily tucked his uttariya into his waist sash as he hurried through the gates.

He wandered through the crowds, ducking under stunning topiaries that made him want to try sculpting for the first time. There, Alok was deep in conversation with someone near one of the bushes. Kunal walked up.

"Alok," Kunal said. "Are—"

"Kunal. Guess who just arrived," Alok said, warning on his face.

Alok's companion turned around, and Kunal did a double take. General Panak.

Why was he here? Was he still looking for the Viper?

He would have to be careful—Kunal couldn't forget how the general had lulled him in last time before demanding a Battle of Honor.

"General," Kunal said, saluting. "I didn't know you were arriving."

"It was a rather sudden decision," General Panak said. "But the king requested my presence, and so I'm here. I've heard you've become one of the champions, Kunal."

"Yes, sir."

"How has it been so far?"

Kunal forced out a laugh. "Certainly not the same as the Fort."

A servant appeared at the commander's elbow, whispering in his ear. He excused himself, and Kunal watched him until he disappeared from sight.

"I don't like it," Alok said. Kunal nodded. "He confuses me. At least with General Hotha you knew to be scared."

Kunal couldn't help the way his shoulders tightened.

Alok sighed. "Sorry, Kunal. I forget you're related to that man sometimes."

"It's all right," Kunal said.

The contestants had started up again, and the sharp notes of a flute punctuated the air. Kunal gazed around the tents, pulling the colors and textures and shapes into his mind, forming them into a layered painting he itched to go back to his room and sketch.

"He would've hated this, you know," Kunal said.

"The contest?"

"He would've thought it useless. All this pomp and circumstance."

"Celebrating our ancestors and history is a way to remember the sorrows of the past. You know down in the artisans' quarter they take the day off to remember the Jansans who perished in the Blighted War."

"I didn't know that," Kunal said. "Maybe there's a chance we can return to our old ways, after all of this."

The thought lifted some of the unease from his

shoulders, reminding him that they knew where Reha was, her exact location. They were one step closer to that future.

The tent suddenly went silent, and Kunal turned around.

General Panak was up on the stage, tugging at his uttariya in discomfort. But it wasn't him Kunal was interested in.

Next to him stood a young woman, the top half of her face covered by a crimson silk uttariya. Her sari was resplendent with gold embroidery that mirrored the night sky. She took a step forward, and the bells of her anklets rang out.

Vardaan stepped out from the shadows behind her, a gleaming smile on his face. "We've enjoyed a night of splendid music from among the most talented of the land. And for them, I have a gift. A treasure I discovered only recently."

No.

Not now. Not here.

"Our lost jewel, the princess Reha."

CHAPTER 22

I t took only one cry to shatter the silence, and chatter filled the room.

Esha reached a hand out to Harun, knowing that his heart was breaking. His sister was in the hands of their enemy.

Was she all right? She couldn't see a cursed thing with that uttariya veiling her face. Esha wanted to go up there and rip it off, refusing to believe this was the Reha they had all worked so hard to save.

But there was still a chance Vardaan's gamble wouldn't work. He needed the public's approval, and right now they looked as disbelieving as Esha felt.

"I welcomed her into our palace as soon as I discovered. But I haven't stopped there. I'm overjoyed to announce that Princess Reha has asked to marry our general Panak and become part of our Jansan family."

Reha stepped forward, her eyes still on the ground. "I am so grateful to the king for welcoming me back into the family. He has my eternal gratitude for finding and saving me."

She had been trained well.

There was a smattering of applause, more than before. Vardaan had expertly maneuvered this. By saying Reha had asked for the marriage, he was invoking the age-old tradition of Jansa's women choosing their own husbands.

Esha raged at the idea that Reha had been forced into this. She already had a family, one that had been searching for her and was sitting right here.

But when she looked at Harun, he looked neither devastated nor confused.

His eyes flickered to hers.

"Don't react," he said.

"How can I not?"

"Esha, put a smile on your face," Harun repeated, his face placid as a still lake.

"This is not the time for you to order me around—"

"It's not her," was all Harun said. Esha tore her eyes away from the stage, where the adviser was reading the official decree that announced the engagement of the general and the newly reinstated Princess Reha.

"It's not her," he said again, with more emphasis.

"How do you know?"

"She was my sister." The tiniest of fissures appeared in his mask. "I held her when she was scared of evil spirits at night. I cleaned her skinned knees and taught her how to hold a knife. I knew her blood song better than anyone. I know *her*."

Esha looked for the king, only to see him walk up to the stage and embrace the princess—fake princess. "Does he know?"

Harun's smile curved downward. "It was Father who gave me the signal to stand down. Vardaan did this on purpose. He's playing us for fools. We can't reveal that her blood song is wrong without betraying centuries of royal tradition.

"Smile, Esha. And clap," he said. "We have to fight another day."

Esha swallowed hard.

"If this isn't her, then who is it?"

"I don't know," he said.

The thought made Esha's skin crawl. "We confirmed last night that the shipment is in the citadel. The whole lower level is cordoned off. We found *jasmine* oil in the citadel where women aren't even allowed." Esha could hear the desperation in her own voice.

Harun sniffed at the air, his eyes flashing yellow as his senses sharpened. "I don't smell jasmine on her."

"So she has to still be there. If this was Vardaan's plan all along, they must have kept this fake Reha in the palace."

"I think so too. The rescue is still on."

Esha nodded, looking away. "Let's confirm with Kunal later. Harun, this changes things. We need to discuss."

"We do," he said, his voice lowering. "But for now, we need to act like we're pleased."

It was harder than she thought to keep her face in that mask of happiness, accepting people's well-wishes on the royal family's behalf, exchanging her own. Dinner was announced, and the fake princess was pulled into a seat beside the general, the two of them staged like plumed peacocks in the king's zoo. Esha wondered if the general knew that he was engaged to an impostor.

She moved to get a glass of lemon water, something to cool the fire of panic and despair that was in her throat. She almost jumped out of her skin when she felt a tap against her arm. Esha spun around to face Kunal's amber eyes and open face.

"Is it her?" he asked. She pulled him half into the shadows so no one could read their lips.

"Harun says it's not. The king agrees." She spoke fast, knowing they couldn't linger together. Not here.

"The king blessed the union with his own two hands."

"Think, Kunal. If we accused him here, now, we'll look like fools. Especially as Vardaan has so carefully orchestrated this by getting an audience of citizens, those who were so desperate for her return. And he's invoked her ancient right to choose a husband."

"I don't think they believe that it's really her." There was a note of uncertainty in his voice.

"Even better. But we can't be seen to be moving on speculation. He raised the bar, Kunal. We need to get Reha out and have her in the flesh to pose a challenge." Tension rose in her head. "Did you see how he set this all up? Having her give that speech as if she had no interest in her birthright? Reha is the rightful heir to his throne and he knows it. Nothing but the woman herself will undo this."

Kunal's mouth softened. "Okay. Then as you said, it's a setback. Not failure."

"Right, a setback." She had to keep telling herself that until she believed it.

Esha took a breath, calming her mind, letting in that coolness that had led her to key strategic decisions before.

"Can you go let the team know?" she said, tapping her fingers against the smooth shell of her knife underneath her sari. "I need to see to Harun."

Kunal nodded and turned away, leaving Esha to her thoughts. She closed her eyes for a second before turning around and walking back into the crowd with a smile.

She found the supposed Reha within minutes, slipping into the gap between two nobles who were waiting in line to meet her. Esha grabbed the girl's hand and bent into a deep bow.

"My princess," she said. "I'm Esha."

The girl tilted her head at her. "So nice to meet you."

"But, Princess," Esha said, holding on to her hand, laying her own over hers. "We've met before. I once tutored you. Perhaps you remember? You used to hate your sums, and I would have to coerce you with a piece of mango every time."

"Oh," the girl said with a quick smile. "But of course I remember. Esha—" The adviser next to her pulled her away, whispering into her ear. "Forgive me, the king is asking for me."

Esha didn't stop staring at her as she left.

The skin on the girl's hand was remarkably smooth despite the blue sapphire ring Esha was wearing, which she had pressed into the girl's palm. No one with royal blood would have been able to stand having their skin touched by such a jewel.

And the Reha she'd known had loved sums and hated mangoes.

Esha found Harun within minutes.

"You were right," she said.

"Aren't I always?"

"About this, oh, Prince."

"You doubted me?" he asked, his voice suddenly heavy.

"No, but we needed real confirmation, and I have it now," Esha said, holding up her hand. Harun immediately recoiled.

"Watch where you're waving that thing."

"Relax, I'm keeping it in a pouch. For protection," she said.

He nodded, and their gazes drifted to Vardaan.

"You know, it could help us get support from the nobles," he said, still smiling as they turned to face each other. There were already new hollows under his eyes. "We'll need to move quicker than before. Rescue and coup all at once."

She hesitated, catching a flash of pale eyes down the way. "We can't forget the ritual."

259

"Of course not, but none of it will matter if we don't have her on the throne. You were right. We can't save the land just to break it with a civil war. We have to move up our timeline."

Esha sighed and tugged at the edge of her sari, knowing she couldn't show her frustration.

"I've already talked to a few nobles I had been in contact with before and reassured them, but I'll need your help. There are too many, and we don't want Vardaan to gain any more traction."

"He already has," a deep voice rumbled. King Mahir came up behind the two of them. "We don't have time to win the support of fickle nobles. We have to take the throne by the end of the Sun Mela."

———◄◦►———

The night air had cooled, adding a chill that hadn't been there before. Fitting after the reveal, a layer of discomfort that matched the feelings of those gathered.

Kunal looked up at the moon, the way it curved into darkness, and thought of the ways he would combine paints to catch that shade. It calmed him, and calm was what he needed right now.

Arpiya and Farhan had taken the news of the impostor Reha well, though he had noticed the hard set of their jaws. He trusted Esha's judgment, even the prince's, but it was too many coincidences at once. Someone had known they were casing the citadel, and now, the reveal of the impostor Reha.

He hadn't been lying before when he had told Esha that

he thought many of the citizens weren't convinced. The applause had been lackluster, enough not to get thrown in chains, but after his time in Ujral and the other towns, he knew the true depth of feeling for the lost princess.

If Vardaan was given the time, he might be able to convince them. How many other nobles had figured it out? If not from the halfhearted speech the impostor had given then from the rather too enthusiastic support from their own king.

Kunal dodged away from two young men who looked like they recognized him from the Mela. He pushed through the crowds, finding his way back up to Esha. The party was winding down, but she was still up on the dais with the king and Harun, ensconced in a small nook surrounded by thickets of plants. He couldn't approach them, not if the king was there, so he waited nearby, using his sharpened senses to focus in on what they were saying.

"Take the throne?" Esha said.

"Father, I've been working on gaining support from the nobles for weeks now. We talked about this, how we need to sign the peace treaty for our people first, before we try to get Reha on the throne. It'll guarantee trade will move freely again."

"Which was a smart play, but irrelevant now," the king said. "We discussed that as a way to make sure the Jansan people don't starve under my brother's watch, but after this move, I'm not so sure he ever had the intention of signing that peace treaty."

"I respectfully disagree, Your Highness," Esha said.

"Not about the peace treaty. Moon Lord, we all know how the last meeting went. But we do need the nobles' support to keep her on the throne. To prevent a civil war."

"One is already coming if we don't move quickly. We put her on the throne by the end of the Victor's Ball or we lose all ability to avoid a war."

Kunal started, his heart beating faster as he realized what the king was saying.

"Vardaan will need only a month to gain support for her, some sort of show of force. Did you see the speech he made her give? Most of tonight's attendees can see through the artifice of politics. But with practice—"

Esha breathed out. "The public. If he takes her to the public, we'll have no choice. It'll become violent."

"Let's give ourselves a choice. Even if he trots her out around the entire city, it will still take time for him to gain support. The people won't be so easily won, not from what I've gathered. And we can't forget the land," Harun said.

"And Dharmdev," Esha said. "This will be the perfect time for him to enact whatever plan they've been working on. Remember how they refused our help? I know that isn't because they're happy with the status quo. The public will be wary, uncertain of this new princess. What better time for a beloved folk hero to come forth and claim power?"

"Is that what they want? Does Dharmdev want to become king?" Harun asked.

"No." Esha let out a frustrated sigh. "I don't know. My meeting with them told me very little as to what their actual plans were. They didn't even seem to know the princess was alive."

Kunal stepped back. Esha hadn't told him that she had met with the Scales. She knew they had been looking for Kunal. And Laksh had said he hadn't told anyone of his identity, but doubt burned in Kunal's veins.

Kunal spun away, fighting his way back through the crowd. He grabbed a glass of wine from one of the servers' platters and knocked it back, feeling it burn as it flowed down his throat.

Why had he come here? To this nest of vipers, as Esha had called it.

Why had he made this choice to save Reha instead of saving his own skin?

It had been about protecting this land, his people. As a soldier, that had been the duty he had ignored. As a soldier and a royal, he owed it to them to do what was right for his people. He'd come here to tip the scales back, right the wrongs he had done, and still somehow, he had gotten caught in a lie. His past used against him even as he did what he could to escape it.

Kunal grabbed another goblet of wine from a passing server and twirled it in his fingers as he brooded.

———◆———

Esha looked over to Harun and his father as they walked, both so similar that in the twinkling lights only their height distinguished them.

"What do they want, then?" Harun said.

"I wish I knew," Esha said irritably. "The only thing I can say for sure is that they will use this moment, somehow. Dharmdev's second, she was adamantly against another Dharkan on the throne. Vardaan has made these people skittish about any foreign influence. A girl who is only half their blood and carries the name of the Dharkan royal house along with Vardaan's approval? I don't think they'll be happy. Especially if people are whispering she's an impostor."

"But soon you'll have my real daughter, won't you, son?"

Neither Harun nor Esha could stop their jaws from dropping.

"You know?" Harun asked. He looked as if he had just eaten a frog.

King Mahir chuckled. "As if I haven't known for years what you two have been up to. Why do you think I've been working so hard to find a way to fix the bond? You took over the work I would have wanted to do, had I been free to. I had plenty of adventures during my own youth. Gauri and I . . ."

Harun blinked in wonder at his father. "You've seriously known this whole time?"

King Mahir laughed and patted his son on the back. "I'm not as old as you think I am. I was your age when I led my first battle against the Yavar invaders during the War in the North."

"Yes, yes," Harun said, looking irritable. "We know. And you should really not call them invaders when they're floating around this room. They could be great allies for our coup."

"The bond," Esha said. "Dharmdev's second mentioned it in passing. She said 'that bonds were meant to be broken.'"

"That could mean anything," Harun said. "The bonds between our countries; the bonds that bind them to Vardaan . . ."

King Mahir had gone silent and still, long enough that Esha looked over.

"My lord, can the bond be broken?"

Harun gave her a look as if she was being ridiculous, but Esha kept staring at the king. He looked up, a tight smile on his face. She'd observed enough people to know when someone had realized something unpleasant. He heaved a heavy sigh.

"Theoretically. But the requirements to do such a thing, to break our only connection to the gods . . . It'd be difficult, to say the least. No one has tried in centuries, not since the Blighted War."

"But someone has tried?" Esha asked, shock coursing through her.

Harun swore vividly. "Great, now we have to worry about that as well. Why in the Moon Lord's blessed mercy would Dharmdev want to break the bond? What good does that do anyone in his land? We'll have to move even quicker."

Esha placed a calming hand on Harun's arm.

"We're working off a lot of assumptions here. Let's not assume the worst before we know for sure," Esha said in her most soothing voice. King Mahir sent her an approving glance. "And anyway, we're moving as quick as we can. The Victor's Ball is our new deadline, before the marriage. And the bond—"

"That's my domain, children," the king said, his voice taking on steel. "You worry about finding and rescuing my daughter. I'll worry about the bond."

Esha and Harun nodded, though Harun's muscles were tense under her hand.

"My lord, this person who tried to break the bond before. Clearly, they didn't succeed. What happened to them?" she asked.

"They didn't succeed," he said. "History remembers him as the man who started the Blighted War."

———◄◦►———

An adviser bustled over to the king and Harun, pulling them away, and Esha bowed in return, taking her leave.

She wandered around the party for a few minutes, searching for Kunal with little luck. The night's events were all jumbling together in a massive storm in her head. The only thing she could do was move forward. That's what she always did when everything went wrong.

They needed to break out the real Reha by the end of the Victor's Ball. But the more time she spent wandering around the gardens the more she wondered—what would truly happen then? Would the country rally around their long-lost princess? Would they find that the reality stood up to the stories that had been told for the past decade?

Or would Vardaan win? Or Dharmdev?

Esha found a semi-hidden seat, covered by cascading tendrils of jasmine.

King Mahir had known this whole time that they were searching for his daughter, and he had trusted them, trusted her.

The guilt that lived hidden under her ribs, that she had chosen to save Reha on the Night of Tears instead of fleeing with her parents, it hurt less in the face of that realization. But still it didn't let go of her. That she might've been able to save them.

Her father, who never failed to have a bright smile for her. Her mother, who held her when the storms had been too dark and scary.

Esha gritted her teeth and stood up, startling the maid standing a few paces away. She hated the idea of letting Vardaan, or any of them, win. They had lived years without judge or jury, escaping the hand of justice as they paraded around the country.

Forgiveness. That's what Kunal would council. It's what he had chosen. And it should be an easy decision—the last thing she wanted to do was to jeopardize the mission again after the peace summit.

But Esha had been remade, forged anew when her parents had died, when her bones had been broken and her heart shattered in the dungeons not far from the palace. And the Viper had been born.

Esha walked up the stairs, past the brightly colored and adorned courtiers, her heart turning heavier and heavier with every step. She wondered if they could see that darkness in her, the way she felt it spreading beneath her breastbone since she had heard about the Falcon Squad.

She had believed there was only one way to stop that darkness and to honor her parents.

But she had seen the Pretender King in the flesh, his humanity and foibles. She had met a soldier, one she had begun to care for despite his armor.

And she wasn't so sure anymore.

CHAPTER 23

Esha jostled her way through the cheering crowd of the fighting ring. She was deep in the thieves' den, prowling for information on what the Scales might be up to. The rest of the squad wasn't as concerned, but Esha had a feeling since she had met with Zhyani that there was a bigger picture she might be missing.

And once the king had mentioned that the bond could be theoretically broken, she realized she needed to gather more information, at least until the encoded letter from the scholars in Mathur could be deciphered. She'd just received the hawk, but Esha was by no means the best code cracker in the Blades. She'd enlisted the Red Squad, but due to the sensitive nature of its contents, she'd split the message up.

The code breaking would take time. The one thing they didn't have.

So far she hadn't picked up much from this crowd. There

was another hall that was connected, the birthplace of many an alliance, or plot, among the Jansan nobles. Esha decided to give it a try when she felt a warm hand on her shoulder. She grabbed the wrist, about to yank the man over her shoulder, when she caught the edge of a wry smile.

"How'd you know?" she asked, sighing, dropping his wrist.

Harun gave her that look of his that both annoyed her and made her tingle. "You think I wouldn't be able to recognize you in disguise?"

Esha chuckled. "Of course you would."

They were near the edges of the crowd that encircled the metal cage in the center of the hall. Tufted seats were strewn about the outer ring, and a number of beautiful maids in rainbow-hued saris danced around the outer ring, refilling wineglasses like attentive bees.

A few of them glanced toward Harun as they approached, blushing and throwing him shy smiles. If she wasn't mistaken, a few of them looked as if they knew him.

"So is this where you spend your free time now?" Esha asked, her lips pursing.

"Jealous?" Harun asked, lifting an eyebrow, his eyes twinkling. Esha flushed, not just because she was indeed feeling the pricklings of jealousy. He had looked at those maids with more happiness in his face than he had shown her in a week. "And no, not here. In the adjacent hall. I suppose the maids split their work between the two."

"Ah, I was about to go there."

"Information?"

She nodded. This was the longest one-on-one conversation they'd had in days.

The crowd began to widen, pushing into the outer-tiered seating, angry about one of the recent fights. Harun caught Esha around the waist, preventing her from being toppled over by a particularly angry fisherman.

She didn't push him away immediately, instead inhaling the familiar scent of almond, indulging in the feel of his calloused fingertips against her skin. She remembered the first time they had spent the night together, how surprised she had been to feel the calluses, how he had told her about his years practicing swordsmanship and learning to play the veena.

"You shouldn't be here alone," she said softly. "It's not safe for you."

"I'm not alone. I brought Bhandu."

"Bhandu?" Why him and not her?

His expression said it all. She cursed herself for bringing it up, having enjoyed the brief moment of normalcy between them.

"Yes, him. And he's going to be mad at me. I slipped him a while ago and stuck him with a noble. If my luck holds, he'll have managed not to kill the man by the time I get back."

"So why are you here?"

He sighed, letting go of her waist to sit down. She took the seat next to him, tugging her uttariya farther over her head. Harun didn't look like a prince tonight, his arms bare and his clothing simple. Only the huge jeweled ring on his finger indicated his wealth—the right move in a place like this. It showed status and privilege to not have to wear your fortune on your neck.

"I've been talking with the nobles," he said. "Seeing how happy they are. Seeing how *unhappy* they are. If Father wants to move quickly, we can't do it alone. I've had to speed up a number of conversations that were in play."

She nodded.

"And you? This is an odd place for a Dharkan lady to show up," he said, a slight warning in his tone.

"Oh, really? You don't think I secretly frequent fighting rings in my free time?"

Harun laughed. "You're wincing every time you turn your torso, which means your wound is acting up. You're wearing your favorite wrist guards, and no one else knew you were coming. You were either following a lead or blowing off steam."

"Fine. I came here to get information on the Scales. I don't trust them." She hesitated, unsure if she should reveal more. She didn't want to keep any more secrets from him.

"Did you find anything?"

"No, not about the Scales," she said, inhaling sharply, preparing herself. She'd realized after the musical competition that with all the secrets and schemes being thrown about, they couldn't afford another. For a decade they had never lied to each other. And she had been the one to break that. She owed the truth to Harun now. "But I did want to tell you something. I'm the reason Vardaan wanted to stall the signing of the treaty, why he increased security."

"Esha . . ."

"I found the Falcon Squad, Harun. The squad that led the coup during the Night of Tears and killed my parents. I had found them, and I was going to find my parents' murderer."

"Did you?"

"No," she said. "Not yet. I was being followed. And the soldier Vardaan mentioned? I didn't kill him. But I had gotten some information off him."

Esha realized Kunal had been right. It was reckless of her to go after the killer when security had become stronger and Vardaan was already on edge.

"I tried again, and Senaps were called to the spot."

"I take it you still don't know the killer's identity."

"No. And I think someone doesn't want me to know."

Harun didn't say anything, simply staring at her with unreadable eyes. To her surprise, when a waitress passed them, he reached over and grabbed two glasses of wine off the closest tray. He handed her one of the glasses.

"I think you need this," he said.

She nodded and downed the glass in one gulp. Harun chuckled.

"Why didn't you tell me?" he asked. "I could've helped."

"I didn't want to burden you," she said, going for the truth. "But now I have. My choice ruined everything."

"Esha, I don't think it was just you. The peace treaty was always going to be a tool for Vardaan to exert his power. But I'm glad you were honest with me," he said, playing with the edge of his glass. "At least now I can help."

"Really?"

He laughed, a low, hearty sound. "I'm not going to officially advise you to kill Senaps on Jansan soil while we're still here, if that's what you're asking. But I can be your prince better if I know what you're doing. I could make sure that the guards are occupied or that you have extra backup. I get it, Esha. You've wanted to deliver justice to the man who killed your parents since I met you. If I could, I'd help you string up the cursed soldier myself."

Harun's skin brushed against hers, and she felt a little thrill. He pulled closer, his body speaking a language she knew so well. He tilted her face up, a familiar gesture she had missed.

"That means a lot to me," she said softly.

"Of course. I will always support you, Esha. Now, let's get back to the Scales—"

She sighed, agreement on the tip of her tongue. But the truth came out, the thing that was weighing the most on her heart.

"Not yet. We can't brush away our previous fight. Pretend it's okay. I messed up."

"You did."

"And I'm sorry."

"I know."

"And I'm not letting you leave until you forgive me."

He sighed and traced his knuckle against her skin. "I forgave you already, Esha. If I'm honest with myself, that is. I wasn't angry, I was . . ."

"Hurt," she said.

He tilted his head. "Sad."

That was almost as bad.

"But do you understand why I did it?"

His nostrils flared. "Because of the soldier. His pretty eyes or something," he mumbled.

"Jealous?" she teased. "Not a good look on you, Prince. And no. Remember when we would talk about your sister? What her shape-shifting might have been like? We'd worry about how alone she'd feel if she were alive. How scared and lonely and terrified of being used."

She swallowed. "Kunal is my friend too, one of my first. Even before you." Harun made an annoyed face. "And I couldn't let that happen to him. I didn't know how you'd react, so I waited. And by the time I knew, it was too late to tell you without betraying him."

"Then you should've betrayed him. You betrayed me instead," Harun said hotly. Anger was good, anger she could deal with.

"I didn't want to betray anyone." Esha couldn't say she would've done things differently, but she knew at least that she'd have considered more options.

"There's a lot of things you might have known, if only you'd asked."

Esha's shoulders dropped. "I know. And I'm sorry for implying you would've done something bad to him."

"If anyone does, I understand what it's like to lose family, to be a royal. I might've been able to train or counsel him."

"You didn't seem to like him very much," she pointed out.

"You dropped a soldier into our laps, Esha," he said. "What did you expect? You offered no context, just 'trust you' and we did. But you didn't trust us back." Harun took a deep breath. "I said I've forgiven you. But it'll take me awhile to forget."

"I don't expect you to, Harun," she said, taking his hand. "I might not be so kind myself if I were in your shoes."

"I'm not being kind. I'm being reasonable."

"Many people never touch reasonable in their reactions, let alone forgiveness," she said. "Harun, your friendship and the Blades mean everything to me. I am no less committed to this mission or to our vision for the Southern Lands."

His gaze pinned her down, boring into her like the heat of the Sun Maiden's fiery bow. Harun was searching for something, and finally seemed to find it.

"All right."

Without realizing it, they had drawn closer, their knees, hands, and heads almost touching. Esha looked into the eyes of the boy she had watched turn into a man, the one who had held her when she had broken down and who had fought beside her through the years.

If she moved a little bit closer, if she moved her hand, they'd be able to rekindle the clear spark between them.

Heal their rift the way they always did.

Gods, she missed Harun. She missed this ease between them.

"We should get back to the palace before anyone notices," Esha said, pulling back. "Especially you. You're blowing the conch for the footrace tomorrow."

He nodded briskly, disappointment in his eyes.

"I can't wait," he said, his voice dry as a bone.

She swatted him on the shoulder. "Come on, let's go."

———◄◊►———

Kunal looked at the little scrap of paper in his hand, eyes flickering to his surroundings as he tried to determine if he was in the right place.

How Laksh had managed to get the note onto his bed, in the citadel, was still puzzling him. On the note was a time and place with the word *tonight*, and nothing else.

He shoved the note into his pocket as the conch shells blew ten. The note said the building with the sign of the bow and arrow. It wasn't very helpful, as a lot of buildings had the sign of Naria's favored weapons. This was Jansa, after all.

Kunal scanned the nearby buildings. The inn was too lively. The restaurant didn't look too crowded, but the guard outside took it out of consideration. That left the ramshackle shop, one that had seen better days.

He strode into the side alleyway and knocked on the door there. A small rectangular piece of wood slid out, revealing a pair of eyes. Kunal hesitated, unsure what to say, when the eyes disappeared and the door clicked open.

"You made it," Laksh said, ushering him in. "I thought it would do us some good to get out, change up our normal meeting spot."

"You mean how you always find me during the competitions." Kunal stepped into the dim room, keeping a hand on his knife. "Say, who is your man? An infantry soldier you bribed? Threatened?"

Laksh grinned. "And you, I'm sure you're getting tired of being cooped up at the citadel."

"While I hate to skip our normal pleasantries," Kunal said, "why am I here?"

Laksh gestured for him to follow him inside. They walked through a long, dark corridor punctuated by many rooms with different doors. It was, by all appearances, empty for the night.

"I didn't bring you here to hurt you, if that's what you're wondering."

"It wasn't." Kunal was confident he could take Laksh on. "But good to know."

"I have something I want to show you. And another request," Laksh said before pushing open the large double doors in front of them.

Inside was a mass of people talking in hushed voices. Most were dressed in plain clothes, but flashes of jewels or guild insignias could be seen underneath their uttariyas, as could knives and swords. It was a mixed group, men and women, old and young, but they all shared one thing in common—the pin of Naria's scales on their uttariyas.

"You brought me to a Scales meeting?" Kunal said, his voice icy. "You tricked me."

"I sent you a note and you came," Laksh said. "Not much of a trick. It's a common meeting, anyhow."

Laksh's voice lost a bit of its airiness. "These meetings are open to anyone, Kunal. I didn't lie to you. Dharmdev isn't here and doesn't know you're here either. I'm letting you see who we truly are. We have the numbers and support from all the classes and guilds in the city. Our country is ready to rise up, without help from anyone else."

"And what, you think this will change my mind?"

"No," Laksh said. "I thought you deserved to meet some of the people, hear what they have to say. You have been working for us, after all. It's only fair."

Kunal couldn't help the scowl that crashed onto his face. But curiosity won out, and he stepped forward, Laksh close behind.

Laksh was right. It was a group of about thirty, all Jansans, and something small in his heart warmed at the idea that these people, his people, were risking their lives and defying the royal decrees to meet. The tone in the room changed, mellowing into a muted silence. There was a faint, excited thrum in the crowd. A young woman caught his eye—she was staring at him as if she knew him. Sharp eyes in a round face, she looked vaguely familiar. Perhaps one of the fans from the tournament or a noble from court.

It was a good reminder that as he watched others, they

were watching him too. Kunal tugged his uttariya lower.

"The Archer," someone shouted.

Too late.

Kunal stepped around a man and hid behind Laksh. Laksh didn't bother helping him as excited whispers went up all around.

"I swear, it was him."

"You've had too many poppy seeds today."

"I think I saw him too. Is he a Scale? Dharmdev's right-hand? How glorious!"

Kunal whirled Laksh around, pulling him into the darkness of a corner.

"Is that why you brought me here? To let others think I'm a Scale? To force me into this?"

"No," Laksh said. He held up his hands as if innocent. "I hadn't planned for that. Kunal, you're famous around the city. Whispers about you are even filtering up to Faor and beyond. 'The Archer reborn.' People are clamoring for legends again, especially in such uncertain times."

"I don't want to be one," Kunal said automatically. But there was a change this time, a feeling he couldn't quite pinpoint. Pride? Duty? It didn't sound like such a horrible idea to be someone his people could look up to. Though if they knew why he had been given that title, the powers that lay hidden in his blood, it might be different.

Laksh watched him, tapping a finger against his chin. "I have something I want to show you," he said. "And then I have another request of you."

"Is that even allowed?" Kunal said. "I'm already getting you the king's boon."

Laksh smiled at that. "I make up the rules, so it's allowed."

Kunal tensed. Alok and him had never let Laksh make up the rules when they played card games, both convinced that Laksh would somehow trick them.

"It's nothing so bad, Kunal. No need to plan how you're going to escape already," he said, his voice a little too light for his words. It was enough of a tonal dissonance that Kunal realized something—Laksh wasn't immune to the crumbling of their friendship. "There's a report that is in the possession of the king. I'd like it to be in mine."

"Why do you need me? Do it yourself, like you did with the general. Murder him and blame it on someone else, a hapless victim," Kunal said.

A chuckle, a mild thing, from Laksh. "Calling the Viper a hapless victim. Love really is a funny thing. The Kunal I knew . . ."

Kunal flushed, worried he had given away something of himself that he shouldn't have. "Perhaps not a victim, but innocent nonetheless."

Laksh seemed unconcerned by such semantics. "No, to answer your question, I have no need of murder and betrayal, not now that I have you."

Kunal glowered, feeling some sort of empowerment from the small movement. "And what is this report I'm meant to steal?"

"A report. With a particular seal—a winged horse with

an arrow curving over its back."

"Just the report?"

"That's all I ask of you."

What did it say about the forced shifting of Kunal's honor that his first thought wasn't shock but rather of how he could sneak by the Senaps who guarded the king's chambers? How he'd be able to slip this lie into the many others he had been telling Esha and the team?

"What was it you wanted to show me?" he asked.

Laksh took his whiplash change in conversation in stride.

"This," Laksh said. "Take some time, talk to a few of your fellow countrymen. Many of them have great theories on how best to defeat the Yavar in the mace competition the day after next. You could learn something. And perhaps they need to hear from the Archer that there is a future better than the present. Weren't you the one who said you wanted to create a new world?"

The crowd began to disappear through a pair of tall, metal double doors.

Laksh beckoned him with a hand, following behind the crowd.

Kunal couldn't forget how Laksh had tried to capture him for the Scales. That he had tried to hurt Esha. These people, his people, had done nothing to harm him, but . . .

It was too much. Kunal turned away.

Perhaps one day he might walk through those doors, but not today.

CHAPTER 24

Kunal cut through the tangle of wet branches with a swipe of his machete. He tugged at the edges of the branches and pulled them apart, creating a hole in the jungle foliage big enough for two people.

King Mahir had set up an extra training before the mace-fighting event tomorrow morning. Kunal still didn't have firm control—or understanding—of all his powers. He had expected a trip to the armory, though, not a journey far outside the city walls.

King Mahir followed him through the opening he had made, and Kunal looked up, swallowing a gasp at the towering temple they found inside the thicket of jungle vines. It was clearly ancient, ruined in some areas, and was made of the same gold-flecked marble and white sunstone that all the Sun Maiden temples were in Jansa.

A sliver of rainbow cut through the white sunstone

as Kunal stepped closer and began to take the stairs. This temple was unlike any he had seen before. Colored mosaics and carvings spread across every wall of the temple, history brought to life.

King Mahir ran his hand along a groove in the wall that Kunal couldn't read until he stepped closer. It was a family tree of the Samyads, and at the bottom, where King Mahir's hand had been, was a small pearl embedded in the stone with the name Gauri carved under it.

Even now, a decade after her death, King Mahir's love hadn't faded. His eyes were misted over as he traced the edges of her name on the stone.

He straightened and coughed, pulling his hand away. Kunal caught a glimpse of another name, one he had been thinking of more and more often.

Payal. His mother.

Her name was inlaid with a ruby, luminescent in the shifting shadows of the temple.

"I went back and forth on this, but ultimately you are one of us," King Mahir said, interrupting his thoughts. "You deserve to know the lore that is passed down to every Samyad. It's a crucial part of every royal's training.

"Do you know of our origins?"

Kunal nodded, reciting words every Southern Lander knew. "In the beginning, the gods made man and sent three representatives to the earth, tasking them with the duty to help mankind—the Sun Maiden, the Moon Lord, and the Wise Child. They made their home on earth, loving and leading the people for eons. But mankind began to fill the earth, crowding it, and the gods grew tired, desiring to return to their celestial home. And so they sought out the wisest, strongest, and kindest of their children. Three demigods were chosen: the twins, Naran and Naria; and Vasu the Wanderer, who journeyed to the lands of the Sea God, churning them alongside the gods and pulling forth what became the Southern Lands."

Mahir patted his shoulder. "Good. That is what they say." He walked toward the wall, his sandals shuffling against the old stone. Despite its age there was no dust. "And the *janma* bond?"

Kunal racked his brain, feeling as if he was with the Fort schoolmaster again. "Each of the demigods chose their home. Naran and Naria split the peninsula, and Vasu the Wanderer went north. We, mankind, learned from the demigods, and they protected and nourished the land with their magic. As long as the demigods touched their feet to it, all was well. Neither man nor animal nor creature wanted for anything. But the God of Death began to claim the land.

"The demigods, who had come to love their people, knew they wouldn't be able to live forever to protect them. They decided to call for help from the gods, their parents, performing the first Ayana. In this first Ayana, or ritual, they asked the gods to bring down the celestial river that gave life to all creatures. On the longest night of the year, the demigods forged a connection with the gods, one that needed to be renewed every year by the royals with their blood. Vasu the Wanderer rejected the connection, preferring his freedom. And that is how we got the Bhagya River, the source of all life, anchored onto the land by a droplet of each twin's blood. Their descendants, the royals, still have their blood and powers to this day."

"Ah, so neat and tidy," King Mahir said. There was a tension in his jaw. "Most of that is true, but there's so much more. History that has been forgotten but that the Himyads and Samyads have always remembered. It's our duty to remember." King Mahir's voice took on the deep, steady cadence of a recitation. "'But for such a boon, the gods demanded more—and offered more in return. The gods saw the good in mankind, but they also saw the potential for evil.'"

"What does it mean?" Kunal didn't recognize the quote, and he'd read every book at the Fort on the origins of their land.

"That's from the text on the Blighted War," King Mahir said.

"I thought all texts from the Age of Darkness were burned or lost."

"Not all. What those texts reveal is something the royals have kept secret for centuries." He took a deep breath. "All humans were born with shape-shifting magic in their blood, Kunal. The original Ayana was performed with simple offerings—food, flowers, milk—and artifacts that each god left behind. It required no blood, no sacrifice. Magic was to be shared by all, to help us connect to the land and be one with that which nourishes us.

"But humanity ravaged the land, our one gift from the gods. And during the Blighted War, men, and one city in particular, sought to control and own the connection to the gods—for power. The gods punished them, claiming the city for the sea, and the original artifacts were lost. Still furious, the gods threatened to sever the *janma* bond as well. But the ancient royals convinced them to forge a new connection, one that didn't need the artifacts or rely on the state of the land. The gods accepted, but only if the royals alone controlled the magic and its burdens. They demanded a price for what they saw as betrayal."

"'But for such a boon, the gods demanded more—and offered more in return,'" Kunal repeated, his voice quieting. Magic had once been everyone's gift, and the people had taken it for granted. What did that mean for the current drought?

King Mahir nodded. "The ancient royals broke the previous bond, forged a new one. It was the only way the gods agreed to renew the connection, especially after the gods' own children and creations fled the land during the Blighted War."

Even ages ago, mankind couldn't control its greed for power. Did this never end? Would they always be stuck in this cycle?

"And the royals have been hiding this from the people?" Kunal asked, anger tingeing his words.

"What good would it do to tell them?" King Mahir said.

"What if some decided they wanted their powers back? Decided to find a way to break the bond? The gods might not forgive a second time."

He wanted to be angry at the deception, at the loss of control, but Kunal also understood. You made hard choices to protect those you loved—even if it meant obscuring the truth. Had he not chosen to obey Laksh's whims to protect Esha, Alok? But it was a burden, one the royals shouldn't have had to shoulder.

"It took centuries of learning for the royals to control their new powers, as well as the jealousy and mistrust that followed. Their people didn't understand why the gods had left them."

"And the royals got the blame. That's a raw deal."

"It's not as if I made the deal, my boy. I share your anger. Do you think I wanted this as a child? I resented it, fought against it. But my brother wasn't going to be the one to continue the traditions—he hated them. He wanted the title and power I had with none of the struggles," King Mahir said.

"It's not fair," Kunal said. "To you, to any of the royals. To the people who have been lied to."

"No, it's not. We carry a great burden in our blood. We carry knowledge so that others don't bear its weight. But our powers are also a gift, and that's why I'm trying to teach you. It's our duty to our people. We must always protect them. As the descendants of Naran and Naria, it is our edict, passed down through generations."

"Do all the royals feel this way?"

"No. There are noble houses with royal blood. Pramukh and Manchi. But they've never grown up with the weight of a kingdom on their shoulders."

"Can they shift, since they have the same blood?"

King Mahir pointed at a mural that showed humans with animal features. Men with large wings, women with talons. The mural told a story of mankind at its glory where phasing was the norm. As the panels went on, the murals changed. And at the end, the same man and woman were completely human, one wearing a valaya, a metal brace-let, the other wearing an anguli, a ring with a sigil. Kunal blinked, trying to understand what it meant.

"The valaya and anguli."

"They have a purpose. Initially, they were used to prevent any latent powers from surfacing. Now, they've become custom. So, no. Only direct children of the queen or king should have powers."

Kunal quieted. "But I'm—I'm a bastard."

"I have my doubts about that, Kunal. Your father would've honored Payal."

"You knew my father?" Kunal's pulse sped up. He had given up hope long ago, remembering only a thick head of hair and scarred hands.

King Mahir tilted his head. "Yes. A good man. Better than most. He'd be honored to know how you've repre-sented the family."

"I wish I had known him. All Uncle said of him was that

he died recklessly," Kunal said quietly.

King Mahir looked at him. "Is that what he told you? Kunal, your father, he wasn't—"

A sharp rustle came from outside the temple, and both men looked up, startled. A monkey appeared through the trees and both of them dropped their hands from their weapons.

Your father, he wasn't— Wasn't what? Kunal wanted to ask more, to hear stories, anything about his father, but the moment had vanished, and the words caught in his throat.

"I think your parents were married, Kunal. In secret. I don't know why that is, but it's a suspicion I have. Otherwise your powers wouldn't have shown. Our powers—the strength, the shifting—those houses will always crave it, without realizing all that you have to give up to shoulder it. I tried my hardest to teach that to Harun, but I think I burdened him too much."

"Harun? Burdened?" Kunal's voice was incredulous.

"Don't judge my eldest too harshly," King Mahir said, chuckling. "He wasn't always so prickly. He changed—we all changed after the Night of Tears."

"How did he change?"

"He was once the brightest light in our palace. He made everyone smile with his curiosity, and his love for his sister filled the palace with joy. He loved philosophy, history. That changed, though. He's since become focused, reserved."

Kunal wasn't sure *reserved* was the word he'd use—but Harun was certainly smart, cunning, charismatic—though the last one pained him to admit.

"Would there be a way to undo it? So it wasn't such a burden?" Kunal asked slowly, thinking back to something Esha had said.

Mahir considered it. "Possibly. If something can be made it can be unmade. Our ancient lore talks as such. But that's not a path we've ever considered. It's a burden, yes, but it's also my duty, Kunal. Our duty."

Kunal nodded along. They all had their duty, but Kunal was beginning to think that his was to question.

What if there was another way?

CHAPTER 25

The towering arena was filled to the brim, with Gwali citizens fitted into every nook and cranny of the gleaming pink sandstone seats.

The sweltering heat mixed with excitement, transforming into a palpable tension. Kunal wiped the sweat from his brow and peeked out into the audience, his heart beating faster at the sight of so many people.

Three matches and he'd be into the next round.

Three matches he'd have to win, against fighters who'd been training the whole year-round for this very competition. But it was the only way for them to continue having access to the citadel—and the way to Reha.

Kunal rolled his shoulders and began to stretch. Mace fighting required strength, but a surprising amount of dexterity as well. The rules stated that if one were to drop their mace, they could pick up one weapon other than a mace, such as a sword or spear, for the remainder of the match. He peeked around at the other fighters. To his right, a man who twirled his mace over his shoulder with ease, lifting a fifty-pound mace like a babe. To his left, a smaller fighter wielded his fifteen-pound mace like a spear. Mace fighting wasn't Kunal's strength, despite training with Chand, so his main goal would be to get his opponent to drop his mace. Any other weapon he was confident against.

Or as confident as one could feel when the weight of the entire mission rested on his shoulders. They still needed to scope out the citadel's defenses, and he'd worked with Alok to shift patrols around so they'd have a larger window of time— now all he needed to do was get into the next round and keep his access to the citadel.

The sun pierced the metal grate that separated the training area from the arena, dotting the ground with blocks of shimmering light. Kunal lifted his mace over his shoulder, spinning it around his torso and then his neck. The movements began to come back to him, the careful precision of the turns, which muscles needed to be used to stabilize the weight of the mace.

He determined that the thirty-pound mace would be best. The perfect balance for him. Kunal took his spot next to the other fighters in his class and sneaked a peek out into the arena boxes, searching for a thick mane of curls.

Esha was a glimmering blur, and Kunal peered closer,

pulling at his power to hone in his gaze and catch a glimpse of her.

"Win," she mouthed.

He smiled.

Esha sat back in her seat, glad that Lord Mayank was deep in conversation to her right and hadn't noticed her leaning forward to watch Kunal.

Esha hadn't much liked Mayank after their initial meeting at the Welcome Ball, but his potential support from House Pramukh would help make up for the manpower the Scales refused to provide. Coups needed armies, and the Blades needed allies.

She tuned back into the conversation to her left, led by Lord Aniket of House Rusala. His armbands were a glittering white ivory, which he showed off with every wave of his hand.

"It's true," he said, holding court with his sister, Lady Mati. "My sister saw it herself."

"I did," she confirmed.

"Really?" another lady piped in, crushing her sari pleats as she leaned in, which drew a disapproving glance from another older courtier.

"Have you figured out what they're going on about yet?" Lord Mayank said, his voice soft enough to startle Esha. He leaned in close to her, not past impropriety, but enough that she could feel the warmth from his skin.

"No clue," she said. "I'm feeling rather stupid, actually."

"You? Never," he said. "I've heard tales of you."

"And what might those be?"

"Now, I can't give away all my stories so easily, can I? You'll never have a reason to talk to me again," he said, smiling.

It was a smile that lit up his entire face. Esha no longer wondered how he had maintained his status as the most eligible bachelor in Jansa. Thankfully, he had dropped the overt flirtations of their previous encounter. Perhaps it had been an act for Vardaan.

"You're not giving yourself enough credit, Lord Pramukh."

"No, no, that would have been my father. I'm far too young for that."

"So, you're not interested in being Lord Pramukh? I've heard many reports to the contrary, my lord."

Lord Mayank raised an eyebrow. "Straight to it, are we?"

Esha shrugged. It was well known that Vardaan refused to entrust Mayank with his father's and family title. The reasons why were unknown, but Esha could guess. Vardaan was either jealous or saw a potential rival in the charismatic, beloved young man. Her theory was likely correct, if Mayank's reaction was any indication.

Esha's eyes drifted below. Kunal was stretching, about to begin his match.

"Interested in sports?"

"I love a good match, yes," she said, keeping her eyes below. The match started in earnest. Kunal narrowly avoided his opponent's swing and started using footwork to knock his opponent off balance. Kunal's opponent was a creature of strength, and her lemon boy had picked up on it.

"Indeed. This one looks interesting. One of the fighters is clearly in a better position, strength on his side. The other smaller but more dexterous. The unassuming ones often win, precisely because they've been underestimated. My coins are on the smaller one. The Senap."

Esha gave Mayank a thoughtful look.

"Mine too, my lord."

A moment's pause. Silence between them, the audience roaring as Kunal knocked his opponent's mace to the ground. Now they were fighting mace against sword.

The smart move would have been to deliver a blow to his opponent's leg, knocking him out, but Kunal wouldn't do that. He was too damn honorable.

To her surprise, Kunal lurched forward, aiming for the leg, before feinting the other way and landing a blow against his opponent's cuirass. The other fighter flew backward from the impact, hitting the ground with a thud. And stayed down. The nobles around them roared in outrage or joy, exchanging coins under the silk folds of their clothes.

"Your reports weren't wrong."

Esha cocked her head at Lord Mayank.

"About me. My title," he elaborated. "But then again, don't we all want what's rightfully ours? And when denied, well, it does make one slightly put out."

Esha smiled. "Indeed. I can understand that, as can the prince. And we would always be willing to help out any . . . friend if we felt they were being unjustly treated. But, of course, there is more than enough time for this sort of talk. I get ahead of myself."

Satisfied that Kunal had passed this first match—and without a scratch—she sat back. Esha realized she and Lord Mayank might have more in common than she had originally thought.

But did they have a common enemy?

A maidservant passed by them with trays of sweet yogurt drinks and assorted fruits. Esha spotted a piece of mango and carefully popped it into her mouth, pondering the question as another noble caught Mayank's attention.

"—my money is on that Senap captain. The handsome one," Lady Seshi said.

"Well, that's a useless description. Most of the Senaps are strong, strapping men," one of the ladies complained.

"No, no, the one who has those unique—"

"You mean the one with the eyes like amber sunstones? He just won magnificently," one of the ladies said, a sigh in her voice. "He fought like a fierce tiger."

Esha snapped to attention as she realized they were talking about Kunal, trying to hide her frown at the idea of any of their eyes on him.

"Ooh, he is handsome. I wonder if he's also like a tiger in—"

The woman to her far right looked shocked, and Esha's face flushed, from the implication and from indignation—for Kunal, of course.

"Runtika!"

"What? We were all thinking it."

"Oh, the Falcon Squad," someone said venomously. "Ruining everything."

"The Falcon Squad is here?" Esha asked, snapping to attention. "I didn't see them here."

"They are guests of honor, and no, they're not here." Runtika leaned forward. "Leela is only groaning because they're having a special Mela ceremony for them tomorrow, and she has to go because she lost a bet. Those ceremonies are terribly boring."

"Sounds like it," Esha said, her words casual even as her mind whirred, a new plan nestling into her. The ceremony. "They'd be wearing their regalia, right?"

Runtika nodded, her mouth full of rainbow sweets. She swallowed quickly and then sighed. "They look so handsome in their regalia."

"Helmets?"

"Yes," the girl said. "Don't love those, though."

Esha murmured in agreement.

She couldn't help it. The uncertainty of the past few days had made her desperate for something to go right. The ceremony was the perfect opportunity. It shouldn't interfere with their plans and she could get lost in the crowds.

Justice would finally be hers. She'd end it during the

ceremony, once and for all. Vardaan wouldn't win. He wouldn't steal this from her, and he wouldn't steal Reha either.

"A brass coin for your thoughts?" Lord Mayank said, startling her.

"Are my thoughts worth so little?" Esha tilted her head at Mayank.

"A gold one, then. A cart of them."

"You wouldn't want to know them, my lord. Just the tedious thoughts of a lady."

"You know, House Pramukh values both men and women," he said. "Our traditions haven't changed in our region, and I'm committed to never let them. The . . . current rule in Jansa may have moved away from this, but I hope you know you can be open with me. We could be friends, as you mentioned."

"I'm grateful for the offer, my lord. One could always use more friends," she said softly.

The competitors below had finished up their match, one of the fighters walking off with a limp, holding his side.

"Come now, Lord Mayank, let's talk of fun things. Tell me one of your stories," she said, turning to her new, potential friend and tucking away her troubled thoughts for later.

<figure>———◦———</figure>

Kunal pulled himself back into the training ring, rotating his shoulder and wincing. A light muscle pull that was aching, but nothing dislodged or broken. He supposed it was the best he could hope for.

The second match had been difficult, and the next one would only be worse as the amateur fighters were eliminated. His strategy had worked with his first opponent, throwing him off-balance and taking his mace out of play. It had taken longer with the second fighter, and he had almost been walloped in the head, his shoulder taking the brunt of it instead.

There was a reason mace fighting had become heavily regulated since the ancient times. It had been the main weapon of Vasu the Wanderer, who had accompanied Naran and Naria on the quest to fulfill the first blood ritual. To this day, Vasu was revered by the Yavar, not just for being their ancestor but for his valor in their quest. It had always puzzled Kunal that Vasu, and the Yavar, revered the gods yet had rejected the bond to the land.

He glanced up to the stands, at the tall, curved spears of the Yavar. They held a festival every year in honor of Vasu and were probably itching to have one of their fighters win. Kunal hoped he wouldn't have to face one.

There were a few more matches before his last one, so Kunal went to fill up his waterskin. The heat was brutal that day, beating down with a viciousness, determined to wring every last drop of strength from him. It didn't help that they were outfitted in metal cuirasses, donned to protect from the steel maces. It was surprisingly civil—usually the competitions were a bit more brutal, though he supposed opening up the tournament to other countries required precautions.

But after the archery tournament, Kunal knew this civility wouldn't last, not in the final round. He wanted to brace himself, but he didn't know what for.

More wild beasts? Different weapons or multiple opponents?

The conch blew, and Kunal sighed, wiping his brow and taking one last drink of his waterskin.

He'd find out soon.

———◁◇▷———

Kunal wasn't sure he'd ever get used to the crowds of the Mela, all there for a chance to see him win—or fail spectacularly. Now that failure had a whole different meaning for him as the Archer.

People had bows painted on their cheeks, others waved flags in his honor. He had people to represent, to win for. They had chosen him, and he couldn't let them down. And they didn't even know the real burden on his shoulders.

The mace-fighting competition was taking everything out of him. Kunal was glad he had spent extra time training with Chand and King Mahir. He inhaled deeply, trying to center himself as he took his starting stance, drawing a line in the sand with the toe of his sandal.

At the sound of the conch, both Kunal and his opponent circled each other like prey. Kunal crouched low, balancing the mace on his shoulder as he assessed his opponent's weaknesses and strengths.

Suddenly, his opponent lunged toward him. Kunal darted away, sidestepping the blow.

A faint circle began to show in the sand below them, created by their footsteps, each waiting for the other to make a move.

His opponent lunged again, and Kunal took the same stance, anticipating it, but saw the feint a second too late. His opponent rammed into his side with his mace, making Kunal fly backward and tumble to the ground.

Kunal groaned, trying to get to his feet before he could take another swing at him, one that would keep him down. He struggled to his feet, protecting his injured side with his mace.

Kunal had miscalculated. His opponent wasn't new or inexperienced. He had been sussing him out as well, tiring him out slowly, and Kunal hadn't even realized.

A tactician, not a brute. He could respect that.

He also knew how to react.

Kunal switched his grip, suddenly breaking the circle between them and standing his ground. His opponent stopped, a moment of confusion across his face.

He started moving from side to side, forward and back, anything to keep his opponent on his toes. When his opponent was finally getting frustrated, Kunal lunged forward.

He rammed into his opponent, landing a blow of his mace again his cuirass, right above the shoulder. The man staggered back a few paces but didn't go down.

Kunal and his opponent ran forward at the same time, locking into a fierce tangle of maces. Kunal pushed forward, putting every ounce of strength he could into the forward drive of his mace. He couldn't even swing it around. They were stuck together, and whichever one of them pulled away first threatened to expose his side.

Kunal took the risk, unlocking his mace to swing around, but his opponent was ready, landing a blow on his already worn shoulder. Kunal lost control of his mace and it went flying.

He scrambled back, rolling across the floor and dodging mace blows that pounded into the earth of the arena, as he grabbed his secondary weapon, a sword.

This was his specialty. He was much defter with a blade, and it was certainly a more precise weapon than a mace. The other man didn't realize that he was in trouble, rushing forward, swinging his mace.

Kunal ducked and dodged, and when he saw the opportunity—he stabbed his sword into the side gap between his opponent's cuirass.

He went down, dropping his mace with a crashing thud that reverberated through the courtyard. A deafening roar went up through the crowd.

Kunal backed up, wiping his brow, exhaustion hitting him like an anvil despite the adrenaline still coursing through his body.

He was done.

He had made it through.

Kunal started to walk over to his opponent on the ground, to offer him a hand up and get him to the healers, when the voice of the official pierced the silence.

"To enter the final round, competitors must kill their opponent."

A hush came over the crowd. Kunal's body stiffened, even as his mind knew exactly what to do. The neck or a blow to the head for a quick death. He *was* a soldier.

But death for entertainment, senseless death, went against everything he knew to be right. And since he had left the Fort, he had lost his taste for the Lord of Darkness's sport. He wouldn't be part of it.

Not like this.

His opponent staggered to his feet, grabbing his secondary weapon as well.

"It's either you or me," he said, coughing.

"No," Kunal said. "I can't."

His opponent gave him a look, a questioning glance between Kunal's face and the Senap armband on his bicep.

"Then I will."

His opponent strode forward, a violent look on his face as he took a running leap at him. Kunal responded as he had been trained to, meeting him with the same ferocity as his body and mind recognized the threat in front of him. His instincts slid into place, where his life was paramount.

He didn't want to kill this man, but he didn't want to die either.

The other man dodged, but Kunal was quicker, sliding under him and slicing his calf and then his side.

He went down, falling to his knees, and Kunal whirled

around and slit his throat, aiming for the quickest possible death.

His opponent hit the ground.

Kunal closed his eyes, overcome. He slowly turned around and dropped to his knees next to the man, reciting the proper prayers over him, holding his hand as he transitioned into the Lord of Darkness's world.

He didn't move away, even as the officials ran forward.

Or as the crowd broke into a deafening roar, chanting his name.

CHAPTER 26

Esha sent a prayer of thanks up to the Moon Lord for hot baths and good maids as she stepped out of the tub, wrapping a linen cloth around her body. Aditi bustled about, ordering maids to braid the jasmine ornaments tighter or to press Esha's sari more carefully in preparation for that night's party, hosted by House Pramukh.

She sank into the plushness of an armchair, sighing as she leaned back and gave in to Aditi's ministrations.

"Aditi, what good did I do in my past birth to deserve you?" Esha asked as Aditi worked her hair into a magnificent crown of curls. "I can't believe I'll have to leave you in only a few days, after the chariot race and the ball."

The girl laughed, but her smile wasn't as bright as usual. "Maybe your ancestors did a lot of penance. I'm still surprised that you didn't have a lady's maid for years. The amount of dirt you track in?"

Esha pursed her lips. "The price of loving gardens. I used to spend afternoons with my father in the gardens. He absolutely loved horticulture and I gained a lot of knowledge from him."

Her voice wavered at the end, unintentionally, and she looked away. She caught Aditi's gaze in the mirror.

"He's gone now, if that wasn't obvious," Esha said, clearing her throat. "But I still love spending my mornings walking among nature."

"I'm sure he'd be proud of the woman you've become," Aditi said softly.

Esha chuckled. "Perhaps."

She wasn't sure he would be. But Esha had become this person, the Viper, *because* her father would never have the chance to be proud—or disappointed—in her.

Aditi tugged at her hair. Esha looked up. "My parents are gone as well. So when I say I understand, I'm not pitying you or offering false words. But I can't believe that your father wouldn't be proud of you. You're kind, generous, and strong. You're an adviser to the prince—who knows, perhaps you could be ambassador one day, in Dharka."

"Oh." Esha had been living in the skin of the Viper for so long that she hadn't considered the impact she wanted to have after she got her revenge. "I've never really thought about it."

"I have," Aditi said, her voice stronger, different. "Do

you believe being a lady's maid is all I want? No, my lady. You're lucky that there are so many opportunities for you in Dharka. As a woman."

Esha turned to face Aditi, taking a good look at the girl. Aditi flushed, her previous brazenness fading under Esha's gaze.

"Not that I'm unhappy here in Jansa," she said quickly.

"It's okay," Esha said, laying a gentle hand on Aditi's arm. The girl glanced up, the fear in her eyes ebbing. "Your secrets and dreams are safe with me."

Aditi nodded slowly. "Thank you, my lady."

"Esha."

"Esha," she said after a brief pause.

Esha moved to get up when Aditi clucked her tongue. "We're not done yet. We still have to weave the jasmine into your braids and rub your feet with sandalwood."

Aditi returned to dressing her hair, weaving and pinning with expertise.

Esha groaned. "Is this really all necessary? Can I wear that ruby necklace and be done with it?"

"Did you not hear a word I said, my lady?" Aditi said, arms akimbo. "We're doing everything the proper way today."

Esha sat back down with a scowl. It was both a blessing and a curse that this girl had come to understand her in a few weeks. "Fine, but I get to wear the diamond-and-gold belt as well."

"Deal."

Esha sat back and let the girl finish, thinking about Aditi's words. An ambassador. She allowed herself a moment of fancy, dreaming of the lands she might visit. The desert-covered lands of the west where there was a fierce queen. The islands to the east with palaces of jade and pearl. The snowy mountains of the Aiforas, even.

There was so much of the Southern Lands itself that she hadn't seen.

And perhaps one day she'd be able to see it all—as just Esha.

———◇———

The smile on Esha's face didn't disappear until the noble had turned his back.

"Tired?" Arpiya said, appearing at her elbow as she stifled a yawn. They'd stayed up all the night before, checking and rechecking the plan for the next day's mission to case the citadel's defenses. They'd get only one shot to do it correctly. Security was growing tighter around the citadel and palace as they approached the Victor's Ball, but they had no choice. The real Reha had to be rescued before the Victor's Ball, before her marriage to General Panak.

"Not really. What's the news from the boys?"

"The citadel really is locked down as tight as we thought," Arpiya said, lowering her voice. "Without Kunal and his access to the citadel, it would take us weeks to figure out a way to get in. And it would probably be messy."

"Messy?"

"There's a hawk's nest at the top of the citadel, where the messengers are trained. It's the only place with an entrance to the citadel that isn't guarded by armor-wearing, spear-wielding humans."

"Ah," Esha said. "Then our new plan for Kunal will be the best one."

Arpiya nodded. "Speaking of Kunal, I meant to tell you earlier . . . When we were scouting, there was another man, one he let into the palace."

"A soldier? Not Alok?" She tilted her head at Arpiya, and they moved over to a corner of the room, where moonlight streamed in through the glass windows.

"Someone. I couldn't be sure." A faint blush crept over Arpiya's face.

"Someone you may have liked?" Esha said, her voice singsong even as she tried to decipher what it meant that Kunal was letting unknown people into the palace. She couldn't remember the last time Arpiya had fancied anyone.

"Perhaps. There was something about him . . . But that's not why I brought it up," Arpiya said hurriedly. "We're trusting Kunal with a lot in this rescue. And I do trust him. Especially after he responded so well to my threats."

"Arpiya!" Esha exclaimed.

She shrugged, a gleam in her eye. "What? You thought he'd get away without one of my talking-tos? The boys probably pray for that. But I thought you should know, as our leader."

"I'm sure it was a fellow soldier, Arpiya." Esha's grin turned wicked. "Which means you think a soldier is intriguing."

Arpiya made a face. "I think no such thing."

"What don't you think?" Harun said, appearing at Esha's side.

"Nothing," Esha and Arpiya said at the same time.

Harun frowned.

Esha craned her head, searching through the crowd for Kunal. At least during this party, it wouldn't be odd for Kunal to introduce himself and talk to them, especially not as the famous Archer. Once she spotted him, she pulled a servant aside and asked him to bring Kunal over to them, at the request of the prince.

"That's sure to give him worry. We don't have the best relationship," Harun mused.

"That's up to you, my prince," Esha said, knowing that he only preferred his title in certain situations. "And probably because of you, if we're being honest."

"You know, if you call me your prince, doesn't that also mean you should be kind to me? Or risk punishment?"

"And what punishment would that be, my prince?" Esha said, a grin on her face.

"Please stop. I don't know what direction this is about to go in," Arpiya said, and pointed at the approaching maid. "We also have guests."

Esha realized she had stepped closer to Harun, and he to

her. A natural sort of thing for them when verbally sparring. She coughed and moved back a pace as the maid returned, Kunal in tow.

"The Arch—the champion, Kunal Dhagan, Your Highness," the servant squeaked out before bowing low and running away. Kunal looked perplexed and a little unnerved.

"Don't worry, soldier. She called you over," Harun said. At least he wasn't glowering at him like he used to.

Kunal relaxed, his shoulders dropping from around his ears. "What is it?"

"We thought this would be a good opportunity to talk in the open. Pretend like you've just been introduced to us, Kunal," Esha said.

"That would mean a bow, soldier. Isn't it great how I can call you that now and it's still accurate?" Harun said, his voice light. Ah, there it was.

"I'll take it as a compliment, Prince," Kunal said, the tone with which he said *Prince* indicating what he truly thought.

"Now, now, aren't you two cousins or something?" Esha shushed Arpiya, and the girl shrugged her shoulders. "Everyone keeps beating around the bush. But you two have more in common than you'd probably like to admit."

"Like what?" Kunal said.

"Both royals, loyal to a fault, hotheaded, territorial, insistent on protecting your land and people, both lost parents at a young age. I could go on."

Harun and Kunal looked ill at the comparison.

Harun reached a hand up to his hair before dropping

it. "She's right," he said. "Though I'm not sure I care for the characterization of being hotheaded."

"Same here," Kunal murmured.

"I'm sorry I haven't properly welcomed you to the family. Even by marriage, you're my aunt's son and there's too few of us already," Harun said, lowering his voice to a whisper.

Kunal responded with a deep bow.

Paces over, a group of nobles broke out into loud laughter, a good reminder to them all that they were still in the nest of their enemies. No matter what they might think, they were constantly being watched.

"The two of you, look pleased. We have things to discuss and we don't want the other nobles to notice anything amiss," Esha whispered.

The two obliged as best as they could.

"Kunal, we'll need you to check the outer walls tomorrow when we're stealing the schematics."

Kunal nodded, though he kept looking away, distracted. Recently, he'd latch onto any indication there was information that wasn't being shared with him. The only thing Esha could see that was interesting around them was Yamini, and that made her frown.

A few other competitors were nearby, and from their hungry looks they were eager to get their own time with the prince of Dharka, if only because Kunal had. It wouldn't do to monopolize his time anyway—they didn't need to draw any more attention.

Esha tucked a note into Kunal's palm as she leaned over,

making it look as if it were nothing more than an accidental touch. To his credit, he didn't startle, but he did turn to look at her, his gaze searing and inquisitive before he walked away.

Two days. They had only two days before their game board would be set.

Which meant she had far less time to accomplish her own goal.

Esha palmed the side of her dress where she had attached a small weapons holder to her thigh, under the stiff folds of her silk sari.

Harun's warm chuckle brought her back to attention, a look around telling her what had brought mirth to his lips. The other competitors were circling like attentive men eyeing a bride to court, nervous, yet eager.

"If you had to pick one of the competitors to back, who would it be?" Harun asked.

"Not that one," Esha said, glancing over the rim of her cup at one who kept darting back and forth. "He looks too nervous. I'm waiting for one of them to take courage and approach us. And you know the answer anyway. Kunal."

"You always did like an unfair advantage," he said lightly.

"True," she said, avoiding the bait. It wasn't Kunal's fault he had royal blood or that he'd been forced into this competition. "My whips are rather unfair."

"Are we talking about you now? Oh no, Esha. There's far more deadly things about you than your whips."

She returned his gaze, lifting an eyebrow.

"You know, if you were in the competition properly, I'd bet on you," Harun said.

One of the circling competitors gained courage and walked toward them.

"Your confidence in me is inspiring," Esha murmured as he approached. Her tone was playful, but Harun's words provided her heart the layer of steel she needed. In the corner of the room was a group of Senaps, chatting and drinking, looking far too happy for her own taste.

She was the Viper, Dharka's legend.

She delivered justice, and she would finish this—tomorrow.

CHAPTER 27

Esha skittered over the rooftop of the merchants' guild-house and came to a stop, looking for her target.

There.

She started to climb down the wall of the guildhouse, but her foot caught on a few loose bricks, and they went crashing to the ground. Her head jerked up, alert.

When nothing happened for a few minutes, she finished climbing down the wall, landing squarely on the dirty alley floor. She patted dust off her dhoti and made sure all of her weapons were concealed.

Satisfied, Esha strode forward into the light of the main road, checking left and right before sneaking across.

She was so intent on her direction that she didn't see the flash of bronze at first.

A Senap in a helmet grabbed her arm and stared down at her.

"We've been looking for you."

———◄○►———

Esha tugged at her chains, her wrists aching under the unfamiliar weight. Her vision was still fuzzy from being knocked out, blood dripping from a cut on her eyebrow.

She stepped forward, trying to keep pace with the Senap by her side, his grip firm on her chains. They approached the outer wall of the citadel, and the Senap nodded at the soldiers who stood guard.

"A prisoner. The one the Senap captain was looking to question."

The two guards glanced at each other, one of them checking a small scroll hidden in his waist sash. He gave his fellow soldier a nod and waved the Senap through.

"The captain is out right now, but you can place the prisoner in the inner ring's rooms for now."

"When will he be back?"

One of the soldiers checked the sundial nearby. "He was called away to the palace but should be back within an hour."

"I shouldn't take him to the captain's rooms?"

The other soldier snorted. "No. No one's allowed into the inner tower if the captain isn't there. Wait for him below."

Her captor looked like he was going to argue but then nodded and yanked at Esha's chains, making her stumble. She bit back a yelp as she lurched forward, following the Senap through the main gates of the citadel.

Memories hit her like a towering wave. She'd been there

before, almost a decade ago, after watching her parents die and helping Reha escape. Her arm ached in response, the bone having never healed properly. A reminder of what the Senaps were capable of.

She slowed down, her feet growing leaden as they crossed the inner courtyard and moved toward the inner sanctum, where the captain's tower and, if she remembered correctly, the dungeons were. The night was silent, except for the squelch of their sandals. Weapons were strewn about everywhere in the courtyard.

Her chains were yanked again, and Esha was only able to stop herself from flying forward at the momentum by digging in her heels.

She'd had enough.

"Stop yanking me about," she said crossly. "We're past the guards."

Aahal turned around, his face contorting in apology under his Senap helmet.

"Sorry! I was worried they wouldn't believe us, and then I got a bit into it. It's kind of heady, having all this power."

"Yes, I know," Esha said, glancing around. "I spent plenty of time with soldiers who felt the same way, in this place."

Aahal's eyes widened as he loosened the slack on her chains. "I forgot. Farhan told me, and I completely forgot. You were kept in the citadel's dungeons, weren't you? After the coup?"

Esha nodded, finding her balance again. They drew close to the inner sanctum and tower.

"It's fine, Aahal. We need to focus." *She* needed to focus. Being in the citadel again was harder than she had anticipated. Her ghosts were louder here. "We have to get through the next set of guards. And then we're in."

Aahal squeezed at the chains in acknowledgment. Esha made herself smaller, slowing her steps and bowing her head like any other prisoner.

A decade ago, she had come here the same way, cowed.

But this time, it was her choice.

"We're almost there," Aahal whispered.

Esha prepared herself.

———◦———

Kunal held back a sigh of annoyance, watching the nobles from the House Ayul chatter and bemoan the states of their shoes—again.

He didn't know what the nobles had expected when they had accepted his invitation to a tour of the citadel. Perhaps they thought they were getting an exclusive look at where the champions trained and soldiers were made, one they could lord over their fellow nobles at the next party.

But they had forgotten that one hundred men had been living and training there, and though the number was dwindling, it was still an area for training and rest. Of course the courtyard would be muddy. This was a ground to practice the art of fighting, not the pristine marble of their palace quarters.

He tried to hide his annoyance with a smile. Why had they even said yes to his invitation? Perhaps they told themselves that it meant the Archer had chosen them as his patrons, was spending an afternoon off with their esteemed presences.

How would they act around him if they knew the truth of his birth and parentage? Would the geniality fade into competition and jealousy? As it was now, he was famous but still below them. Only a soldier.

Kunal motioned at the crowd of Ayul noblemen and -women, mostly young, though a few old. He had gotten special dispensation for this tour. In fact, the captain had encouraged it, saying it would make their army stand taller in the eyes of possible benefactors.

"This courtyard is used for training, as you might be able to surmise from the discarded weapons. I promise we're better behaved at the Fort," Kunal said. They tittered in amusement.

He caught a glimpse of a Senap helmet and a man in chains down below and steered the nobles away.

One of the noblewomen gasped. "There's a prisoner over there," she said, aghast. "I thought it was only champions in the citadel during the Mela?"

"And the Senap captain, my lady," Kunal said. That was something they had only discovered a few days ago, after one of Alok's scouting trips. It was said that he had been positioned there to protect the soldiers, but Kunal knew better. "As added protection for the champions."

"You don't really need any protection, do you, Senap Kunal?" one of the ladies asked, her gaze dragging down his body. Kunal flushed, and he hid it with a cough, his discomfort only seeming to make her more interested.

"We could all use a little help. Did you know that last Sun Mela, a woman tried to capture three Mela champions?"

"Why?"

"She was a fan and had been following them since the start of the competition. The Senap captain caught hold of her, though, and released the champions."

One of the noblemen huffed. "We never heard of this."

"Of course. We didn't want to alarm anyone."

They entered the outer walls of the citadel, where the champions weren't allowed at night. The guards there caught sight of Kunal and waved him in, a scroll with his approved request for a tour tucked in their belts.

Two guards at the outer door and two at the inner door. Kunal noted it for later.

They turned in to the outer walkway, winding up a narrow staircase to what Kunal and Alok had identified as the only natural exits in the citadel.

A few nobles huffed and puffed behind him. Kunal strode up the long staircase as if it were a morning stroll, counting the arrow notches and taking note of how many soldiers there were and where they were positioned as they arrived at the top, on the upper ramparts of the citadel. This was where the majority of the citadel's impressive defensive advantage lay.

It had been Esha's idea to lure the nobles in with a promise of secrets and danger, to use them as cover as they scouted.

Kunal was already putting together a mental sketch of the compound's defenses and number of soldiers stationed.

Aahal and Esha should be en route to steal the captain's schematics of the citadel, which would reveal any routes or hidden tunnels they could use. Farhan and Arpiya were scouting the armory to determine how much weaponry the citadel had—just in case.

Despite overhearing Esha discussing the need to take the throne at the musical contest, she hadn't come out and told him yet, only hinted. He couldn't deny that he was frustrated at still not having her trust.

"And these are the men of the Kestrel Squad, strong infantry soldiers and honorable, good men," Kunal said. He patted one of the soldiers on the shoulder. The men puffed out their chests and gave exaggerated bows to the nobles, who lapped it up.

He tried not to roll his eyes. He was now sure he hated politics, but he did see the benefit of understanding people and playing to what they expected—or wanted—him to be.

Kunal cleared his throat.

"Shall we continue?"

The nobles gave an enthusiastic response and Kunal continued ahead, scanning the walls as he went.

———◁◦▷———

Esha laid the thin parchment over the schematics and rubbed the dark chalk in as Farhan had shown her, taking care to not disturb or mar the original schematic plans.

Aahal bounced on his toes nearby, looking out the window.

"Esha, we're almost out of time."

"One more second," she said. The chalk trick was beginning to work. Dark lines and cross sections began to show through as Esha kept at it.

"Esha."

"I know."

"Esha." Aahal's voice was sharper now and she glanced up.

"What? By my calculation, we still have five more minutes."

"And yet, I see champions coming back in. The Senap captain won't be far behind."

Moon Lord's fists. Esha rubbed harder, willing the lines to solidify into the clarity of the schematics below.

Only another minute . . .

Anxiety rose in her belly as the chalk refused to cooperate. There was still a whole wing she needed to transfer over to the parchment paper, and Aahal was looking increasingly agitated.

"We need to go."

"One more—"

"Now."

Esha finished the last section of the map and rubbed the dark chalk in as fiercely as she could. Aahal grabbed her shoulder as the impression began to seep through, finishing off the layout of the citadel.

They'd done it. Esha wanted to collapse to the floor, but her feet and adrenaline kept her moving. A glance out the left window revealed what had caused Aahal's concern—a wave of champions were almost under the tower, the plume of the Senap captain's helmet not far behind. These were no longer coincidences, not when her information had been good a half day before. She had the feeling that someone was watching her, following her every move.

"Other window," he said, and she nodded.

They grabbed the rope Aahal had tied minutes before and shot off the window ledge, plunging into the darkness.

CHAPTER 28

The rooftop of the eastern wing's residential quarter was scorching, and Esha slipped her feet into her jeweled sandals before the tiles could leave singe marks on her bare feet.

"Moon Lord, those tiles are steaming," she said, adding a choice Dharkan curse under her breath.

"I warned you," Harun said. They had arrived early for the festivities so that it was only she, Harun, a few scattered Dharkan and Jansan nobles, and their servants.

"Not well enough."

"It's not my fault you only listen to half the things I say."

"Oh, you figured that out?" Esha said, grinning.

Harun looked slightly better than he had the day before, some of the life coming back to his face after hearing that their scouting mission had been a success.

She was glad for it. She'd been able to corner Arpiya later

325

that day and get it out of her—Harun hadn't been sleeping well and he had asked her to get a draft. Esha could only think he had hid it from her, hadn't asked her to get it, because he didn't want her to worry.

Which was stupid. As if she couldn't already tell something was off.

"What's the plan?" Esha smoothed out her sari under her twining gold necklace carved with roses. It matched the dusty-rose sari she wore with a thick gold border embroidered with peacocks. She held a spool of thread in one hand, a small kite in the other.

"We split up. You'll talk to Mayank, and I have a few nobles on my list. If we can get them confirmed, we'll be that much more secure when we move in a few days' time."

"Think of what we could've done with a week's time, or a month."

Harun made a noise that indicated that he had been thinking of it. It was probably the cause of his sleeplessness. He looked over at the spool in her hand, which she was spinning.

"Why did you even bother bringing a kite? You know they'll be providing some for the kite flying," Harun said, reaching for one of the kites and spools that a servant had laid out on a low table nearby.

"I like this one."

"Because you think you beat me that one time with it? I can't believe you brought it all the way from Mathur."

Esha scoffed. "Because I *know* I beat you that one time

with it, Prince. You were so certain you'd win. I still remember your face when you lost."

Now that had been something she'd never forget—or let him forget.

"I definitely got a prize later that night, though," he said, his voice low as a grin spread across his face. Esha flushed, remembering as well.

"If that's what makes you feel better for losing—"

"Oh, it definitely made me feel better—"

She gave him a sharp look but was glad to see him smiling again.

"I challenge you," he said suddenly, holding up his kite. "We arrived early because you demanded we get a good spot. Let's race before the others arrive."

"And what will they think then?"

"That the prince of Dharka is a normal young man." He lowered his voice. "And it'll show that we're not bothered by the recent happenings."

"You really want everyone to see you lose horribly?"

He rolled his eyes. "Are you in or out?"

"In," she said, hiking up her sari to cross over the small partition from the edge of the rooftop.

Harun followed, both of them ignoring exclamations from servants behind them, who rushed to offer help. Aditi wasn't there despite Esha having seen her at the musical contest. The servants' schedules were a mystery to her.

"I'll be fine," she told one of the servants. "If I'm close to tumbling over, I'm sure the prince will save me."

"I don't think he found that very reassuring," Harun said as soon as the servant turned away.

Esha smoothed out the lines of the kite, checking the string and tightening its connection to the kite. She looked up to find Harun watching her and she made a face at him.

"Shouldn't you be preparing your kite?"

"The kites are fully made, tied together and everything." He laughed. "Do you really think the nobles will have any idea how to put a kite together properly?"

"But you know better," she said.

"Of course. I'm the one who took you to your first kite-flying contest, don't you forget."

She tightened the knot on the kite, kneeling down on the ground to get the correct angle. She heard a gasp from behind her, but while Esha felt comfortable among all the baubles of the royal court, she couldn't resist a moment of freedom from her childhood. Or a competition.

"I'm pretty sure you'd never let me forget," she muttered.

"What was that?" Harun asked, craning his neck around to look at her kite.

She swatted him on the shoulder. "No cheating."

He gave her only an impish look in return.

The rooftop behind them was still rather empty, which worked in their favor. But it wouldn't remain that way for long, despite how late the nobles of both courts preferred to arrive. One could almost add an hour to the start time for any event during the Mela and still find themselves among the earliest to arrive.

She finished tying her kite together and tested it, lifting it a few times in the air. It took longer than usual—Harun kept trying to look over her shoulder, making her have to turn away every so often.

Finally, she turned around, hiding her kite behind her back.

"Let's go," she said.

Before he could respond she had launched her kite into the air, feeling the tension as it caught its first gust of wind. She quickly tightened the line, making sure the spool didn't grow lax as she flew the kite over another gust.

It felt as if she had wings of her own, controlling the kite over the air. She wondered if this was what Kunal felt like when he flew. He would've loved being up this high, pure air at his back and the wind in his face.

A kite careened into hers, knocking her off the air stream it was on, and she glanced to her right with a frown on her face. Harun was quickly slacking and then tightening his thread, concentration etched into his brow.

Esha grinned, taking note of the way his body swayed. He still used the motions they had been taught by that kite flyer in the artisans' quarter in Mathur. Kite flying was the main event in that part of the city for the Moon Festival, and Harun had taken her down there once, years ago, after she had complained that she had never flown a kite.

But Esha had learned a few new tricks since then.

She tilted her body, leaning her kite away from his, and then cut across. The sharp rebound made her kite slam into his, knocking him off-balance. He stepped forward, bouncing on his toes to keep hold of his string.

"That was dirty," he said, giving her a look of appreciation. She winked at him.

Harun inched over toward her, keeping an eye on his kite. "Where did you learn that?"

"I don't tell you all of my secrets," she said, before realizing the implication of her words. His arm brushed against hers as they both fought for control, a huge gust of wind threatening to topside both of their kites.

"I'm learning that," he said after a few moments of silence. She glanced at him, trying to gauge his tone. "You could've told me about your parents' killer, Esha. Even if we were fighting," he said, dropping his voice.

"There was enough on your mind," she said. "I wasn't going to add more."

"That's not how this works," he said. "You don't get to pick and choose what I know, not if we're truly friends."

"I'm sorry," she said quietly. "Again."

He didn't say anything for a long moment, the silence settling over them like a blanket in the summer.

"It's all right," he said, but the tension in his shoulders was new, as if he was holding something back. She bumped into him, making him step back, breaking him out of his thoughts. He blinked a few times, his thick eyebrows knitting as he looked down at her.

"What is it?" she asked.

"Kunal knew." No accusation, no anger, a simple statement of fact.

"He found out." She shrugged, accidentally letting her kite careen off to the left. She tugged it back. "More accurately, he got in my way."

Harun released a deep, unencumbered laugh. "He's braver than most, then."

"Well, his first encounter with me was as the Viper. I think it's all been uphill from there for him."

"True, he didn't know you when you were a runty little teenager trying to boss everyone around. That was a pleasure I had all to myself." He snorted.

"Trying to?"

"I'll admit, you were pretty good at it." Esha looked up at Harun, both of them wearing matching grins, and she felt something in that moment. A spark, a rush of warmth, an emotion from moons ago.

"Prince Harun, Lady Esha," a voice called out. Esha snapped to attention, moving away from Harun as he did the same. Unfortunately, it only caused their kites to tangle together.

"Lord Mayank," she called, untangling her kite as best as she could. A servant rushed forward to help as they brought their kites down. "Are you excited for today's festivities?"

"Clearly not enough to arrive as early as you both," he said. "I've actually never been kite flying."

Esha bowed to him in greeting, her hands together. He responded in kind, the gesture looking a bit stiff on his frame.

"Today will be perfect, then. You'll be able to try a tradition of Dharka."

"One of our most fun," Harun said, untying his kite with deft fingers. He had mentioned that he had spoken to Mayank a few times since their introduction, mostly in casual settings. But that's how these friendships were made. "My favorite."

"Though one might wonder why, given how spectacularly he's been beaten in the past," Esha said.

"Really, you're going to do this in front of our dear guest?" Harun said.

"Technically, I'm not *your* guest," Mayank offered.

"There you go," Esha said. Harun rolled his eyes.

Mayank looked between the two of them, a curious expression on his face. "The rumors are true, then."

"What rumors?" Harun asked.

"You two are quite close."

"That's not a rumor, my lord. It's truth. I was raised as a ward of the palace after my parents died," Esha said. Common knowledge to any of the Dharkans, but old enough that none of them truly talked about it.

"I see," he said. "I'm sorry for that."

"The royal family treated me very kindly," she said, glancing at Harun. He was looking at her, with that inscrutable expression he had developed recently. She hated not knowing what he was thinking, whether good or bad.

"I'm not surprised. I've heard of their kindness before," Mayank said. Both Harun and Esha looked at him. "What? King Mahir, the Arrow of Dharka, had quite a reputation after the War in the North."

Harun winced.

"No need to worry, Prince. Many of us remember the olden days, when the Southern Lands were united in fighting threats, protecting our borders." Lord Mayank leaned forward. "It was a better time, I say. You're half Jansan yourself, my prince. I'm sure you agree. Jansa has changed, but the Jansan people are the same. While we value honor and strength, we don't value might over reason."

Esha nodded slowly, understanding why Harun had marked him.

An alliance between House Pramukh and Dharka. It had been an idle thought before, more in preparation, but now Esha was glad that she had the forethought.

"My lord, if you're curious about kite flying, I'd be happy to show you myself," she said, bowing again and holding out her spool.

"Please. I'd like that," he said. "If you'd like to join, Prince?"

Harun gave them a rueful smile. "I already promised my time, but I'll find you later."

Mayank tilted his head in farewell before turning to face

Esha. She swept a hand out, indicating for him to follow her. They walked a few paces in silence, weaving through the growing crowd.

"There's a spot up there where we'll have room to fly," she said.

He nodded, following close behind her. "I hope I wasn't too forward with your prince."

"Not at all. Harun appreciates a straight arrow."

"I'm not sure I'm one of those," he said, grinning. "Harun? I think you're rather closer than I had thought."

"I'm not sure what you had thought, Lord Mayank, but we are friends."

He looked skeptical at that. "So I won't be expecting a royal scroll inviting me to your wedding."

Esha tried not to make a face. "No, don't hold your breath for that."

It seemed everyone at court believed those rumors now.

She took a kite and a spool from one of the trays nearby and began to show him how to tie them together. He was a bit clumsy at first but quickly got the hang of it.

"It's rather like tying string together for a horse fence," he said, growing excited.

"Not sure I can verify that, but sure," she said, laughing. "Have you spent a lot of time fencing horses, my lord?" Her tone was teasing but, to her surprise, he nodded.

"Our region borders on the mountain plains, and we were gifted with horses from the Yavar generations ago, as one of our prizes. I learned how to take care of my horses before I learned how to fight," he said, a hint of pride in his voice. He looped the string through the rest of the holes on the kite and started to lift it up.

Esha reached up in a swift movement to grab the kite before he let it loose, dragging it back down. "If you do that without attaching it to your spool, you'll never see your kite again."

"Truly?"

"The wind is not as forgiving as one might think," she said. She started to show him how to wind it together and stay clear of the razor-sharp edges of the kite string by holding it loosely.

Once it was all secure, she showed him how to catch the wind, and he followed suit, a radiant smile breaking across his face as his kite flew proudly in the air.

"I'm impressed," she said. "You picked that up as quickly as a Dharkan."

"Us Jansans are rather smart. You know regions in Jansa hold kite-flying competitions."

She winced, realizing that she might have offended Mayank.

"Don't fret, I'm not offended. I just like to put 'you Dharkans' in your place sometimes," he said.

Esha was unable to hold back her laughter at that. "Oh, really? You should hear some of the jokes we have about Jansans, my lord."

"You should hear ours," he said. "And please, stop calling me 'my lord.' I keep thinking my father is behind me.

If we're going to be talking alliances, you have to call me Mayank."

She pulled her kite back sharply to avoid another, turning to glance at him. "And why would you think we'd be doing that?"

"I was there when the princess Reha's marriage was announced. I've seen enough changes in power to know that this was a play, and I know enough about family to understand your prince's reaction." A shadow passed over his face, but he didn't elaborate. "Don't worry, everyone else bought it."

She was silent for a few moments, considering everything he had said.

"Let's be plain, then. We'll need men," she said, drawing out her words, waiting to see his reaction.

"I have plenty of those. But will it be enough?"

"For?"

"I thought we were speaking plainly," he said.

"I meant you should speak plainly," Esha said.

His brow smoothed and he snorted. "You're an interesting woman, Lady Esha. I think you should tell me what you're thinking so I don't put my foot in my mouth."

"If we're speaking plainly, then I don't have to make clear the secrecy of this, right? We're going to move the night of the Victor's Ball to put Reha, the real Reha, on the throne."

"The real Reha?"

"We believe this one is an impostor."

"And do you have any proof of this claim?" he asked, his

voice indicating that he thought it was a large assumption to make.

"Yes," was all she said.

Mayank pulled at his kite, struggling to make it turn away from another. "And if all goes right?"

"We'll have returned the rightful heir to the Jansan throne. Once she's settled, I'm sure she'll feel most generous to the people who helped. Dharka would too. Even generous enough to send troops to help you find your rightful place, if necessary." Esha kept her voice low but steady, knowing this was the key part of their negotiation.

"My rightful place." Mayank's voice was equally low, but there was a note of humor in it, as if he was musing on the idea. "Indeed. And if I needed something other than troops?"

"I'm sure that could be arranged. Friendship can come in many forms."

"Friendship," Mayank repeated. "Now, that I can't decline." He angled his body so that his mouth couldn't be seen by others, a trick she recognized because of the amount of times she had herself employed it. "Let me talk to my house, see how many men we could gather. The Victor's Ball isn't far off."

"I know. It's a risk. I won't deny it," she said, bending her head as if she was focused on fixing her kite. "But we'll have the rightful heir. We can reset the balance of the Lands. It's a chance we have to take."

"Does King Mahir know of this?"

Esha hesitated. "Only recently."

Mayank gave a small laugh. "I take it you only found out how much he knew recently. I was always skeptical that the king wasn't involved in the Crescent Blades."

Esha tried not to look surprised. "The Crescent Blades?"

"I've connected the dots, Esha. I've been listening for any and all information as to the Blades and their mysterious leaders. I also keep an eye on court politics in both Dharka and Jansa. You only began to come up in conversations recently, this new lady. But when I dug deeper, I realized you had been around for a while, on the periphery of court. I put two and two together."

Esha considered her options. Mayank knew she was part of the Blades, and yet was still willing to work with her. He had to have made further connections, but as of now, he wasn't using them against her.

"I'm impressed at the deduction," she said slowly, smiling. "And surprised that you would still be entertaining an alliance given this belief of yours."

"I don't see the Crescent Blades as the villains in the tales I've heard. Merely as people dedicated to restoring balance, fighting injustice. If anything, I have more faith in this . . . plan of yours as a result. Normal politicians are rather ineffectual. Sometimes, they become bullies," he said, his voice becoming hard. "To effect change, sometimes you have to be the catalyst and that requires action."

It was risky to trust a Jansan noble, and one who was such a darling of the court, but she knew he had more grievances against the king than anyone—more to gain from helping them. He had proven to be trustworthy so far.

"I agree," she said. "Sometimes hard choices have to be made."

He nodded, looking out to the distance of the city and the sea beyond. "Indeed."

"There's something else," she said, thinking of the other part of their plan. "We need help to discredit this Reha."

"Help?"

"A well-placed whisper by anyone will bloom and grow like a weed."

"And you need a whole forest of whispers," he said, nodding his head. "Especially seeing how soon the Victor's Ball is."

Esha looked away for a moment, over the tops of the buildings of Gwali, all the citizens who lived in the sprawl below. Did they truly believe the lost princess had returned?

She knew there were many who didn't, and the Red Squad, stationed in the city proper, had been encouraging those rumors, seeding dissent wherever they could. All squads within a few miles had been recalled to Gwali as well, as soon as Esha had realized Harun and the king had been serious about overthrowing Vardaan. They only had a few days to cement the distrust and to gather troops outside, and inside, the city walls.

Mayank stood to her side, and she wondered what they looked like together, what whispers might have already started. They'd have to cut their conversation short soon, make sure that it didn't drag on longer.

"Some citizens are planning to voice their distrust at the chariot race," she said, revealing information she had gathered recently from her sources. "A few allies would help."

"To incite a riot?"

"No," she said. "We're merely encouraging the people's right to ask questions of their leaders."

"And what if they get hurt?"

"Vardaan wouldn't dare punish unnamed citizens during the Mela," she said with more confidence than she felt.

"He has no fear of the gods."

"He does have an image to uphold before the peace treaty. He will do it merely to save face. Mayank, I don't want anyone to get hurt. But we must show the people that they are not alone in their distrust. That seed of doubt will be all we need."

Mayank was silent for a moment, contemplating the sky. "I might be able to spare a few of my people. In exchange, I want my warrior, Punohar, to win the chariot race."

She blinked at him. "But why?"

"Vardaan offers a boon, does he not? Perhaps I want it. Or I want the honor for my House after being shamed. Maybe I want to see the look on the king's face. I'll share that with you as soon as you tell me your real role in all of this, my lady," he said, emphasizing the title.

"I don't know why you think I can make that happen."

"You don't have to do much other than make sure your man doesn't win. My warrior will do the rest."

"My man?" she said, her heart racing faster than a thousand horses.

Mayank smiled languidly. "I'm sure you have one. Judging by your face, I'm correct."

She turned her face neutral as he chuckled. As long as he didn't know about Kunal specifically, she could handle a hundred innuendos. She swallowed a sigh, realizing that she wasn't left with much bargaining power if she wanted to see this through.

Finally, she nodded.

"Then we're agreed. I'm glad I can be of help. And thank you for the lesson." Mayank winked at her and turned to leave. He made his voice louder. "I'm feeling a bit unwell from the heat and I feel I must retire. I'm sure I'll see you at dinner tonight."

Her eyes flashed in understanding as she saw the group of Jansan noblemen who had drifted over to them, only a few paces behind them.

"Yes, of course," she demurred. "We can continue our conversation then."

With that he bowed and left, leaving her with her thoughts.

CHAPTER 29

Kunal wiped his brow, exhaustion from training getting to him. He'd tried all morning to phase, to hold on to both forms at the same time instead of one, hoping that something would click in him. He hummed his blood song again, letting the notes float around him, envelop him, picking one or two to focus in on.

Sharpened eyesight. Talons. Wings.

At least talons. Kunal squeezed his eyes shut, ignoring the beads of sweat rolling down his face. He tried again, focused harder.

"You're pushing too much," King Mahir said, from his seat to the side. He was finishing up his chai and dabbed a napkin to his lips and beard.

"Last time you said I was pushing too little."

"It's a balance," the king said. He cocked his head at Kunal. "Perhaps we should take a break."

Kunal resisted groaning. The last thing he wanted to do was take a break. At the Fort, if he struggled to master a new maneuver, he'd spend all day in the training courts until he got it. That's what his uncle had taught him—focus and discipline, until you achieved. It was a matter of breaking down the core of the move. Perhaps his footwork was wrong or his balance was off. There was always something to be fixed.

But magic training was different. There was no "correct" way to do it but, rather, the correct way for you. He almost wished someone could just tell him what to do so he could do it properly.

"All right," Kunal said. He was about to sit on the floor when King Mahir shook his head.

"Sit next to me, Kunal."

"Your Highness?"

"Uncle." That was something Kunal still hadn't gotten used to. Knowing he was royalty still unnerved him.

Kunal took the plush seat next to King Mahir, leaning against the gold-bordered back. The metal was cool against his skin. King Mahir passed him a small cookie studded with dried mango. Kunal ate it in one bite. King Mahir raised an eyebrow and passed him the entire tray.

"I forgot what it was like to be your age." He laughed. "Always hungry. In more than one way."

"Is that what you felt?"

"Oh yes. I wanted to make a name for myself during the war. I also couldn't be allowed near the mango orchards in the palace or the gardeners would find them all gone."

So that was where Esha got her love of mangoes from. Esha's childhood must have been pleasant if she had been a ward of the king. He was everything Kunal had imagined the ideal father would be. Patient yet firm, kind yet challenging, and, above all, protective.

"You must have passed that down to Esha," Kunal said.

King Mahir laughed, slapping his knee. "I'll take the blame for that. That's the only way I could get her into the training courtyard at first."

"Really?"

"She wanted to spend all her time with the dance troupes, hiding away. But I feared she'd lose herself. So, I got her into lessons with Harun and that was that. She took to the weapon master like a fish to water. After a bushel of mangoes as a bribe, that is."

Kunal smiled, thinking of a round-eyed and full-cheeked young Esha. She'd probably charmed everyone's sandals off back then too.

"I haven't had as much time with her, and Harun, recently, though."

"You've been focused on maintaining the bond, haven't you?"

"Esha told you?" the king asked. Kunal nodded. "I have."

"Is that something I, or Harun, could take over?" Kunal said hesitantly.

"No, child. I wouldn't want you to," King Mahir said.

"And the ritual requires blood from a Himyad man and a Samyad woman."

Kunal thought back to their previous conversations, a slow thread unfurling in his mind. King Mahir had mentioned earlier that the original ritual required artifacts. He had cut himself off, but Kunal could've sworn he had mentioned looking for them.

"Your Highness—"

"Uncle—"

Kunal hesitated. "Uncle, tell me more about the artifacts. The ones you've been searching for."

"What makes you think I know anything?" The king arched an eyebrow but also shifted in his seat.

"A guess." Kunal looked the king in the eye. "You said the original artifacts were once the main conduits to renew the bond, before the deal the royals struck to save the people. But now those artifacts are lost. And according to Esha, you've disappeared for long periods of time and come back tired, withdrawn."

King Mahir exhaled a deep sigh. "Yes. It's why Harun has taken over my royal duties so much, as I've gone looking for the original artifacts."

"Have you found them?"

"No, I fear we might be on our own," King Mahir said. But there was a note of dissonance to his voice.

"If we had more people looking, perhaps we—"

"Don't torture yourself, Kunal. We need our blood to do

the ritual. That's unavoidable at this point. And while I've been able to re-create some of the offerings from the original ritual, it's not an exact science. And we've long ago lost the ability to talk to the gods directly."

Kunal placed a half-bitten cookie down. "I know you've been doing something with your blood to hold the bond from breaking."

King Mahir rubbed the bridge of his nose, a gesture that looked more weary on the king than it did on the prince. "It's a temporary hold I developed with the scholars. I've been giving more and more blood, in my human and animal form. It's made me weak, yes, but I don't want you or Harun to take on the burden, because this is not a solution. It's a quick bandage—we cannot have our royals spilling their life force at increasing amounts to barely hold together the *janma* bond. Dharka cannot afford that."

"Then what?" Kunal asked. It was the one question that had been bothering him since the king had told him about the bond's history.

"Reha," he said. "My daughter. We can only hope that her blood will be the other missing half." King Mahir looked as if he was going to say more, and Kunal waited, but nothing else came from the king.

Kunal knew the king was trying to tell him that Reha was their one hope, but Kunal couldn't help but think there was more to it. All knowledge could be rediscovered, relearned. Secrets were meant to be unearthed.

He believed that. More than that, it was his duty.

King Mahir rose to his feet and indicated that Kunal should do so as well. "Let's try again. One more time for today. And remember, phasing is about balance, seeing both sides of yourself and allowing them to simply be."

Kunal nodded and walked into the center of the tiled square. He closed his eyes and, this time, he heard his animal song, wild and feral, but he heard another one too. His human song joined in, intertwining with the other to create a full picture. Freedom, strength, love, honor—and duty.

When Kunal looked down, he saw talons instead of fingers and gasped.

"Go deeper," King Mahir said, his face alight with joy. "One more step."

Kunal sank into the notes, feeling them, tasting them on his lips and skin. Wings burst from his shoulders, and he took an unsure step forward. They beat, once, twice, unsteadily as he got used to the new weight of them.

And unlike every time before, Kunal felt no pain, only a sense of completeness.

Of being whole.

———◄◦►———

The bazaar was a nice change of pace from the walls of the palace. Esha felt as if she could breathe more freely. She'd decided to put everything out of her mind for a few hours and go shopping for the Victor's Ball with Yamini, who had requested her help. They had been spending more time together at the nobles' parties, and Esha enjoyed the Yavar heir's company.

It was odd being back in a bazaar, the labyrinth of stalls calling to mind her escapades with Kunal only a few moons ago. The situation was more dire, though. There was no soldier after her, but everywhere she turned she heard whispers of more deaths as the river faded up north. Riots, as well. It only confirmed their course of action to secure Reha.

Esha picked up a delicately crafted pair of bangles, two snakes intertwined together, their tongues making up the clasp. She looked up, ready to haggle with the seller in the bazaar, when she saw Yamini puzzling over a necklace, a finger to her lips.

"Having trouble, Yamini?"

"I hate shopping," she said, making a face. "I wear whatever my lady's maid picks."

"I'm sure she loves that," Esha said, laughing. She walked over to where Yamini stood, picking out a few necklaces that would match her coloring.

"Gold, for your complexion. No silver. Ever." Yamini looked like she wanted to ask a question but nodded instead. "What color do you want your sari to be?"

"Blue?"

Esha tried not to smack her hand against her forehead. "Which type of blue?"

"Does it really matter which type of blue?" Yamini asked, bewildered.

"Have you truly never picked out any of your clothes or jewelry before?" Esha asked. She was rather astonished, but she supposed being the heir presumptive meant a life of not having to make decisions if she didn't want to.

"No," Yamini said. "Not that I couldn't, I just never cared. And I worried that if I acted like I was interested in such things, then the men wouldn't take me seriously. My father wouldn't take me seriously."

There was something so refreshingly open in Yamini's honesty that Esha couldn't help but respond.

"I was the opposite way," Esha said. "I used beauty and clothing as my armor. If they thought I was just a girl, then I'd be just a girl. But then they'd never see me coming."

Yamini cocked her head, considering her words.

"I like that. Not sure I could pull that off, but . . ."

"Nonsense, fashion is for everyone."

They made their way over to a new stall, and Esha picked out some more jewelry for Yamini.

"My mother loved all of this," Yamini said.

"Your mother. She passed into the Lord of Darkness's realm," Esha asked softly.

"Years ago," Yamini said. "Her favorite color was cerulean. That's a type of blue, right?"

Esha nodded, her throat suddenly choked with emotion. Another death, another loss that had shaped a young girl.

Yamini and Esha weren't so different. None of them were.

"Then you'll be wearing cerulean in two nights at the Victor's Ball."

————◄◦►————

Kunal rose amid the clouds, wheeling through and toppling down, letting his wings carry him along the currents of air.

The wind that night was calm, as if the moon had stilled the whole night sky with its milky splendor.

Kunal wanted to stay there, revel in the feeling, but knew he had to get to the king's office as soon as he could. The sooner he got the report Laksh wanted, the sooner he could be done with it all.

He abandoned the cloud he was breezing through, diving down to catch a lower air stream that carried him silently over the palace courtyard. The people below looked like specks of dust now, mere dots on a canvas.

Kunal flew close to the open window near the office, beating his wings as he came to a stop. There was no one inside, and he nudged the curtain open with the edge of his wing. He tumbled inside, shifting into his human form.

Kunal caught himself as he fell, bracing his weight, and any potential sound, with his hands. He winced and rolled over, clutching at his wrists and shaking them out.

He shook his head and moved toward the desk, crossing the distance in two strides. Instead of rummaging through, Kunal tried to concentrate, thinking back to his own uncle's room. Where had he kept recent reports? Sealed ones would have been left in his desk, unsealed ones would have been read and burned or hidden away.

There was no second compartment on the underside of the desk, no other hidden area in the office. Kunal could only pray to the Sun Maiden that Vardaan hadn't gotten so suspicious as to take things out of his office.

Kunal tugged open the desk drawer, rifling through old

scrolls for anything sealed. Everything here was notes, scraps of paper in old Jansan or another dialect Kunal couldn't transcribe. Biting back a growl of frustration, Kunal moved to the bookcases that lined the office, tapping gently for any hollow sound.

He tapped the entire wall to no avail. His luck had run dry.

Kunal dug his thumbs into his temples, sharpening his senses in the hope that it'd help, though he didn't know how. Maybe the mistake was in thinking like his uncle. Vardaan and his uncle had been close friends, but in the end, they weren't as similar as Kunal had thought. That he had seen firsthand.

There was an arrogance to Vardaan, cultivated to mask a cunning that he didn't want people to notice. As if he were hiding in plain sight.

Kunal dove back to the desk, rummaging through the stacks of papers on its surface. An administrative map was laid across the top, what looked like a book of figures under it. Kunal picked up the stack only to realize it was a small box cut in the form of a thick book.

It was hollow. Kunal quickly undid the lock and opened the box to reveal a carved-out inside in which the report was tucked, among many others. Kunal tugged out the replica scroll he had brought and quickly changed it for the real report. He noticed the other reports in the box and his heart skipped a beat as he considered all the information that could be in them. Kunal sorted through the scrolls, looking for anything that grabbed his attention.

Taxes, taxes, bargaining with the merchants over a grain shortage, reports from the Senaps, an illegible note in a different dialect with symbols, more taxes. Kunal doubled back, picking out one of the reports from the captain and the letter with that symbol.

It was hard to decipher, a mix of ancient Jansan and Dharkan. Whoever had written this report had taken the time to translate the contents into something almost indecipherable. The symbol on the seal caught his eye. He could've sworn he'd seen it before.

Kunal tucked the information away for later as his sharpened senses picked up footsteps two rooms away. He could wait to see if they'd turn in this direction, or he could call it a night. He had the report, didn't he?

It would have to suffice for now.

Something caught his eye out in the courtyard, and Kunal stepped closer to the railing, looking down below. A dark figure moved in the gardens, weaving through the intricate paths. Only his keen eyesight allowed him to narrow in, focus on the way the figure moved, and recognize the shape of her body.

Esha.

Kunal was getting tired of running after her.

CHAPTER 30

Esha crept through the outer gardens of the palace, darting behind shadows as she trailed the Senap out of the gates.

Since the king's reveal of the fake Reha, security had been tightened. He greeted another pair of Senaps, and Esha took the opportunity to vault herself over the gate, sliding down the walls.

From there she ran along the street edges until she arrived at the location she had gotten from her contact. She would have to do things the hard way after her failed attempt to draw the Falcon Squad out at the citadel. No playing around, no games.

This would end tonight at the ceremony. She'd have her justice.

The Falcon Squad would be exiting this building before

they traveled with the Senap squadron to the medal ceremony. She turned and ran in the opposite direction until she came to an alleyway.

Esha clambered up the side of a sweets shop, inhaling the smells of pistachio and cashew, dates and jaggery, trying not to let her hunger get to her. She sped over the rooftops, crossing from the merchants' quarter into the thieves' and then on to the martial, tracing a circuitous path so she couldn't be followed this time.

Finally, she reached her destination and crouched down low over the rooftop, wrapping the end of her uttariya fully around her face so only her eyes could be seen.

Then Esha drew out a smaller bow, one that was specially made for long-distance shots, and notched a short, poison-tipped arrow.

———◁◦▷———

Kunal ran through the streets leading between the palace and the citadel, knowing that Esha wouldn't go down one of the main ones. But which one?

Crowds of people were going in the opposite direction toward the medal ceremony. He cursed himself. Of course she would come here, choose tonight, the night her parents' murderers were being honored for the Mela.

He closed his eyes and sorted through all the various noises that surrounded him, as King Mahir had taught him, until he heard one that didn't fit.

The crack of a bow being pulled back, a crossbow by the

sound of it. Not a weapon any of the Senaps would be using.

Sun Maiden's spear. If Esha was embodying the Viper tonight and he arrived too late, someone would surely be dead. And if the Senaps found her again, not only would she be in mortal danger, but the entire peace treaty could be tossed aside. The Mela potentially canceled and the citadel shut down. Their mission ended before it even had a chance.

It hadn't taken him long to figure out more about the squad of men Esha had been trailing the night at the citadel. And from there Kunal had slowly pieced it together with all he knew. There was only one thing that would make Esha endanger everything she was working for, that the team was working for.

Her revenge.

Kunal thought back to what Harun had said about Esha in Gwali and her need for revenge. That it was the only thing that would fill the hole in her heart.

Was it even his place to stop her?

But he knew the darkness of something like that would spread. It'd be a stain, a killing unlike the others. No matter the tales, she had said that the Viper didn't kill for fun.

But who was he to tell her how to mourn?

Kunal turned the corner of the street and clambered up the building side once he saw her on the rooftop, clad in inky black. He landed on the roof and she turned to face him, only her chestnut eyes apparent through the misty moonlight.

"Kunal," she said quietly.

Kunal stepped forward. "How do you keep escaping?" he asked lightly, his voice barely above a whisper.

His attempt at humor didn't do much to change Esha's murderous expression.

"My lady's maid. She thinks I have a secret lover."

Kunal shifted tactics. "What are you planning to do, Esha?" He stepped forward, and she still didn't move a muscle. "Do you even know which soldier did it yet?"

"No, but I'll figure it out. I could kill them all. It's not as if they're innocent," she said.

"Five soldiers? Just like that?"

"I've done worse, Kunal." The way she said it chilled him. Her face was blank, lost in memories, and she was pure Viper. He couldn't see a hint of Esha.

"And endanger everyone? The team? Harun?"

"Of course not," she said, her eyes flickering in outrage. Esha pulled out a horse brand, one that looked like a Scales, tossing it between her hands. "I thought it might come in handy."

"You're going to frame them?"

"No worse than what they did to me."

"Yes," he conceded. "But you are better than them."

"It's not as if I had been planning it since the beginning," she snapped.

"What if someone innocent dies?" He drew closer, taking a measured step toward her.

Esha gave him a look, like no soldier could be innocent, and his face flushed. "Collateral damage." But he saw her grip on the bow loosen.

"Esha . . ." Kunal's ears caught the sound of a door cracking open and he shifted, walking over to the edge of the rooftop. If he distracted her long enough, the Falcon Squad would pass and there'd be no danger.

He glanced down, sharpening his eyesight to make sure none of the Senaps surrounding the squad had noticed anything amiss.

That was when he caught sight of a familiar face on the squad. Could it—

No.

Kunal didn't have time to register the new information because Esha stepped forward, poised, her bow at the ready.

"I'm the Viper. I was forged in the rage and grief of seeing my parents murdered in front of my eyes. And you want me to forgive? That soldier has haunted me for ten years. Even now, I dream of his face in that helmet. Those owl eyes and smirking grin. Never."

———◇———

Esha expected a lecture, harsh words, disapproving eyes, but Kunal had none of that in his expression. His face was open, the understanding in it painful to see.

"I can never forgive." She kept her bow raised. If she dropped it, it would all be over. She would have failed.

"We all deserve mercy. You forgave me," he said quietly.

"You didn't murder my parents, my unborn sister. You didn't strip my life away with two careless swipes of your blade."

"I've killed someone's son. You've killed someone's son. Is it necessary to keep this cycle going, Esha?" She tried to look away, but he strode up to her, cupping her face and forcing her to look at him. "End the cycle."

His eyes were as soft as the moon's caress, coaxing her to believe him. That there could be peace in forgiveness.

There had certainly been no peace in her anger.

"And he gets away? No justice for his crime?"

"Justice is an unsteady thing. It won't return your parents. It won't take away the pain you've endured. But you are more than your revenge," he said.

She pulled away. "You don't know me that well, Kunal. I am not more than revenge. I am not more than this aching, gaping hole in my heart that this *soldier* left."

"What then? Will you take your revenge at the expense of our mission, your country's peace and security? Or are you becoming your own nightmare?" She said nothing and he kept going, his voice deepening. "Is this who you want to be? Or do you simply not have the courage to be better?"

Every word was a slap.

"You chose this pain, and you can choose to let it go," he said, reaching for her.

"It's not so easy for some of us to forget our pasts and abandon who we are."

"And who are you, Esha?"

She was the Viper. An orphan.

Or that's what she would've said. But these past months with Kunal had shown her a glimpse of something more, something complex and whole and *dangerous*.

Hope.

And it was terrifying because the moment she reached for that hope was the moment she had to stop living in the past and had to face the future.

Who did she *want* to be?

Her grip on the bow faltered and Kunal caught it before it clattered to the roof tiles.

"This doesn't mean I'm going to suddenly forget what happened," she said shakily.

Kunal brushed a lock of hair from her forehead. "I never thought that. Your family is as much of you as your heart is."

Esha rose to her feet. Maybe she'd change her mind—maybe she wouldn't. Esha didn't know. All she knew was that Kunal's words had struck a chord inside her chest.

"You're right," Esha said softly.

"Can I get that in writing?" Kunal said.

Esha ignored him, her heart still pounding with adrenaline. "This was a reckless attempt. Unfitting for the leader of the Blades. Next time I'll plan better."

"Esha."

"I'm not going to go after him. Not tonight, at least."

They stood there for a long moment, one stretched as

far as the sea in the distance, simply staring at each other. Finally, Kunal nodded and turned around, but not before holding a hand out to her.

She stepped forward and took it, letting him lead her away from the rooftop, the barracks, and her revenge.

Kunal was saying she had a choice, that she could be the Viper or Esha.

The question was, who was she?

CHAPTER 31

Esha entered the small closet of a room, slipping in and shutting the door behind her. She turned around and nearly jumped out of her skin.

Kunal was lounging against one of the shelves, staring down at the floor as he did his magical exercises. His eyes were flashing between amber and yellow, his body rising and falling in a steady rhythm.

He looked up at her and a moment of hesitation passed between them, mirrored in each other's eyes. She glanced at his lips, the soft curve of them, and the set jaw underneath. His eyes were warm on hers as he took up the space between them.

"How are you?"

"I'm alive. No Senaps have discovered our plan and the mission is still on," she said with false cheer. Last night might have been her only chance at finding her parents' murderers and bringing them to justice. Even if she got their names after this Mela, they would disperse across Jansa and she'd have no reason to go after them.

No reason that wasn't utterly selfish.

And she didn't want to wallow in her own grief, allowing the past to steer her into the future. She didn't and yet . . . the choice wasn't easy.

Kunal saw right through her attempt at positivity. He reached across to her, but she pulled away as the door creaked open and Aahal's and Farhan's heads poked around the side.

"Did we interrupt something?" Aahal asked as he slid in, sounding gleeful at the idea.

Esha glanced at Kunal. "Not at all."

"Good, because the others are right behind us," Farhan said.

Bhandu made a face as he squeezed in behind Aahal. Harun and Arpiya entered the room next, their heads bowed together, breaking apart as they took spots on opposite sides.

"Let's get started. We don't have much time," Harun said. "You said you had updates?"

"Exit plan is set," Arpiya said, tossing her short hair back.

"And we've made some new friends down in the servants' area," Aahal said, shooting a look at his brother. "The night of the Victor's Ball will be perfect with everyone else distracted."

Bhandu moved forward, placing a scroll on the table.

"The names of the squad that will be on duty that night for the lower level in the citadel."

Kunal moved toward the scrolls. "That's great work, Bhandu. I'd been trying to get that information for days."

"Did you ever try bribing them?" Arpiya asked, raising an eyebrow. "I'm pretty sure that's how Bhandu got it."

"Close. I won it in a round of dice," he said, grinning. Kunal looked appalled.

Esha's focus shifted to Harun as he read through the scrolls. There were hollows in his face that hadn't been there weeks ago, a tension in his body that hadn't left since he'd entered the Pink Palace.

"This is a great start. Before we review our mission plan, does anyone have any concerns?" Esha asked, crossing her arms.

"No. I do have a question, though," Kunal said. "What's the plan after the rescue? We get Reha, and then what?"

Esha frowned, unsure why Kunal was bringing this up now. She'd hinted as much as she could to him already.

"We're planning on rescuing my sister, overthrowing Vardaan, and setting the real Reha on the throne," Harun responded.

"And that's it?"

"That not enough for you?"

"It's enough for me," Bhandu said from the back.

"And how are you planning on doing this?" Kunal asked.

"Don't concern yourself with it, soldier," Harun said.

"We have it under control."

Esha bit her lip, unsure whether to interject. She knew Harun was trying to protect his team, but for Kunal, who was tied to his duty and honor, it wouldn't be a soothing answer.

"I want to help—"

"Kunal, we'll pull you in when—" Esha cut in.

"This is my land," Kunal said, ferocity in his voice. "I've become the Archer, I've won the competitions, I've killed a man for this mission—I deserve to know. Do you think I can stand idly by while you decide the fate of it?"

Esha felt her face flush. It was as if he didn't trust them—didn't trust her. But she also hadn't realized how much being in the Mela as the Archer was weighing on him. It made her reassess his ability to be on this mission. Would he do what needed to be done?

"No," Harun said, stepping forward. "I don't. You're a royal, and you want to protect your land. I can understand that, admire it, even. But there are things going on beyond what you know, and we need to focus on the rescue first, as a team. If you want to be a part of this team, then you'll have to follow what we say."

A war raged across Kunal's face.

"Fine," he said tersely.

Esha found herself releasing a breath. Kunal was an instrumental part of their team now—an unofficial Blade, whether he liked it or not.

She ignored the voice inside her that whispered that her feelings for him might be blinding her, that he was still a soldier.

That bronze would always shine through.

———◇———

Kunal waited for her as everyone straggled out of the meeting room. Esha waved Harun ahead when she spotted Kunal.

She stood in front of him, raising an eyebrow. "Spit it out, soldier."

He cleared his throat. "Are you going to tell me what the plan is after we break Reha out?"

That wasn't what she had expected. A comment on how much time she was spending with Harun, maybe. "We introduce her as the real princess," she said. "The people will see reason."

"Will they? You're planning on taking the throne," Kunal said, his expression hardening. "You withheld the information from me before. I was looking for you during the musical contest and I heard what King Mahir said."

"I didn't withhold. It was a need-to-know—"

"And I didn't need to know?"

"No," she said. "The squad needs to focus on getting Reha out. Only Harun and I can gather support—"

"Oh, only you and Harun?"

"What's that supposed to mean?" She lifted her chin to stare him in the eye. Kunal exhaled sharply.

"It doesn't matter," he said. "I should've been read in on this. I'm not like the rest of the squad."

"No, you're definitely not. You forget, Kunal, that I'm the leader of the Blades. I don't owe my every decision to the team. My job is to lead and protect them."

"I'm not a Blade," he said emphatically.

She stepped back. "You don't need to say it with such spite."

"I'm not saying it with spite. I'm trying to get my point across. Which is that you should've trusted me. I shepherded nobles around for a day. I could've bent the ear of any one of them, if you'd only mentioned it to me."

"You'd hate doing what I do." She laughed. "You've told me that."

Kunal looked mulish. "Perhaps, but you shouldn't have hid it from me. I'm not going to take orders and not ask questions. How many men have you gathered?"

"I can't say," Esha said. "And I'm not ordering you around, Kunal. What is this really about?"

"It's about what I'm saying," he said. Despite his words, Esha had a feeling this wasn't about Kunal not knowing how many weapons or troops they had amassed in support. He was expecting her to treat him differently, which wasn't fair. He couldn't have it both ways.

"And what about you? Arpiya mentioned you let someone into the palace last week, someone she didn't recognize. And you directly disobeyed us during the archery tournament. You were reckless."

"We weren't supposed to have secrets between us," he hissed. "Yet I found you climbing out of a second-story window. You want to talk about being reckless? Have you told your prince about that?"

Esha bunched her fingers into a fist by her side. "I don't appreciate the way you said 'your prince.'"

"He is, isn't he?"

"He's my friend—"

Kunal made a disbelieving noise.

Esha strode forward and poked him in the chest. He grabbed on to her wrist and pulled her close, feeling her anger like waves of heat off her.

"You have yet to even say how you feel about me. You don't get to—"

"I haven't said how I feel?" Kunal's voice dropped to a dangerously low whisper. "Why would I be here, trying to argue with you for your trust—"

"Why did you even join us? You don't want to be a Blade, but that's what we are," she said, her voice becoming tight.

———◁◦▷———

Kunal growled in frustration. How could she not see how much he wanted, cared for her? She couldn't—or wouldn't—see that, yet she gave Harun passes.

"Well, maybe joining was a mistake."

Esha looked as if she had been slapped. A moment of silence stretched between them.

367

"If that's how you really feel—"

Kunal let out a frustrated sigh, reaching for her. "No. It's not that simple."

"It is, Kunal."

"No, it's not."

She turned to leave and he went after her, grabbing her wrist.

"Esha, don't leave. I'm sorry. I'm sorry."

She stopped at his words, turning back to him. Her face was a mask of hurt and anger and frustration.

"You don't get to say that," she said.

"I meant that this hasn't turned out the way I had thought—"

"What, that you're having to take orders from me? A woman?"

Kunal did a double take. That was the last thing he meant.

"No."

He hadn't meant that the mistake was in following her, not for a minute. But rather that he wanted to be in that inner circle and part of him worried he never would be. Especially after seeing her and Harun together, plotting out the rescue of Harun's long-lost sister.

Where did Kunal fit in that story?

He wanted to be the hero, but he felt lost in this world of politics and alliances. He felt like a soldier of old, clinging to his duty to protect, his desire to change the world.

"I wouldn't ever think something so stupid. You are

the smartest, fiercest— How could you think—" Kunal unleashed a sigh of frustration and pulled her into a kiss.

She kissed him back, channeling her anger into the kiss, shoving him against the wall. He pulled her closer to him, so close he felt her breath on his eyelashes as he kissed her neck. They broke apart minutes later, both their breaths coming in rough. Esha pulled back to look him in the eye, her voice heavy.

"This hasn't turned out the way any of us thought. It was supposed to be much simpler. We were supposed to have time." Her voice became insistent even in its softness. "That's all. I've been spending every moment with the nobles trying to find alliances. But I'm not in a position to tell you everything. Ultimately, that's Harun and King Mahir's decision. You have to trust us—trust me."

Kunal leaned his forehead against hers, closing his eyes. That was the problem, wasn't it? He trusted her, but he didn't know if he trusted the Blades. Or the Scales. Or the prince. Or Dharmdev. And he was sick of sitting back, taking orders, and being the good soldier. He wanted to make his own choices.

"I trust you, Esha. But don't keep things from me again," he said. "I want to help and be of use. How can I do that if I don't know what we're up against?"

"As if you don't have secrets, soldier?" It was clear from her expression that she was teasing, but Kunal froze. He had become a hypocrite.

He had reams of secrets now, ones that might have been

used directly against the Scales. He was the scum on the bottom of a sandal and he'd never forgive himself for lying to her about Laksh.

But the alternative was worse, wasn't it?

If Laksh told anyone he knew the identity of the Viper, Esha would be in danger. She was still wanted for the general's murder. For a moment, he wanted to reveal everything to her, unburden himself.

But he was carrying the burden so she could remain safe.

If anything happened to her . . .

"I do have secrets," he said, his voice turning serious. "I never told you I'm not a huge fan of mangoes."

Esha gasped. "Liar. You ate two of them when I wasn't looking in the jungle."

He grinned, pulling her close to nuzzle into her hair, whispering into her ear, "You caught me."

With a heavy sigh she pulled away and held him at arm's length.

"I won't hold back anything else from you. It's my natural instinct as the leader of the Blades, you have to understand. Presenting disparate pieces of information to the team can be confusing. I like to come in with a plan. Otherwise, I put the burden of leadership on all of them."

"I understand that." And he truly did. It was easy for him to forget all that she did, that she had done, at this age. Leading a team of rebels, ones who would lay down their lives for her—that was no easy feat. "I saw the burden of leadership at the Fort."

"You were fine with not knowing everything before. What changed in the last few weeks?"

Kunal felt himself stiffen. He hadn't wanted it, but his time with Laksh had opened his eyes up, for good and for bad.

"Nothing. You don't like that I'm starting to get opinions of my own," he said drily, masking the roil of emotions in his belly.

"No, I quite like this new fiery side of you," she said, pulling his face down to hers.

Kunal sighed. "Esha, you can't solve everything with a kiss."

"No?"

Her eyes twinkled, and the corners of his own mouth turned up, unable to resist her charm.

Kunal's smile masked his thoughts, the certainty with which he felt that there was now a crack in their relationship. Lies and mistrust and suspicion. Esha believed it could be mended with a kiss.

He hoped she was right.

CHAPTER 32

This time when Laksh found him, Kunal didn't even bother to act surprised.

Kunal was on patrol in the bankers' quarter near the citadel, near the squat buildings and tall homes that bordered the merchants' quarter, lively at all times of night and day. It was there that Laksh showed up, appearing from the shadows of an alleyway.

"Hello, Laksh," Kunal said. He didn't bother to look up and continued polishing his spear. He was taking a moment of rest to sand off a small nick he had found on the underside.

"Still as fastidious as ever," Laksh said in greeting. "You put everyone to shame at the Fort. The weapons master never gave us full marks after looking at yours."

"Perhaps you didn't deserve them."

"We probably didn't. But come on, it didn't help the 'perfect Kunal' image."

Was that why he was here now? To make him feel bad for a previous life? If this was all a way to take Kunal down a few pegs, Laksh needn't have bothered.

"No need for that stare of yours. I was just . . . reminiscing. I'm allowed to do that, aren't I?" There was something honest in Laksh's defensiveness, enough to make Kunal look up at his old friend and put aside his spear.

"I'm not the one ordering you around."

"Is that how you see this? I view it more as a partnership, so to speak," Laksh said. "How was the musical competition?"

"Delightful. I enjoyed the milk sweets, thought the saffron rice was quite delicious as well." Kunal couldn't help the slight smile on his face as Laksh frowned.

"I'm glad to hear it. There wasn't anything else interesting?"

"They did have a new dish, made with fermented goat's milk. Perhaps to honor the Yavar. It was an interesting choice."

"Indeed." Laksh's lips pursed. "And your digestion wasn't impacted at all by the announcement that the princess Reha is alive and marrying our dear general Panak?"

Kunal hid a grin, feeling a thrill at having been the one to force Laksh into speaking plainly. It was a small victory, but enough for Kunal.

"It would have been if I believed it to truly be her," he said, taking a gamble to gauge Laksh's reaction.

"Do you have proof it's not?"

"If I did, would I be here?"

They stared at each other for a moment.

"I'm sure it's not her," Kunal said finally.

"I'm not surprised," Laksh said. "That Vardaan would do this."

Kunal had expected a bit more of a reaction, but it was always hard to tell with Laksh. He may have already heard the rumors. Half the city was speaking the same words.

Laksh leaned forward. "And if she's still out there, we still have a chance for the land. Don't we?"

Kunal shrugged. He was willing to tease out the Reha information to see what else Laksh knew, but he'd not betray the Blades' plans.

Especially when they both knew the truth.

But Laksh's first words had been about the people, the land. And it brought back all the frustration and helplessness of talking to Esha and the team earlier. He still believed they'd do better working together, the Blades and the Scales. But both sides were too keen on their own plans, whether it be rescuing Reha or whatever was up Laksh's sleeve.

"You know the answer to that. But I will say this. The land and our people are the most important, always. So, if you know of anything—" Kunal cut himself off before he could say anything else, wary of edging into betrayal.

Laksh tried to hide the momentary satisfaction on his face, but Kunal caught it, tucked it away for analysis later.

"I'm pleased you were able to get the report. Did you read it?"

"No," Kunal said, though he wondered why he hadn't. He tugged it out of his waist sash and handed it to Laksh. "I want no part in your schemes."

"Bit late for that. Are you ready to win the chariot race— the Mela? This will decide it all, won't it?"

"For you, you mean?" Kunal said.

"For you as well, Kunal," Laksh replied. "It's a simple thing, isn't it? You use your already formidable skills as a soldier and mix in a bit of that supernatural power you have. It should be easy for you," Laksh said.

"It's not the difficulty I'm concerned with. Why do you want me to win?"

"I already told you," Laksh said.

And he had, but something told Kunal there was more to it. The king's boon, the report, sneaking into the palace. What did it all mean? And what had he inadvertently done?

"I'm not an idiot, Laksh. I know there's something you're not telling me. It doesn't make sense."

"There's nothing else," Laksh said. No evasion or mocking tone. But his fingers twitched, rubbing together under his uttariya. His tell during cards.

Kunal realized Laksh was nervous that he might still say no. Hadn't Esha once told him that he always had a choice? So then why was he still listening to others blindly? He still took orders like a soldier.

For once, the thought unsettled him. He wanted to be a man of honor and action.

Finally, Kunal nodded, and Laksh relaxed a bit.

"Fine. I'll see the competition through till the end, and then? We'll be done."

Laksh raised an eyebrow but nodded. "Do this for me, finish this out and get me the king's boon, and then yes. We'll be done."

Laksh held out his hand and Kunal grabbed it, but he held him there.

"I'll do it. But I have a request," Kunal said, holding Laksh's hand in limbo.

"And what's that?"

"Take me to your next Scales meeting," Kunal said.

Laksh smiled, broad and wide.

———◆◇◆———

There was a brief break in the crush of people, and Kunal darted across the gap, slipping his way through the crowds and taking a shortcut to the stadium locker room before the start of the chariot race. He got there as the first conch blew, sweaty and frustrated.

He looked both ways before sneaking into the corridor that led to the outer hallway, where the audience sat. A glance up told him the pathway to the upper boxes of the arena were guarded—he noted who was on patrol.

Kunal found Esha a few minutes later, seated in a side box that was out of use. The outer window was covered, but they could still hear the shouts and cheers of the audience outside, readying themselves for the last, and most violent, competition of the Mela.

She was peeking around the window covering, searching for something.

Kunal cleared his throat.

———◄◌►———

Esha sat up instantly and then relaxed.

"Hello," Kunal said in greeting, closing the curtains behind him.

"Hi."

She could already notice it, the tenor of their greeting this morning, as if something were different between them. Strained since their last conversation.

"Did you sleep well?"

"It could've been better," she said.

Kunal's mouth curved downward. "And I'm the cause."

"Yes," she said. Esha felt herself freeze up as soon as she admitted it, her Viper mask returning. "Though I would've slept better if you were there."

Kunal raised an eyebrow. "You're doing it again. Didn't I say you can't solve everything with a kiss?"

"I haven't kissed you."

"It's the same thing."

Esha huffed. "It most surely isn't. If you think a bit of flirting is the same as a good kiss, I'm not sure I can help you. By the way, was I your first kiss?"

"Esha."

"If not, tell me her name, and I'll find her. No killing, I promise."

"Esha."

"What?" she said.

She felt everything careering toward a disaster she couldn't control, and as the Viper, that meant she typically used her whips, but here? Now? She didn't know what to say to Kunal.

"Stop. You don't need to pretend," he said, sighing. "We fought. It's all right. You don't have to act like it didn't happen."

There were still unspoken words that needed to be said. It was clear from Kunal's face that he had slept as poorly, if not worse, than her.

"I'm not," she said. He gave her a disbelieving look. "Fine, Kunal. What do you want me to say? I'm still angry and hurt over what you said. I'm not good at forgiveness, like you. There. I'm horrible and selfish. Are you happy now?"

Her breath heaved as she finished. Would he turn away?

———◄◊►———

"No," he said. "I didn't come here to make things worse between us."

There was silence between the two of them.

"You look very official," she said first.

"It's the armor."

"I've seen you in armor before, soldier."

She stood up, approaching him slowly. Kunal didn't move, treating her like a jungle cat he didn't want to spook. Esha came up to him and ran a finger down his armor, her expression inscrutable.

He was about to say something, apologize, but Esha jumped up on her tiptoes and brushed a kiss against his lips. He kissed her back, letting his hands curl into her hair. At least this was familiar.

"How are you feeling about today?" Esha asked.

"I don't know," he said, shaking his head. He couldn't tell her about Laksh, that he suspected something was going to happen but he didn't know what or when.

"It's nerves. But everything is set for today, for the race and the Victor's Ball. You have nothing to worry about."

But that was the thing. He did. She just didn't know. And he couldn't stop worrying, because this wasn't simply a mission to him. This was what he risked his entire future for—this was the future of his land. He couldn't leave that up to chance.

"I do have something to tell you, a request for today's event. Don't win the race," she said, something urgent in her eyes. "That's why I asked you to come here before the event."

"And why's that?" Kunal asked, thinking of Laksh's order. And here he was, receiving another one.

Esha paused, biting her lip. "You asked for the truth, didn't you? We're building a potential alliance, and for that to be successful, I need you to step back. Let House Pramukh's man win." Esha held up a hand before Kunal could say anything. "Do not sabotage the others. All you need to do is finish alive," she said. "Which, given the past nature of these races, might be harder than you think."

Kunal chuckled. "I've been watching chariot races since I was a child. You forget I'm trained for this."

"You are? I thought only the charioteers were."

"Senap training covers all four branches. And I had a particular interest in it, so I'd sneak out to watch the charioteers practice."

"You? Sneaking somewhere?" she said, her eyebrow rising. "I'm shocked, Kunal."

"I wasn't all boring."

"You're not boring at all, lemon boy."

"And the mission?"

"Everything's the same. Whether you win or lose, we'll still have tonight to make our move. The champions won't be moved out of the citadel until tomorrow, and by then, we'll be long gone." She pushed at him, stepping away. "Stay alive. I won't be pleased if you don't."

Kunal gave a strained laugh, forcing himself to focus on the new problem at hand—did he do what Laksh wanted or what Esha asked? And what did he ultimately want?

He hadn't asked himself that question in so long, not since the moment Laksh had escaped in the jungle, when everything had changed.

Esha tilted her head, a smile breaking out on her face. "Have I told you how glad I am that you're here? This mission . . . it's different."

"I'm glad to be here." His mouth softened as he remembered everything that had brought them here. "I would've never had the opportunity if I hadn't met you. Esha. . . ."

"Yes?"

"I know you told me to be careful, but the same applies to you. Don't do anything rash." It was all he said for a beat, but she understood.

Don't go off alone again.

"I might not agree with you on getting justice, Kunal, but I won't endanger the mission again. I promise."

"It's not that. If something happened to you . . . I don't know what I'd do. And tonight will be dangerous, until we've rescued her."

"Don't be ridiculous. You'd probably be better off. Find a pretty girl, settle down somewhere boring, have beautiful kids and paint them all," she said, though her face belied the flippant words.

"If I had any choice, I'd never spend a moment away from you. Not now and not . . . It would have to be the world ending to take me away from you," he said.

"Let's pray it never ends," she whispered, no longer trying to hide the emotion on her face. "Once this is all over . . ."

"Once we can be in the same room and actually speak . . ."

"Once we tell the team . . ." She winced as she said it.

"Gods, that will be interesting to see."

"Everyone's going to be so happy when I reveal I've been lying about my feelings for months."

Kunal stilled, looking up at her. "And what might those be? Those feelings."

"If something happened to you, I don't know what I'd

do," she said, repeating his words softly.

He wanted to say something, capture the fledgling feeling between them in a few poignant words. But they stuck in his throat, unable to come to life.

"Now go, before they disqualify you for not showing up during warm-ups."

She sent him one last quick glance before turning the corner, leaving him alone with his muddled thoughts. Kunal took a deep breath, stilling his center as King Mahir had taught him. Every word Esha had said made sense, yet he couldn't shake his frustration and restlessness.

He jogged back into the training room and slid past the guard who was distractedly looking out into the arena.

Kunal craned his neck around to catch what the guard was looking at—the impostor Reha standing in the center of the stadium.

CHAPTER 33

Esha hurried back, lifting up the skirts of her sari to run faster through the corridors that wound up to the box seats. Being late wasn't typically suspicious, but she didn't want to draw any attention today.

She got to the open-air level of the arena, slowing her steps down to something appropriately ladylike, when she heard it.

A girlish voice down below.

Esha looked over to see the fake Reha in the center of the arena, giving a speech of some sort. She was too far up to hear Reha's words clearly, but the arena was silent.

Esha smiled, the audience's silence an indication that some of their plan had begun to work. The people of Gwali were naturally suspicious after years of rule under Vardaan. It hadn't been too difficult to stoke that fire, even in the few days they had.

A low hiss started in the crowd, one that grew and crescendoed into a wave of jeers that made the impostor princess stutter and look up. To her credit, she continued on, rushing through the end of her speech even as the boos increased and other citizens became emboldened.

She almost ran off the stage at the end of her speech, and it took the announcer the better part of ten minutes to calm the crowd.

Esha signaled to a waiter, grabbing a goblet off the silver platter he was carrying. She raised the chilled buttermilk to her lips and looked over to where Lord Mayank sat across the way. He lifted his glass ever so slightly in her direction.

Their alliance was off to a good start.

———◄◊►———

The cheers of the crowd were deafening, echoing through the open arena, surrounding them all.

One of Chand's horses whinnied and he reached forward, a worried look on his face. The other competitors fared better, wearing varying degrees of apprehension or arrogance on their faces.

Kunal rubbed his hand against one of his horses' necks, calming it down as he attached the reins to its back. He whispered into the horse's ear, trying to find their connection and tug on it. The stallion blew air out of its nose and shook its mane, turning to stare at Kunal. Kunal stared back, blinking only once.

A stallion like this needed to be shown dominance and be able to work with the others. That was the hardest part about chariot racing—keeping the horses in tune and working together.

The sun beat down on the arena floor, creating pockets of blinding light. Kunal would have to avoid those spots if he wanted to keep a strong rein on his chariot. However, he *could* maneuver the other charioteers into it.

While he was against dirty tricks, he wasn't against smart play. But should he win or lose?

Either option left him with a taste in his mouth that reminded him of the Fort.

Esha didn't trust him. Laksh sought to use him.

He bit down on his cheek, thinking hard and fast.

The conch shell blew, a warning before the thrice-blown conch that would signal the opening of the gates and the start of the race.

Kunal jumped into the chariot, securing the ropes and wrapping them around his forearms. It was a trick his uncle had taught him, a way to more naturally feel the way the horses moved and to move with them.

That would be the key, anticipating the horses' movements.

That would also be where Kunal would have an advantage. He closed his eyes for a second, feeling the rush in his blood, the feeling of fire in his veins. His body inched toward shifting, but he pulled back, only calling on his sharpened sight and ability to sense.

"Good luck," Chand said. "Hope to see us both alive at the end of this."

The conch blew three times and Kunal barely had time to thank Chand before Chand pulled at his reins and was off, flying down the circumference of the arena. Special barricades had been put up in the center and on the sides.

Kunal flew after him, holding tight on to his reins as they took the first lap. This would be the calm lap, the one where they assessed their opponents and determined who to take out. Kunal came out of the gate fast, as did Chand and another, but as they approached the corner, he pulled back.

He'd let them fight it out first, giving his horses the chance to get their bearings.

It was a good move. Seconds later, two of the chariots in front of him locked together, each competitor reaching to knock the other out of his seat. Kunal took up the back, watching it all as they rushed past the seat tiers of the arena. The audience broke out into a deafening roar.

But Kunal didn't escape notice for long. One of the competitors close behind turned his chariot into him, threatening to ram Kunal off course. He tugged sharply at the reins at the last second, and the competitor crashed into the inner barricade. Kunal looked back to see the competitor alive, breathing, and pulling his chariot back on track.

Five laps and Kunal would be done.

Five competitors to beat if he wanted to win.

Kunal glanced behind him, focusing in on a competitor's chariot, noticing the loose connection of one of the wheels.

If he took a sharp turn, he'd be able to knock the chariot out of play, leaving one fewer competitor—for himself or for

Punohar, the House Pramukh warrior Esha wanted to win. Kunal's eyes narrowed, his heartbeat pulsing.

He could hear the approach of the chariot from behind and see another from the right. If he leaned the right way . . .

A huge crash rang out in the stadium as the two chariots behind him collided. Kunal let a look of glee take over his face. His first ploy had worked.

Chand was ahead of him, battling with another competitor who was trying to edge him into the barricade. The Senap's face was contracted in fierce concentration, his attacker's face contorted in maniacal delight.

Kunal took the opportunity to slip past them on the left, urging his horses on as he turned the corner, keeping the reins taut.

One more lap.

Kunal's joy at being in the front position receded as he heard a scream from behind. He whipped his head back to see Chand doubled over, Pramukh's warrior in the chariot across from him having rammed the edge of his knife into Chand's chariot wheel.

His blood roared in his ears—a dirty move. They weren't allowed weapons during this race—they only allowed them in betting races. He must've sneaked it past the guards somehow.

Had Esha known?

He let instinct take over as they approached the last lap. Despite the dirty move, Chand had kept control of his chariot and was locked together with the Pramukh warrior.

Neither was able to break the hold—in a few seconds, both of their chariots would go flying into the barricades on the turn, leaving Kunal, paces ahead, the winner.

Unless he got them unlocked.

Kunal slacked his grip on his reins, reaching out to Chand's horses with his powers, nudging them to slow down enough for the chariot to unlock.

Chand soared up, only a few paces to the side of him.

"Best man wins, Kunal," the soldier yelled. "No tricks."

"No tricks," Kunal agreed. He glanced at his fellow Senap, an idea dawning on him.

Imperceptibly, Kunal pulled back on his reins, guiding his horses to match the pace of Chand's horses, their chariots traveling side by side.

Inch by inch.

They crossed the line together, flying over the finish line at the same moment. Both flags went up on either side of the finish line.

A conch shell blew, long and hard, its finality bouncing around the arena and announcing the end of the race.

———◈———

The entire arena hesitated, the only sound in the hush the trampling of their horses' feet as they slowed down. They wondered what would happen now, with two claimed winners.

Would there be a brawl? Another fight?

This was unprecedented, as Kunal knew. And so he decided to make a new precedent in that moment. Their horses slowed to a stop, and Kunal brought his chariot close to Chand's. He reached a hand over to Chand, who looked stunned, his grip on the reins slackening.

He looked at Kunal's hand and then at Kunal's face, his eyes wide and uncertain, before taking his hand. Kunal raised their clasped hands in triumph, showing the entire arena.

Finally, the citizens of Gwali erupted in a wild roar of applause and cheers, uplifted by their show of unity. It surrounded Kunal like a cocoon, warming him until he let go of his worries about what would come next.

Right now, right here, he had followed his heart, his intuition.

And it hadn't led him astray.

Kunal and Chand had barely lowered their hands when they were overrun by handlers, grabbing at their reins and pulling them off their chariots, shoving them onto the dais to have the award presented to them.

It was only then that Kunal had a moment to think. He had been so caught up in the rush before that none of it had settled in.

What he had done and what it might mean.

Kunal fingered the gold medallion around his neck. Chand was at his side, talking to one of the announcers as they went back into the training rooms.

A few handlers rushed forward to help him as he began to take off his armor, chatting with some of the other competitors to see how they were faring. Dirit had taken a particularly nasty fall, and a bruise the size of Kunal's fist bloomed over his ribs.

Kunal reached to put away his leather cuirass when he saw a familiar face among the handlers bustling to and fro. Laksh smiled when he saw Kunal had noticed him.

Kunal instantly tensed as Laksh approached. He took ahold of Kunal's forearm, tugging at the guard he had been struggling to take off earlier.

"You should've won, Kunal," Laksh said quietly.

"Is a tie not a victory? I still crossed the finish line first." Kunal tried to pull his arm away, but Laksh didn't let go, his grip tightening.

"You basically gave the other man the trophy to share with you," Laksh said.

"It's not my fault my horses began to get skittish. I fulfilled our deal. I came in first. I'm not sure why it matters that someone else did as well."

Finally, the forearm guard came off, leaving a red burn on Kunal's skin. Laksh tossed it on the bench and looked at him, thoughtful.

"A deal's a deal, and you did win. Our business is done," he said. "But what happens later? That's on you."

He swept away as the gates opened and the audience from the arena surged out. Laksh faded into the mob before Kunal could even register his words.

The crowd swelled around Kunal, lifting him and Chand off their feet, ushering them into the main arena stage to be crowned.

CHAPTER 34

Esha could get used to this. The palace hallway was awash in splendor for the Victor's Ball, with gold statues, jeweled decorations, and swathes of silk adorning every inch, creating an air of opulence.

She patted her thigh for her whips and knife, more out of habit. If all went well tonight, she'd never have to use them.

Esha walked back to a tray of desserts, stopping to swipe a peda, a milk sweet studded with pistachios. She took a bite out of it, enjoying the moment of sweetness, looking around the hall for one person in particular.

The man of honor. Who was nowhere to be found.

A little flicker of frustration rose in her as she thought of her lemon boy. She realized losing wasn't in Kunal's nature, and once he had seen the dirty trick the Pramukh warrior had used, she had known all bets were off.

It had taken her the better part of lunch to convince Mayank that Kunal would give him the boon, something she'd make sure happened in order for them to seal their deal.

Perhaps it had been her own fault, not explaining the importance of her request to Kunal. But Esha could've sworn she had seen Kunal pull back, help Chand win. Esha took another bite, considering the layout of the room and the two exits available.

Tonight was the night. Everything was in place for them to break Reha out of the citadel's lower level. Arpiya was on her way, and Farhan and Aahal were already in place.

Harun claimed they had recruited more men to their cause, but he hadn't provided further details—another reason for the small crease in her brow. He was standing to her left, resplendent in his royal regalia. His role was the least involved tonight, as his absence would be noticed.

Harun glanced over at her, sending her a quick wink. She grinned back. In a few hours, they'd have Reha and the palace. Everything they had worked toward for years.

Esha spotted Kunal hidden in a crowd of people and broke her gaze away. His cowinner was to his right, telling what looked to be a lively story. Kunal moved away from the crowd, shaking a few hands as he went.

Harun frowned as she walked away, but she'd have only a few minutes to check on Kunal before he disappeared and headed for the citadel. Kunal looked tense as she walked over, an inscrutable look on his face even as he smiled and greeted everyone who approached.

She arrived in front of the winners, a few nobles moving out of her way. Finally, she could walk up to him without notice. It wouldn't be odd for her to greet and congratulate them, strike up a conversation.

A servant came up to Kunal's cowinner, as she had arranged, and whispered in his ear.

The soldier turned and nodded, quickly bowing. "My apologies, the captain is calling for me."

Esha bent her head. Once he had left, Esha turned to Kunal, an eyebrow arched.

"Congratulations, Senap Dhagan."

He bowed slightly, placing four fingers against his chest. "Thank you."

His shoulders were still tense. She moved a little closer, lowering her voice.

"Nervous?" she asked.

"A bit," he admitted. His hands played with the tassel on the hilt of the sword in his waist sash.

"You'll have to leave once the food arrives, in a few minutes. I overheard the servants confirming the time. Are you ready with your story?"

"If I'm found I'll say I thought I had left my medal back in the citadel and that some courtiers had asked to see it."

She smiled. "Better than a fake headache, which is what I'll plead as I make my way to the ladies' room, with a slight detour."

Esha brushed her finger against his hand, the lightest of

touches. A stream of servants arrived in the hall with trays of steaming food, signaling the start of their plans. Kunal's body tensed as he saw them. Esha lifted two glasses off a tray and handed one to Kunal.

"Good luck, Kunal. See you on the other side," she said.

He lifted the glass to his lips and drank down the rest in one go before bowing to her. Esha watched him walk away before turning to place her glass on an empty tray and surveying the room. The nobles were preoccupied with their revelries that night, so she only had to look around the room twice to ensure no one was watching her.

Esha strolled out of the ballroom, taking care to appear as if she were in no hurry. Once she was outside the main hallway, she swept into a smaller corridor, throwing a careful glance behind her. This was the way to the ladies' room, but she didn't want anyone who might be following her to see where she went next.

Another turn to the right and Esha stepped into a little nook of a hall, quickly unlocking the door and letting Arpiya in.

"We only have a few minutes," she said after shutting the door. "You can take the main way to the courtyard to set your distraction."

Arpiya grinned at her. "Like old times?"

"The same. And the others?"

"Right on schedule," Arpiya said. "Stay in the hall for another five minutes and then go to the corridor. We should be out of there by then."

Arpiya slid away, pulling her stolen uniform tighter as she left.

———◆———

Esha hurried back to the main hallway in time to run into Harun.

"Harun, what are you doing out here? You're supposed to be in there, mingling before Arpiya sets off the distraction. The gates will be opened in half an hour for our and Mayank's men," she whispered.

"I had to find you, Esha. Before all of this. So you'd know it wasn't an afterthought," he started saying hesitantly, and then with more confidence.

"What?"

"Walk with me," he said.

"Harun, there are eyes and ears—"

"Let them talk," he whispered back hotly.

"They'll start to say we're involved, that there is something between us," she said with a sigh. "It does matter."

"We are involved, Esha," he said, stopping and putting his hands on her shoulders, his touch hot against her skin. She looked up at him; his hooded gaze was entirely focused on her. "We've been involved for years."

"Okay, but is this the time to be having this discussion?"

"When else? I was too stupid before and then you were always on missions and I fear there's no other time. This fight between us, it made me realize a lot of things."

Esha's heart stuttered, a hint of hope surfacing despite the years she had buried it. Even if it was too late now.

"It made me realize how much you mean to me, Esha. How much this means to me. You are everything I need, you are the only thing that makes me better. For years you've been by my side, and I have only become who I am because I've been able to be your friend."

Her throat began to close, heat rising up her cheeks.

"That's very flattering—"

"Be my queen, Esha," he said, the sincerity in his voice turning her throat to ash. "After all of this is over."

"Harun, you've had too much to drink."

He grasped her arm, pulling her a bit closer. "I haven't had a sip."

"It's the only reason you'd ask me this. Now. Here."

"I'm sorry for that. And I know this is backward."

"It is. Especially after making it clear for years that you had no feelings for me," she said. She didn't even know why she said that, except that she had wanted him to—for years.

"Did I really do that? Or did you assume? You were fine with our arrangement."

"Only because you were fine with our arrangement! I buried my heart for years, thinking yours wouldn't be mine," she said, her words sparking embers. Her mouth tightened as she realized how much she had given away. Esha turned to leave, ready to bolt, but Harun moved to block her path.

"Esha . . ."

"Go ahead. Laugh at me."

"Why in the Moon Lord's name would I do that?" He

moved closer, his hands on her shoulders. "It seems we both made assumptions."

"You never challenged them," she said.

"I was young, stupid. I thought I had to keep myself apart to lead."

"You're still young and stupid," Esha muttered.

She tilted her chin up, and Harun took the opportunity to lean in, placing a light kiss on her lips. It was a shock to her system, and she stood still, staring at him. He reached down and pulled her into another kiss, and she didn't resist. Not when her body responded before her heart could catch up, familiarity and passion flooding her limbs.

She broke it apart seconds later, pushing him away.

"I can't."

"Why?" The simple question was so distraught, so heart-broken, that Esha looked up at Harun. His dark eyes were wide, his hair mussed like it used to be after one of their romps. But it was the expression on his face that broke her.

"Because of Kunal," she said, shaking her head.

Because I think I love him.

He stepped back, folding his arms. "I had a feeling," he said quietly. "Though I thought it was a passing interest."

Esha didn't say anything, not trusting her own voice at that moment. "I think I owe it to myself to figure that out," she said finally.

"And what about us?"

It was a good question.

It was also when she finally broke.

"I can't do this, Harun. We had years and we never got it together. Years," she said, her voice desperate as she remembered nights when she had stayed up, curled in his arms, mornings she had left, carrying her heart in her hands.

He rubbed his face with his palms, covering it for a moment before pulling away. "I thought we'd have many more, Esha. I truly did. I didn't think this would be the end of our story."

"This isn't the end of our story," she snapped. She tried to calm down, giving a light laugh. "Don't be ridiculous. We still have to finish this mission, and after that, don't think you'll get rid of me that easily. You're still one of my oldest friends."

Harun looked as if he wanted to respond to that, his face contorting. He sighed. "I can't say I'm going to give up on you. On us."

Esha looked away, trying to force back the wetness that was collecting at the corners of her eyes. Even in this, the gods teased her.

She could still imagine, with great detail, a life by Harun's side, and the past month here at court with him had only made it clearer. But that had been before she had met Kunal.

"That's your choice, Harun. As your friend, I can't say I advise it."

"Good thing you're not my official adviser, then," he said, his voice strained.

Esha didn't know if she was either. She was the Viper,

co-leader of the Blades, used to searching for every edge case and playing them against each other, and yet, she hadn't seen this. Or she had willfully ignored it, gods knew why. Perhaps to save her own heart from the uncertainty of loving a prince.

He ran a hand through his hair, unsure of what came next.

"I'm sorry," she said quietly.

"Don't be," was the immediate response. "It's not your fault I waited."

"Part of me wishes you hadn't," she said. "But what's happened can't be undone."

He nodded, looking away.

"It's getting late—we should get in place before the team arrives from the citadel," Esha said, turning to go.

"Esha." Something in his voice made her stop. "I loved you—I love you, you know that?"

She shook her head, words suddenly difficult. She tilted her face away, up to the Moon Lord, asking him for strength.

Harun was outlined in the moonlight, the only thing visible the quirk of his mouth.

"I won't say anything else. Not now. I'll see you on the other side, Esha."

He turned away, and she found herself unable to tear her eyes away, or move.

"I loved you too," she whispered, quiet enough that only she could hear, as she walked the opposite way.

CHAPTER 35

Esha paced outside the entrance to the Great Hall, trying to compose herself before she had to go back in and face any more courtiers. She took a deep breath, trying to find her center and push away old memories of the past that refused to let her go.

Tonight was about Reha, the future.

Esha's hands clenched and unclenched, missing the weight of her whips and the surety they always brought her. She stepped forward, staring down the hallway Harun had taken, weighing a decision to follow him, swallow her previous words, when a rush of voices flooded down the hall. Esha pushed herself flat against the wall, sliding into the nearest nook.

Two soldiers turned into the small area, their voices hushed.

"—I saw them going that way."

"Well, King Vardaan wants them back immediately."

"But, sir, one of the servants told me to escort them to the eastern wing."

"You're taking the word of a servant over mine? I'm your captain. Bring the Falcon Squad back—we'll be presenting the boons in an hour. The king wants to speak to them beforehand."

Esha's grip on her belt knife tightened, the sharp, cold steel cutting into her palm. The sliver of pain drew her out of the rage that swallowed her every time she heard the Falcon Squad's name.

She had stepped away that day on the rooftop. Kunal's argument had resonated with her, stayed in her mind since that day. And she could hear it still.

But today?

Harun's expression, lost and sad, haunted her. She'd abandoned her past once already today.

Everything was in place, the squad was in position, and they'd have Reha by the end of the night. What harm was there in a small visit?

Esha waited for the soldiers to leave before quietly following them down the hallway.

———◇———

The night breeze whipped around Kunal as he flew to the meeting point, careening downward. Bhandu and Alok were already there, specks against the ground.

Kunal dove down, picking up speed as he went, until the end when he pulled up short, rolling onto the ground and into human form. He bounced up onto his feet, brushing off a few twigs and some dirt as he walked over.

Bhandu and Alok were staring at him with their mouths open.

"It's odd when you see it in person," Alok said. "Compared to in your imagination."

"Agreed," Bhandu said, eyeing Kunal like he would shift back at any moment.

"At least I can land now," Kunal muttered.

"What?" Alok held a hand to his ear.

"Nothing. Let's move. We need to get to the outer wall before Arpiya's signal."

The other two nodded.

"Farhan and Aahal are set up below. They'll be lookout once they're done," Bhandu said.

"How will they let us know if they see anything?"

Bhandu tapped his nose. "I'll know. It's an old signal we've had since we first started going on missions together."

Kunal tried not to huff, deciding he didn't have time to push Bhandu on this. They needed to move if they were going to be in place in time for Arpiya.

"You both ready?"

The quickest way to the outer wall would be to fly to the top of the parapet, like he had scouted before. From there, they'd make their way down.

Kunal closed his eyes and found the harmonies of his song. When he opened his eyes, large golden wings sprouted from his back, engulfing the other two men. A surge of energy coursed through him, renewing his strength.

Bhandu and Alok exchanged nervous glances.

———◄◦►———

The soldiers carved a path diagonal from the main hall, taking Esha farther away from the party and Harun.

Once she had started following them, Esha found she couldn't stop. Not when she was getting closer and closer to what she had wanted this entire time—to find her parents' killer.

But every step forward was beginning to feel like it was also dragging her backward.

"Who was this servant? I'll have their hide for this."

"Sir, she was just a girl. Probably got the wrong order from someone else." The other soldier sounded worried.

"Doesn't matter, she's risked the king's ire by delaying the ceremony. Plus, no one is even supposed to be in the east wing. It was closed off this morning due to an incident."

"Sir—"

"There's only ten minutes left till ten."

Esha stopped and whipped around. Ten minutes till ten. She had lost track of time, and Kunal and the others would soon need her to be at the walkway.

She'd been so preoccupied in her haze of revenge that she'd almost forgotten. She needed to turn back *now*. But if she gave up this chance, would she ever be able to forgive herself? Would her past ever let her go?

The answer came almost immediately. She had the ability to choose.

And she knew the one thing she'd never forgive herself for would be endangering her team. They were the family she had found, ones she had cherished and who had cherished her back. If her parents were here . . .

But they weren't. And that was a pain that would never fade, that would be constant. But she had love, and she had family, and right now, they needed her.

She cursed, quickly looking around the palace hallways to orient herself. There'd be time later to berate herself. Now she needed to find her way back.

Esha tucked the end of her sari into her waist so she could move faster, sprinting back down the hallways. She reached the end of a hallway, one she could've sworn had two corridors, but there was only one and she took it, speeding up.

The same thing happened again at the next hallway, like the second corridor had simply vanished. Esha slowed down and backed up to where the other corridor had been, reaching a hand out to touch the walls.

A streak of gray came off onto her fingertip. Paint.

She spotted a hastily tied rope below a window to the right. Esha walked over quickly and bent down to move a box that was pushed against the wall, tracing a finger over the dusty footprints underneath. A light breeze gusted through the window, and Esha stepped back as she put it all together.

Sudden shouts and screams filled the air, from the direction of the main hall, rending the peace in two.

Esha ran toward the hall, taking a sharp turn right and away from it as she came closer, heading for the kitchen cellars instead. She found the small closet that Aahal had mentioned previously and clambered into it.

Esha's heart hammered in her chest as she leaned over and looked through the small window that peeked into the main hall from the kitchen. It was barely more than a slat, but it was enough.

The main hall was overrun by men and women in animal masks, wielding blades and bows. Half the guests were slumped against the floor, drugged by the looks of it, spears held to their throats by those in servant uniforms. The rest of the nobles were looking around in terror, goblets of spilled plum wine clattering against the floor as they raised their hands in surrender.

Esha saw what had caused the screams.

The doors and windows were blocked—by the limp bodies of soldiers and servants, haphazardly stacked into a wall.

A large flag with the titled, golden scales of Naria had been planted where the table of food had once been. The table was shattered, the delicacies strewn about the ground like fallen soldiers.

In the middle of the room stood a tall lady in an ornate sari, a tiger mask on her face. She turned and the light caught the angles of her mask, a scar etched down one cheek.

Zhyani.

The Scales had infiltrated the palace.

Kunal could tell Alok was trying not to scream as they flew. Bhandu had actually been the easier, though heavier, of the two. He'd enjoyed flying and hadn't resisted, while Alok felt like a weight in comparison.

They neared the top of the parapet, and Kunal slowed down as he gently placed Alok on the stones. His friend sagged in relief.

"Let's never do that again," he said, leaning over the wall to dry heave.

Bhandu bounced on his toes. "Don't know what his problem is. That was amazing. You think you could fly me to the sea?"

"We can figure that out later," Kunal said, motioning them over to his side. They were hidden behind a stout column of stone, a flue for smoke from the smithery below.

They moved to the right, where a second staircase led to the fifth-floor rooms. They'd timed it so that no one would be on patrol here. They arrived at the window, and Kunal tugged at the lock, one he had loosened yesterday.

It took a few tries, but the window opened, and they ducked into the room. It was recently empty, a few teacups half filled on the table, the sheets rumpled. Alok moved forward, checking the four corners of the room before giving the signal for all clear.

Bhandu nodded and moved forward.

"You know our Fort hand signals," Kunal whispered.

"Spent a month learning them while I was in j—" Bhandu paused. "There's a lot you don't know about me, cat eyes. Take me flying after this and I'll tell you my stories."

Kunal chuckled, low. "Deal."

They walked through empty rooms, creeping down the levels one by one. Kunal caught Alok as he walked in front of him, grabbing his arm.

"Alok, I never asked you much about how you came to the Fort or your time before."

"And now's the time?"

Kunal waited, and Alok sighed.

"I was drafted. When I was thirteen."

Kunal calculated quickly. "So you arrived at the Fort before me, before the coup?"

Alok swallowed, his jaw tightening. "The general picked me out. I was even on an elite squad with your uncle, before I realized that I hated the things I had to do to stay there."

Kunal inhaled sharply. The suspicion that had hit him the night he had stopped Esha was coming to full life. "The Falcon Squad."

"How'd you know?"

"Guests of honor."

"Oh yes," Alok said. "I wasn't officially part of them, just tagged along on the night of the coup. I never told you, did I? The things I've done . . ." A sorrowful expression came over Alok.

Kunal gripped his arm. "Tell me later, after we survive

tonight." Kunal could only hope he was wrong. That Alok hadn't been the soldier who had killed Esha's parents.

"Are you two done chatting?" Bhandu barked. "I already checked this corridor."

Alok moved ahead to scout, and Kunal and Bhandu brought up the rear. They stopped when they arrived at the circular stairwell, one that led to the hidden second entrance into the lower levels. They'd found it on the schematics.

This was how they'd get down below. But once they got there, they'd be swarmed with soldiers, which is why they needed to wait for Arpiya's signal.

While they had planned their movements around the patrol schedules to avoid any soldiers, this sort of quiet made the hair rise on Kunal's arms. They'd barely needed to dodge any soldiers.

Kunal looked out the large window at the top of the circular staircase, at the twinkling lights of the palace and beyond.

Were they missing something?

————◇————

Esha didn't believe in coincidences. Dharmdev and his followers had known that they had chosen tonight.

Esha looked back and forth, most of the Senaps posted outside having gone in at the first shout. She dashed across the hallway and slipped into another corridor that gave her a better vantage point over the hall and the chaos beyond.

They had till the end of the night to get Reha out and

to take Vardaan into custody. It was the only way they'd be able to see their coup through.

She rushed forward to the walkway the squad would come through, which led to the throne room and beyond. A booming noise went off.

Moon Lord.

Her eyes darted to the left, to the tall, looming outline of the citadel, and then to the eastern entrance where Mayank had brought his men. The men who would be streaming into the eastern gate right now, toward the main hall—and directly into a trap.

They needed to know what they were getting into. Kunal and the team could handle themselves from here.

Esha sprinted through the hallways toward Lord Mayank's rooms.

———◇———

Kunal signaled for the others to follow him, and they crept down a level on the staircase, peeping into the adjacent hallway. He stepped gingerly into the hallway, one he hadn't scouted before due to strict patrols.

But something was setting him on edge, an unease he couldn't place. Alok and Bhandu stopped behind him.

"What's wrong?" Alok said.

"Something feels off," Kunal answered.

They surveyed the whole hallway, checking the nearby corridors.

Nothing.

Perhaps he was being paranoid. They'd planned this thoroughly, from the routes they were taking here to the distraction and the exit plan. And so far, everything was going—

Kunal's eyes darted to the door they had passed.

A fresh streak of red was smeared against the bottom. He pushed it open. The mangled body of a soldier slumped against a nearby wall, with two more beside him.

"Three soldiers down," Alok said in a strangled voice.

"That we've found," Bhandu said, leaning down to check the pulse of one of them.

Kunal grunted. "We're not alone," he said, giving voice to the thoughts churning in his head. Someone else was in the citadel.

Friend or foe?

And then a deep boom cracked through the stillness of the night, rushing in from the direction of the palace.

Kunal ran to the nearest window and narrowed in his sharpened eyesight, trying to see what he could. The sky was dark, only the lights of the Great Hall twinkling— exactly as they had planned it.

Kunal cursed.

His first instinct was to run over, see if Esha was all right. But he knew that if something was going wrong there, it was even more important for him to be here and find Reha.

"What in the Moon Lord's bleeding—" Bhandu stopped suddenly and cocked a hand to his ear.

A faint cooing, a few low shouts, and the smell of smoke. Arpiya's signal.

"We have to move," Kunal said. "We're not the only ones here. Get to the lower levels before they do. Quickly, while Arpiya's fire is still a distraction."

Alok and Bhandu nodded, and they hurried out of the room. Kunal turned back toward the deceased soldiers and said a quick prayer for their souls.

———◄○►———

Lord Mayank's room was mostly dark, except for a lone candle highlighting a turbaned figure hunched over the desk.

"Thanks to the Moon Lord," Esha said, breathing heavy. "Mayank, you're not safe here. We need to go—"

The figure shifted in the dancing shadows, and Esha realized her mistake.

It was two figures near the desk, Mayank limp on the ground and his attacker hunched over the desk, with a knife in hand. His attacker turned, removing a foot from Mayank's chest, and Esha froze.

The betrayal hit her like a crumbling wall, shocking and then burying her.

Even with the turban, Esha would recognize her. A round face and bright eyes stared up at her.

Aditi.

It had to be a mistake.

But there she was.

Her lady's maid was standing over the lord, with a

vicious grin on her face and a knife still in her hand as if she had been born to hold it.

Mayank took the moment of distraction to lunge at Aditi, knocking her down, her turban falling off and long hair spilling around her. A knife clattered to the floor where she had been.

"She's got a mean arm," he said, drawing in a raspy breath. He was panting, holding a hand to his arm and wincing as he tried to stand.

"Aditi?" Esha said.

"Lady Esha," she said. Her voice was the same, still calm and slightly good-humored, but with a slight edge to it now.

"Why are you here?" Esha got no response. "Why are you here with a knife, and trying to murder Lord Mayank?"

"Not murder. Capture," she said nonchalantly. "We need him."

"We?" Esha racked her brain before the realization slammed into her. How had she not seen it? "Are you one of the Scales?"

"You could say that."

She had trusted Aditi.

And she was a Scale. No wonder they hadn't wanted their help. They'd already found a way to use the Blades— through her.

"I saw your friends and the wall of bodies they made in the hall. How can you work with them?" Esha said, trying to understand. This wasn't the girl she had come to know over the past few weeks.

"Work *with* them?" Aditi said. "I expected better of you, Esha. Or should I say, Viper? You of all people should know that looks can be deceiving."

Aditi stepped into the light, and Esha saw that the girl was wearing a glittering pin. Two scales tilted to the right, the sigil of the Lord of Justice.

Lord of Justice.

Aditi was Dharmdev.

"You've figured it out now, haven't you?" She shrugged. "It's always the same look of disbelief."

Esha's vision darkened. "You've been lying to me. This whole time."

That stopped Aditi. "I regret that. You've been kind and generous, more than I expected. I almost feel bad." Her voice was flippant, but Esha caught the way she shifted her stance. "We could use someone like you, Esha."

She paused for a second, searching for something in Esha's face. "Esha, I know who your parents' killer is."

Esha's heartbeat stuttered.

"My—you lie. I've been searching for the past two weeks and they've evaded my grasp."

"It doesn't do me any good to lie," the girl said, shrugging. Despite the nonchalant gesture, her face was keen, focused in on Esha's reaction. "Your parents' killer isn't gone, Esha. He's in the palace. Right now."

"I don't believe you," she said. She couldn't trust Aditi—Dharmdev.

"Give me Mayank. The Scales already have the palace.

No need for you to die too."

Esha hesitated.

"Esha, I was there when you woke up from your nightmare. I know your pain. I have my own ghosts and nights that haunt me. You owe nothing to this noble," she said, spitting out the last word.

Esha tightened her jaw, fighting against the tide of emotions in her chest. This was about more than her own pain or her past. She was building a future for them all, one with Reha safe and Vardaan gone.

And to do that she'd have to sacrifice her revenge, the one thing that had kept her warm for all these years. But for the first time, it wasn't the only thing that fueled her.

Hope.

She had hope that things would be different. That *they* could make things different, and this was the first step.

"No deal," Esha said, her voice growing steadier. "You tricked me, lied to me, framed me, and now you think you can manipulate me. The Scales only have the hall, not the palace—yet."

There were a few more surprises the Blades had in store. Harun's backup troops would come in handy now.

"Your pyre. I warned you."

Esha braced herself for an attack, shielding Lord Mayank with her body, but none came. Instead, the young woman gave her one last lingering look before throwing her rope out the window. Esha hadn't missed how her eyes had flown to her weapon for a second. But she hadn't moved to unleash it.

Aditi had decided not to attack Esha, to spare her life.

Esha didn't think twice. She ran for the window, lunging to grab ahold of her.

But Dharmdev had already disappeared into the pitch black of the night.

CHAPTER 36

Kunal crept along the dimly lit corridors of the staircase. Alok's breathing was heavy behind him.

A low fire of fear and worry simmered in Kunal's belly. Nothing was going the way it was supposed to. He had known something was off from the beginning.

And now they'd found three soldiers dead and an explosion had gone off near the palace. Was Esha all right? Lord Mayank would be there with his men, as would Harun. He hoped it would be enough.

He kept his sword at chest level as they wound down the staircase. Shouts of fire and the stench of burning wood were beginning to float down from the top. Right now it was chaos outside, but in a few minutes they'd enact protocol and order would be restored.

They needed to be down in the lower levels by then.

Kunal reached one of the windows on the first-floor

landing and took a moment to look outside, keeping an eye out for Arpiya. She was nowhere in sight, but multiple fires were alight in the courtyard and in the rooms of the inner ring and outer wall.

He focused in for a quick listen, trying to see if any of the soldiers knew what was happening at the palace. One ran into view, yelling about a breach at the palace.

A squad of soldiers broke off, thrusting buckets of water at nearby soldiers. They sprinted away.

All Kunal had been able to hear beneath the crackle of fire with his sharpened hearing was two words.

Dharmdev's Scales.

Laksh's words came back to him.

What happens next is on you.

Kunal cursed, filling in Alok and Bhandu.

"There's nothing you can do for her now," Alok said softly. "Except to get Reha out. We have to make sure that even if they take the palace, they won't have her."

Kunal nodded, pushing aside his worries. Esha could take care of herself. He was here to rescue Reha, the one chance they had to save his land, his home.

"Cat eyes?" Bhandu was down near the door to the lower levels, his hand resting on the knob. "We need to move."

———◄○►———

The throne room was swathed in darkness except for the dim glow from a lone torch on the wall.

Esha had sprinted there after sequestering Mayank away, showing him another entrance in and out for him and his men. Their reinforcements should be arriving soon to present a real challenge to the Scales presence. The Scales may have had the element of surprise, but Mayank's and Harun's additional troops would have the strength.

Esha waited for Vardaan.

She stepped deeper into the shadows as voices drifted in from the far corner of the room. Three figures rushed into the room: one Senap, a disheveled adviser, and Vardaan. The adviser ran to light a few of the other torches, but King Vardaan held out a hand.

"Don't," he said. "We need to stay as covered as possible."

A rush of adrenaline flooded Esha as she crouched to the ground, pulling out her whips and getting into position.

He wouldn't leave in one piece.

"Your Highness, we need to get you out of here. The palace is not safe," the Senap said, looking around with a nervous air.

"No, we need to wait. They said they'd be here. I need to finish this."

Esha peered closer at the king, trying to make sense of his words.

"I must insist—"

"Stand down, soldier," the king said, his voice firm. He moved away from the Senap, taking two steps that brought him inches closer to Esha.

She palmed her whips, adjusted her grip.

The Senap strode forward, trying to block the king

from the windows. Esha looked around, determining what she could use. She needed to take out the Senap first—the adviser she wasn't worried about.

She was calculating her next move when King Vardaan stilled.

Moon Lord's fists. He could hear her.

Time to move.

A huge chandelier hung above the Senap, and Esha acted by instinct, lashing out her whip to wrap around it. She tugged, once, twice, and it loosened. The Senap barely had a chance to look up before it came tumbling down to crash. Esha took advantage of the distraction to run up behind Vardaan and wrap her whip around his throat.

He roared, and she could feel his body readying for a shift. She dug her ring into his neck, the blue sapphire's terrible effect working immediately. He dropped to his knees, releasing a growl that sounded barely human.

His eyes flashed at her as he took in who she was. "Lady Esha? I knew there was something off about you."

"Viper, Your Highness," she spat out.

His eyes bulged, the veins in his neck looking more prominent. "You've been a cursed nuisance."

"I could say the same about you."

Esha kept the whip secure around his neck, fishing out the sapphire-encrusted cords she had bought to tie his hands, trussing him up.

"And what is your plan? Kill me in my own throne room?" he asked, coughing.

"*Your* throne room? Don't you mean the throne you stole?"

"How nice it must be to have such a simple way of looking at things," he said, the disdain in his voice clear despite the blood pooling at the corners of his lips. Esha dug her ring in more, anger coursing through her.

"If you keep doing that, he'll die."

Esha spun around to see Laksh striding across the room, two Scales in fox masks trailing behind him. There was a faint hint of purple at his temples, hidden under his curling hair. The poison hadn't escaped him after all, though he had survived.

"Is that a problem?" she spat out. But she did release her hand from Vardaan's neck, Kunal's words echoing in her mind. Somehow, Esha couldn't shake what he had said.

End the cycle.

"You don't want to start a civil war, do you?"

Esha hesitated. She had already decided she wouldn't kill him, not when the country deserved a fair trial. But she didn't need to tell Laksh that.

"Are the Scales really asking me that? After all you've done to lead us to one? Framing me for killing General Hotha, storming the palace, and killing nobility."

The king let out a throaty laugh. "My suspicions ended up being true."

"We saw an opportunity and took it, Viper," Laksh said, circling around her. "I told Kunal that whatever happened next was on him. If he had done what I had told him— Where is Kunal, by the way?"

Esha started, checking herself before she lost her grip on the cords.

"Kunal? You've been in contact with Kunal?"

Laksh gave her a wide smile. "Oh, there's so much you don't know, Viper. Your soldier turned rebel isn't who you think he is."

His eyes flickered to the king, who was struggling against his bonds, blue tendrils bulging at the sides of his temple every time he moved.

Vardaan gave a throaty laugh. "So much potential and so much bickering. What might have happened if your two sides worked together?"

"Shut up," Esha growled, yanking at the cords. "You thought you had played us all with the fake Reha, gaining power so you could rule forever."

But Vardaan didn't struggle anymore. In fact, he had gone stock-still, looking at the corner of the room. "You fools. Did you really think that? I've been protecting her."

"Protecting? If you really think we're going to believe—"

Vardaan held up a hand to silence Esha.

His breath hitched. "They're here."

CHAPTER 37

They opened the door to the lower level, a blast of cool air hitting them from the vents. The dungeons were kept ice-cold below. Kunal moved forward, holding up five fingers.

Five soldiers all together.

Kunal went right, and Alok and Bhandu went left. Kunal's fist was in the soldier's throat before he even saw it coming, an elbow in the exposed side of his torso under the armor, and an uppercut thrown to his face.

The soldier slumped, and Kunal caught him, letting him down gently toward the floor. He crept up behind another soldier and lunged, grabbing him with a chokehold. This one had a knife on him. Kunal ducked out of the way as the soldier's arm flew wildly, thrusting his fist into the soldier's mouth as he tried to scream.

The knife clattered loudly as it fell to the ground, but

Kunal could already hear the sounds of fighting to his left. Whoever would be alerted was already aware.

The soldier finally went limp and Kunal eased him down. Two more infantry soldiers ran into the hall. Kunal took them down with four hits from his sword pommel.

Over to his left, Alok and Bhandu were pulling the soldiers up against the wall, tying them up. It had been Kunal's request to not kill them.

Kunal could hear footsteps, still three levels above but gaining quickly. He rushed to the door they had identified as Reha's, tugging at the lock. The night sky poured through the windows, reminding Kunal of the time they had already lost.

Esha and the others should be waiting on the other side, if the explosion hadn't changed everything. Kunal took a deep breath. He had to go on as if the plan were the same, which meant there was no time to lose.

He struggled to lift the bar of steel, only managing to move it an inch. It was worse than he thought. Bhandu appeared on the other side of the bar.

"We can at least get this first mechanism open," Kunal said.

Together they lifted the bar, inching it up as fast as they could. Footsteps pounded behind them, and Kunal shifted his head to look out.

Alok was running toward them at full speed, the key they needed in his hands.

"I got it," he said, triumph in his voice. "It was on the

guard you had in a chokehold. You were right."

"Perfect," Kunal said. "Now slide it in."

Alok did so, sliding it behind the two metal bars. It gave them enough leverage to twist the mechanism and dislodge the lock.

It went flying, skittering across the stone floor, but Kunal couldn't care less. They were already too far gone to care if anyone heard them at this point.

Except the door still wasn't opened.

He looked at the others, trying to hide his panic.

Kunal waved them away, calling on his strength and senses to find the exact part to hit. He moved backward, giving himself space. With a burst of speed, he sprinted at the lock, using his awareness to send a targeted kick at the mechanism, ramming into it until it shattered.

They stood there for a heartbeat as the door swung open, looking at each other in disbelief.

They had done it. They were in.

A faint cough came from the inside. Kunal took a step into the dungeon.

"Not so fast," a soft voice said from behind them.

A figure launched out of the darkness, striking Bhandu and then pivoting to send a knife into Alok's leg. He went down with a yelp, and before Kunal even registered it, the figure had clocked Alok on the head. Bhandu and Alok lay still on the floor. Kunal's senses returned to him and he lunged toward the attacker.

The figure neatly sidestepped Kunal, an uttariya tossed

over its head and wrapped around its mouth.

"I'm so glad to have found you, Kunal," his attacker said. "I'm Dharmdev."

The figure walked into the light, revealing sharp eyes and a small curved mouth.

Kunal froze. Dharmdev?

Then the words hit him. *Found him?*

"Laksh has told me so much about you. The infamous lost prince," she said. "It's nice to finally meet you."

———◇———

Esha yanked harder on Vardaan's ropes.

"What are you going on about?" she demanded.

"Reha," he said. "I never had her. I've been lying this whole time to protect her from the real enemy." He caught her look. "I've been playing a shell game, and they almost believed it. I was *this* close to getting them to believe it."

"And I'm supposed to take your word?" she scoffed. "That you've now found honor?"

"Believe it or not, Viper," Vardaan spat. "Everything I've done is to protect Jansa. The country welcomed me when my own didn't want me. It valued me. I would do anything for it. But I've made mistakes. And now they've come to collect."

"Who?"

Laksh's eyes had gone wide, though, and he stood frozen in his spot. What was going on? What did Laksh know that she didn't?

"Tell me," Esha said, shaking the cords. Vardaan closed

his eyes for a moment, whispering something below his breath.

"Tell me, or he dies." Esha drew her knife quickly against Vardaan's throat, feeling a sense of pleasure as his throat bobbed, his body tensed.

Laksh jerked into action, thrusting a hand forward.

"Ahh," she said. "My suspicions were right. You know, it's curious to me. Why would the Scales want to keep the king alive?"

Anger flashed in Laksh's eyes. "Don't be so high and mighty, Viper. We want to ensure a simple transition of power. Jansa has seen enough pain. An obvious usurpation would only lead to more destruction, more factions."

"Transition of power? To whom?"

Laksh said nothing.

Esha tightened her grip on Vardaan, drawing her knife closer. "If you don't feel like talking, that's fine. We have no use for him."

Laksh's eyes flickered, but it wasn't his voice that spoke next.

"I wouldn't do that," a low voice said from the shadows.

"I told you they were here," Vardaan whispered. "And now we're all done for."

"We still have use for him," the voice said, sounding more familiar with every clipped word.

Two figures emerged from the shadows and archers appeared, as if conjured, to surround the exit.

Yamini looked like the warrior she was, dressed in full

battle armor on top of her cerulean sari, the one Esha had picked out.

Her ceremonial sword rested against the bob of Harun's throat. She pushed him forward, walking behind him.

Harun's eyes flashed at Esha's with a clear direction. *Don't.*

Esha resisted every inclination she had and kept herself still.

"The Yavar," Vardaan said. "The real enemy."

"I had hoped it wouldn't come to this, but he's been evading us for days now. Ever since he announced that cursed marriage. We've come to collect our due."

"The Yavar?" Esha looked to Vardaan. "But why?"

"I was younger, brash. I lived through the war in the north." His eyes turned glassy, haunted. "It wasn't as glorious and honorable as everyone said. We had to make choices, hard ones, despicable ones, but we did it to save our people. I took the throne to protect us. Queen Shilpa was a good woman but a weak ruler. She could've saved thousands of lives if she had been stronger. Setu and I, we had a vision."

"A vision the Yavar helped you with," Yamini said. "Once it became obvious you wouldn't be able to hold the throne alone."

"I've regretted it ever since. The deal I made."

"You got the throne. We got a pawn. I'd say it was a pretty good deal for you," Yamini said.

"I thought you'd demand an army. Jewels or our trade route. Not Reha. Not our land." Vardaan rose as tall as he could. "I will not be known as the king who destroyed Jansa by inviting in the northern invaders."

Esha's head was swimming with all this new information. She had seen that fire in Vardaan before, at the peace summit, and despite every part of her body wanting to say otherwise, she read his words as true.

He really thought he had been protecting the land. He really believed that.

Esha knew the lies they could tell themselves to think they were right.

"Your time is over anyway. Esha, I had hoped you would be here. Perhaps you could help us, do what the king refuses," Yamini said.

"Why in the Moon Lord's name would I do that?" Esha spat out.

Yamini stepped forward. A drop of blood inched down Harun's throat from where Yamini's knife was, falling onto his white uttariya.

"I gather you care about your prince," she said. "And whether he keeps all parts of his body."

"If you hurt him, I'll—"

"Where is the girl?"

"What girl?"

"No need to pretend, we've been watching your every move." Yamini glanced at Laksh, who was surrounded by arrows. "And yours too. Ridiculous, these divisions you Southern Landers create between yourselves."

"You're one to talk," Esha said.

"True. We do have clans. But we come together when there's a need." Harun struggled against his bonds and Yamini tightened her hold, a blue sapphire bracelet flashing against her wrist.

Esha cursed.

"Don't help them," Vardaan croaked. "They want to break the bond permanently. Reset it."

For a second, Esha thought she had misheard him. But the firm set of Vardaan's mouth brooked no argument. Reset the bond?

The impact of that was unknown, potentially catastrophic. Without the bond, rivers could dry up, crops would follow, and the resulting famine would be endless. It was madness.

"No. You're lying." Esha shook her head. "You've always been a liar."

Yamini shrugged. "The old man is right. We have nothing to hide anymore."

Esha couldn't believe it. They'd risk the wrath of the gods—for what?

"But why?"

Esha racked her brain. It couldn't be a normal grab for territory. If the Yavar wanted to expand, they could've planned another invasion. This was new.

Vasu the Wanderer had chosen to leave the connection to the gods behind. A nomadic life was prized by the Yavar, had been for centuries, eras.

Was there more to the story?

"The girl," Yamini said, her voice ringing through the room. "I'm getting bored by all this talk. Give her to me now."

"I don't have her," Esha said.

"Lies."

"It's not a lie," she said. "We don't have her—yet. The rest of the team is supposed to arrive soon. They'll have her."

Esha tried another tactic. "Take Vardaan. But give me the prince."

She hoped the desperation in her voice wasn't apparent. Fear for her friend, for the man she loved, was filling her lungs until she felt like she couldn't breathe.

Harun tried to shake his head at her. But she swallowed, holding firm.

"Oh no," Yamini said, glancing between Harun and Esha, watching their interaction. "Now I want the girl. The girl—and the king as well. That seems fair to me."

A smile spread across Yamini's face.

"Or your prince dies."

———◦———

It took a moment for Kunal to understand.

"Dharmdev?"

The girl looked nothing like how he'd imagined the leader of the Scales. In fact, she looked familiar. Kunal's eyes widened.

"I've seen you before. Around the palace," he said.

It only made her grin. "One of my many faces."

"What do you want?" he asked. He glanced at the exits, trying to determine how many beats he'd need to run and shift to escape. "I fulfilled my debt to Laksh. He promised I would be left alone."

"No, you didn't. Not really. We—they—had grand plans for you, Kunal. You were to be the victor of the Mela, so beloved by the people that when we revealed you were a Samyad, the public would accept you. Adore you. Choose you."

"What?" Kunal couldn't believe it, the game that Laksh had been playing right under his nose. He thought back to every task he had done, how it had all led him to be crowned the victor.

If he hadn't messed it up.

Anger rose in his throat like a snake, cold and vicious.

"I will not be taken to be used by all of you. Everyone seems to be more concerned with who sits on the throne than with the people who are to be protected." He stepped closer to the girl, Dharmdev, whoever she was. "Move."

"No, Kunal—"

"I came here, to this cesspool of a palace, to save our land. And that's what I'm going to do. You can have your petty squabbles away from me," he said.

Dharmdev sighed. "Listen—"

"I don't even know your real name. Just that you've played me, like everyone else."

"Listen." The girl stepped forward, firmness in her voice. "And look."

Kunal glanced down at her hand, which was reaching for him. It matched the hand he had clenched, talons digging into his skin.

Hers were different, claws or talons, he couldn't tell. And when he looked up, her eyes flashed yellow, and then a russet gold.

Eyes like his, with that feral gaze that he'd only seen in a mirror.

Kunal listened and heard her heart beat, her eyelashes flutter against her cheeks. And then he heard her blood song—wild and free yet proud and fierce.

Samyad and Himyad.

Similar and yet so different from his own song.

This girl was Reha. Dharmdev was Reha.

Kunal felt his eyes widen as he looked at her in disbelief and then at the locked cell in front of them.

"Then who's in there?"

CHAPTER 38

Reha stepped toward the dungeon, disappearing inside to pull out a bedraggled-looking girl.

She peered at them both with weary eyes. "Is it time for my meal yet?"

Kunal stepped forward and then wished he hadn't. Alcohol. She was drunk, and from the looks of it, this was a familiar state for her.

"How many more days of this?" she said, sniffing. "I'm getting bored in there."

"My guess is an actress," Reha said.

"Vardaan knew we were coming for her. He also knew the Yavar were coming for me."

"How?"

She held up the report he had stolen for Laksh. "Recognize this? Laksh mentioned you hadn't read it. It says that Vardaan made a pact with the Yavar years ago to secure this

433

throne. They've come to collect their payment—me. I don't know why, but I'm not sticking around to give up my life to the Yavar."

"But he announced your marriage. Took you public."

Uncertainty flickered on Reha's face. "Perhaps he changed his mind, gained a conscience. But that's not the point."

Kunal remembered where he was and with who. Reha, Dharmdev, whoever. This was the person who had started all this, endangered his life and those of the people he cared about.

She registered the shift in his mood, holding up her hands in peace. "I came here to talk. I need you, Kunal. We can save this land. You and me. Together."

Kunal paused, staring at her as if it would somehow put the puzzle together.

"The land?"

"Why do you think I'm here? Tonight's our one chance to get away. I didn't anticipate the Yavar attacking tonight, but it's the best distraction."

"You mean the night when your people decided to infiltrate the palace?" Kunal asked, trying not to raise his voice.

"It was supposed to be *you* on the throne. Laksh has been giving me full reports. I thought you'd understand more than anyone."

"Why not you? Where have you been all these years?"

She looked at him sidelong, as if she didn't want to answer, her mouth set in a firm, almost angry line. "I only found out recently about my parentage. I thought I was a gutter orphan. Apparently, I'm the mystical *lost* princess destined to save everyone."

Suddenly, she was angry, coming up to him, fury on her face.

"You think I wanted this? I'd been working as a lady's maid, and I was this close to getting the information we needed, to setting you up as our figurehead for the true rebellion. I had finally worked my way up to being Dharmdev. I had power. I was doing something. And then I grabbed that cursed blue diamond ring Esha had. Since then . . ."

"Are you able to control the shifts?" he asked suddenly.

"No," she said.

"I can teach you," he said, before shaking his head. "Why am I even bothering? You've been planning to use me, to hurt the Blades who wanted to rescue you."

"True, all true. Except the hurting part. Laksh and I have been trying to convince you, but yes, if you weren't cooperative we would've coerced you."

"And I'm supposed to trust you?"

She looked impatient. "Look, I only took over the Scales recently. I'm not even the first Dharmdev— You know what? You ask too many questions."

"How do I know you're not lying?" he demanded again.

With a vicious grin she pulled out a pouch and dropped a ring into her palm. She bit her lip, her flesh sizzling. Her eyes flashed, red and gold, green and blue. Colors he had never seen.

How was it even possible? King Mahir had found him in the palace. How had he missed her?

"The king should have noticed you, heard your song. He found me out within minutes of meeting me." Kunal rushed forward and knocked the ring out of her hand, grabbing her palm to see the damage.

"I'd have to actually get within one hundred paces of the king for that to happen, wouldn't I? And no one notices a lady's maid," she hissed, pulling away. "Do you know what it feels like? To find out your entire life was a lie? That your body wasn't yours?"

"Yes, I do," he said back, anger rising in him as well. "And what did your people do when you found out? Used me, threatened me."

Fury rose in Kunal's blood.

"Why do all of this? You murdered the general, my uncle," he spat out.

She shook her head. "I didn't found the Scales and I didn't make those decisions."

"But you allowed them."

She shrugged. "Look, cousin. I'm not here to apologize to you for your past hurts or to right them. What's done is done. But I'm trying to look forward. I came here instead of just running, risking my own skin, giving up my entire life and identity because of this new one that was thrust on me."

"Why?"

Reha looked away for a moment. "The Scales will never follow me now. The lost princess is too Dharkan, too entrenched. And if everything I've worked for is gone and if I am the cursed lost princess, I should do something with it. There are decisions the Scales made, not ones I agreed with. Now I can do something. Protect the land. The people."

"Why me? Why not go alone?"

Reha looked as if she might just do that. "My magic is unstable. I've read every book I could find, but it's not enough. Laksh noticed your control, how it's developed."

Kunal paused, recalling the unnatural colors of her eyes. Her song, it was uneven. "Then what are you suggesting?"

"We leave. We journey to the mountain and complete the ritual. Let these people squabble among themselves." She laughed, giving him a slow, coiling grin. "And they will. When I left the palace there were already reinforcements on their way. The Blades planned better than we had expected."

She reminded him of another girl, one who he was moving farther and farther away from with every step he took. His heart threatened to shatter at the thought, but his duty held him in a firm vise, refusing to let him go from the burden that was now his.

His land. His people.

Was this the right solution?

"And everything else? Your rebels attacked the palace. Do they know you're here?"

She shifted uneasily, which was his answer. "*Your* rebels were about to take over the throne."

"How'd you even—" Kunal's eyes widened. "Esha. You've been the one following her."

Her eyes narrowed. "Don't have a tantrum. No one knows about this. No one could. I didn't even until a few weeks ago." Reha tossed aside a lock of hair from her forehead. "This was my own plan. Now the question is, can you put this all aside? We have to heal the land before time runs out."

"It wouldn't matter. You have the Samyad blood of a queen, but not the blood of a Himyad king."

Reha held up a little vial with a few drops of blood. "Why do you think Laksh was in the palace?" she said. She had thought of everything.

Kunal's breath stuttered. If he did this, he would be abandoning Esha, the Blades, everyone.

But his honor demanded he do what was right, despite the consequences. Was that not where his uncle had failed?

Kunal looked up at Reha, the slight girl who commanded the Scales. He didn't know her. He couldn't trust her either. But on this, they were aligned.

"Decide, cousin," she said in a harsh whisper.

"Can't we tell the others? Leave them a note?" His voice was desperate, but all Reha seemed to recognize was the hope of agreement. She stepped closer, her eyes glittering in the flickering light.

"And lead them right to us? No, we go alone. If all goes as planned, we'll be back soon enough. They'll be fine."

"You don't even want to reunite with your brother? Your father?" he asked.

"My father?" Her voice hitched. A flash of longing sped

over her face. "There'll be time enough for reunions later, if we leave in time. If not, it won't matter."

Her fingers clenched around the spear she held. She was still a girl, despite the conviction with which she spoke. A girl who was choosing her country above all else.

Choosing her duty above all else.

Kunal glanced back at the palace, at the new friends he had made and the girl he had come to love, and then at the lights of the city that illuminated the fading green and gold of the land beyond.

His home. The one that they could save.

"What'll it be, cousin?"

———◦———

Esha tried not to lunge forward and claw at the throat of the girl who had feigned friendship with her, offered her comfort just days ago.

Yamini chuckled. "Your control is very good. I wouldn't expect anything else from the Viper."

"I'll make you another deal," Esha said.

"Are you sure you want to?" Yamini said.

"Yes." Esha couldn't afford hesitation right now.

"The king thought the same years ago. But the Yavar don't take deals lightly. The one King Vardaan made with my father was not forgotten by our clan. And we're here to claim our price now."

Esha's mind whirred as she tried to catch up. "Then your conflict isn't with us."

"It wasn't. In fact, I rather liked you, *Lady* Esha. Liked

you even more when I found out you were the Viper. I don't really care who gives her to me, but I want the princess."

"My team is coming. They'll come back and bring the princess." Esha swallowed. "You'll have her. Don't harm the prince."

Harun struggled against his ropes. "Esha, no. I'm not worth it. Don't give them Reha."

"You're our future, Harun," she snapped. "Kunal is coming with the team soon."

"Is he?" Laksh said, his voice raspy and unkind. "Last time I saw him he didn't seem beholden to any team or allegiance. And time is running out. Wasn't he supposed to be here by now?"

"He'll come," she said sharply, wondering how he knew so much of their plan. "Kunal will come."

CHAPTER 39

"We have to return to the palace first, let the team know," Kunal said, trying to find a way to make it all slow down.

"No. No deal. Make up your mind, Kunal."

"I'm not going to leave them here." Kunal indicated Alok.

"It's either them or the land." Reha's voice shook as she spoke. "If the Yavar want me, they have some sort of plan for the *janma* bond, and it won't be good for either of us or our countries. That should be enough to convince you. But if it isn't, let me say this. This is your only chance to come. Otherwise, I'll go myself. I want your help, Kunal, because the gods know I don't understand these new powers of mine. I could also use backup. But I don't *need* you. I have my blood and this vial, more than anyone ever has had before. If you say no now, good luck finding me again. If I've hidden under all of your noses for this long as Dharmdev—"

"You'd really—" Kunal's voice was rough, harsh, disbelieving, until he caught sight of her eyes. Eyes that were awash in fear.

He had forgotten that she was only sixteen. The same age Esha had been when she had taken on the title of Viper, the same age he had been when he had led his first campaign.

Young and yet not young at all.

"You didn't know," he repeated, everything somehow hanging on her answer.

"No, I didn't," she said. "I already said that."

Kunal took a deep breath. She had only found out recently too, she knew what it felt like, he could see it in her eyes. How scary and lonely the realization had been, the world no longer the one you knew. Your life torn before your eyes. She was as new and untested as he was, suffering from living a life that was a lie. And if he didn't go, she'd be alone.

And their chance to protect the land would be gone.

"Fine," he said quickly, before he could take it back. "Just let me make sure he's okay."

Alok was beginning to wake up when Kunal crouched near him.

"I have to leave. Tell her I'm sorry," he whispered into his ear. "But I have to do this."

Alok stared back, recognition slow on his face.

"We have to go. Now," Reha said.

"Wait," he said. "I need to do one more thing."

<hr />

A noise sounded in the outer room, and Esha's breath caught. They'd come. Kunal hadn't failed her.

Footsteps clattered against the stone, followed by a faint trailing groan.

Esha dropped Vardaan as she caught sight of Bhandu and Aahal dragging an injured Alok. Farhan and Arpiya were running in behind them, closing the door to the tunnel.

"No! Don't close—" Esha tried to slide toward them and got a spear to the throat for her outburst. It was too late. The team walked into the room, into the waiting arms of the Yavar.

"Esha. What are you still doing here? The squads are on their way up the stairs to retake this wing. We need to go to—" Farhan said.

"Farhan, step back," Arpiya said, sussing the situation instantly.

"What happened?" Esha asked sharply, searching for Kunal.

Arpiya glanced behind Esha, at the Yavar princess. "I'm curious myself. Where is this Kunal? Where is the girl?"

"Gone," Aahal said. "Kunal left with her."

Esha felt the words like a slap in the face.

"With who?"

"With Reha. Though apparently she's been going by another name. Dharmdev."

Laksh's face went white even as Esha struggled to catch up.

"No," Laksh whispered as if he had finally seen the light. "It can't be real. She told me she was going to the citadel to secure the princess. *She* told me to come to the throne room. But why?"

"He left?" Esha repeated.

Kunal had betrayed them, run off with Reha—their key.

And now Harun's life was in danger because of him.

Sounds of battle filtered into the room, growing louder and closer by the minute. The Blades and their reinforcements had arrived.

Yamini realized this as well, backing up with big steps, her warriors encircling her and Harun, who looked close to fainting. Blue swirls etched up his temples like twining vines, but he managed to catch Esha's gaze for a fleeting second.

"Seems this didn't work out well for any of us. Whoever this Kunal is, I don't care. But now he has what we want. And until we get what is ours . . ." Yamini glanced at Harun, tugging him upright. "I think we'll keep this prince as collateral."

"Take Vardaan," Esha said, preparing to shove him across the way. "You have no need for the prince. With the king you can keep your deal."

"I don't think that'll be enough incentive," Yamini said.

"I've seen how the prince looks at you. Question is, how do you feel about him? I think you'll be far better to make a deal with."

"This isn't a deal," Esha spat out.

Yamini shrugged. "Coercion, then. Either way, I get what I want."

The sounds outside intensified, and when Esha blinked, the Yavar had disappeared into the night. She began to run after them, but a commotion started behind her and she turned in time to see Vardaan throw off his cords and shift into a large lion.

He roared and charged off. Esha shouted at the Blades closest to the door to follow him, switching directions to chase the king.

But he was too fast and Esha had to stop, watching Vardaan leap out of the lower level of the palace and onto the outside grounds. A few of the Blades still chased after him, but she felt a pit of despair open in her chest.

She had let Vardaan live, and he had escaped.

Harun was gone. Her friend, her teammate, her prince.

And it was all because of Kunal.

She slid to her knees, the marble floor cold on her skin.

CHAPTER 40

Kunal didn't know what forced him to look back, searching for one last glimpse of her. Perhaps to see her face once more before he left.

But in that, his eyesight failed him.

Kunal turned away, holding his memory of her like an ember of light for the darkness ahead of him. He looked at the girl in front of him tugging at the bundle of cloth across her back, a stubborn frown on her lips.

The darkness ahead of *them*.

He was doing this for Reha—for Jansa.

He could never spend a life, deserve a life, with Esha if he didn't set things right first. Not after all he had turned away from. He wouldn't take the easy path, not like his uncle.

He'd sacrifice, make the hard choice, because that was who he was. He was no prince, but he knew the ritual, and Reha needed help.

He could do this. He could help save them all.

Esha would come to understand. He turned back to look up at the balcony one last time.

But Kunal knew she wouldn't, that this could break what was between them.

But not sever it.

He had to believe that.

———◀◎▶———

Bhandu shook her shoulder, calling Esha back to reality as she stood at the marble balustrade overlooking the palace courtyard.

By then the other Blades reinforcements were in the room, surrounding Laksh and the Scales. She got to her feet, brushing off Bhandu's hand.

Lord Mayank's men had found them a half hour after Vardaan's escape. The extra Blades she had stationed with them had finished off the job, taking back control of the main hall and setting up posts across the palace.

The Pink Palace was now in the control of the Crescent Blades.

"We've collected everyone we could, every single one of the Scales, and brought them here. The entrances and exits are ours and are secure, thanks to Lord Mayank's men. And the Senap guards are tied up—the few that are still alive," Bhandu said.

"Good," Esha said. "You've covered all the bases."

"What's your order?" Bhandu asked.

"My order?"

"You're in charge, Esha. Acting leader," he said, his tone almost regretful. "Lord Mayank agreed as well."

Rage filled her. This wasn't a role she wanted. And she was still burning with despair. Kunal had been holding back, had hidden Laksh—or protected him. And now he had created his own plan. Had she been so involved in her own troubles that she had ignored his?

She could understand someone leaving her. But her team hadn't deserved his betrayal.

Only a day ago he had been kissing her, promising her a future. Was this treachery in his heart even then?

Maybe he hadn't known the consequences of his actions. Maybe she had done something to indicate that he had to hide the truth from her.

After everything she had given him. Freedom. Choice. Now he left her with none. Her heart begged her to trust the boy she had come to care for—even love.

Love. She almost spat. What a lie.

She was the Viper, the leader of the Blades, their source of light in the dark. She pulled herself together. Her prince was in chains, and the fate of this entire country, and her own, rested in her hands.

"Give the Senap guards an option to join us for a reduced sentence. As for the Scales—" she said.

"Kunal lied to us too, Viper," Laksh said, lifting his head to look her in the eye. "He may have worked for me, but never *with* me. He never betrayed you."

"Until he did," Esha shot back, before turning to her

team again. "Keep the Scales in the eastern wing. Locked up, but comfortable. I'll deal with them myself soon."

"Anything else, Viper?" Bhandu asked.

Esha's heart was warring in her chest, threatening to tear itself out and lay near her feet.

How stupid Bhandu must think her for having ever trusted the soldier to begin with. She looked up at him. But it wasn't recrimination on his face. Rather, he looked as if he himself had been kicked in the gut.

And worry. It shone in his eyes. She turned her face, not wanting to see it directed at her.

There was nothing to worry about.

With every passing moment her feelings for the soldier receded into the dark space that lived in her chest. It left her cold, but she welcomed it, ushering it back into her heart.

The Viper reared her head, ruthless and unencumbered.

She placed a hand over her pulsing heart, turning to look at Bhandu and the other Blades.

"Hunt down the soldier."

ACKNOWLEDGMENTS

A second book is a wild thing. It's still a dream, but one that's seen a glimpse of daylight (and reality). Which is my way of saying that this book was hard. Really hard. So many people were crucial to bringing this story to life, and I'm forever grateful to all of them.

To Mabel Hsu, my intrepid editor: thank you for taking the meandering ball of yarn I gave you and helping me knit it into something real. Your insight and thoughtfulness are a treasure and a gift. To the fabulous team at Katherine Tegen Books and HarperCollins, I couldn't have asked for a better home. Thank you to Katherine Tegen, Tanu Srivastava, Jon Howard, David Curtis, Ebony LaDelle, Aubrey Churchward, and all the tireless sales, marketing, and publicity people who have worked on this book and series.

To Kristin Nelson, my agent extraordinaire: as always, it's an incredible pleasure to have you and the whole team at NLA behind me. Thank you for your wisdom and support—I couldn't do any of this without you. I'm so proud to be a part of the NLA family.

To Amma, Nanna, and my Akkas: thank you for understanding when I stop talking midsentence to write something down or ask random, odd questions to get more "character insight." You've always humored me, my whole life, and I'm the luckiest daughter/sister.

To Aakash: thank you for always helping me see the silver lining and forcing me to take breaks and eat food. You keep me human.

To Chelsea, Crystal, Madeleine, Rosie, Tanvi, my wildcats: the fact that you still tolerate me and my endless writing neuroses is still a mystery to me. Thank you all for being my constants in an uncertain world and for always treating my stories with kindness and care.

To Meg, Katy, Akshaya, Kat, June, Elizabeth, and Deeba: thank you for your kindess, support, and friendship, not to mention all the laughter and fun. I couldn't have asked for better writing buddies in this city (and beyond).

To Meghana, Mayura, and Nikki: thank you for always seeing me and never flinching.

And lastly to my readers, I'm so grateful. Thank you for taking a chance on this story and walking this journey with me.

GLOSSARY

Anguli—A sigil ring worn by all Jansans.

Chai—Indian tea, often heavily spiced with ginger, cardamom, or masala.

Crescent Blades—A rebel group based out of Dharka with the aim to bring down the Pretender King.

Cuirass—Armor for the upper body that includes a breastplate and backplate welded together.

Dhoti—A garment worn by men. It's a long, unstitched piece of cloth that is worn as pants by wrapping the cloth around the waist and through the legs.

Himyad—The royal house of Dharka.

Jalebi—Thin strips of fried dough drenched in syrup.

Janma Bond—The magical bond between humans and the Southern Lands, gifted by the gods.

Naran and Naria—Twin demigods who pulled the Southern Lands from the sea and founded Jansa and Dharka.

Samyad—The royal house of Jansa.

Sari—A garment worn by women along with a blouse. It is a long piece of unstitched cloth, often embroidered and printed with beautiful designs, that is wrapped around the legs with the end thrown over one shoulder.

Senap—An elite squad of soldiers in the Jansan Army, trained as trackers and stealthy warriors.

Uttariya—An upper garment worn by men and women. It is like a shawl and is typically made of cotton or silk. It can be worn over the shoulder or around the neck. The modern form of an uttariya is the dupatta.

Valaya—A steel bracelet worn by all Dharkans.